E X T I N C T

ALSO BY RR HAYWOOD

The Undead Series

The Undead Day One-Twenty

Blood at the Premiere: A Day One Undead Adventure

Blood on the Floor: An Undead Adventure

Demon Series

Recruited: A Mike Humber Novella

Huntington House: A Mike Humber Detective Novel

Book of Shorts Volume One

Extracted Series

Extracted

Executed

E X T I N C T

EXTRACTED BOOK 3

R R H A Y W O O D

Published by 47North, Seattle

www.apub.com

Amazon, the Amazon logo, and 47North are trademarks of Amazon.com, Inc., or its affiliates.

ISBN-13: 9781503902459
ISBN-10: 1503902455

Cover design by Mark Swan

Printed in the United States of America

-LF-
(Miri)
What you did, you did first.
Thank you.
Rich

Prologue

A tourist turns to smile at Konrad and Malcolm from the corner at the junction. His tourist guide and map clutched in his hands and his face showing the confused, harassed look of someone lost in a strange city.

'Er . . . do you speak English?' the tourist asks clearly and slowly with hope in his eyes that someone might be able to communicate with him.

Malcolm grins. 'You're a bit lucky, mate,' he chuckles. 'You lost?'

'You're English!' the tourist says with evident relief. 'I have no idea where I am . . . Apparently this building should be a museum,' he adds, looking at the building on the corner.

'Let's have a look,' Malcolm says, nodding at the map. 'Where you trying to find?'

'Gentlemen, say a word and you die right here,' Alpha says, showing them the pistol held under the map. The genial look vanishes in a second. His eyes dart between the two stunned men.

'Just stay still,' Bravo says almost politely, walking briskly towards them with his own squat black pistol held partly concealed.

Men come in from all sides. All of them dressed in normal civilian clothing. Malcolm flinches. His heart jack-hammering in his chest. Konrad spins, seeing the net closing in.

'Don't move,' Alpha says.

'Easy, mate,' Malcolm says, rushing the words out.

'Mistake,' Konrad blurts. 'Seriously . . . don't do this . . .'

'Shush,' Bravo whispers, moving to stand behind Malcolm.

'Mate,' Malcolm says. 'Don't . . . you don't know who they are . . .'

'They'll fucking kill you . . . all of you . . .' Konrad adds.

'Do as we say and you live. Understood?' Alpha says, his tone calm, his manner relaxed.

'No.' Malcolm grimaces at having to argue. 'Don't do it . . .'

'Listen to him,' Konrad urges. 'You won't get a—' He stops speaking with a gasp as the ultrathin point of a stiletto blade sinks a millimetre into the flesh of his right thigh.

'Not another word,' Bravo mutters, holding the blade while apparently trying to see between them to the map being held by Alpha. 'The blue light. Is it the device?'

A flash of red snaps everyone's heads over, followed a split second later by the boom of a large-calibre sniper rifle. Bravo's head is removed. A second shot and Alpha is taken out, while Delta flies back from the rounds of the assault rifle slamming into his chest. More shots are fired in rapid succession, killing the agents surrounding Malcolm and Konrad with a swift and brutal assault.

'Ere, Kon. They got a red one.'

'I can see, Malc. Who's that with them?'

'No idea, Kon.'

'That's him!' Emily shouts, pointing at Malcolm. 'The one on the left.'

'You sure, Emily?' Ben asks.

'Yep, definitely him.'

'Can't be,' Ben mutters.

'Blimey,' Malcolm says, looking round the street. 'They killed everyone, Kon.'

'We did warn 'em,' Konrad says, nodding at Malcolm.

'We did,' Malcolm adds, nodding back at him. 'We said what would happen.'

'Don't stand there bloody gawping,' Safa snaps. 'The toilets are blocked up, we've got shit floating everywhere and a dead Nazi in the bunker.'

One

The Bunker, Monday morning

'There are too many variables,' Ben says. 'I mean, we're talking about the concept of predestiny. The whole fabric of life, the whole of everything . . .'

'It's a toilet,' Safa says, standing next to him in the bathroom.

'A blocked toilet,' Emily says from next to Safa.

'Tried a plunger?' Ben asks.

'Yes, Ben,' Harry says, holding the dripping plunger in his hand.

'Didn't work then.'

'No, Ben,' Harry says simply.

'Hmmm,' Ben says, lifting his mug to sip his coffee. 'Just use another toilet.'

'They're all blocked,' Emily says.

'Hmmm,' Ben says again. 'Hang on, why are you plunging this one if they're all blocked?'

'We didn't know they were all blocked,' Emily says. 'Harry did this one and I went for a wee next door . . .'

'I see,' Ben says slowly while very aware of Safa staring at him. He turns his head to look at her, waiting for the comment. The same comment she has made every few hours for the last few days. 'Not saying it?'

'I don't need to say it,' she says.

'No.'

'Yes.'

'No.'

'Stop no-ing me. The toilets are all blocked. We need Malc and Kon back.'

'And there it is,' Ben says with a groan.

'And there's no hot water,' Emily adds.

'I know, but the same thing I have said every other time still counts . . . Bringing Malc and Kon back could have countless consequences that could devastate . . .'

'I vote yes,' Safa says, cutting across him while holding her hand up.

'Aye,' Harry says, holding the plunger up.

'Aye,' Emily says, holding her hand up.

'No,' Ben says, shaking his head.

'Outvoted,' Safa says.

'Good luck telling Miri that.'

'Good luck telling Miri what?' Miri asks from the doorway behind them.

'Toilet's blocked,' Emily says.

'Tried a plunger?' Miri asks.

'Aye,' Harry says, holding the plunger up.

'And there's no hot water,' Emily adds.

'No,' Miri says flatly.

'Told you,' Ben says mildly.

'We need Malc and Kon back,' Safa says, her tone already growing firmer in readiness for the battle.

'And then what?' Miri asks.

'And then what what?' Safa snaps.

Ben groans, Harry sighs and lowers the plunger before rubbing a hand through his beard. Emily leans back against the sink.

'Safa,' Ben says slowly and very carefully. 'We've been through this lots of times . . . Lots and lots of times.'

'We take M and K away from that situation, then the British never track the device to Cavendish Manor and we never do the things we did to extract Bertie and Ria . . . *and* Tango Two,' Miri says.

'It's Emily,' Emily says quietly.

'I don't believe it,' Safa says stubbornly. 'Roland said you can't unknow something . . . He said that . . . So we go get Malc and Kon and Emily will still be here.'

'And what if Tango Two ceases to be here?' Miri asks.

'It's Emily,' Emily says quietly.

'It doesn't matter,' Safa retorts. 'You two overthink everything and we haven't even checked yet if it worked and if the world still blows up in twenty-one one one . . .'

'Twenty-one eleven,' Ben mumbles, earning another glare from Safa.

'The bunker is falling apart,' Safa says, her voice dropping a notch, 'but more than that . . . Malc and Kon are mates and we can't just leave them dead. Ben came back for me and Harry . . . Didn't that mess the timeline up? And if it did, we fixed it . . . same as we'll do if getting Malc and Kon messes anything up.'

A moment's worth of pause in reflection at the new angle being worked by Safa in the ever-continuing debate, either that or the tiredness from the assault on Cavendish Manor and the multiple incursions into governmental war rooms just a few days ago are taking their toll.

Ria killed her own mother and currently lies sedated in her bed with a gunshot wound to her stomach. The hot water has stopped working and half the shutters in the bunker are either jammed shut or jammed open. The filtration system on the back door is whirring with a noise it shouldn't be making. The electrics are flickering, the lights fading, doors squeaking and mould growing in the corners of rooms from the lack of sunlight and ventilation.

They killed scores of people during a sustained, prolonged and exhausting day of days that stretched them physically and mentally. They knew what they were going in for. It was a mission, a job, a thing that had to be done, and their faces and bodies still show the bruises, cuts and wounds. They can process and deal with all of that. They can spend long hours on Bertie's island under the Aegean sun and swim in the warm waters of a pure unpolluted Mediterranean Sea. They can decompress and let the raw, brutal energy wane and recover. They can heal and go forward to the year 2111 to see if it's still apocalyptic and if it is then they will fix it, but there is a line, and blocked toilets cross that line.

'Harry's a big man,' Safa says, breaking the silence.

'What's that got to do with anything?' Ben asks.

'Big men do big shits,' Safa replies, staring at the toilet.

'Oh,' Ben says mildly as Harry tuts in admonishment at the crass mention of his daily motions.

'I'm going for a wee outside,' Emily says, but stays leaning against the sink, staring at the toilet and the still water an inch below the rim. 'Where does it go?'

'What?' Safa asks.

'The waste. Where does it go?' Emily asks again.

'Where does the waste go?' Safa asks Ben.

'Why you asking me?'

'You're an egghead.'

'I'm definitely going for a wee,' Emily says, moving towards the door.

'Shit,' Ben says with a sudden wince. 'Malc and Kon wouldn't have risked raw sewage going outside . . . Must be a tank somewhere that we've never emptied.'

'We've been here months,' Safa says, screwing her face up.

'Miri,' Ben says, looking across to the older woman edging aside to let Emily pass. 'We really need Malc and Kon back . . .'

Emily snorts a laugh, walking out into the corridor and down towards the doors at the end with a big yawn and a stretch of her arms over her head that makes the yawn sound gargled and strained. Moisture in her eyes that she blinks away. Her muscles are still sore from two days ago. A general feeling of fatigue and a few painful points from the bashes and bumps. She pushes through the double doors into the main room, flooded with natural light, and ducks as she walks to see through the window at what the weather is like outside.

A blue light flickers behind her, instantly forming a square doorway of shimmering iridescence and a man running through it whose voice comes to hearing mid-scream.

'. . . ILY . . . EMILY . . . GET HIM!'

She spins with years of practice drilled into her core and her eyes hardening to read the threat. The man looks terrified. His face bathed in sweat, but his eyes fixed on her.

'EMILY!'

He runs deeper into the room, veering away from the portal with a glance behind as a second figure comes through with a snarl etched on his face. Blond hair, square jaw, blue eyes, grey clothing and a black pistol gripped in his hand that lifts to aim at the first man.

Everything on instinct. Everything on gut reaction. Emily snatches a plate from the big table and sends it flying at the man holding the pistol. He fires as the plate smashes into his face, knocking him back, the boom of the gun so loud and sharp in the confined space.

'Get him, Emily!' the first man yelps, diving for cover.

She grabs another plate and throws it hard, then launches across the room. She knows neither of the men, but the first is unarmed, terrified and shouting her name. The second is angry, uniformed and holding a gun. The second plate hits his elbow as he plucks another shot. With a shout, he tries to aim at Emily, but she's closed the distance and first feints left then goes right and low while kicking out with a leg sweep designed to take him down.

His reactions are fast and he almost jumps the kick, but tangles at the last second and starts to topple while plucking the trigger. He twists as he drops with an obvious intent to slam his body weight into her. She rolls to the side and kicks up to drive the heel of her naked foot into his groin with an explosive impact that sags him mid-fall. He slumps down with a yelp and tears in his eyes, but still he tries to aim and fire. She vaults up and slams that same heel into his face, snapping his head over, then drops to grab the hand holding the gun to ensure the aim is away from her.

'CONTACT! CONTACT!' She bellows the words, knowing the shots will already be bringing the others towards her. The man fights her grip, suddenly lunging to sink his teeth into the back of her hand while scrabbling to pull a dagger from a sheath on his belt. He slashes out wildly, scoring the blade across her arm. She twists and yanks to free the pistol from his grip as he stabs up with the knife. No time to move away. No time to do anything other than point and fire. She sends two rounds into his chest, killing him instantly.

'Oh my god . . . thank you, thank you . . .' The first man runs to her side, his face still frantic with fear and worry. 'Emily, thank you . . . you're a bloody lifesaver.' He leans in fast to kiss her cheek with an action so natural and unexpected she doesn't even think to shoot him. 'I hate this bloody job . . . I'm Malc, by the way . . .' he yells as he runs through the portal that shuts down just as Safa bursts into the room.

'HOW MANY?'

'ONE DOWN,' Emily shouts back, still aiming the pistol at the body. 'The Blue was here . . .'

'I saw it,' Safa says quickly.

'What?' Ben asks, rushing into the room with Harry and Miri.

'The portal . . . It was open . . . Two men came in . . .' Emily reports.

'Two?' Miri asks, seeing one body on the floor.

10

'One went back,' Emily says. 'He said my name . . . the first man . . . He ran in, he was scared . . . He shouted *Get him, Emily* . . . Then this guy ran in and fired at the first man. I got the gun off him . . .'

'Fuck me,' Ben says, coming to her side to look down at the body.

'He, er . . . the first guy,' Emily says, turning to look behind her again. 'He said his name was Malc . . .'

'Malc?' Ben asks as the others snap heads over to stare at Emily.

'He kissed my cheek and said he hates this bloody job,' Emily says.

'Malc?' Safa asks. 'Malcolm kissed you?'

'He said he was Malc . . .' Emily says, looking back round the room. 'Brown hair . . . average build . . .' She trails off on seeing the hard stares coming from Ben and Miri. 'What? I'm not making it up . . .'

'I saw the portal go off,' Safa says, clocking the way Ben and Miri are staring at Emily.

'You're still here,' Ben mutters. 'He said his name was Malc?'

'He said Malc,' Emily says. 'Why are you looking at me like that?'

'Safa, did you see him?' Ben asks while Miri looks on with a growing frown.

'No, I just saw the portal going off as I came in.'

'Couldn't have been Malc,' Ben says.

'He said Malc,' Emily asserts again.

'If Malcolm is alive to run in here, then he doesn't die in Berlin,' Ben says. 'Which means they don't track us to Cavendish Manor, which means your team don't meet us and you don't end up here—'

'Bloody hell,' Safa exclaims. 'You shot a Nazi . . .'

'What?' Emily snaps, finally looking down to take in the details.

'A Nazi. You shot a Nazi.'

'What on earth?' Doctor Watson blurts, rushing into the room while pulling his trousers up. 'Are we being attacked? I heard shots and— Good lord!' he says, coming to a sudden stop on sight of the body. 'Is that a dead Nazi?'

'Um . . . dunno. We got a doctor anywhere?' Safa asks.

'The toilets are blocked, by the way,' the doctor says, staring down. 'That's definitely a Nazi.'

'Doc, check the IP,' Miri orders.

'IP?' the doctor asks.

'The Nazi,' Ben whispers. 'Check the Nazi.'

'Oh, right, yes, yes of course . . . I was on the toilet.' He lowers stiffly to a knee and pushes his fingertips into the man's neck. 'They're blocked, by the way. Did I say that?'

'You did,' Ben says.

'Stormtrooper,' Harry says.

'What is?' Emily asks.

'He is,' Harry says, pointing his plunger at the body.

'He was,' the doctor says. 'He's a dead Stormtrooper now, I'm afraid. What does IP mean?'

'Injured party,' Ben says. 'I thought doctors knew that.'

'Of course I knew,' the doctor says quickly. 'Shock.'

'Have a chocolate bar,' Safa says. 'That's good for shock.'

'That's the worst thing for shock,' the doctor fires back.

'I was taking the piss.'

'Harry, you know how to use this?' Emily asks, looking at the pistol in her hand.

'Aye,' Harry says, swapping the plunger for the gun. 'Luger, nice weapon in its day.' He lowers down at the head of the body wearing a uniform once so familiar as that of the sworn enemy. A blond-haired, square-jawed master of the Aryan race. Broad shoulders, thick limbs and no doubt as brainwashed and fanatical as the rest. He grabs the dead man's hand and slides the dagger free. Standard SS issue. Sleek and evil-looking with a hilt shaped like a reversed hour glass. Words etched on the blade: *meine ehre heisst treue.*

'My honour is called loyalty,' Emily says, resting a hand on Harry's shoulder as she leans over to read the words.

Harry grabs the dead soldier's collar to pull him closer, inspecting the insignia as old habits kick in. He rips the tunic open with a hard yank to reach in and feel for the inside pocket, ignoring the blood smearing his fingers. A sheaf of papers neatly folded and what should be standard identification documents, but the layout of them is different and not a design he has seen before. A sepia picture of a pretty fräulein with blonde-ringlet hair and a stern expression. Harry instinctively looks for anything of note that could reveal positions, formations or orders. He doesn't read German, but he recognises certain words and was taught the styles of papers and forms, and none of these matches what he has been trained to look for. Then he remembers his war is over and he's in a bunker in the Cretaceous period and blinks while shaking his head. 'Papers are different,' he says gruffly. 'Not like how they should be . . . Uniform is different too. The insignia on the lapels isn't right.'

'You think he's a fake?' Ben asks.

'No. Just different,' Harry says, pushing a hand through his beard. 'The Luger and the dagger are right . . .'

'So why have we got a dead Nazi in here?' Safa asks.

'Cos Emily shot him,' Ben says.

'Quiet,' Miri orders, stepping away, her head cocked over.

Harry and Emily rise quickly to their feet as Safa and Ben move out, all of them straining to listen.

'What?' Ben whispers.

Miri lifts a hand, silencing him. She heard a noise. A low metallic sound. 'Get armed,' she orders quietly.

Safa runs through the door towards the armoury as another clang rings out, this one louder and followed by a solid thump that seems to rattle and roll through the bunker from one end to the other.

'Pipes,' Harry says, feeling vibrations through his bare feet that send a thrumming sensation, increasing quickly, that rises to a crescendo then stops and ceases as though it was never there. Silence follows save for a sudden yell from Safa and a prolonged vent of foul words being shouted.

They respond swiftly, running through the doors into the corridor leading to the rear door into an overwhelming stench of faeces and urine coming from the murky brown water pouring from an open doorway, and the sight of Safa pushing at the back door while gagging and swearing, her arms coated in filthy liquid that exploded from the toilet as she ran past the doorway of the bathroom into the armoury. She staggers outside to bend double and vomit as Ben and Harry rush into the closest set of rooms to see the bathroom dripping filth and the toilet purging water from the bowl.

Emily gags. Miri coughs hard with tears in her eyes. Even the doctor, well-experienced in the smells of the human body, gags and covers his mouth and nose as he splashes through the sewage to the back door.

'Ria,' he says quickly as though remembering. He veers off to Ria's room, quickly leaning in to see her room looks clean and untouched and the dark-haired girl still heavily sedated in the bed. He pulls the door closed and wades out to see the others coughing and gagging with Miri bracing herself against the outside wall.

'We're getting M and K back,' she gasps.

'Oh, now we're getting them back?' Safa asks.

'Safa?' Emily says.

'What?'

'You've got some shit on your face.'

Two

'We only popped out for coffee,' Konrad says. 'What the hell did you do?'

'Is he dead?' Malcolm asks, leaning over to look down at the body in the main room.

'Bloody hell,' Konrad says, slowly turning to take in the main room that ten minutes ago was austere, sterile and filled only with furniture of basic functionality but is now adorned with deep leather sofas, side tables bearing tiffany lamps, rugs on the floor, art on the walls, armchairs and a table big enough to seat a dozen people. 'Malc, you seen all this?'

'I have, Kon. It's a dead Nazi.'

'What is?'

'That is,' Malcolm says as Konrad finally looks down at the body.

'Ten minutes,' Konrad mumbles. 'We've been gone ten minutes . . .'

'You just woke up from the ocean rescue,' Malcolm says, looking from Safa to Harry and feeling very weirded out at them both grinning at him. Ben, too, standing there with a huge smile as though they haven't seen each other for a while. The penny drops at that point and his eyes widen. 'Now hold on a bloody minute! How long have we been dead?'

'Few days,' Ben mumbles.

'Days?' Konrad asks.

'Maybe weeks?' Ben suggests lightly.

'Weeks?'

'Months then, but . . . you know . . .'

'Been busy,' Harry booms.

'Busy,' Ben says.

'Very busy,' Harry adds.

'Super busy,' Ben says. 'You know . . . saving the world and . . . But hey, here you are . . .' he adds brightly.

'Months?' Konrad squawks, gathering himself up from Harry's warm welcome. 'Malc? He said months.'

'You got Harry and Safa back in ten days . . .' Malcolm says. 'Ten days . . . Look at this room . . .'

'I said, we've been really busy,' Ben says again.

'Busy?' Konrad asks. 'Busy? Too busy to pop out for five minutes? I got stabbed in the leg!'

'Where?' Ben asks, looking down in alarm at Konrad's legs.

'S'tiny but that's not the point . . . No, I mean it was the point, but just the point . . .'

'Not too busy to go shopping either,' Malcolm says, looking round at the furniture.

'Ria did that,' Safa says as Ben and Harry wince.

'What?' Malcolm asks.

'Ria?' Konrad asks.

'Roland's Ria?' Malcolm asks.

'Ria Cavendish?' Konrad asks.

'Hi! I'm Emily,' Emily says, offering her hand to Konrad, who gives it a weak shake. 'Hi,' Emily grins, stretching to shake Malcolm's hand as well. 'You kissed me a few hours ago after being chased by that dead guy.'

'It was definitely him then?' Ben asks with a puzzled frown.

'Oh yes,' Emily says, staring at a wide-eyed Malcolm.

'I didn't kiss you!' Malcolm sputters. 'I didn't . . . I never met you and I don't know nothing about a Nazi chasing anyone . . .'

'You did,' she says, pressing a fingertip to her cheek. 'Right there.'

'I never did! I didn't . . . Honestly . . . I was here an hour ago with Kon and Ben and . . . Kon, tell her, tell her I wasn't kissing . . .'

'Months?' Konrad asks again. 'Bloody months? Oh, that's lovely, that is. Really lovely. Where's Roland? Why did Ria . . . ?'

'I didn't kiss you.'

'M and K?' Miri says curtly. 'R is dead. We need to debrief. Suggest redeploy to Bertie's island for refs.'

'What?' Konrad asks.

'What?' Malcolm asks.

'Takes a bit of getting used to,' Ben says. 'But, um, so . . . Miri, this is Malcolm and Konrad and, er . . . this is Miri.'

'I know,' Miri says.

'Miri's the OIC now,' Ben says.

'Oh, I see?' Konrad asks.

'Officer in charge,' Ben says.

'Oh, I see,' Konrad says with a sudden grin. 'Get it? *Oh, I see?* No?'

'Some tumbleweed just went past,' Emily says.

'I didn't kiss you, miss.'

'How are you still here?' Ben asks Emily.

'R?' Konrad asks. 'Is that Roland?'

'Yes,' Miri says.

'Roland is dead?' Konrad asks.

'Yes.'

'Oh, I see,' Konrad says.

'Nice one,' Emily laughs, then stops when no one else joins in. 'Sorry, I thought he was doing the, er . . . joke thing . . . erm . . .'

'When are we getting him back?' Malcolm asks. 'Few months? Few years? Maybe a decade? You know . . . busy with shopping and everything and what's that awful bloody smell?'

'I told you,' Safa says. 'The toilets exploded, there's no hot water, the lights are flickering, there's mould growing on the walls, half the shutters are jammed and the filter thing at the back door is making a weird noise.'

'Right,' Malcolm says.

'Oh, I get it,' Konrad says, looking at Emily. 'You thought I said *oh, I see* as in OIC . . .'

'Yes! I thought you were joking again.'

'And that Nazi chased you through the portal, before you kissed Emily and legged it,' Safa adds, pointing at the dead body still on the floor.

'I did not kiss her! I didn't . . . I really didn't . . .'

'Oh, and we got Bertie and Ria out from their house,' Safa says, 'and Roland too, but it went tits up so we went back to help us the first time and ended up killing the guys that we just killed in Berlin, but that was in the UK. Confuses the hell out of me. Anyway. Ria killed her mum and got shot in the belly but she was pregnant with Derek's baby from America . . . He worked in McDonald's but was joining the Marines and then Bertie made a red time machine thing. Er . . . then Miri killed Roland, but Ria and Bertie don't know that, they just think he sodded off. I think Ria knows, but she hates him now. Bertie doesn't seem bothered though. Er . . . that's it really. Oh, yeah . . . we threatened just about every country that has nuclear weapons, but we haven't checked if the world still blows up in twenty-one eleven. We were going to do that today, but the toilets exploded and Miri finally agreed we could come get you.'

'Right,' Malcolm says into the stunned silence that follows.

'And we're millionaires,' Safa adds.

'Right,' Malcolm says again.

'We stole loads of money from smurfs.'

'Smurfs,' Malcolm says.

'Money launderers, not the little blue people.'

'Right,' Malcolm says. 'I didn't kiss you though,' he adds with a look to Emily.

'Been busy then,' Konrad says.

'I did say that,' Ben says.

'Oh, I see,' Konrad says, smiling at Emily.

'Yeah, not funny this time,' she says politely.

'Tough crowd. How did Roland die?'

'Shot him,' Miri says.

'Who shot him?' Konrad asks.

'I shot him.'

'You shot him?'

'Yes.'

'What for?'

'To kill him. We will redeploy and debrief.'

'What about him?' Ben asks, pointing at the body.

'To be decided,' Miri says simply, walking over to the portal set in the main room to save them having to keep venturing into the sewage-filled corridor. She pulls the tablet out from a pocket and starts thumbing the screen with practised hands that Malcolm and Konrad both spot. 'Stay armed from now on,' Miri adds as the Blue shuts down then comes back on.

'I'm not lugging this bloody Barret about everywhere,' Ben says.

'Sidearms will suffice, Mr Ryder,' she replies, before disappearing through the portal.

'Did we just . . .' Ben starts to speak, then tuts when he realises she won't hear him. He goes through after her, wincing at the bright sunshine and the wall of heat from the instant transition in time and space. 'I said did we just undo everything at Cavendish Manor?' he asks again, shielding his eyes to look at Miri lighting a cigarette.

'That is to be established,' she says.

'But Emily is still here,' Ben says.

'MIRI! BEN . . .' Bertie shouts as he runs towards them, bare-chested and his hair dripping wet from swimming, with a huge smile that grows bigger as Harry, Safa and Emily come through to the island until he stops dead with the face of a child showing sheer delight. 'Malc . . . Kon . . .' he gasps before charging to hug both at the same time.

'I think we just proved something significant,' Ben says, resuming the quiet conversation while the attention is focussed on Bertie. 'Except I don't know what it is. Theoretically we just undid . . .'

'They thought the world was flat,' Miri cuts in. 'That was a theory. Theories mean jack shit until proof is obtained. Emily is still here but Ria is still shot, Roland is still dead and one thing is sure as shit . . . time is definitely not fixed . . .' She sucks air in as though just speaking has left her breathless.

'Definitely not fixed?' Ben asks.

'Definitely not fixed,' she repeats before inhaling deeply on the cigarette again. 'I witnessed M and K being killed.'

'Do what?' Ben asks. Instant silence falls. Everyone staring at Miri and Ben and even Bertie stays quiet.

'I saw it.'

Ben's head drops as that look crosses his features that still makes Safa cock her head to one side as she watches him closely. He rubs his jaw, scratches his forehead, then the tip of his nose before looking up. 'It's not possible. But it just happened . . . so it is possible . . .' He trails off to stare at Bertie.

'S'just binary,' Bertie says with a shrug. They all look at him, knowing he'll be able to understand the whole of it with ease, but also that what's in his head does not translate to his mouth in a way anyone else can understand.

'Miri, right, listen . . .' Ben says, holding his hand out. 'You were there. You saw Malc and Kon being killed, then blew the warehouse, then all that stuff happened at Cavendish Manor . . . but we just went back to that point and stopped Malc and Kon being killed.' He points at Malcolm and Konrad as he speaks. 'Time *isn't* fixed then. It *can* be changed . . . which suggests our detachment from the timeline renders us immune to the changes within it.' He looks at Bertie, who grins and nods eagerly.

'You overthink it,' Safa says. 'We're here. Malc and Kon are here. Now we go figure out why a dead Nazi chased Malc into the bunker.'

'Agreed,' Miri says.

'First time for everything,' Safa says in surprise.

'Bloody hell,' Ben says, shaking his head to rid the confusing thoughts as another idea pops in his mind that prompts a new suspicious look at Miri. 'Have you been forward?'

'Negative,' Miri says instantly. 'I told you there was no point seeing what the world looked like until after we finished.'

'That was two days ago. Plenty of time for you to take a little trip and go forward.'

'Check the tablets. The usage is all recorded.'

'Devices can be manipulated.'

'We are in an entirely reactive position now,' she says, shaking her head at him. 'I would never give consent for M and K to be re-extracted, but we obviously did for M to appear . . .' She drags on the smoke as Harry lights up a few feet away with Emily and Safa both chiding him for smoking.

'Hmmm,' Ben says. 'Guess we've got some work to do then.'

'We need to see twenty-one eleven,' Miri says, grinding her cigarette out under her boot before pulling the ziplock baggie from her pocket and lowering slowly to a knee to retrieve the stubbed butt.

'Miri, do you enjoy this?' Ben asks, still watching her closely for reaction.

She holds her eyes on his for a second and maybe, just maybe there is a twinkle and a fleeting flicker of a smile.

'Bloody knew it,' he says, arching an eyebrow at her.

'We'll debrief,' she says, pushing up to her feet. 'Then *I* – she pauses to give Ben a very faint smile – 'will decide the next steps.'

'You're a tyrant,' Ben says.

'This is not a democracy, Mr Ryder . . .'

Three

The windows are mirrored so anyone glancing at the GCHQ building will not see them staring out across the River Thames to the twelve-foot-high holographic 3D image of Tango Two giving her finger to the heavens above.

'Rather apt,' Mother mutters.

The man at her side stays silent, secretly agreeing with her and wishing she would just go.

The assault on Cavendish Manor was only a year ago, but already the world is a vastly different place. Borders sealed. Alliances shattered. Trust gone. NATO in tatters. The UN a laughing stock. The EU on the brink of collapse. A new global cold war with walls going up on hard borders equipped with heavy weapons. Satellites hacked and spies turning up dead every week.

Maggie Sanderson used a time machine to simultaneously appear in dozens of government war rooms at the same second with a truly American show of absolute power designed to bring total shock and awe.

She certainly brought about world peace as not one single nation has fired a shot at another in the guise of war. Instead they have murdered, poisoned, drowned and gone back to covert methods of secret messages written with invisible ink on edible paper while riots raged in nearly every city as the masses rose up in emulation of the heroes that held guns to the heads of their oppressors.

Mother sips from the long-stemmed glass of champagne. Her eyes now more hooded and the bags deeper and darker. The lines on her face more pronounced. 'World peace,' she snorts bitterly.

'Indeed,' the man at her side says.

She looks at him, hating him, detesting every ounce of his creation and existence. Then she smiles warmly. 'So,' she asks, taking another sip. 'How does it feel?'

'Feel?' he asks politely.

'To be Father. How does it feel?'

'Oh, I won't be Father,' he says, turning back to the window. 'It's been agreed that such terminology is too closely associated with the, er . . . well, with the bad old days.'

She glares at the side of his head. 'That's a good idea,' she says amiably. *You smug cunt*, she thinks.

'Yes,' he says deeply, rocking on his heels in a way that makes her want to slam his face into the window. 'Plenty to be getting on with,' he adds, hoping she'll take the hint.

There certainly will be, she thinks, draining the glass and watching the heavily armed paramilitary police unit arrive to batter the people away from the holographic projection, using boots to stamp the plastic cube to bits, making Tango Two flicker for a second before blinking out in a way Mother wishes was true and real.

'Well, it's not my concern anymore, is it?' Mother says, turning from habit to stalk back towards her desk, then remembering it's not her desk anymore. It's his. Roger Downtree. The new head of the British Secret Service. And Mother knows that not one single person within the organisation will be sad to see her go. They'll have a party. They'll celebrate and rejoice that the witch is gone.

'Anyway,' Roger says brightly, turning away from the window to hold his hand out. 'On behalf of His Majesty's government, may I thank you for your service?'

She shakes his hand and waits expectantly. Staring at him. He falters. Unsure of what she is waiting for.

'Well, go on then,' she prompts.

'What?' he asks, narrowing his eyes.

'Thank me for my service.'

'I just did.'

'You said *May I thank you for your service*. You never said thank you.'

'Right. I see. Er, okay then. Thank you for your service.'

'You're most welcome,' she replies icily, holding his hand until the moment becomes uncomfortable, reading the point when he is about to ask for his hand back and ever-so-politely suggest she should leave.

'Cunt,' she hisses sharply, making him flinch and pull his hand free as an urgent knocking comes from the door being pushed open by a harried-looking woman blanching at the sight of Mother.

'Mr Downtree, sir . . . there's, er . . .' The woman hesitates. Her gaze flicking from Roger to Mother. 'We have an urgent situation developing, sir . . .'

'I'll see myself out,' Mother says, striding past the woman and out of the building for the very last time to be driven through the sullen streets of London for her final debrief with the PM, passing soldiers standing sentry on street corners with drones whirring near silently to keep the masses under scrutiny, and three more times she sees the glowing holographic image of Emily Rose shining in the air.

A symbol of freedom that the massed public took to their hearts. A lone female armed with an assault rifle making a stand against gunships and armies. A taunting reminder that not only did Mother fail to stop Maggie Sanderson securing the device, but that she also failed to stop that very image being hacked and released from what should have been a secure satellite feed.

At Downing Street, she walks alone past the soldiers stationed every few metres and looks up the road to the tank sitting massive outside the gates.

A glance to the side of the street where the press pack once dominated. Now banned since the terrorist attack in which Safa Patel *apparently* died protecting the then PM.

'Mother,' Colin Brough says in formal greeting, ushering her in through the main door. An aide to the PM and so full of his own self-importance it makes her want to claw his eyes out, but her attention focusses on the hub of noise and the sight of aides and advisors rushing from room to room clutching tablets and holding rushed conversations. Something is happening. Something big.

'Through here, please. We'll try not to keep you waiting too long . . . but the PM is somewhat busy right now . . .'

A look of horror shows on Mother's face as she walks into the waiting room to sit in humiliated isolated silence. She is Mother. She practically ran this country and has never even seen the inside of a waiting room in Downing Street before, but now sits like a toxic pariah in true isolation until the door opens and the same aide rushes in, his manner worried, his whole being now very preoccupied.

'Colin? Where's the PM?' she asks, standing up to glare through those hooded eyes that once made men quake in their shoes.

'My apologies,' Colin blurts. 'The PM is, er . . . dealing with something, but she has asked me to pass both her highest regard and her personal gratitude for your service . . .'

The reaction shows on Mother's face that floods with deep offence at the insult, and she storms to the front door through the clamouring chaos and out into the silent street, suddenly filling with more soldiers, to be taken home on the last journey she will probably ever make in an armoured government vehicle.

'What's going on?' she demands of the driver and guard in the front of the Range Rover as the vehicle speeds through the London streets to her private residence. They don't answer but then they don't have to now. She's not Mother anymore.

They pull up outside her private Georgian residence and she waits for the driver or the second guard to get out and open the door.

'When you're ready, love,' the front-seat passenger says rudely, turning to motion for her to go.

She goes to fire back, to wither his crass insubordination with a diatribe of abuse, but she is not Mother now. She is nothing and so for the first time in years she opens her own door and gets out to stand and watch as the Range Rover speeds away.

She walks briskly to unlock her front door, then stops at the alarm panel set on the inside wall, lowering her head for the biometric scanner to read her iris while her thumb presses on a small panel. 'I am home,' she says quietly for the benefit of the voice-recognition system.

'System deactivated,' a soft automated voice announces inside while she turns to absorb the ambience of her cold and empty house that will never be a home, and again she pauses, her eyes narrowing, then flickering to the grandfather clock off to her right.

She strides forward a few steps and stops facing the open door to the downstairs toilet, staring in at the white-tiled room in silence.

Seconds pass. A minute. A flicker of irritation, then both things she was expecting happen at the same time. The bathroom fills with a green glow as the tablet in her pocket vibrates with an incoming call.

She pulls it free, holding it in her hand while taking in the way the white tiles reflect the green shimmering iridescent doorway of light. A figure comes through, marked with blood spatters and holding a pistol. Mother lifts a hand, indicating to wait.

'WHAT?' the figure shouts before pulling out ear gels that give off the tinny sound of loud rock music. 'I was listening to music . . . What did you say?'

'Wait,' Mother says, showing the tablet vibrating. 'Is it all ready?'

'I'm here, aren't I?' the person replies. 'Are you answering that?'

'I am indeed,' Mother whispers, swiping the screen to activate the call.

'*Mother?*' an urgent voice says through the secure connection, one she instantly recognises.

'*PM,*' Mother says.

'*Please,*' Veronica Smedley says, the British Prime Minister and the person that deflected the full responsibility from the government to the shoulders of Mother when it all went so horribly wrong. '*Mother, please tell me you have nothing to do with this . . .*'

'*With what?*' Mother asks while the waiting figure taps a foot and hums patiently.

'*Mother, I am asking you now. Are you behind this?*' the PM asks, her voice hardening.

'*Behind what? You sacked me, remember . . . How do I know what's going on? I'm the toxic fucking pariah that has been humiliated the world over and hung out to FUCKING DRY . . .*' Mother screams the last two words, her face twisting with rage.

'*Oh dear god,*' the PM whispers. '*Please . . . please don't do this . . .*'

'*Tell me,*' Mother hisses. '*Did you honestly think I wouldn't find out? Did you really honestly think I wouldn't know?*'

'*Mother, please . . .*'

'*It's in front of me right now, Veronica, and what a nice shade of green it is. Who chose the colour? Was it you?*'

'*Full re-instatement. Full control,*' the PM says quickly. '*I will make a public apology and exonerate you of all wrong-doing. You can have the project . . .*'

'*What project?*' Mother asks, switching to an innocent tone while the figure holding the gun in the bathroom looks at the blood spatters and tuts mildly. '*Do you mean the secret time machine you've built, Veronica? That project? The one I now have control over? That one? The one I am going to use to hunt down and kill that cunt Maggie Sanderson? That one? I'm going now, but, please, try not to worry, I won't do anything stupid . . . Sleep well, PM, because it won't just be Maggie standing over you in the dark . . .'*

'*MOTHER!*'

She cuts the call off with a simple swipe of her thumb and exhales long and slow with a blast of air rushing through her nose.

'Feel better?'

'Indeed,' Mother replies. She turns, marches to a cupboard and pulls out the bag she packed earlier, then heads into the bathroom to stare quietly for a second.

'Go through,' the figure says.

Mother walks through the solid green light, stepping from her bathroom in London to a brightly lit room with freshly painted concrete walls and a floor littered with dead bodies lying in pools of blood.

Small anterooms lead off it and a set of double doors give way to a wide corridor as brightly lit as the room she is in.

Movement behind her as the other person steps through and walks to a fixed stand to operate a screen that shuts the portal off.

'Where are we?' Mother asks.

'About fifty million years in the past. Do you want the precise date and location?'

'No,' Mother replies, looking at the bodies.

'That's Gunjeep,' the person says, pointing at the corpse of a big bearded Indian man in a white lab coat. 'Or rather it was . . . They're all dead anyway.'

'Good,' Mother says. 'Where's the canteen? I want a coffee.'

'Up the corridor. I'll show you . . .'

'No need. Get this cleaned up. We've got a lot of work to do . . .'

'Yes, Mother . . .'

Four

How such a big man can move so silently speaks volumes to his training and experience. Miri still hears him coming, but then she is also highly trained and experienced.

'Sergeant,' she says without looking round.

Harry's lips twitch in a fleeting smile as he comes to a stop next to Miri and stares out at the inky black sea. Warm and humid and the stars overhead shine bright and glorious. Night-time in the Cretaceous period is good, but Harry can't remember anywhere matching this now. Northern Africa maybe.

There was no choice but to spend the night on Bertie's island away from the stinking bunker. Malcolm and Konrad were brought up to speed within an hour, but then Miri has that ability to make grown men listen and take in what she is saying.

'Help you?' Miri asks.

'Wanted to ask for a pass, ma'am.'

'A pass?'

'Aye, ma'am.'

She thinks for a minute, processing the different military terminology and what it could mean. 'Do you want leave, Harry?'

'Aye.'

'Why?'

A barely noticeable shift in his position as he stands at ease with his hands behind his back, and although he stays impassive that lack of reaction speaks volumes. 'Killed a lot of men, ma'am. Mission was difficult. Be good to get drunk . . . and . . . well . . . Not been home in a long time, ma'am.'

She frowns in thought while looking up at him. Harry is the least demanding of all of them. The most dependable too. Unflappable. Fearless and selfless to a fault and that's the problem with honourable men: they'll do the bad thing, all right, but they'll suffer for it afterwards. Not on the surface, but deep inside. A niggle that can turn into a nag and eventually leads to a noose or the barrel of a gun.

In the blink of an eye she brings knowledge of his life to the forefront of her mind. Harry was engaged to marry Edith. He is an Alpha-type male. Fit and healthy. He has been confined to the bunker for months. Safa and Emily are both very attractive women and although Harry has more honour in his little finger than most men have in their entire bodies he still has the same needs and desires as everyone else.

'You cannot go home,' she says firmly. 'Our extractions are permanent.'

'Understood.'

'But yes to a night away and getting drunk. Some' – she pauses to choose her words carefully – 'decompression wouldn't go amiss. We'll get through tomorrow and reassess.'

'Aye. Thank you.'

'Anytime,' she says quietly as he nods smartly and walks off back towards the lights glowing outside the shack and the others sitting at the large picnic table.

'Everything okay?' Emily asks as the big man sits down.

'Aye,' he says simply.

'Beer?' Safa asks, passing a bottle down.

'Aye,' he says just as simply while taking the bottle.

'Aye,' Emily says, deep, hearty and mimicking a gruff look that makes him smile. She holds his eye for a second and inclines her head with an unspoken question hanging in the air between them. He shakes his head. She frowns lightly. He shrugs minutely and takes a sip of his beer as she reaches over and rubs his arm. 'Tell me later.'

'Nowt to say.'

'What's up?' Ben asks, seeing the interaction between them.

'Nowt,' Harry says, taking another sip from the bottle.

'We're sleeping under the stars tonight,' Emily says, pointing her bottle at Harry, 'and you're my pillow.'

'Aye,' he says, looking away to the flat surface of the sea.

'Awful state,' Malcolm calls out. The attention on Harry moves to the two workmen walking into the clearing. 'Bloody awful . . . You haven't changed the filter in the filtration system and the tanks haven't been emptied in months, so the outlet valve in the outside wall is actually dripping poo . . .' He trails off from his mini rant on seeing Emily watching him. 'I didn't kiss you.'

'You did.'

'What concerns me,' Konrad says, taking over from Malcolm as he grabs a bottle of beer from the case and twists the top off, 'is the mould growing in the corners . . .' He swigs a mouthful, tries to suppress a belch and looks round. 'The inside of the bunker is effectively a modern environment, right? The filtration system is the barrier between the two worlds, right? Is the mould,' Konrad asks, holding his bottle up in emphasis of his question, 'is it modern fungus growing in a Cretaceous environment or Cretaceous fungus growing in a modern environment?'

'Er . . .' Ben says.

'Because, either way, with that filtration system knackered we could have altered the state of the entire world as we know it,' Konrad adds with a nod and a big glug from the bottle. 'Only takes a spore . . . a seed on a shoe . . . bacteria or . . . or whatever and that's it. Your T-rex never happens and instead we get something between a goat and a dog as the master race.'

'I'm sure it's okay,' Ben says.

'I'm not,' Konrad says. 'Wouldn't be obvious either. Could take generations to have an effect.'

'We'll add it to the list of shit to worry about,' Ben says.

'Dead Nazi being chased by Malcolm,' Safa says. 'Put that on the list.'

'He wasn't dead when he was chasing him,' Emily says. 'He wasn't a zombie . . .'

'Semantics,' Ben says. 'Anyway, what outlet valve?' he asks Malcolm.

'Outside, on the back wall. It's low down, hidden by the long grass that hasn't been cut . . . We had a hose in the warehouse in Berlin. Coupled it on and stuffed the end down the sewage drains. God knows how we'll drain it now without a hose.'

'Add buying a hose on the list of shit to worry about,' Emily says, waggling her bottle of beer at Ben.

'Miri?' Ben calls out.

'What?' Miri calls back.

'We need a new hose.'

'And a list of shit to worry about,' Safa says to a few chuckles.

'We always have a list of shit to worry about,' Miri's voice floats back.

'Want a beer, Miri?' Emily shouts.

'Minute.'

'How's Ria?' Emily asks.

'Awful mess,' Malcolm says sadly.

'Awful, bloody Roland,' Konrad says. 'Greedy, selfish sod. We told him. We told him, didn't we, Malc? We said he's out of his depth. We said he shouldn't be doing it.'

'Never listens,' Malcolm says.

'Never bloody listens to anyone,' Konrad says. 'Not an evil man.'

'Not evil, just selfish.'

'And a coward too. Left his wife and kids. Ran off and left them to die.'

'Awful,' Malcolm tuts sadly. 'Mind, though, Kon, Ria went back of her own accord, she did.'

'She did,' Konrad says as the others play conversation-tennis and look from one to the other. 'Always headstrong was our Ria.'

'Headstrong,' Malcolm adds.

'Immature sometimes,' Konrad says.

'Kids today, Kon,' Malcolm says with another tut. 'Got another beer there? What we doing with that dead Nazi then? He's still in the main room.'

'You can't leave him there,' Emily says in disgust.

'Can't put him outside, miss,' Konrad says. 'Get a hungry dinosaur eating him? Change the world that could. Only takes a spore or a seed . . . or eating a dead bloke from the twentieth century . . .'

'Another one for the list of shit to worry about,' Safa tells Ben.

'Noted,' Ben replies.

'My great granddad was in the German army in the war,' Konrad says.

'Was he really?'

'Got shot in the foot at the start. We still had his uniform when I was a kid. It looked a bit like that dead bloke's. The dead guy was SS, though. My granddad was just regular army.'

'I thought the SS wore black,' Malcolm says.

'Some,' Harry says, giving them both a look that thereby signifies the end of that conversation.

'Fuck me,' Ben says softly, nodding at Konrad to pass another bottle of beer down. 'Lot to think about.'

'It certainly is,' Miri says, looming from the darkness to take the bottle Konrad was reaching for. She pops the lid one-handed and holds it out to be passed down before taking another for herself. 'HB state, report,' she adds, looking at Konrad.

'What's the HB again?' Konrad asks.

'Home base, Kon,' Malcolm says. 'And it should be condemned. The bloody thing isn't fit for purpose now.'

'Not an option. Repair?' Miri asks.

'Repair she says,' Malcolm mumbles into his bottle.

'We can patch it up,' Konrad says.

'Good. We used Milwaukee twenty ten as our supply source, but that is now negated.'

'Why Milwaukee?' Malcolm asks.

'The locale suited purpose with access to the services and function we required.'

'Great,' Malcolm says weakly, trying to decide if Miri is more intimidating than Safa.

'Why's it negated?' Konrad asks. 'Because of Ria and that lad?'

'That and if two new members of our team deploy from the vehicle in that parking lot it will draw attention,' Miri says. 'The van needs to be forensically destroyed.' She lowers herself slowly to sit at the table and places the notepad down in front of her.

'So we need a new supply source,' Ben says.

'We do,' Miri says. 'And it's called a staging area.'

'We had staging areas all over the world,' Emily says.

'Every government has staging areas all over the world,' Miri says.

'I know, Miri. I was just making a comment,' Emily says primly.

'Was it true about the basement in London?' Ben asks, looking down the table to Miri.

She feigns ignorance for a split second with a lifetime of habit ingrained at being asked a direct question about her past. Then she remembers where she is and who these people are. 'Affirmative,' she says.

'What basement?' Safa asks, looking from Ben to Miri.

'Legend has it,' Ben says, 'the US intelligence services back in the late nineteen seventies or early eighties bought a house in London. Right in the middle of a part of Chelsea before it became so upmarket. The house was said to have been bought through offshore companies registered to other companies and all sorts of stuff. Anyway, they had the house renovated from top to bottom, but while that was going on they secretly built a big secret underground bunker thing, but with a secret entrance hidden somewhere away from the house. The house was then rented out on short-term lets through a local agency while the CIA used the secret basement as a staging area for covert operations in London.'

'Oh, we knew all about that,' Emily says. 'Worst kept secret ever. We even gave it a postcode and pinned a Christmas card on the *secret entrance* once,' she adds with a laugh, while making speech marks.

'That true?' Safa asks Miri.

'Emily is ahead of me in time, but, yes, that staging area was known.'

'Bit shit, then,' Safa says before downing her bottle.

'Just a bit,' Emily says with a laugh.

'Hang on,' Ben says, looking at Miri and seeing that carefully hidden smug look. 'Decoy?'

'Who knows, Mr Ryder?'

'Eh?' Emily asks as Ben bursts out laughing. 'What? What's funny?'

'How many?' Ben asks.

'Four,' Miri replies. 'Chelsea was blown on purpose, so the UK intel services felt comfortable. The other three were never discovered in my time . . .' She leans forward to look at Emily and the smile slowly fading from the younger woman's face as everyone else laughs.

'Oh, fuck off,' Emily says with a huff. 'We probably did know about the others.'

'Still a two,' Safa laughs.

'Stop saying that! It was a lack of promotion that—'

'Okay, okay,' Ben says, cutting in with a wave of his bottle. 'So Milwaukee is out. Where then? Needs to be an English-speaking country . . .'

Miri flips open the front page of the notepad and starts leafing through the sheets until she finds a list she made several months ago.

'What's that?' Ben asks, craning over to look and reading New York, LA, Dallas and more US cities, along with years and sequences of numbers recorded against each. 'Population density?'

'Yep,' Miri says, resisting the urge to tell him to move away and stop reading her notes.

'LA's a bit risky,' he remarks. 'You're from California, aren't you?'

'Spoken like a true Brit,' Miri remarks.

'Eh?'

'California is bigger than Great Britain.'

'Someone once said if you stand in Piccadilly Circus in London you'll meet everyone you ever knew,' Ben says.

'That's because the UK is tiny,' Miri says with a flash of a smile that makes the others laugh at the look on Ben's face. 'Priorities,' she continues in a tone that suggests no one should interrupt. 'The sewage tank in the bunker needs emptying, correct?'

'Yep, but we don't have a hose,' Malcolm replies.

'Orders,' Miri says. 'M and K deploy with Harry and Emily to Milwaukee . . .'

'Eh?' Konrad asks. 'We don't need babysitting . . .'

'You have no counter-surveillance training,' Miri cuts in. 'You will deploy with Harry and Emily to the construction depot. Ben and Safa will deploy to the mall to buy supplies for the next few days until we can establish a fresh staging area . . .'

'Ooh, can I go with Safa?' Emily asks, earning a glare from Miri at a trained agent requesting to alter the orders. 'Not being a girl, but a construction depot isn't very interesting,' Emily adds, 'and I've never been shopping with Safa.'

'I hate shopping,' Safa says.

'Shush, you'll love it,' Emily says, waving a hand at her.

Miri just stares. This would never happen in her former life.

'It's fine,' Ben says easily. 'Harry and I can go with Malc and Kon . . .'

'Maybe I want to go to the builders' centre,' Safa says. 'Sexist dicks.'

'Do you?' Ben asks.

'God no,' she snorts. 'I'll go girlie shopping for hairbrushes and tampons.'

'Are we doing this tomorrow?' Ben asks.

'No. Now.'

'Now?'

'Now, Mr Ryder. Tomorrow we are going forward to twenty-one eleven.'

'Camera!' Ben says, clicking his fingers. 'Just remembered. We need one of those endoscopy things. The construction depot will have one . . . you know . . . the little camera on a long pipe thing they shove down blocked drains and gutter pipes. We need one of those.'

'It's a bit late for that, Ben,' Konrad says. 'The bunker's not blocked anyway, it just needs emptying.'

'No, for twenty-one eleven,' Ben says to the blank faces. 'We make the portal tiny and shove a camera in first to have a look and watch it on a screen.'

'Hey, that's clever, that is,' Malcolm says.

'Clever,' Konrad echoes.

'Bright spark, aren't you?' Safa says, grinning at Ben.

'Good,' Miri announces, pushing up from the table. 'Deploy now . . .'

Five

Siberia, 2060

Siberia, even in summer, is not a pleasant place. This city certainly isn't. A dire, nasty, grim place full of hard men and harder women. He sits in his usual place drinking his usual tea and reading his usual newspaper.

The café owner had the tea waiting for him. That's the sign of a good embed when the locals start thinking of you as a piece of the furniture.

The same café owner strolls out, lights a cigarette and tuts heavily at the scene across the road.

'What's going on?' the man at the table asks casually, only half-interested.

'Fucking politician,' the café owner says bitterly, but in a quiet voice and with a glance round to make sure no one else can hear him.

'Politician?' the man at the table asks, turning the page of his newspaper. 'See they're finally doing repairs on the main road by the gas station,' he adds by way of conversation.

The café owner glares at him, tutting again. 'For the fucking politician. Not for us. Everything has to be clean and working for the fucking politician, then he'll fuck off back to Moscow and we'll go back to having fucking broken roads and fucking . . .'

'What politician?' the man at the table asks, showing confusion.

'Visiting the hospital,' the café owner says, as though the answer is obvious. 'I told you last week.'

'Did you?'

'Did I? Are you my wife? She doesn't listen either.'

'Am I your wife?' the man at the table asks, showing some slight concern and earning a quick grin.

'Fool, drink your tea.'

'I would, but someone is moaning about a politician and disturbing my day.'

'Find another café then!'

'I would if your tea wasn't so good . . .' the man says, glancing over at the security team climbing out of the dark four-wheel-drive vehicles. Men in suits wearing sunglasses and carrying sub-machine guns. Big men too. Shaved heads and mean looks. They set up a perimeter, flanking the main door to the hospital, and busy themselves intimidating anyone within the immediate vicinity.

'Gorillas in suits,' the café owner snorts. 'Not a clue. Look at them. Not a fucking clue.'

The man at the table shrugs. 'They look good to me,' he says.

'Look good?' the café owner sputters. 'You never served, did you? I was fifteen years in the army and that is not how to guard a perimeter. Look at the gaps! They're not paying attention. Look at those two talking to that pretty girl. Shameful. They need to move out and gain a greater angle of view.'

'Go and tell them,' the man says, smiling at the café owner.

'And get shot by gorillas in suits? I think not! Let them fuck it up and if anything happens I will tell them what they should have done.'

The two men lean forward at the sound of engines screaming down the closed main road. A flotilla of dark four-wheel-drive vehicles driven at speed and no doubt done to impress the locals with a show of power and might.

'Fools,' the café owner says, still tutting and shaking his head. 'Too fast. Where is the view ahead? They'll have to brake sharply now or risk collision.'

He's right too. The convoy do brake fast and have to veer and steer away from one another to avoid a concertina effect. To the untrained eye, it might look good. Fast vehicles, heavy braking and rakish angles, but to anyone with experience of such things it's bloody awful. The café owner laments on this while the man at the table nods and remarks that he thinks it looks good.

The two bicker quietly as the politician sweeps out from his vehicle, surrounded by heavily armed men, and is escorted into the hospital, while a TV crew and photographers follow behind. A quietness ensues for twenty minutes while the man at the table drinks his tea, reads his newspaper and continues to bicker with the café owner and while the politician – a maverick, outspoken young man who is becoming very well known for his anti-western views – continues his tour of the hospital.

'Right,' the man at the table says. 'Enough of your moaning. I'm going.'

'Good riddance,' the café owner says. 'You're like a bad smell.'

'This place is a bad smell.'

'See you tomorrow.'

'Unfortunately, you will,' the man says, stretching and yawning while paying no particular attention to anyone or anything. He strolls out from the café as the politician exits the hospital and walks swiftly to his vehicle just as a very big fuel truck driven by a very drunk Russian comes careering down the middle of the road. The driver is a frantic man, but then anyone in his situation would be. His family are being held hostage. His wife and children have guns at their heads. He must do this or they will die.

The man leaving the café hardly glances at the fuel truck. He has his routine and walks on, as though deep in thought. He hardly glances when the fuel truck swerves towards the hospital and the four-wheel-drive vehicles pull away. He hardly notices when shots ring out from the sub-machine guns firing at the truck, killing the driver, and he only glances round when the truck slams into the rear four-wheel-drive vehicle and explodes in a huge detonation triggered by a small switch in his pocket. Everyone dives for cover, even the café owner, but then he is ex-military and so maybe he has some experience in these things.

The politician is killed instantly. So are his guards and the press officials covering the event. So are several nurses, doctors and hospital workers and several more bystanders. The truck driver was struck with bullets a second before the impact. Later it will show he murdered his family and drove the truck in a crazed wild attempt to kill himself.

An assassination months in the planning. The man from the café will not go back for tea tomorrow. By tomorrow he will be back in London being debriefed and hopefully having a few days off before the next job. This mission was a hard one. The infiltration took a long time, but then he is the best at it. That's why he is Alpha.

He reaches his small apartment a few minutes later to a backdrop of sirens. All he needs to do is grab his already packed bag and he's off. A few hours' drive into the next city to the airfield. A pre-booked commercial flight to Japan and the man he is now will cease to be as this legend is finished and another one begins.

He walks through the communal hallway to his apartment door. A prickle on the back of his neck as he pushes his key in the lock. Something is wrong. A detection of a change in air pressure. A lifetime of experience that tells him someone is waiting in his apartment.

'Come in,' a female voice calls out.

He blinks once, unlocks the door and enters quickly to see her standing in the tiny landing.

She looks different. Older. Her hair is greyer. The lines on her face deeper. The bags under her eyes darker.

'Mother,' he says quietly. His senses ramped. *Why is Mother here?* He looks past her to his small bedroom bathed in a green light.

'So,' she says, smiling at him. 'Harry Madden, Ben Ryder, Safa Patel and one of our own agents called Emily Rose killed you, but guess what? The British Government found a scrap of paper in the ruins of Cavendish Manor and used it to build another one.'

He listens and doesn't show reaction, while outside more emergency vehicles swoosh past with sirens screaming and lights flashing.

'Maggie Sanderson has a time machine. They used it to threaten every government in the world. You're dead, but now you're not dead and all of this happens in your future, but in my past. Confused?'

'Slightly,' he says quietly. 'Green light?'

'Time machine.'

'Right.'

'I just told you. Maggie Sanderson has one, but now we have one too.'

'Time machine?'

'Yes, Alpha. Fucking listen. A time machine. I say we have one. *I* have one.'

'I see,' he says, nodding slowly. 'Is this a test?'

'No,' she says while looking round the dingy apartment. 'I don't miss covert ops. How long have you been here?'

He hides his reaction at the question. She sent him. She is handling him personally. He spoke to her yesterday by way of an encrypted call.

'I'm from the future,' she says, understanding his hesitancy. 'About six or seven months from now. I remember this mission. This was your last before Berlin. The politician visiting the hospital. Yes, of course. Anyway, enough reminiscing. Are you coming? We have work to do. Extraction, they call it.'

'Extraction?' he asks as she turns to walk into the bedroom.

'Extraction. Taking someone from their timeline. I am extracting you from yours.'

He follows her into the bedroom, which is a strange thing in itself, to be in a dingy little bedroom in Siberia with Mother. He winces inwardly at the sight of his soiled undergarments on the floor, but then he had to maintain an exact persona as part of the mission. A scruffy, unkempt Russian man working as a temp for a digital software company. Then he stares at the green portal shimmering at the far side of the room and swiftly forgets about his undergarments.

'The concern was, of course, that by extracting you now, before Berlin and before Cavendish Manor, we would stop those events from taking place, but it turns out time is not fixed. You see, to me, those things will always have happened and regardless of what I do, or what we do, Maggie fucking Sanderson still has a fucking time machine and that' – she snaps her fingers at Alpha – 'cannot happen. I'm going too fast. Come on, I'll debrief you. It doesn't hurt, see.' She waves her arm into the green light and Alpha observes, without expression, how her arm disappears. 'Follow me.' She walks through, vanishing from the room and leaving a still expressionless Alpha staring at the portal and he still doesn't show any reaction when she leans back through to appear from the chest up in the room. 'Hurry up, we've got work to do.'

He grabs his go-bag and looks round.

'Don't worry about this place,' she says, seeing him commence the final visual check. 'What we're going to do will make all of this meaningless. Coffee?'

Six

The Bunker, Tuesday morning

'Ssshh, it's okay,' Malcolm says, rubbing Ria's back. 'Come on, lie down. The doc said you shouldn't sit up yet.'

'Ria, come on, love, lie down,' Konrad says, bending over to kiss the top of her head.

'I killed my mum . . .'

'You saved her,' Malcolm says.

'He's right, Ria,' Konrad adds. 'You listen to Malc.'

'They would have hurt her more.' Malcolm carries on gently stroking her back while she sobs in his arms. The raw emotions pouring out of the young woman.

'Ben told us what happened,' Konrad says. 'You poor love. Your mum wouldn't want you to be like this.'

'I killed her . . . Oh my god, I killed my mum . . . I can see her face . . . She . . . she . . . They hurt her and I killed her . . .'

'Come on now,' Konrad says firmly. 'You've got to lie down. The doc said, Ria.' He guides her back into the pillows with Malcolm helping.

'There you go,' Malcolm says, wiping his eyes but giving her a warm smile. 'It'll all be okay. It will. They should have got us before . . .'

'Oh, that doesn't matter, Malc. We're here now.'

'We are, Kon. We're here now.'

'And we're not going anywhere,' Kon says, smoothing thick strands of hair from Ria's forehead.

'Nope, we'll be right here nagging you to eat grapes and chicken soup.'

'I lost my baby,' she whispers, her eyes fixed and imploring on Malcolm then switching to Konrad.

'You're young,' Konrad says. 'Plenty of time for all that stuff.'

'Plenty of time,' Malcolm adds.

'Kids are expensive anyway.'

'And messy.'

'And noisy.'

'And they smell.'

'And they cry. You did when you were a tiny one,' Konrad says with a slow smile.

'Cor, did she,' Malcolm says. 'Ria Ria, smelly dear.'

The first smile breaks through at the rhyme she grew up hearing from the two men. They've always looked the same to her. Always older, wiser, funny, warm, familiar and down to earth, and always there too.

'I'm glad you're back,' she whispers, reaching out for their hands.

'Now you rest,' Malcolm says.

'Here, you did a cracking job with all that furniture.'

'Looks lovely,' Malcolm says.

'Very nice.'

'You rest,' Malcolm says quietly as her eyes start to droop from the meds kicking in.

Another few seconds and she slides into a deep drug-induced sleep. The two men slowly pull their hands from hers and move quietly to the door and up the corridor that smells of pine from the hard scrubbing and mopping last night after the sewage tanks were emptied finally using an ill-fitting hose gaffer-taped to the outlet valve and fed into a

Milwaukee drain. It was a busy evening, but it all got done and again the difference between Roland in charge and Miri was stark and clear. Everyone worked, for a start, including Miri.

Harry and Ben drove the van from the parking lot in Milwaukee to a disused warehouse identified by Miri. The van was doused in fuel and set alight, then the two men stepped back into the bunker, grabbed mops and joined in with the cleaning.

◆ ◆ ◆

'How is she?' Emily asks as Malcolm and Konrad walk into the portal room bathed in red from the island portal shimmering open with a live link.

'Looks terrible,' Malcolm says with a deep sigh.

'She's alive,' Safa says bluntly, chucking them each a white coverall. 'These are old crap ones meant to be worn with gas masks, but it's all we could get.'

'Um, so what's the point in wearing them?' Emily asks while Harry grimaces as he pulls the zipper up over his huge chest, drawing the old-style white biological and chemical warfare protective clothing up to his chin. He tuts again when his beard gets trapped in the zipper, an exhalation of air pushed through his nose that makes Emily turn and grab his hands.

'Let me,' she says softly. 'You'll yank the hair out.'

'Too tight,' he grumbles.

'No, you're too bloody big is what it is,' she says quietly, pulling the hairs free from the zipper. 'Lift your chin up a bit . . . bit more . . .' She starts smiling at him, seeing the tension in his gaze and tweaks his beard. 'Needs cutting.' She holds his eyes on hers, trying to find the smile that's normally there. 'Let me do it later?'

'Aye,' he says, offering a tight smile. 'Done?'

'Yep, all done.' She pushes the zipper up under his chin then reaches to put the hood over his head. He stoops down, letting her. He's not right. The man who lifted Alpha off his feet one-handed. The man who held an army back at the top of the stairs in Cavendish Manor. The man who was shot in North Korea but didn't flinch and carried on working. She slept on him last night on the island after mopping through the bunker. They lay side by side with her head on his chest and her arm draped over him. That she adores him is obvious. She kisses his cheek nearly every day. She hugs him, holds him and seems drawn like a satellite to his centre of mass, and right now she detects that Harry just isn't himself. There is a disquiet. A sense of all not being well.

'Working?' the doctor asks, waggling a bendy stick about while Ben stares at the screen of a large tablet.

'Nope,' Ben mutters. 'Ah, there it is!' he calls out as the screen comes to life with a close-up of Doctor Watson's face looming from the camera hovering in front of his nose. 'That's good quality,' he adds, looking at the doc then back to the screen.

'Fisheye lens,' the doctor says, turning the long bendy pole to record the room as they watch the screen.

'Fisheye?' Harry asks.

'Wide-angled,' Ben says.

Everything done for this point now, to see what the future is like, to see what the world is and how it was broken. To find the fault and fix it. To save humanity.

'Activating,' Miri says, her voice somewhat gruff from coughing so much. She presses the device in her hand to turn on the tiny blue shimmering light as the tension in the room increases. The doctor holds the radiation counter bought from the survival store and bends closer to the small blue light.

'No change,' he reports.

Ben waves his hands in front. 'No change in temperature . . .' He leans closer to sniff the air of the blue light. 'Can't smell anything.'

'Don't sniff the bloody air!' Safa snaps. 'Could be chemicals . . .'

'Fair one,' Ben says, easing away. 'Camera then . . .'

'Finally,' Safa mutters under her breath. 'Faffing about . . .'

They watch as Ben feeds the camera towards the blue light. The long, thin bendy pole looming at the portal. The tablet screen fills with the iridescent blue light as the lens works to refocus until suddenly the device is within the blue and the screen grows darker. Ben frowns, blinks and gently pushes forward, feeling resistance on the other side. 'Not going through,' he says quietly. They watch the screen, seeing just blackness and the odd streak of blue as Ben pulls back a little and tries to guide it forward again. 'Blocked,' he says with a shake of his head and a look round to Miri. 'You sure you put the right coordinates in?'

Miri checks them and nods. 'Confirmed.'

'Could be rubble,' Ben says, pulling the camera out. 'We're a day after Bertie went here . . . so maybe his drone or his presence disturbed something.'

'Redeploy then,' Safa says to Miri. 'Move back a few feet.'

'Is that an order, Miss Patel?' Miri asks.

'Er . . . yes?'

'Are we needed?' Malcolm asks politely, glancing at the door.

'Yes,' say Miri and Safa at the same time, looking at each other with narrowed eyes for a split second.

'Teamwork,' Safa says.

'Your expertise may be required,' Miri says.

Malcolm and Konrad nod, but stay quiet as Harry tuts at the zipper under his chin and the suit too tight across his chest.

Ben picks up the second tablet, thumbing the screen to take the footage recorded by Bertie on his original trip to 2111 back to the beginning, looking for obstacles that could have shifted. He watches the screen showing the pock-marked ground littered with chunks of concrete, bricks and parts of houses crumbled and broken.

'Stand by,' Miri says, working out the fresh longitude and latitude coordinates. The Blue goes off and the room fills with the sound of breathing and the rustles of small movements made by people waiting quietly. 'Five metres,' Miri says as the tiny blue light comes back on.

Ben grabs the camera and once again starts feeding it towards the light. All eyes stay on the screen, which fills with colour, then instantly fades to black as Ben guides the end of the pole through. That darkness disappears as light fills the screen, but everything stays blurred as the lens works to focus. Ben twists the bendy pole, working to angle the lens down to the ground, but moves too fast for the focus to stay sharp. The screen blurs again, streaks of grey, black and green.

'Fuck's sake.' Safa snorts a laugh. 'You wouldn't make a surgeon, would you?'

'Piss off,' Ben chuckles. 'It's a bit hard to make it bend . . . I think that's down . . .'

'Something moved,' Emily says urgently, staring at the screen.

Movement on the screen. Something close to the lens that morphs into grey then hues of purple and white with a rocking motion that is strangely familiar.

'Pigeon,' Emily blurts. 'That's a pigeon.'

They watch the bird bobbing its head forward and back as it struts about in front of the camera. A flutter of movement and another bird lands next to the first one and bobs forward to stare into the lens. The grey feathers hued with purples, whites and blacks all so organic and all so familiar to every person in the room watching them.

'Grass,' Safa says. 'Pigeons walking on grass,' she adds with a smile.

'Shit,' Ben mouths, glancing with Miri to the tablet showing Bertie's original footage where everything is dead and ruined. No grass, no birds, nothing.

Rapid motion on the live feed from the pigeons suddenly giving flight and bursting away. Feet land in their place, small and clad in red shoes, followed by a tiny pair of hands bracing on the grass as the face of a grinning child looms at the camera, shouting something excitedly.

'ABORT NOW!' Miri shouts.

The child grabs the lens, tugging it forward while Ben feels the pull from a hundred million years in the future.

'He's got it,' Ben says frantically.

'Pull it back,' Safa says, lunging to grab Ben's hand. He yanks hard, wrenching the bendy pole from the kid's grasp with a wince at causing a child pain.

'Turn it off,' Ben says, getting the camera back through the blue.

'NO!' Emily shouts as the child's hand plunges into the blue light and starts waggling about in the bunker, knocking the poles askew and making the portal stretch higher and wider.

'Push him back,' Safa says, pushing at the kid's hand to get it back into the future, but the poles widen as the kid's head looms in, breaching the light to stare round in obvious delight.

'DAD! DAD! IT'S GOBLINS AND . . .'

'FUCK!' Safa yells.

'THEY SWEAR, DAD! DAD . . . DAD . . . THE GOBLINS SWEAR . . .'

'Push him back,' Miri orders.

'Bloody trying,' Ben says, gently pushing his hands through the portal to try and force the child back.

'Get him out,' Emily urges.

'Sorry, kid.' Ben pushes the child, who falls back and away from view, but clearly rallies, lunges forward and leaps through the portal to land bodily in the bunker to a stunned silence of white-suit-wearing adults staring at a small blond-haired child with red shoes.

'So cool,' the child mutters and is off, running for the door. 'GOBLIN HOUSE . . .'

'GET HIM!' Ben shouts.

They burst for the door, all of them trying to get through at the same time, cursing and pushing at each other while the child runs down the corridor in glee.

'GET THAT CHILD,' Miri shouts angrily.

'KID . . . COME BACK.' Ben gets into the corridor first.

'GOBLIN HOUSE . . .' The boy yells, running on through the doors into the main room as Ben blunders after him, pushing in to see the boy climbing over one of the big leather sofas and clapping his hands as he jumps up and down on the big cushions. 'Goblin chairs and goblin sofas and . . .'

'Kid, no, no, no, come here,' Ben says.

The boy laughs, leaps off and runs on round the sofa towards the main table, going under and crawling the length of it before popping out next to Miri. She tries to grab him, but her body doesn't respond fast enough, and the boy laughs happily at her arms closing on thin air as the others give chase and call out.

The big, bearded goblin finally captures the boy. Clamping an enormous goblin hand on his arm and swinging the laughing boy up into the air.

'Got you!' Harry says, grinning at the boy, who laughs and stares in wonder at Harry's big beard. 'Time to go home.'

'NO, NO, NO . . .' the boy yells out, squirming to get free, but still laughing in the throes of the game. 'Do it again . . .'

'We goblins have got work to do,' Harry says.

'I wanna be a goblin . . .'

'When you're older,' Harry says, pausing in front of the Blue. 'Now you go on home and when you're bigger you can be a goblin too. Off you go . . .' Harry leans through the Blue, planting the boy down and looking round before quickly drawing back as Ben thumbs the screen to switch the Blue off.

'Holy shit. Did that just happen?' Safa asks, grinning in stunned amusement.

'Report, sergeant,' Miri orders. 'What did you see?'

'Street, houses, vehicles parked. No damage, nothing like that,' Harry says, pointing at the original footage still playing on the screen.

'Did we save the world then?' Safa asks eagerly, looking round at Ben and the others. 'Yes? No?'

'I don't know,' Ben says quietly, thinking while looking at Miri.

'What's not to know?' Safa asks. 'Bertie saw it was ruined and now it's not ruined.'

Ben thinks. It makes sense. Bertie invented the device then went forward. The world was fine. He went forward again and it wasn't fine. Something had changed the timeline. Then everything else happened. Has that now fixed the timeline or changed it from what Bertie saw the first time? Does it even matter? The world isn't ruined in 2111. A happy child just proved that. He glances at Miri, both of them locking eyes with the sudden realisation that whatever they have done appears, at this stage, to have prevented the world being over.

'We need to see more,' Miri says. 'But . . .' She trails off quietly, filling them all with hope.

'Um,' Emily says, lifting her hand as though to ask a question. 'Dead Nazi?'

'Oh, cock it,' Ben groans as Miri tuts and walks off towards her office.

'Sorry,' Emily mumbles, wincing while Harry tugs at the zipper trapping his beard again.

Seven

Somewhere in Africa, 2060

Rounds ping the ground, ricocheting from rocks and stones. More whizz overhead. Bravo holds position on one knee behind a bank of earth. His face covered in a layer of grime and filth as he purveys his troops hunkered down, taking cover. Heat shimmers hang over the land and the air feels dry and hot.

Weeks of training a local militia ready to become government-backed troops working to overthrow a breakaway faction of army rebels who, in their infinite wisdom, decided that they didn't like their land being raped of oil by Western countries.

Those evil rebels took control of the refinery in a very well-controlled assault. Those same rebels then pushed out into the surrounding townships and enforced a rule of law that brought hardship and suffering to the masses.

That's the strapline anyway. That's the headline used to whip up support in the UK for involvement in yet another overseas skirmish.

The British Secret Service was sent in to make the problem go away and train the local militia while someone else ensured they would be government backed by the time the assault began. Now that assault is almost over and the last little town lies ahead. A small place, but the buildings are modern, made from concrete and provide excellent cover. Nothing is ever simple, is it?

'I SAID NOTHING IS EVER SIMPLE, EH?' Bravo shouts happily at the man nearest him. A broad-faced Nigerian, strong and fit. Sergeants' stripes on his arm given for working hard throughout the training programme.

The sergeant stares blankly, then smiles and nods. 'This is simple. Yes,' he says earnestly.

'Indeed,' Bravo mutters. 'Well, come on . . . RIGHT, YOU LOT. UP AND AT THEM . . . EARN YOUR BLOODY MONEY, EH . . . GO ON . . .'

As Bravo rises to lead the charge of his platoon, the buildings ahead, a small cluster of a half-dozen houses, blow sky high with a huge roaring explosion that sends flames scorching up and debris flying out.

'WHO DID THAT?' Bravo roars, grabbing his radio. '*WHO BLOODY DID THAT? CHARLIE?*'

'*Not me.*' Charlie's voice comes back through his earpiece.

'Maybe they do this,' the sergeant says, staring in awe at the size of the explosion a few hundred metres ahead.

'They're army rebels, not bloody fanatics,' Bravo says, his privately educated voice strong and cultured.

Gunfire ahead. An assault rifle giving burst fire. Bravo looks at his own assault rifle, knowing the gun firing in the ruined complex is the same as the one he is carrying, and not the god-awful things the rebels are using. A frown starts to show. A puzzled look as he starts weighing up options. If Charlie is on the far side, who is inside the complex?

From the swirling dust, smoke and debris, Bravo spots the outline of a lone figure walking between the now-ruined buildings. The flash of muzzle-fire comes a micro-second before the sound of the assault rifle firing as the figure shoots to the side of him, and the frown on Bravo's face shows deeper.

'Stay here,' he orders the sergeant.

'*Bravo . . . you seeing this?*' Charlie's voice asks through the secure radio network.

'*I am, old chap,*' Bravo replies.

'*Er . . . what's Alpha doing here?*'

'*I rather think we should go and ask him,*' Bravo says, jogging towards the lone figure he knows so well.

'BRAVO?' Alpha shouts, shielding his face from the dust still whirling in the air around them.

'WHAT THE BLOODY HELL ARE YOU DOING HERE?' Bravo calls out, a hint of humour in his voice, but his finger rests on the trigger of his weapon, which is held ready and aimed. 'SHOULDN'T YOU BE IN SIBERIA?'

'IS CHARLIE WITH YOU?' Alpha shouts.

'INCOMING,' Charlie calls out, striding towards Alpha from the other side of the complex. 'DID YOU BLOW THE VILLAGE?'

'YES,' Alpha shouts, turning to see Charlie, then waiting until the two men get closer. 'Thought you could do with a hand,' he adds with a casual air.

'Well, that is jolly nice of you,' Bravo says.

'Lower the weapons,' Alpha orders, knowing they'll be suspicious. 'New mission. Mother's orders. Immediate redeployment. This area is negated.'

'How did you blow it?' Charlie asks, looking round. Smoke billows all around them. The stench of chemicals from different materials on fire. Solid dry heat, a choking, nasty air, and Bravo notices a tinge of green light showing in a wide section between the buildings.

'I prepped a few hours ago,' Alpha says. 'Long story but I knew . . . well, Mother knew from your post-mission debriefs that you would both be here at this time, so it made sense to use this as the point of extraction.'

'Extraction?' Bravo asks, confused by the word.

'I'll explain. Come with me. We're getting Delta and Echo this afternoon.'

◆ ◆ ◆

Italian Riviera, 2060

She is so beautiful. So heart-achingly beautiful. That he is being paid to do this is just crazy. Some missions see you covered in filth and shit. Some missions have people shooting at you. He heard Alpha is on a covert embed in Russia and Bravo and Charlie are somewhere on the African continent training troops to fight army rebels. Poor sods. Delta grins at the thought.

'What's so funny?' she asks in a lilting Italian accent.

'Just thinking,' he says softly, still smiling at the thought of the others having such a bad time while he is here with a warm breeze blowing gently over his naked back. He even shivers pleasurably, but that's more from her fingernails tracking so lightly up and down his spine.

The bed is soft. The light is perfect. The doors to the balcony are open and outside the sound of the Italian Riviera gives a backdrop of perfection. An Italian heiress. Her father a multi-billionaire media mogul who needs to understand that the British sometimes need positive reflections to certain political stories reported on his twenty-four-hour news channels.

This is proper James Bond stuff, this is. *Woo the woman, earn her trust and worm your way into her family to find dirt and leverage.*

It worked too and the last few weeks have been some of the best of his life and now, in the golden afternoon of a perfect day, he is about to make love to the most beautiful woman he has ever seen.

She smiles coyly, fluttering her heavy eyelids. Dark-blonde hair spilling over her shoulders and splaying across the pure brilliant-white pillows on the pure brilliant-white bed. A full voluptuous figure. Radiance in her cheeks and her blue eyes so caring, so deep and searching his for validation of the love she is feeling. He doesn't even have to fake it. He feels it. He actually feels it and slowly lowers to press his lips against hers and they both sigh as they kiss with hearts booming and passions igniting, and it takes but seconds for their breathing to become heavier and their bodies to start pushing harder.

Slowly, while kissing, touching, searching and seeking, they become naked on the pure brilliant-white bed and the yearning builds as they grind and kiss and then, without warning, without concern or worry, he is inside her. She gasps and freezes. Her eyes fixed on his. She must know he loves her. She must know she is not giving something away that is special and real and that her heart is not lying.

'I love you,' he whispers.

The love shines in her eyes that fill with moisture as a single tear breaks free to roll down her cheek. 'I love you too,' she whispers. 'Will you stay with me?'

'Forever.'

'For always?'

'For always and forever.'

The knock at the door comes heavy and hard. They freeze. Coupled. Clinging to each other.

'Not now!' he calls out while already feeling a prickle of concern. This hotel is the most expensive in the region and there is no way a hotel employee would knock on the door. They'd call the room first. The knocking comes again. Louder and harder.

'Please, not now,' she calls out this time, pushing into him for fear of breaking this perfect yet fragile moment.

'Oh, I am terribly sorry,' a strong, cultured voice calls out from the other side of the hotel door.

Delta freezes then recovers instantly without showing the utter surprise he feels inside at the voice he knows so well.

'Be two seconds,' he says quickly, grabbing a pillow to cover his groin before running for the door. He wrenches the thing open and steps out to see the grinning faces of Alpha, Bravo and Charlie. 'What the fuck?'

'Hi,' Bravo says cheerily.

'Seriously . . . what the fuck?' Delta asks, looking up and down the corridor.

'Nice pillow,' Charlie says.

'What's happened?' Delta asks. 'I'm on a job.'

'Job?' Bravo asks. 'We were in Africa getting shot at and Alpha was embedded in Siberia . . .'

'So,' Delta says with a defensive shrug. 'Missions are different . . .'

'Is she in there now?' Charlie asks, leaning to peer past Delta through the open door.

'Yes, now what's going on? What's happened?' Delta asks.

'Recall,' Alpha says. 'New mission.'

'Right,' Delta says. 'Now?'

'Yes, now.'

'Okay. I mean . . . right now?'

'Yes, right now.'

'Of course. Er . . . so you mean absolutely right now? Not, say . . . in ten minutes?'

'Ten minutes!' Bravo snorts. 'You doing it twice then, you rampant sod?'

'Seriously fuck off . . . She's lovely,' Delta says. 'Give me an hour.'

'You just said ten minutes,' Charlie says.

'We can grab a coffee,' Alpha says, making Delta stare in stunned amazement. 'Hour? We're in room seventeen.'

'That's my room,' Delta says.

'We know,' Bravo says obviously. 'We are spies too, Delta. Anyway, need a hand in there?'

'No! An hour . . . Thanks, Alpha.'

'Wear a condom,' Bravo says as Delta runs back inside.

'Is everything okay?' the Italian heiress asks, sitting up in the pure brilliant-white bed with her hair cascading down her shoulders and her breasts without a hint of awareness of her own nakedness.

'Yep,' Delta says eagerly, ditching the pillow. 'Wrong room . . . Where were we?'

Eight

The Bunker

'Just ditch him in an ocean somewhere,' Safa says, staring at the dead Nazi wrapped in a sheet pushed into a corner of the portal room.

'Doesn't seem right,' Ben says.

'Well, we can't exactly take him back, can we,' Safa says. 'For a start we don't know what bit of the war he came from, or where in the war . . . or where in the world for that matter.'

'Acid bath,' Konrad says as everyone else in the main room slowly turns to look at him. He shrugs back at them. 'Just a suggestion.'

'Bit morbid, mate,' Ben says.

'Morbid?' Safa says. 'Fucked up more like.'

'Pigs,' Malcolm says. 'They eat everything . . .'

'Aye,' Harry says thoughtfully.

'We don't have any pigs or acid baths,' Ben points out.

'No, no, no,' Konrad says, 'what you do is you take the body to the pigs, see. You don't need to bring the pigs here. Just find a big pig farm somewhere.'

'Big pig farm?' Emily asks.

'Yeah, big pig farm,' Konrad says.

'You're messed up,' Safa tells him.

'I'm just trying to move the issue to the solutions table. Can't stay at the problems table forever now, can we.'

'Ready?' Miri asks, striding into the room and glancing round at their casual clothing of shirts and jeans, all in muted colours. 'Ben and Safa will deploy first. Unarmed. They will reconnoitre the immediate area and assess the suitability of deployment for the rest.'

'Okay,' Ben says slowly, giving Miri a confused look. 'I thought it would be me and you first?'

'You and Safa are a couple,' Miri says. 'You look like a couple. The profile is better.'

'Ah, okay, yeah, that makes sense,' Ben says thoughtfully.

'That is why I said it, Mr Ryder, and you are more than capable of conducting an initial assessment without me,' Miri says, picking up the Blue's portal tablet. 'Coordinates?'

'Ah, right, yes,' Ben says, handing Miri a sheet of paper. 'Electrics and maintenance room accessed by an underground car park in a building between Haymarket and Regent Street,' he adds as Miri reads the GPS settings on the paper. 'I did a job there a couple of years ago. Some chap slipped on a wet patch and tried to sue the building owners. They brought us in to investigate the claim.'

'And?' Safa asks to the silence that follows when he finishes speaking.

'Leaking pipe. They settled quickly.'

'Oh,' Safa says. 'I was expecting a bit more of a story then.'

'Yeah, I was too,' Emily says.

'Sorry,' Ben says as Miri starts thumbing the numbers into the device.

'Are we using the camera again?' Emily asks.

'Nah,' Ben replies. 'Just go straight in, be fine . . . That room is only accessed every six months for a safety check.'

'Okay,' Miri says, bringing everyone's attention to her while her thumb hovers over the button to activate the portal. 'Time is early evening . . . There not here, Tango Two,' she adds when Emily turns to look out the door as though seeking validation of the time of day.

'I was just looking.'

'Date is a week after the previous deployment. Central London. Summer. Expect densely populated streets. Ben, stay alert and watchful. Look for clothing. Do you blend in? Are people staring at you? What is everyone else wearing? Shoes, legwear, upper-body clothing, hair styles. Will any of us stand out as we are now if we deploy. Clear?'

'Got it,' Ben says. 'I am surveillance trained, Miri.'

'I am sure you are. Safa, your role is to risk assess and look for signs that anyone is observing you. Clear?'

'I'd do that anyway,' Safa says.

'You are team leader for mission deployment but do not engage unless absolutely—'

'Yes, we know, Miri,' Safa cuts in.

'Activating.' Miri presses the screen. The Blue comes on.

Safa goes forward with Ben right behind her. The two of them stepping through to central London and what should be a maintenance room accessed by a door from an underground car park.

'THREE FISH, HOLD THE SAUCE ON ONE AND THE VEGAN WANTS . . .'

'SERVICE! SERVICE! GET THOSE FUCKING PLATES OUT . . . THE SAUCE IS BUBBLING . . . WHO THE FUCK ARE YOU TWO?' the head chef screams at Safa and Ben appearing at the end of his kitchen.

Plumes of steam everywhere. Ovens, gas hobs, hot plates and heated lamps. White-suited chefs running back and forth as penguin waiters scurry from the service table carrying plates loaded with fresh meals towards the heavy swing doors at the far end.

'Mind out, mate.' A thin man in chef's whites pushes in front of Ben to reach a pan of bubbling sauce that he stirs while tossing another pan full of vegetables with the other hand.

'Toilets?' Ben asks.

'GETTHEFUCKOUTOFMYKITCHEN . . .'

'Who you fucking shouting at—' Safa snaps, going towards the bellowing chef as Ben grabs her hand to pull her back through the Blue.

'Abort . . .' Ben says quickly.

'Aborting.' Miri thumbs the screen, ending the Blue.

'That cheeky twat,' Safa says, still bridling.

'We walked straight into a commercial kitchen,' Ben relays to the others. 'Chefs and waiters everywhere.'

'Redevelopment?' Miri asks.

'Must have been,' Ben says.

Harry tuts mildly and pushes off the wall he was leaning against as he pulls a packet of cigarettes from his pocket and heads towards the door. 'Call me when you're ready.'

'I'll come with you,' Emily says, following behind with Malcolm and Konrad.

'Let me see,' Ben says, looking from the sheet of paper he passed to Miri to the tablet in her hands. 'Maybe I wrote the numbers down wrong . . . Hang on five minutes. There's an alley just off Piccadilly we can use.'

Outside, Harry inhales and blows the smoke into the warm clear air while staring down at the vast herds of enormous diplodocuses grazing far below on the plains of the valley floor, moving slowly between glittering lakes and forests of trees.

'Ever been down there?' Emily asks.

'Who are you asking?' Malcolm asks, when neither Harry nor Konrad reply.

'Anyone.'

'We haven't,' Malcolm says.

'Nope,' Harry says.

'Shame really,' she says. 'I'd like to see them closer.'

'Big distance,' Harry says. 'Take a day to walk.'

'So? We've got time,' she says.

'Aye,' he says quietly, inhaling on the cigarette.

'What's wrong?' Emily asks him. 'You're not you . . .'

'Beardy,' Safa says, stepping into the line staring down into the valley. 'Stop smoking . . . It stinks.'

'Aye,' he says, still smoking.

She tuts and blows air from her cheeks. 'They're bickering over where to go next.'

'Rio,' Harry says.

'Rio?' Safa asks, shielding her eyes to look up at him. 'We're going to London.'

'Rio was a good night,' Harry says deeply, quietly.

'Oh, oh, right . . . Yeah, it was good,' Safa says.

'The carnival?' Emily asks. 'You said you went there.'

'Should go again,' Harry says.

'We'll go tonight if you fancy it,' Safa says easily.

'Aye.'

'Yeah? You fancy a night with dancing ladymen in Rio, Beardy?'

'Aye. Do,' he says, looking down at her. 'Not the ladymen though.'

'You loved the ladymen. Done. We'll go later. You two bell-ends up for it?' Safa asks, looking at Malcolm and Konrad.

'What about Miri?' Malcolm asks.

'What about her?' Safa asks.

'Will she let us?' Konrad asks.

'Why wouldn't she? We're not prisoners. I'll tell her in a minute.'

'Brave that is, Kon,' Malcolm says.

'She is brave, Malc,' Konrad says.

'WE'RE READY,' Ben shouts from inside.

'Bet we're not,' Emily mumbles as they turn and file back inside, each pausing for a second under the now-fixed filtration system.

'Right,' Ben says, smiling as they walk back into the portal room. 'Piccadilly Circus, same time, same date . . . early evening during the summer. The portal is opening in a back alley I know. It should be empty, as it's only used as a fire-escape route for a load of offices. We're appearing right at the far end . . .'

'Piccadilly will be packed,' Emily says.

'Yeah,' Ben replies. 'That's why I chose it. Hide in plain sight and all that.'

'Great,' Safa says, holding a thumb up. 'Let's get on with it then. Oh, we're going for a night out in Rio later, Miri,' she adds as Malcolm and Konrad hold their breaths and Emily winces at the blunt tone.

'Good idea,' Miri says, working on the tablet in her hand as Malcolm, Konrad and Emily exchange shocked glances. 'Ready?'

'Yep,' Safa says, moving in front of the portal.

'Activating,' Miri says.

'On it.' Safa waits for the Blue to shine, then steps through with Ben behind her.

Central London. Early evening in summer and they should be walking into an alley tucked up behind the giant display boards in Piccadilly Circus.

'It's not an alley, that's sure as hell,' Safa says, looking round at the huge plaza.

'Abort.' Ben grabs her hand again to launch back into the portal after snatching the same view of an enormous pedestrianised area packed with thousands of people walking in all directions. 'It's not Piccadilly,' he tells the others in the portal room. 'Like a massive plaza . . .'

'Plaza?' Emily asks.

'Yeah, like a huge square . . . buildings further back but it was too quick to recognise anything,' Ben says.

'Couldn't have been Piccadilly,' Emily says. 'Must have been Trafalgar Square.'

'Wasn't Trafalgar,' Safa says. 'I've worked Trafalgar.'

'Something has changed then,' Ben says.

'We'll deploy further out,' Miri says.

'Piccadilly is gone?' Malcolm asks.

'We are not in the guessing business, Mr Phillips. We will deploy further out from the centre of the city.'

'Did anyone see you?' Emily asks Safa.

'Oh, only about four or five thousand,' Safa says.

'Seriously?' Emily asks, snorting a laugh at the way Safa said it.

'Okay,' Ben says, his head dropping as he rubs his jaw and thinks back through all the insurance investigations he conducted in central London. 'There's a gardener's hut on the edge of the Serpentine Lake in Hyde Park. One of the ground-workers sliced a finger off. It's quite big, plus . . .'

'The finger's big?' Safa asks.

'No, the gardener's hut and, believe it or not, it's actually a listed building so it shouldn't have moved . . . Mind you, half of Piccadilly was listed too.'

'Hyde Park in summer?' Miri enquires.

'Evening though,' Ben says. 'Gardeners don't work in the evening . . . It's not far from the café there. It'll be busy, but at least the Blue will be hidden.'

'M and K, get the camera rigged and ready,' Miri orders. 'Take five while we get the GPS.'

'That's worrying,' Ben says, following Miri into her office. 'Piccadilly, I mean.'

'We will see,' she says bluntly, reaching for another tablet filled with world atlas, maps and GPS data of every inch of the planet Earth. 'It confirms the first location was correct.'

'The kitchen? Yeah, I guess it does. London is a big city and redevelopment is common but somewhere like Piccadilly wouldn't be touched.'

'You are the investigator, Mr Ryder. I am sure you will find out. Did you see clothing?' she asks, working on the tablet to find the coordinates.

'Glanced. Nothing outrageous from what I could see,' Ben says, thinking back to the snatched view he gained. 'Did you double check my GPS numbers?'

'Don't second guess yourself,' she says, 'but check this is the right location.'

'Don't second guess yourself,' he says, checking both sets of numbers. 'Yep, they're fine. Safa? We're ready.'

'WE HAVEN'T MADE A BREW YET.'

'HAVE ONE IN A MINUTE,' Ben calls back. 'Hyde Park,' he explains as they walk back into the portal room. 'Harry, grab that side, mate. We'll shrink the portal down again . . . Bit more . . . Yeah, that should do it. Right, try that . . . Camera on?'

'It's on,' Konrad says, pushing the end up his nose as Emily screws her face up in distaste at the perfect view of his hairy nasal passage on the screen.

'Activating.' Miri switches the portal on and any sense of occasion vanishes as Ben takes the camera from Konrad and shoves it through the Blue while turning to see the screen filling with the image of the inside of a gardener's hut. Tools hanging from the walls. Coveralls and clothing on hooks. Weird-looking machines rest on the floor with a bizarre blend of new and old.

'Looks empty,' he says.

'What's that?' Konrad asks urgently, taking a step closer to the screen with an expression of sudden focus that makes the tension in the room increase as Miri readies to end the connection.

'Where? What did you see?' Ben asks.

'Back to the left a bit,' Konrad says quickly, waving his hand at Ben while studying the tablet screen showing the live feed.

Everyone stares at it. Seeing the hand tools fixed to the walls in the darkened interior of the hut.

'Bit more . . . Bit more,' Konrad whispers. 'Just a bit more . . . There! See that?'

'What?' Ben asks, his tone urgent and his hand tensed to pull the camera back.

'Malc, see that?'

'Bloody hell,' Malcolm says slowly while shaking his head. 'Well, I never.'

'Never what?' Safa snaps. 'What the hell are we looking at?'

'That,' Konrad says, pointing at the screen, 'is an anti-grav ride-on hover mower. Unbelievable. We heard they were in testing in our time but, bloody hell, they've actually done it, Malc.'

'They have, Kon. Looks good too,' Malcolm says.

'You bloody twat,' Safa says as everyone else releases their held breaths. 'A sodding lawnmower?'

'Not just a lawnmower,' Konrad says, holding a hand up to Safa as though to stop her talking. 'That is a magnetic displacement mower. Uses the earth's gravitational wotsit to . . . well, to . . . See, right, what it does is it hovers over the ground—'

'Like a hovercraft?' Ben asks.

'Yeah, a hovercraft,' Konrad says, nodding at Ben. 'No! Not a hovercraft. Not like with air blowing down. That doesn't have air . . . It . . . You know . . . Like magnetic and . . . You know when you get two magnets and they sometimes push away from each other? It's like that . . .'

'Oh wow,' Ben says, genuinely impressed. 'Seriously?'

'Yeah,' Konrad says, nodding more eagerly. 'So no physical touching but, right, well, we heard in our time they was testing it so the magnetic resistance thingy could be weakened to make the vehicle sit lower or ride higher . . . cos a lawnmower's got to be low, hasn't it . . . to cut the grass . . .'

'Yeah, sure,' Ben says.

'Will vehicles be the same?' Harry asks.

'I bet they will be,' Konrad says, looking to Malcolm. 'If they're using something like that in a place like Hyde Park you can bet they're using them on the roads too . . . Hey, maybe there's, like, no roads now at all! Maybe everything just hovers above your head and . . .'

'I saw . . .' Ben says quickly, looking at Safa who points back at him.

'In Piccadilly,' Safa says, 'some people were holding handlebars . . . like kids' scooters.'

'Yes! Did you see that?' Ben says.

'Er . . . I just said it,' Safa says.

'Grav boards,' Konrad says, nodding knowingly while adopting a general manner of knowingness.

'Right, I really want to go in now,' Ben says, pulling the camera back. 'Harry, you grab that side . . . Got to try a grav board . . . Are they actually called grav boards?'

'No idea,' Konrad says brightly.

'Bring one back with you, Ben,' Malcolm says.

'I'll try. We might be able to hire them from somewhere, like they did with the bicycles in London . . . er, you know, after we've, er . . . checked everything,' he adds, spotting the look from Miri. The Blue extends out, warping in shape as the four corners are moved to make the doorway-sized portal. Ben leans in, checking the inside of the hut with the naked eye before popping back into the portal room. 'Yep, looks clear. Me and Safa again?'

'Confirmed,' Miri says. 'Check the view outside the building, the perimeter, is there a view inside through windows . . .'

'Got it,' Ben says. 'Safa?'

'Yep.' She walks through to the inside of a gardener's hut on the edge of the Serpentine in Hyde Park, Central London, in the year 2111. She looks round, seeing grimy barred windows clearly made from toughened safety glass. 'Alarm,' she tells Ben as he comes through after her. 'Don't move for a minute.'

Motes of dust hang in thermals that smell of cut grass, oil and machinery. The air is thinner too and not the oxygen-rich atmosphere of the bunker. An instant difference in temperature, humidity and their place in the world. She looks round for PIR sensors or any alarm system that could be triggered by motion or movement within the hut. Nothing. She waves her arms. Nothing.

'Can I move?' Ben asks.

'Yep,' she says quietly, looking outside to a limited view of close trees and shrubs. Sounds of voices. Music from a distance. All normal and steady. She goes to the window on the other side of the hut, while Ben looks closer at the hover lawnmower. She sees the same view outside. Trees, shrubs and grass. 'Clever.'

'It is,' Ben says, looking at the machine.

'Not that,' she chuckles. 'Outside, they've let the shrubs grow right up to the windows to prevent people getting in. Those prickly ones too with the big thorns. Good security.'

'Ah, right,' Ben says, standing up. 'So, can we go out?'

'Alarm might go off,' she says. 'Can you see an alarm box anywhere? Places like this always write the code in pencil somewhere near it.'

'Er . . .' Ben looks round, not seeing anything that looks like an alarm panel. 'Nope.'

'See any cameras anywhere?'

'Nope.'

She moves to the back to an ancient wooden desk clearly used for whatever small admin the gardeners have to do. A large screen tablet is chained to the table.

'Didn't log off,' Ben says from behind her, reaching past to touch the screen.

She turns her head to kiss his cheek as he smiles at seeing the icon marked alarm and the simple *on / off* settings. He clicks it *off* then bursts out laughing as Safa sticks the tip of her tongue in his ear and turns to look at her, seeing the humour in her eyes and the sense of play etched on her face. She tilts her head back a fraction, biting her bottom lip as she glances round with a sudden urge taking over. The muted light coming through the windows. The dust particles hanging in the air. The backdrop of noise and being alone with Ben in the real world away from the bunker and everyone else.

'What the . . .' he whispers in shock, his eyes widening when she reaches out to pull him in to kiss hard.

'We're just kissing,' she says breathlessly, pulling back a fraction after a minute.

'Just kissing,' he whispers.

'Just kissing,' she says.

A few minutes later they step out onto a well-worn track that leads down to a wide tarmacked path snaking through the three hundred and fifty acres of Hyde Park in the heart of London.

A man and woman walking hand in hand glance up at Ben and Safa staring round with glowing rosy cheeks, sweaty foreheads and hair tussled as they straighten clothing. A shared look between them all. Man to man. Woman to woman. No words needed as all four chuckle and dip heads with knowing smiles.

'Nice evening?' the man calls up.

'Very nice,' Ben calls out, grinning widely. He takes Safa's hand and walks down to the path to stroll in the beautiful warm sunshine of a summer evening. 'My legs are still trembling,' he whispers.

'Mine too,' she says with a laugh. 'We'll be stuffed if we have to run anywhere . . . I can't believe we just did that. I've never done anything like that before . . .'

They walk slowly on, hand in hand while trying to take everything in, both of them scanning people and clothing.

Some things stand out instantly. Men in skirts and loose sarong-type wraparounds and Ben spots a muscular bearded guy wearing a vest top that shows the plunging cleavage of his impressive breasts. Ben focusses to hide his surprise, then spots more rugged-looking men with breasts and an obvious fashion for heavy eyeliner worn by both genders, thick kohl under and over their eyes. Everyone looks healthy and fit. Toned muscles everywhere. Tattoos on display on nearly every patch of skin. A young boy and girl run past, the girl chasing the boy, and both laughing in delight while their mum calls out for them to slow down. Both children have tattoos on their arms and legs and the heavy eyeliner, which suggests to Ben that the tattoos aren't permanent. He spots men hand in hand. Women hand in hand and, as ever in London, all races, colours and creeds. Mixed races everywhere. Hints of Asian, Chinese, Japanese, Indian and African and, in that regard, it's all familiar and normal.

He inhales as he thinks and only then realises that the air, despite being thinner, is sweet and untainted with vehicles fumes. Instead he can detect the perfumes and aftershaves of the people around him.

'Grav board,' he says with a big grin at the sight of child gliding silently by on what looks like a hovering skateboard. He has to resist the urge to drop down and look for wheels.

'Another one over there,' Safa says, pointing to the outside area of a café at the side of the lake. Chairs and tables dotted about under awnings and umbrellas. People drinking from cups and clearly passing food to their mouths. Ben laughs in delight as he sees more and more people using the floating boards. Some with handles to hold like scooters. Some without anything, and he frowns while trying to understand how they gain momentum, or even where the power comes from. The frame is thin, too thin for any style of battery he knows of. He blinks and rubs his jaw, turning this way and that with his eyes narrowing and widening.

A few minutes later they slip discreetly back into the hut and close the door before going through the portal into the dingy damp-smelling bunker.

'It's fine,' Ben says, sharing a look with Safa that everyone else detects, along with their rosy cheeks and glowing faces, as Miri ends the connection.

'Been for a run?' Emily asks lightly.

'No, we had sex,' Safa says honestly. 'What?' she asks in the stunned silence as Ben turns away to rub his face. 'It was really nice . . .'

'Clothing? Styles?' Miri asks bluntly. 'Anything that would make us stand out?'

'We were a bit over-dressed,' Safa says. 'It's hot, like a summer evening. Everyone else is in shorts and skirts. Men too . . . Wearing skirts, I mean.'

'Pardon?' Harry asks.

'Skirts,' Safa says. 'And make-up, like really dark eyeliner, but even the kids have got that on and a few blokes had big boobs.'

'Boobs?' Konrad asks.

'Yeah, boobs,' Safa says.

'What, like, transgender?' Konrad asks.

'Funny that, but we didn't ask them,' Safa says.

'Did you see anyone without the eyeliner?' Miri asks.

'Plenty,' Ben says, finally turning back to face everyone. 'It's got to be a fashion thing and there's always people that refuse to follow the mainstream, so it'll be fine. You remember that movie, *Pirates of the Caribbean*? The Johnny Depp character, that sort of eyeliner, like, really dark and thick but coming out more on the sides of the cheeks . . . Like Egyptian . . . Like Jack Sparrow, but Egyptian.'

'Thorough explanation,' Emily says as Ben trails off. 'Thanks for that, Ben.'

'Have we seen that?' Harry asks, looking at Emily.

'The movie? Yes, we watched it on holo. You liked the first ten minutes then you fell asleep with popcorn in your beard . . . It's not there now, Harry,' she adds with a laugh when his hand automatically moves to check his chin. 'I ate it.'

'You what?' Safa asks. 'You ate popcorn from Harry's beard?'

'Yeah, why?'

'From his beard?'

'What?' Emily asks, looking round and seeing the others showing expressions of distaste. 'It was only, like, one or two bits and he'd had a shower before the movie.'

'Oh my god, you two are, like, an old married couple.'

Miri clears her throat with a not-so-subtle gesture of irritation at the lack of focus. 'We need to blend. Change clothing. Back here in five.'

'Change into what?' Safa asks before anyone can move.

'Summer style,' Miri says.

'And what exactly is that?' Safa asks.

'Shorts. Skirts.'

'Skirts? You think I own a skirt? Do you own a skirt?'

'Yes,' Miri replies, dull and hard.

'You can't fight in a skirt without everyone seeing your knickers and I haven't shaved my legs,' Safa announces to the room. 'Look . . .' She bends over to tug the hem of her jeans up, showing a few inches of ankles above the tops of her boots. 'See . . . I'll look like Harry in shorts.'

Miri rubs her face, easing the tension from having to manage someone like Safa. Fearless and brave beyond question, with skills that would shame nearly every man Miri has ever worked with, but totally and utterly inept at anything that even hints at a social situation.

'I've got some summer trousers you can use,' Emily says. 'Put some sandals on and that nice yellow top you've got.'

'I don't have a yellow top.'

'You do. I got it for you in Milwaukee.'

'Did you? I thought that was for you?'

'No, it was for you, but you were busy glaring at that man who winked at you.'

'Ten minutes,' Miri says, following Ben out the room.

'You coming this time?' he asks.

'I am, Mr Ryder . . .'

Nine

The Complex, Wednesday

The chatter dies the second Mother walks into the large briefing room filled with tiered seating facing a small raised stage.

They all know who Mother is, and she is the last person any of them ever expected to see, but the sight of the chief technical officer Gunjeep Singh walking with her lessens the worry.

The five agents file in behind them. Alpha, Bravo, Charlie, Delta and Echo. All of them armed with pistols and wearing black combat clothing. The agents stay by the door to stand easy with hands clasped in front while Mother and Gunjeep take the stage as the whispers and quiet comments ripple through the room.

'Settle down,' Gunjeep calls out, a big Indian man with a thick beard, his accent distinctly London British. The chief technical officer for the complex, who is used to standing on this stage and briefing these same people, normally with a ready grin and a barrage of jokes, so his sombre, serious mood makes them all pay attention.

'You are all dead,' Mother snaps, making every man and woman in the audience flinch while her agents stare round with interest. A large flat screen behind her comes on as she presses the tablet in her hand. 'Today is Wednesday. On Monday morning I was informed this facility had been attacked . . . This is what I found on my arrival . . .' She steps aside as the screen behind her changes to a view of the main corridor running through the complex littered with bodies lying in pools of blood.

Gasps sound in the room. Others stare in horror while some turn their heads away as the pictures on the screen change to show their offices and rooms filled with their own dead bodies clearly shot and killed. Tears flow, faces become instantly pale and Gunjeep shakes his head when the screen changes to the portal room and the sight of his own dead body lying next to the green shimmering light.

'That,' Mother snaps with anger radiating from her, 'was done by Maggie Sanderson . . .'

The ripple of surprise spreads out. Muttered comments, heads shaking, people clearly in shock and struggling to understand.

'A blueprint was found in the remains of Cavendish Manor,' Mother says. 'That blueprint was used to develop a time machine and this complex was built to house that time machine. I sanctioned that development along with Roger Downtree and the Prime Minister. Everything you saw on the news about me being discredited was to make Maggie Sanderson think we are in disarray and to deflect attention away from this project. Gunjeep, you built the device. Many of you have worked here since the project began and some have joined more recently as it reached the final stages . . . so you are all familiar with this facility and you know the security measures in place . . .' She pauses, waiting to make sure they understand.

'Settle down,' Gunjeep says again. 'We're not dead now, are we?' He tries to smile, forcing a weak joke that falls flat, but the quietness spreads once more as Mother continues.

'Maggie Sanderson and her team came here and killed you all. We believe they kept one of you alive to operate the security system to wipe all the camera feeds. They then executed whoever that was and, at the same time, they appeared in Downing Street and killed the Prime Minister and most of the cabinet office, including aides and staff . . . QUIET!' she shouts at the growing noise. 'Maggie Sanderson told us not to build a time machine. We did. She found out and that was her response . . .' She points at the screen, knowing the impact it will be having, cementing the fear within them. 'It was determined that I would take control of the complex now,' she continues. 'To that end, I extracted Alpha from a mission I knew he was on before any of this happened. In turn he extracted the other agents who then extracted all of you.'

'But . . .' a woman says from the audience. Her face as stricken as everyone else's, a shaking hand rising as though wishing to make a point, then looking like she instantly regretted calling out.

'What?' Mother demands.

'They could come back,' the woman says, sending another ripple of fear through everyone.

'No,' Mother says firmly, looking at Gunjeep.

The big man clears his throat and steps closer to the centre of the stage. 'What none of you knew was that this complex wasn't just built to house a time machine . . . This complex *is* a time machine. The same technology was fitted to the outside and has now been activated. We are currently about fifty million years in the past . . .'

Alpha shares a look with Bravo, both of them staying impassive as they watch the scientists and staff in the seats react.

'Heavy stuff,' Bravo whispers.

'Say that again,' Alpha replies. The agents were told everything as soon as they entered the complex, from Berlin to Cavendish Manor then to Maggie Sanderson finding this complex and killing everyone while murdering the PM.

'Why didn't they kill Mother?' Bravo asks quietly while Gunjeep and Mother let the audience have a few minutes to absorb it all.

'She was on the move apparently,' Alpha says. 'No precise location to fix on.'

'Oh, I see. Damned lucky then, I'd say,' Bravo says as the others nod. 'I can see our Delta is eyeing up a few of the fillies in here.'

'I'm bloody not,' Delta whispers quickly.

'Mucky sod,' Bravo tells him.

'Okay, settle down,' Gunjeep calls from the stage. 'From this point on the mission is live. This entire site is now sealed to the outside world and we are not going home until the mission is complete, no matter how long that takes, as per the agreements you all signed. None of you have families or children so we are in it for the long haul . . . Mother?'

'Thank you, Gunjeep.' She presses the tablet to change the image on the screen to those of Maggie Sanderson, Ben Ryder, Safa Patel, Harry Madden and Emily Rose. Each picture carefully selected to make them look hostile and angry, even brutal in the case of Harry. Images taken from archives or pulled from the satellite feeds of the assault on Cavendish Manor. A rogues' gallery of criminals with hard eyes and scowling faces.

The five agents look harder at Tango Two. One of their own. Mother explained what happened, but still.

'They are the enemy,' Mother announces. 'They have a time machine invented by this man, Bertram Cavendish.' The screen changes to show an image of Bertie. 'Our mission is simple. We will locate and kill them and recover or destroy the device they hold. We will not stop until that is done. They are not the saviours you have been told by the media, they are terrorists and we must lure them out . . . and mark my words . . . there is nothing we will not do to catch them . . . Terrorism knows no rules and for the purposes of this mission, neither do we . . .'

A heavy silence. Weighted and awful. The faces of Maggie and the others glaring out from the screen, people they all thought were heroes but who came here and killed them.

'You can go and get a drink,' Gunjeep says after a nod from Mother. 'Be in your stations in one hour so the agents can be taken round for introductions . . . and one more thing before you go. The agents are active operatives. Do not ask their names. Do not ask them anything. If they want to talk to you, they will.'

◆ ◆ ◆

'Nineteen twenties, nineteen thirties . . . forties and so on . . . Each section is clearly marked for decade and nature of use, be that casual, formal or business . . .'

The agents listen intently, nodding and making sounds to show they understand, but then they all know Gerry. A small, neat man, fastidious in his attention, who was several years into his career with the BBC costume department when he was quietly approached by the British Secret Service to provide very discreet technical help with details of clothing, props and equipment for various missions.

'This way,' Mother says, holding the door open. 'Thank you, Gerry.'

'Anytime,' Gerry calls out as the five agents follow Mother down the corridor to the next set of rooms.

'Kate and Rodney, history department,' Mother says, not bothering to knock before pushing the door open.

'Hi!' A pretty blonde-haired woman stands quickly from a desk filled with glowing tablet screens. The same woman from the audience, who asked if Maggie Sanderson would come back. She still looks shaken to the core but is clearly trying to be brave and friendly as the agents peer round at the shelves on the walls filled with old-fashioned books and the maps from different eras pinned to the walls. She looks nervously at the agents, her gaze lingering on the handsome Delta with his chiselled jaw and deep brooding eyes that have the whole pained, vulnerable *snap-your-neck-with-my-bare-hands* thing going on. Then she looks at Alpha, swallowing at the sight of him.

Bravo grins, striding ahead to shake her hand. 'Well, hello, my dear. I say, do you like Italian?'

'Jesus,' Delta groans as Charlie and Echo chuckle quietly.

'Kate is an expert in English and European history,' Mother says. 'We've got every event ever recorded at our disposal.'

'Won't it be relative?' Alpha asks.

'Relative?' Mother enquires.

'May I?' Kate asks quickly, half lifting a nervous hand then dropping it when the five agents look at her. 'So, er . . . Gosh, right . . . History *is* relative to the viewpoint of the one experiencing it, yes. And, er' – she swallows, seemingly very aware of the agents' hard gazes – 'tests have shown us that even if we become detached from the timeline *our* history will always be our history. Does that make sense? It baffles the shit out of me. I said shit. I meant poo. Not shit. Poo. Oh dear . . . I am so sorry.'

'Understood,' Alpha says as the other four agents give a single confirming nod. 'Thank you, miss.'

'Physics in there,' Mother says, pushing open the next door to show several bearded men huddled over a table. 'Don't even bother speaking to them unless it's life and death,' Mother adds, closing the door without a single bearded man looking up. 'Medical bay in there run by Doctor Holmes . . .'

'Not Doctor Watson then?' Bravo asks.

'No, I just said Doctor Holmes . . . This is Gunjeep's office.'

'Chaps,' Gunjeep says, ushering them in. 'Everyone being nice, are they? I bet they are – the sight of you five is enough to scare anyone. The shock will wear off in a day or two and they'll be back to the noisy, chattering sods they normally are. For my part, the only thing I really need to say is don't break my fucking portal. Seriously, they are the nastiest, hardest most bastard things to make ever. We had a scrap of paper all burnt at the edges. Have you seen it? Did Mother show you?

Look, it's on my wall. Come on in and see.' He points at a single sheet of paper pulled from the ruins of Cavendish Manor.

'That's it?' Alpha asks, leaning forward. All five agents are intelligent, with developed skills in many areas, but four of them shake their heads, not understanding a word on the crumpled, marked sheet. They all look to Bravo, who lifts his eyebrows and blasts air through puffed-out cheeks.

'I can follow maybe two or three per cent of that,' he admits.

'Heady stuff, that's for sure,' Gunjeep says. 'And I tell you what, chaps, credit where credit is due for our British Secret Service. I had no idea Mother knew and that whole public disgrace thing was incredible. I feel awful now the way they did that,' he says earnestly. 'But all for the greater good, eh?'

The agents nod and make the same noises as Alpha clocks the tension in Mother's face. Whatever they did to sell the ruse, that she was responsible for the failings has clearly taken its toll on the woman.

'Living quarters down there for the general teams,' Mother says tightly a few minutes later as they continue the tour of the brightly lit, well-ventilated, ultra-modern bunker. 'All of the women here have been injected to prevent pregnancy . . .'

A nudge from Bravo to Delta as the other agents smile discreetly and follow Mother through the tour.

'That's enough for now. You're all good at what you do, despite Berlin and Cavendish fucking Manor . . .' She stops to glare, making them hold still. 'We will be starting first thing tomorrow with a test on the timeline so we can fully grasp the complexities of what we are dealing with.'

The five wait, knowing Mother well enough not to interrupt without very good reason.

'Your time is your own until then,' she says curtly, walking into her office and slamming the door.

'Great,' Bravo says, the first to speak. 'Coffee, chaps?'

Ten

The Bunker, Wednesday

Silence in the portal room. Harry stares down at his hairy legs poking out of the tight denim shorts cut down by Emily with a pair of scissors. He glowers, huffs, breathes out noisily through his nose and finally glances up.

'Don't look at me,' Ben tells him bluntly, also in denim shorts cut from normal jeans. He fingers a shred of fabric hanging down and tries to yank it free but just ends up cinching the material together. 'Cock it.'

'This is shit,' Safa mutters.

'You look lovely,' Emily says.

'I don't,' Safa says. 'Too baggy,' she adds, tugging the material of the trousers out from her legs. 'These are like pantaloons . . . I'll take off if I run or kick anyone.'

'Don't run or kick anyone then,' Emily says, the only one out of all of them feeling remotely comfortable.

'You've cut Harry's too short,' Ben grumbles. 'He looks . . . You know . . .'

'What?' Emily asks with an arched eyebrow.

'You know what,' Ben says, grumbling again.

'Don't be homophobic.'

'I'm not being homophobic. I just meant his jeans are too short.'

'You were going to say he looks gay,' Emily says.

'Well, yes, because he does . . . That's not homophobic.'

'It's so homophobic,' Emily fires back.

'Alright?' Malcolm asks, walking into the portal room with Konrad.

'What the fuck?' Ben asks as the others turn to look at the two workmen dressed in coveralls with tools belts hanging from their waists.

'What?' Malcolm asks, stopping dead at the looks.

'We look like the Village People,' Ben groans.

'Now that's homophobic,' Emily snaps.

'We're in disguise as workmen cos, er . . . well, you know . . . it's a workmen's hut,' Konrad says, pulling a wrench from his tool belt.

'Least you're not wearing the Widow Twankey's pants,' Safa says.

'Are we looking for the YMCA?' Miri asks, balking at the sight of them all as she walks in.

'Is that a skirt?' Safa asks, staring at Miri's bare calves poking out from under the knee-length denim skirt.

'Good observation, Miss Patel. Ben and I will take the lead with Safa . . . Hairy will . . .' Miri stops to stare at Harry's huge thighs bulging from the shorts.

'Who?' Ben asks.

'Harry,' Miri says, aware of what she just said and choosing to ignore it, which also means everyone else should ignore it.

'You said hairy,' Safa points out helpfully.

'*Harry* will follow behind with Emily and keep line of sight on the gardener's hut and the portal. M and K will remain within the hut ready to deploy back here. Clear?'

Miri activates the Blue and steps forward ready to go first as Safa does the same, the two women staring at each other in full expectation of the other giving way. Neither does.

'Team leader,' Safa states.

'CO,' Miri counters.

'It's a mission,' Safa states.

'Of which I am a part,' Miri counters.

'A part, not leading, Miri. I go first . . .'

A second's worth of thinking and Miri steps back with a sudden switch to a warm grin. 'Of course . . .' she says happily as Safa goes forward. 'Cannon fodder . . .'

'What did you bloody sa—' Safa snaps, her voice cutting off as she steps through the portal.

A few minutes later and the Village People covertly exit the hut to blend, by way of experience and disguise, into the local population in Hyde Park on a balmy summer evening. A place full of families with children chasing balls and older kids weaving and snaking through the strolling crowds crouched low on grav boards while older citizens ride the same things with wider platforms, seats and handlebars to hold.

'Excuse me, Affa, can we get through,' a woman asks, making them turn to see a smiling woman and man trying to get past with a hovering baby basket a few inches in front of them. They pass by with polite nods in a world that has moved on and evolved with a hundred or more fascinating things to see and watch.

Miri and Ben take it in with Ben pointing out things he saw earlier and Safa checking back towards the others with a snort at the sight of Harry looming over Emily in his tiny denim shorts and tight white top.

'Third one,' Harry mutters.

'Third one what?' Emily asks, looking round with interest.

'Man.'

'Man what?'

'Winking at me,' the big man says gruffly.

'Oh no,' she says, bursting out laughing. 'Oh bless, you look so unhappy . . . Come here, hold my hand so people think we're a couple.'

'Hi there, Affa,' a man says, nodding at Harry with a quick smile as he walks past.

'Blimey,' Emily says at Harry pulling her closer to his side.

'Denial,' the man calls back, laughing at Harry. 'Revolt and be happy.'

'We're together,' Emily calls out, lifting her hand in Harry's to show the man.

'Sure. Did you choose his outfit, honey?'

'Yes, I bloody did actually,' Emily calls back. 'Now piss off . . .'

'*UNKNOWN ADULT FEMALE. THE USE OF REVOLTING, ABUSIVE OR INSULTING WORDS IS PROHIBITED IN THIS PUBLIC PLACE.*'

An automated female voice booms clearly from every direction making Emily look round in surprise as Ben, Miri and Safa stop and hold position, ready to abort and run for the portal.

Everyone else walks on, paying not the least bit of attention other than a few smiles and eye rolls. A few more tut and show irritation with nuances picked up on by Ben and Miri, but those nuances are directed at the automated voice, not the offender.

'No swearing,' Miri whispers.

'It's like that film *Demolition Man*,' Ben mumbles.

'Well, that was classy,' Emily says sheepishly, walking with Harry over the grass towards a raised bank. 'How is it I get told off for swearing and not Safa?'

'You hear that, Kon?' Malcolm asks, peering out the open door of the gardener's hut. 'They got a voice telling people off for swearing, they have . . . Kon?'

'Huh?'

'Kon, you can't do that,' Malcolm says in alarm, rushing back inside at the sight of Konrad taking the engine cover off the hover mower.

'Benches,' Miri says, making for a series of low wooden benches situated at the edge of the lake and close to the café seating area.

'Bloody hell,' Ben mutters to himself. He lowers down on the bench between Safa and Miri. 'Seen that? In the café . . . now that's clever.'

Ben stares over to a hatch in the side of the café building and observes a member of staff place a plate down on a tray, then tap something on a screen on the wall. As the worker steps back so the tray rises and sets off on a short unmanned flight across the café to the waiting table where it lowers with a piped automated voice warning, '*Do not touch . . . do not touch.*'

They sit quietly, observing, to absorb and see it all as their minds work to understand the world around them.

People with distant, far-away expressions on their faces with a distinct pattern of their eye movements, looking left then right, up then down. Ben looks round to see more people doing it and spots a woman mid-way through a conversation muttering an apology to the man with her before adopting the far-away expression and weird eye movement. A few seconds later the man does the same.

'Retina interface,' Miri says quietly. 'Has to be a retina projection linked to an operating system . . . like a smartphone interface only they can see.'

'From contact lenses,' Ben says. 'Makes sense . . . Haven't seen anyone pay either. Everything must be automated.'

'A personal system unique to the user,' Miri murmurs. 'We're not far from it in our time.' She takes in the sweep of the café seating area extending round and seemingly over the water. A tranquil gorgeous evening and a marked change from the bunker or Bertie's island. Noises of people, the smells of people, the essence of a city.

'This isn't what Bertie recorded, that's for sure,' Safa says. 'Are you sure we're in the right place?'

'Definitely,' Ben says. 'We both checked it,' he adds, looking to Miri. 'Something we've done must have put it back to how it should be.'

'Should be?' Miri asks. 'There is no should be. Perhaps the world Bertie saw was the original timeline and what we are seeing now is a result of our interference.'

'Don't be so picky. You know exactly what I mean,' Ben says. 'Bertie went to twenty-one eleven and saw a dead world. We're now in twenty-one eleven and it's thriving.'

'We are in one part of the world, Mr Ryder. We cannot form a full judgement from seeing one café . . .'

Safa tuts softly, smiling to herself at Miri and Ben descending into another deep discussion. She sits content in the warm evening air, half listening to them while watching the world around her. She used to spend hours standing static guard in a silent house, waiting with dread in her gut for any chance encounter the PM might engineer to trap her alone. Those days seem a lifetime ago and without thinking she moves her hand to press against Ben's thigh simply for the pleasure of the touch. He looks down, then smiles at her before returning to counter whatever Miri just said.

Harry sits with his back against a tree, tutting at the winks and smiles from men passing by while Emily lies down with her head on his leg so they can both see the others and the gardener's hut. She reaches out to take his hand, entwining her fingers in his huge hand, then laughs when someone whistles at Harry and calls out 'Hey, Affa'.

Harry was here before, in this same park. He was on a few days leave. It looked so different then. Anti-aircraft batteries everywhere and it wasn't summer either but mid-winter. Cold, bleak and bitter. Remembering that makes him think of Edith and he frowns as he tries to recall what she looks like. It's getting harder to summon her image and hold it clear in his mind. Whole days and weeks will go by, then he'll realise he hasn't thought of her and be flooded with guilt before forcing his mind to focus on the job at hand. Now he looks out to a London that doesn't have a war going on. A London in the distant future from his own time where things float and men wear make-up. The same but different.

'That's nice,' Emily says quietly, tilting her head back to look at him.

He glances down, unaware that he was drawing circles on her arm with his fingertips. An absent-minded thing born from the familiarity of constantly being next to her on the big leather sofa watching holo movies.

'Kon, now that's enough . . .' Malcolm says, casting a nervous glance at the door. 'If Miri catches you stripping it down . . . Is that it? That's the engine? Now that is a thing.'

'It is, Malc. Look at that. Anti-Magnetic Field Displacement Unit,' he reads from the side of the exposed inner engine. 'Now I bet it's the same as what powers all those grav things out there.'

'Not very big, is it?' Malcolm says.

'Wonder how it works exactly,' Konrad says, staring at the unit with a look in his eye that Malcolm has come to recognise. 'I reckon we can have that off, Malc.'

'No, Kon. We ain't having anything off.'

'We can put it on Ria's bed, float her outside or to see Bertie. Like a medical thing, yeah? Might help her get better . . . Keep an eye out, Malc. Take me a jiffy to have it off.'

At the café Safa tunes back in to the conversation between Ben and Miri, leaning forward a touch to watch them. 'Can't we just bring Bertie here and ask him?' she says.

'Pardon?' Ben asks.

'He went forward twice, right? The first time it wasn't ruined, the second time it was, which to be totally honest confuses the hell out of me, but why don't we just bring him here now and see if this is what he saw the first time?'

Silence for a second as both Ben and Miri reflect on why the hell neither of them came up with that solution.

'Yeah, I was waiting for someone else to think of that,' Ben says, sighing heavily with a self-effacing wince.

'Idiots,' Safa laughs. 'You two overthink it all too much.'

'I think we do, Mr Ryder.'

'I think she's right, Miss Sanderson. So my suggestion is we check it a bit more, look at Piccadilly and make sure it's all safe, then bring Bertie here . . .'

'Cheeky twat, I just said that,' Safa says, swatting his leg.

'Er, excuse me, I'm not the cheeky twat . . .'

'UNKNOWN ADULT MALE. THE USE OF REVOLTING, ABUSIVE OR INSULTING WORDS IS PROHIBITED IN THIS PUBLIC PLACE.'

'Bet that was Safa,' Emily says, smiling up at Harry.

'Bound to be Safa,' Malcolm says, frozen in position staring at the door while Konrad grunts to free the engine from the hover mower.

'Stop swearing,' Miri whispers again.

'Sorry,' Ben says as Safa laughs at him.

Miri looks round, seeing the same lack of reaction to the automated voice. It looks fine and Ben is correct that this appears to be life as it should be. Something doesn't feel right though. A nag inside. A disjointed unsettled feeling that the game isn't over yet, but then, right now, it looks like it is. Is that what she wants? For it to be over so soon? What now? Retirement again?

'And the world being fixed doesn't explain why we have a dead Nazi in the bunker,' Safa says by way of casual observation.

Ben tuts in reaction, thinking for a second it was over and done, while Miri's eyes twinkle and her lips twitch in the hint of a smile at the lure of a new game.

'Piccadilly then?' Ben asks. 'Might as well go and look if we're here.'

'Agreed,' Miri says, pushing up from the bench with Ben.

'Not agreed,' Safa says firmly, going after them. 'We're going to Rio. We can do that tomorrow.'

'Mission first,' Miri says.

'We did the mission,' Safa says firmly, all trace of humour now gone. 'Cavendish Manor was the mission. This is a new mission and we need a night off.'

'This first, then Rio,' Miri says.

'No,' Safa says. 'Harry needs a fucking night off. I need a fucking night off. We all need a fucking night off . . .'

Miri and Ben pause, waiting for the automated voice to boom out but it doesn't come.

'He hasn't smiled in days,' Safa whispers angrily as Harry and Emily stroll down the bank towards them.

'Safa, this is important,' Ben says. 'This is what we came here to do . . .'

'This is work, Ben . . . Being here is work. We need a night off. We're having a night off . . .' she says as Harry and Emily reach them.

'What's going on?' Emily asks.

'They want to see Piccadilly now,' Safa explains. 'And I said no because we need a night off.'

'I agree,' Emily says, glancing at Harry.

'I mean this is as important but, fuck me,' Safa says as everyone else waits again for the automated voice, 'we trained solidly for weeks for Cavendish Manor. Give us a break . . . Actually, sod it. As team leader I am saying my team is not fit for duty until we've had some downtime.'

'Nothing,' Ben says, looking round. 'How the fuck are you . . .'

'*UNKNOWN ADULT MALE. THE USE OF REVOLTING, ABUSIVE OR INSULTING WORDS IS PROHIBITED IN THIS PUBLIC PLACE.*'

'Hey, Affa,' a man says with a nod at Harry.

'I AM HOLDING HIS HAND,' Emily snaps.

'Alright, love,' the man says with a defiant sneer.

'It's predatory,' she fires back. 'The poor bloke can't have a simple stroll without men coming on to him . . .'

'He's six foot five and built like a fucking tank,' Ben says.

'*UNKNOWN ADULT MALE. THE USE OF REVOLTING, ABUSIVE OR INSULTING WORDS IS PROHIBITED IN THIS PUBLIC PLACE.*'

'Fuck's sake . . .' Ben mutters.

'*UNKNOWN ADULT MALE. THE USE OF REVOLTING, ABUSIVE OR INSULTING WORDS IS PROHIBITED IN THIS PUBLIC PLACE.*'

'I'm just saying they should bloody leave him alone . . .'

'*UNKNOWN ADULT FEMALE. THE USE OF REVOLTING, ABUSIVE OR INSULTING WORDS IS PROHIBITED IN THIS PUBLIC PLACE.*'

'. . . especially when he is holding hands with his bloody girlfriend . . .'

'*UNKNOWN ADULT FEMALE. THE USE OF REVOLTING, ABUSIVE OR INSULTING WORDS IS PROHIBITED IN THIS PUBLIC PLACE.*'

'You're not his girlfriend,' Safa points out.

'They don't bloody know that . . .'

'*UNKNOWN ADULT FEMALE. THE USE OF REVOLTING, ABUSIVE OR INSULTING WORDS IS PROHIBITED IN THIS PUBLIC PLACE.*'

'Covert,' Miri whispers angrily. 'We are covert.'

'Yeah,' Safa says with a smug look. 'So stop fucking swearing, you two . . .'

'Nothing,' Ben says at the silence. 'How?'

'Cos I'm special,' Safa says as they stroll up the bank to the gardener's hut and a frozen Malcolm looking very nervous while behind him Konrad stands in front of the hover mower now in bits while holding the inner engine block behind his back.

'What the fuck?' Miri snaps.

'*UNKNOWN ADULT FEMALE. THE USE OF REVOLTING, ABUSIVE OR INSULTING WORDS IS PROHIBITED IN THIS PUBLIC PLACE.*'

'Covert?' Safa points out. 'Gosh, you lot are just awful at being discreet . . . It's a fucking embarrassment . . .'

Miri rubs her forehead, looking round at the state of the hut and Emily and Ben still glaring while Harry looks ready to jump off a cliff. 'Night off . . . We need a night off.'

Eleven

Thursday, Day four

'Bit bloody cold on the old chap though,' Bravo says, rubbing his hands together while Charlie, Echo and Delta snort quiet laughs that blast mists of air from their mouths and noses. 'I think he might withdraw inside like a tortoise,' Bravo adds, reaching down theatrically to check his penis is still there.

'Aren't you wearing boxers?' Charlie asks him. 'I've got boxers on,' he adds, looking round at the others.

'Same,' Delta says.

'And me,' Echo adds.

'I was told we need to be authentic,' Bravo says with a comic shrug.

'When do they invent trousers?' Charlie asks Rodney.

'Good question,' Bravo says. 'We should ask that nice filly Rodney works with in the history department. Eh, Delta? Mission for you, that is. Infiltrate the trouser secrets of the history department.'

'They've already invented them,' Rodney says, blushing deeply at Bravo's joke and the five agents all staring at him.

'Then why the buggering hell are we in skirts, my dear Rodney?' Bravo enquires.

'Tunics,' Rodney says. 'People wear tunics here and wrap their legs in wool to tie off with string. It's correct to the era,' he adds quickly as the five agents look down at their bodies. Rough woollen tunics, undyed and the colour of faded straw. Untreated woollen wraps on their legs held in place with bindings. Socks made from rough material stitched together. Ill-fitting and nowhere near as good as modern thermal protective clothing.

'Wasn't it a thing for the Romans?' Charlie asks Rodney. 'To show how tough they were by always having their legs bared.'

'That's just a myth,' Rodney says, turning round to look again in the vain hope of seeing just a glimpse of the newly constructed Hadrian's Wall. 126 AD.

A frozen mud track snaking between tall trees with barren branches and the ground covered in patches of snow. Northern England close to the border of Scotland. Rodney blinks and gently bites the inside of his cheek to remind himself this is happening, that's it's not a dream. He is actually here, in Roman Britain, dressed to the exact specifications of the era. That he feels conflicted is hidden behind the excitement of being on a live mission. On the one hand, this is a historian's wet dream; to have a working time machine and visit points of history. On the other hand, and the cause of the internal conflict, what they are doing goes against every moral and ethical bone in his professional body. He didn't think anyone other than the agents would actually deploy outside the complex too, but Mother said it would do him good to *get some field experience.*

'Wish I could see it,' Rodney murmurs.

'The wall?' Alpha asks.

'Be amazing,' Rodney says eagerly. 'Hadrian's Wall in use? Oh my god. Like . . . just oh my god . . .'

'Like, totally oh my god,' Bravo mimics, giving Rodney a wink as the young historian blushes again.

'Be, like, totally rad,' Echo joins in.

'Like, epic dude,' Charlie adds.

'Sorry,' Rodney mumbles, dropping his gaze in shame.

'Only playing, mate,' Delta says, patting Rodney's shoulder.

'Maybe we should see this wall if we get time,' Bravo says, looking at Alpha.

'We'll see how it goes,' Alpha says.

'How far is it?' Echo asks.

'One point three kilometres that way,' Rodney replies instantly, pointing down the track.

'Bloody hell, he is eager,' Delta says.

'Sshhh,' Alpha says, striding out a few feet as Rodney blinks at the instant change in the way they switch from genial men chatting and joking to hardened agents glaring down the road with heads cocked while they strain to listen. 'Incoming,' Alpha says calmly. 'Positions.'

'Go down the bank,' Delta tells Rodney, motioning with his head towards the green shimmer reflecting off patches of snow on the ground in the tree line. 'Stay out of the way.'

Rodney rushes to do as he's told. Sliding and tripping down the verge with a thrum of adrenaline. He runs into the tree line, his breath misting rapidly as he breathes faster before tucking up behind the wide base of a tree. His heart booms and thunders and the blood pounds through his skull, but he hears feet crunching within a few seconds. A perfect rhythm of men marching at a fast pace and the sound seems to carry far and deep in the still winter air.

It takes time for them to come into view. Time enough for Rodney to see Alpha and Bravo adopt a stance in the middle of the track with Charlie, Delta and Echo seemingly disappearing into the undergrowth on both sides.

When they do come into sight, Rodney's eyes go wide and his mouth hangs open. Every term of reference goes out of his head and right now he couldn't tell a cohort from a legion. A Decanus from a Centuria. What he sees is a real Roman officer leading a unit of real

Roman soldiers. He expected a Centurion in full battle gear with plumes of red feathers standing proud on a shiny metal helmet. He expected big red shields, men in tunics with interlocking armour, gleaming swords and a standard bearer holding the golden eagle aloft to carry forth the power and might of Rome.

What he sees is an unshaven mean-eyed man in the lead with filthy woollen leg coverings underneath a tunic that could have maybe once been red but now looks more brown. A heavy cloak wrapped over his shoulders and a dull, metal, somewhat battered helmet without any feathers at all.

The dozen or so men behind him look the same. Dull colours. Dull helmets. The shields are big and square but without any decorations at all and there is no standard bearer either. They look dirty, hardened and suddenly that sharp dose of reality kicks in as Rodney thinks they've made a very bad mistake and checks the distance and route to the portal a dozen or so metres away.

He hears a shout and looks up to see the lead officer of the Roman unit yelling at Alpha and Bravo in a harsh tone. Latin is a dead language, but the intent is clear. The officer is screaming for the two men to move aside and those orders are getting louder the closer they get with an expectation that everyone moves aside for the Roman army.

Alpha and Bravo do not move, but stand with their feet shoulder-width apart and their hands behind their backs. They project an air of disinterest. As if being faced with such a thing as a dozen armed men marching at them is entirely without alarm or concern.

The officer screams again. His eyes set. His facial expression twisting. His cloak moves aside with a vicious yank of his arm to show the two men the pommel of his sword. They don't flinch or move. The officer grips his sword pommel, ordering them to move aside, but still they don't comply. He is pissed off, cold, tired and his hands and feet have chilblains from being posted in such a vile, nasty, disgusting horrid place as this. Northern Britain is the worst posting in the Roman world.

There is nothing good about it and now he has two idiots trying to defy his right to pass unhindered. Everyone must give way to the army. There is no question about this.

'HALT,' he screams. The soldiers behind him come to a perfect stop. 'YOU TWO,' the officer shouts, turning to look at two leading soldiers in the column under his command, 'BEAT THOSE IDIOTS ASIDE . . .'

Rodney watches the two soldiers run out, both swinging their shields into position and clearly intending to use them to batter Alpha and Bravo aside and the belief that this is a mistake only amplifies. The Romans number more than a dozen heavily armed men. He can't believe Alpha and Bravo aren't turning to flee. They don't move a muscle, but simply wait as the two soldiers charge at them.

Until the last second that is and to Rodney's eyes the two agents seem to blur in motion as they sidestep and lash out with blades that scythe across the throats of the soldiers causing two arcs of blood to spurt in the air as the soldiers drop with barely a gargle.

'AMBUSH, AMBUSH,' the officer screams, pulling his sword free as his men quickly scramble to bring shields round to the front.

Delta moves in from one side, Charlie the other, Echo from the rear, Alpha and Bravo from the front. Five agents armed with modern, high-tensile, surgically sharp combat knives against a dozen battle-hardened Roman soldiers.

They don't stand a chance. The agents move too fast and have two thousand years of collective skills behind them. They are well fed, healthy, physically fitter, stronger and trained to a far, far higher standard too, and Rodney watches with his stomach dropping and twisting as the agents slaughter the men with brutal ease and the snow on the ground becomes crimson with blood.

'Alpha . . .' Echo says, his voice calm and controlled. 'Last one,' he adds, backing away from the single surviving soldier hiding behind his shield.

Delta and Charlie move away too as Bravo crouches to wipe his blade on the cloak of the fallen officer.

'Go,' Alpha says, waving his hand at the surviving man. 'Go on . . .' His words are not understood but his meaning is clear and it's all the soldier needs to turn and flee. His feet crunching as he pounds down the track back towards the last checkpoint.

'Nice,' Bravo says, rising to his feet holding the officer's short sword. 'Good balance. Rodney? Do you want a memento?' he calls out, turning to look down the bank at Rodney gasping for air with the contents of his stomach now at his feet after bending double to puke at witnessing the casual killing of a dozen men.

'Think he's a bit busy,' Echo chuckles.

'Take it for him for later,' Delta says to Bravo.

Rodney heaves and wants to tell them he doesn't want the sword. He doesn't want anything from here and he doesn't even want to see Hadrian's Wall either.

'Ah, sweetcorn,' Charlie says, placing a hand under Rodney's arm to help move him on. 'Always sweetcorn in vomit.'

'And carrots,' Echo says, taking the other arm.

'We did warn you, old chap,' Bravo says from behind. 'Oh, there he goes again . . . Go on, get it all out . . . That's it. Heave ho . . . I got you a present, by the way . . . Nice sword . . . Bit of blood on it, mind. Oh, there he goes again.'

'All well?' Mother asks, watching the five agents come back through the portal and barely showing any reaction to the ashen-faced young historian held between Charlie and Echo.

'Mission complete,' Alpha reports. 'One survivor as agreed.'

'Good,' Mother says. 'Get cleaned up. I'll tell Kate to check . . . Someone get Rodney to the medical bay.'

'Ah, he's alright,' Gunjeep booms, pulling Rodney upright. 'MAN UP, SON.'

'S'blood,' Rodney says, his face contorting with a precursor to another round of vomiting.

'Let me see that gladius,' Mother says, holding her hand out towards Bravo, who passes the Roman short sword over. 'Very nice,' she says, rotating her wrist to feel the weight and balance. She heads off through the bunker, carrying the sword and glaring at passing workers showing puzzlement at the weapon in her hand. She pushes through the door to the history department. 'Done. Go with Alpha and check it . . .'

Mother strides off as Kate grabs a heavy book from the shelf and rushes down the corridor to the portal room, slowing on sight of Alpha and the other agents dressed in tunics still chuckling round Rodney.

'All set for you,' Gunjeep tells her, nodding at the portal. 'Alpha?'

'One minute,' Alpha says. He strips off unselfconsciously, shedding his Roman clothes to tug on simple modern clothing. A secure holster on the back of his belt covered by shirt tails. 'I'm with you,' he says, looking at Kate staring open-mouthed at having just seen him in his boxers.

'Great,' she says too loudly. 'I like your underwear . . .' She squeezes her eyes closed at hearing the words tumble from her mouth, wincing as the agents laugh.

'Back in five,' Alpha announces, ushering the woman through the portal into the darkened interior of an office at night-time made to look a weird shade of green by the shimmering portal.

Kate balks, blinking rapidly while looking round. 'Oh my god,' she whispers.

'What?' Alpha asks quickly, his hand reaching round to grip the pistol butt.

'It's different.'

'Different?'

'The layout, the windows . . . the desks . . . like . . . like the same but different . . . Shit . . . Oh my god. One thing. We changed one thing.'

'Do you still need to check?' Alpha asks.

'Oh god, yes,' she whispers urgently. 'I worked here for years . . . it's like a second home and . . . and it *feels* the same. The air . . . it feels the same, the ambience, the smell too, but the layout is all changed. The windows were square-framed before. Now they're rounded . . .' She trails off, turning this way and that while staring in awe.

'What are you looking for?' Alpha asks with a calm manner despite the mass murder he led a few minutes ago and while his hand rests behind his back gripping the stock of the pistol.

'Bookshelf . . . It was right here,' Kate says, pointing at an area given over to desks.

'Behind you?'

'Pardon? Oh shit. Haha! Right behind me. Bit embarrassing. Right so . . . erm . . . Oh my god, the covers are all different . . . the authors too . . . I've never seen this one before . . . or this . . . One thing. We changed one thing.'

Alpha stays quiet, listening and looking round, then stepping over to join the woman and catching the scent of her perfume. He inhales, realising it's his favourite, and watches as she lowers the book she brought through to a desktop, then fumbles to open one taken from the shelf. Alpha helps, smiling politely at her mutterings and nervous small talk. '*Timeline of Roman Britain: A Concise Evaluation*,' Alpha says, reading the spine of the new book.

'I've got the same thing here,' Kate says, holding the first book out. 'So we can compare . . . Just give me a minute to . . . Got to work through the decades and . . . timelines . . . Ah, so . . . okay, see this? So both show the same dates . . . see here? Caratacus is captured in AD fifty-one . . . Same details really, same events go on from that all the way up until— Oh my god . . . look at that! Right here. It's right here. One-two-six AD. The mini revolt! They've got a name for it. The mini revolt. "*The mini revolt started when a patrolling Roman unit were believed to have been slaughtered by oppressed locals. This act has been credited as leading to the civil uprising and is the start of the term 'Affa' being adopted into international language with multiple meanings, namely 'in defiance of', 'in anger of', 'in reaction to' or, more commonly in the latter parts of the twentieth century in the UK, as a general term of endearment."* Jesus! Did you hear that. Affa . . . the one you left alive must have heard them calling you Alpha . . . OH MY FUCKING GOD, THAT IS SO COOL . . . Oh, sorry, did I shout? I am so excited right now.' She clamps an enthusiastic hand on his arm while she reads. 'Oh wow, it says they had to bring in extra garrisons and units . . . Full-on warfare by the looks of it, and, see here, the timeline after is warped. Some of the same things happen but the dates are wrong. Talk about throw a pebble . . .'

'Great. Take the book back . . .'

'What? Are you nuts? We'd cross-contaminate our own history. God no. No, no, no . . . Shit, sorry, Mr Alpha. I didn't mean to say no to you . . . Please don't kill me . . .'

'I'm not going to kill you. We need to go back.'

'Right, but you've seen this, yes? So we can vouch to Mother.'

'Confirmed,' Alpha says.

'Wow, that's like proper agent talk,' Kate says in a quiet awe-filled voice.

'Are we done here?' Alpha asks.

'Confirmed, Mr Alpha, sir. Er, can I ask a stupid question?' she asks, staring up at him.

'Go on,' he says.

'So, like . . . how do we know Maggie won't take her team to onetwo-six AD and walk through our portal while you're out there being all heroic and dashing . . . ? I mean, we don't have any guards or anything so they could just walk in . . . S'very scary,' she says with raw innocence.

'Because it's a memory,' Alpha says. 'We need them now, as they are now, and they need us as we are now. We could have gone back to Cavendish Manor or Berlin and killed them, but it's just the memory of them. We could even get through their portal, but it's not them now. It's clear from what we know that Maggie Sanderson has a very firm understanding of this, so there's no point in either side attacking a memory . . . and this test proves what you said.'

'What I said?' she asks, seemingly mesmerised by the lead agent.

'Changes to the timeline don't affect us. I don't remember anything from history about Affa. Do you?'

'Wow,' she says softly, watching him speak. 'You're really smart . . .'

'Thanks,' he says, smiling almost coyly. 'We should get back.'

They head through back into the complex and up to Mother's office where Alpha grips and weighs the gladius while Kate reports.

'And, like, after one-two-six AD it was all warped and different,' Kate explains, bent slightly forward, tapping the history book open on Mother's desk, while Alpha and Gunjeep try not to look at her backside. 'Even the office was different. The layout, the windows were different . . . Books I hadn't seen before.'

'Good,' Mother says.

'Good? It's, oh my god, so amazing and it totally confirms it,' Kate says, standing up to look from Mother to Gunjeep to Alpha. 'We're immune to changes.'

'Didn't we already know that?' Gunjeep asks.

'Confirmed affirmative,' Kate says promptly, making Alpha pause while testing the sword's weight distribution.

'It's just affirmative,' he says, 'or just say yes.'

'Gunjeep, Kate, you can both go,' Mother says.

'Affirmative,' Kate says with a quick grin to Alpha while rushing for the door.

'Want this?' he asks, offering the pommel to her.

'Are you shitting me?' Kate blurts. 'I'd love it . . . Thank you so much.' She goes out behind Gunjeep swishing and slicing the air.

Alpha watches her go, smiling to himself before turning back to see Mother glaring at him. 'Sorry,' he says smartly, the smile fading as he stands a bit straighter.

'Now we wait,' Mother says quietly. 'Maggie will see the change and react . . .'

'Understood,' Alpha says.

'Good,' Mother says, watching him closely and seeing the tiny nuance in his eyes. 'Speak freely, Alpha.'

'Sorry, I just need to be clear on this . . . We're waiting for Maggie to see the changes we made to the timeline?'

'Yes.'

'Roger. But you don't want surveillance on that area?'

'No.'

'Roger,' Alpha says, his face an impassive mask. 'How do we catch them then?'

'Maggie Sanderson will be expecting surveillance.'

'Understood. We are luring them into a false state of confidence whereby they think we're not thorough enough to place surveillance and eventually they make a mistake we can exploit. Is that right?'

'Yes, Alpha.'

'Understood. Orders in the meantime?'

'Do you need a list of things to do, Alpha?' she snaps icily with a flash of the woman Alpha knows only too well. She turns away to the glowing tablet screens on her desk, instantly losing interest. 'I don't care what you do. Now fuck off.'

'Yes, Mother.' He about-turns and marches smartly towards the door, pausing with his hand on the handle at the muttered tones coming from behind.

'I won't be fucking beaten . . . fucking cunts . . .'

He goes out quietly, closing the door behind him to widen his eyes and think for a second, then snorts a laugh at the voices sailing down the corridor.

'Careful, Kate! You almost had my eye out . . .'

'Sorry, I didn't see you . . . Look, it's a gladius . . . Alpha gave it to me.'

Twelve

The Bunker, Wednesday evening

'I'm worried about him. He's so quiet,' Emily says, perching on Safa's bed.

'He's Harry. He's always quiet,' Safa replies, pulling a top from her clothing rail and holding it out towards Emily. 'This one?'

'No. Try wearing something other than a black vest for once,' Emily says. 'Does he ever mention Edith to you?'

'He never mentions anything. Not, like, from his life . . . I mean, he'll say when he had a scrap in a pub or a mission he went on, or, like, the food he likes, but . . .'

'Yeah, I know what you mean,' Emily says quietly, moving to the clothes rail to flick through the garments. 'Rio's hot, isn't it?'

'Very. Maybe he just needs sex,' Safa says with a chuckle. 'He's been here for months.'

'Harry?' Emily asks, blinking at Safa in shock at the thought that Harry would even have a sex drive.

'Why not?'

Emily tries to think why not and finds the concept both alien and weird. Harry is Harry. He's superhuman so therefore the normal human traits everyone else has don't apply to him. 'No,' she says quickly, shaking her head. 'No . . . Harry?'

'What's that?' Safa asks, turning to look at the garment held out by Emily. 'Am I fuck wearing that . . .'

They gather in the main room. Malcolm and Konrad grinning and laughing with the others at the stern telling-off from Miri when they got back from Hyde Park.

'Then she said it was enterprising and she likes ingenuity, but if we ever do it again she's nailing our balls to the floor,' Konrad says.

'Bertie's got the engine now,' Malcolm explains. 'Should have seen his face. It was like all his birthdays at once.'

'Orders,' Miri says bluntly, striding into the room.

'It's a night off,' Safa states, looking down at her glittery clothes. 'I look like a disco ball.'

'You look lovely,' Emily tells her.

'We still have orders,' Miri says. 'The Blue will be in the same position as your previous trip to Rio. We are one day after that trip. The size of Rio and the dense population during carnival time means it is highly unlikely you will see the same people. We work for an oil company undertaking consultation investigative security at ground level, which explains why we will be reluctant to discuss our work with anyone else. I have a small sidearm on an ankle holster. Doctor Watson is staying here with Ria. Bertie is staying on the island. Ria is sedated. Understood? Good. Then we can deploy. I have the money too.' She looks up as the Blue comes on, then nods to Safa. 'After you . . .'

'About bloody time,' Safa says, walking through the Blue to the same alley from so many months ago filled with sound and light reflected off the walls from the dancing and crowds at the end. Instant noise, loud and solid, like a real tangible thing that can be touched. The smells of cooking wafting in the humid air and not the damp, sewage stench of the bunker.

'THIS IS SO GOOD,' Emily shouts at Harry.

Samba beats in the air. Fast and furious. Rhythmic music pulsing, some of it distorted from speakers, but that only adds to the instant ambience of the place they are in. A different sound to the last time too with a military-style drum beat within the music.

'HOW DO I LOOK?' Safa shouts in Ben's ear. She watches him look down then back up with a big smile. 'It's a jumpsuit . . . see? It looks like a dress but it's shorts . . . Emily said I can still run and fight in it without anyone seeing my knickers but that it looks feminine. I said she was a twat . . .'

'You look amazing,' he mouths, blinking at the raw brutal honesty that is Safa Patel, and the night off begins. The down time they need so badly. To decompress. To drink and dance. To absorb in a place of noise and light full of thousands of smiling human beings clad in outrageous outfits.

They killed. They took life. They slept, ate and breathed that mission and although something obviously happens, what with Malcolm being chased by a Nazi and all that, tonight they can relax and push those things aside.

With her trailing hand holding Ben's, Safa breaches the end of the alley, pushing through the dense crowds with the others stretched out in a line behind her. She grins at the noise now so loud, at the beats in the air and the flashing lights of all colours and shades. She sways a little to the music, spearheading a path in the general direction of the bar they used last time. The beat is so good. She remembers being at police training college and the drill they undertook that used a military-style drum to help the cadets learn to march in time. Left, right. Left, right. Dum, dum, dum. She adjusts her feet to fall in with the beat, laughing at her own actions and guessing Harry, Emily and Miri will be doing the same. It's impossible for anyone trained in marching not to fall in time to that music.

The building line on her left drops back and away. This is where they stopped last time, but it's busier now and the crowds are too dense, so she keeps going and doesn't notice that the awning over the bar that was white-and-red stripes before is now blue. She doesn't notice the change to the front of the building either and the fact the bar is now open to the street thanks to the concertina-style window that wasn't there the last time. She doesn't look inside and see the shape of the bar is different.

Instead, she goes on past packed bars to seek a gap somewhere and finally spots a thinning of the crowd and a perfect position to watch the procession, and as she turns to signal the others, so the crowd starts chanting with voices in unison calling out at the procession going past.

'*AFFFFA. AFFFFA.*'

They go closer to the edge of the road, pushing through the gaps to see scantily clad men and women dressed in mimicry of Roman soldiers, with plumes of bright-red feathers glued to their heads and backsides as they march in time to the drum, and as the samba music grows to overtake the military beat so the chanting grows louder.

'*AFFFFA. AFFFFA. AFFFFA.*'

Behind the near-naked Roman soldiers come more women and men. These dressed in tiny tunics, just scraps of material that cover breasts and groins. Sandals on their feet and the contrast is clear. Soldiers and slaves, but while the soldiers march, so the slaves dance and writhe to the music as they work to steal up behind the scary soldiers who pretend not to notice and the excitement in the crowd grows as those watching chant '*AFFFFA*' faster and louder.

Ben watches with keen interest, not having a clue of the term of reference or what it represents. Miri the same.

The slaves attack. Running amok with giant feathers as swords to slice and stab the Roman soldiers who burst out to dance in the street and sides. A heady, gaudy sight of flesh and skin on show and Harry watches beautiful women go by while trying to discreetly see if they really are women.

The float passes, but next is a permutation of the same thing. Roman in theme. Soldiers leading slaves by leashes and almost erotically dominatrix in appearance and design. The word 'AFFA' etched in sequins on the arses of the slaves that get patted and smacked by the soldiers. The word 'AFFA' spotted on the sides of the floats too. On banners and on flags and one gorgeous woman stops in front of Ben to shake her boobs tattooed with the letters 'AF' on one breast and 'FA' on the other, all in flowing script. Ben stares open-mouthed, earning a dig from Safa in the process, but it wasn't the ample cleavage he was staring at but the word. The same word seen everywhere. This is 1999. Why doesn't he know what the word 'AFFA' means? They said it in Hyde Park in 2111 too. He turns to look at Miri, who makes a drinking motion, then nods to the bar behind them. 'I'M GOING TO THE BAR WITH MIRI . . .' he yells at Safa.

'GOOD. GO LOOK AT MORE BIG TITS.'

'I WASN'T LOOKING AT HER TI— BOOBS.'

'YOU BLOODY WERE. I SAW YOU.'

'NO, I WASN'T . . . I MEAN . . . I WAS LOOKING AT THE TATTOO ON HER BOOBS . . . NOT HER ACTUAL BOOBS.'

'SURE. FUCK OFF. GO FIND A WOMAN WITH BIG TITS.'

'I WASN'T STARING . . . I'M GOING TO GET THE DRINKS.'

'WHATEVER,' she says, flicking a middle finger up while staring ahead.

He tuts and turns to see Emily shaking her head in admonishment.

'I WASN'T LOOKING AT HER BOOBS,' he yells.

'SURE,' she yells back, giving a sarcastic smile and an even more sarcastic thumbs up.

He walks off behind Miri towards the building line and the various wide doorways of the bars. The smells of beer and cigarette smoke hang in the air. The heat of people packed together.

'You seeing all this?' Ben asks, putting his mouth to Miri's ear to be heard.

'Confirmed,' she says. 'Observe for now.'

Miri simply holds up seven fingers and shows a banknote to a young man behind the bar, who snatches it from her grip before rushing off while she nudges Ben and points at the bottles on display. Whiskeys, rums, vodkas and all different spirits. Ben spots only one label he recognises. All the others are different, with brands he has never seen before. A big sign above the bar proclaiming AFFA BEER SOLD HERE in English and Portuguese.

'What's affa mean?' Safa asks him when Ben and Miri go out with the drinks, apparently now having forgotten the buxom woman Ben was staring at.

'No idea,' he shouts back.

'Ben?' Malcolm pushes into his side. 'What does affa mean? We've never heard of it.'

Ben shrugs, then turns back to face the procession and drink the beer in his hand.

Harry downs bottle after bottle, but then he is a big man and able to consume such quantities. He starts smiling and laughing too and dances in the road with the men and women that go by. He dances with Emily, lifting her off her feet with his hands on her waist and making her squeal in delight at being hoisted up so easily.

Miri goes for more drinks, noticing the banknotes held by others are slightly different to the money she has but at least the same colour and size. She aims for the busiest section, knowing the bartenders are too frantic to check the notes.

She returns with two crates of beer and a bottle of rum that gets passed round with something akin to ritualistic swigging by a group forming a bond while all around them are signs and logos they have never seen before.

'Roman,' Miri says, nodding at Ben. 'S'definitely Roman.'

'Roman,' Ben replies, nodding in response. 'S'got to be.'

'Affa? Affa? I don't know it. Do you know it?' Miri asks him a few seconds later.

'Nope, I don't know it . . . I keep thinking . . . I keep thinking affa? I don't know affa . . .'

Emily takes the bottle, carefully wiping the opening with her arm before glugging a few big mouthfuls of rum. 'I mean . . . you know . . . I just worry. I do. I worry. That's who I am? You know?' she tells Safa earnestly.

'Sex,' Safa says knowingly, winking at Emily in such a way that Emily sprays her drink. 'He just needs some nookie . . .'

'Safa! He doesn't . . .' Emily says, wiping her chin.

'Bet he does,' Safa says. 'OI, BEARDY . . . ARE YOU HORNY?'

'WHAT?' Harry roars, turning round in the way of a mountain rotating on its axis and thereby shifting several people caught in his gravitational field.

'HARRY, YOU DICK,' Safa laughs as Harry wraps his arm round her and Emily, lifting them both off their feet in a huge bear hug.

'GOING AFT,' Harry strides out to join in with some scantily clad Roman soldiers and tunic-wearing slaves with Safa and Emily still in his arms. The women laugh hard, bouncing along as Harry dances, spins and turns with the men and women.

'Oi, piss off,' Konrad yells, seeing a man taking a bottle from one of their crates of beer.

'Hey, buddy,' the man says, standing upright while holding several bottles. He smiles at Konrad, showing even white teeth in a square jaw underneath buzz-cut hair. Wide shoulders, muscular arms and clearly very American.

'I said piss off,' Konrad says.

'Come on, buddy, it's carnival,' the man drawls, laughing as he passes some of the bottles to his mates.

'Hold my beer, Malc,' Konrad says, passing his bottle to Malcolm.

'Er, he's a big lad, Kon,' Malcolm says, blinking in alarm.

'No, no, hold my beer . . . Bloody cheeky Yank . . .'

'Come on now, Kon . . . I'm sure he'll put it back . . . Oh, he's taking more. Ere, mate, that's a bit naughty, that is. You put them back.'

'The US Navy requires these beers . . .' the American says with a line that makes his shipmates burst out laughing. 'Aw, come on, Affa, quit whining . . . We'll leave you one . . .'

Konrad gives a gargled yell and takes it upon himself to defend the beer supplies against the blatant theft underway by the US Navy. He charges fast, crossing the short distance, while the Americans laugh and look at each other in mild surprise as E-3 rating Culinary Specialist Seaman Gibowski, a former college fullback, reels from the forehead of a half-British, half-German workman from the future slamming into his nose.

Gibowski goes down hard with the bottles of beer falling from his hands as Konrad stands victorious for a long second while the other E-3 rating US Navy Culinary Specialists stare on before lunging at Konrad.

'KON!' Malcolm shouts, then charges in to help his mate.

Harry spins and dances with Safa and Emily still laughing in his arms, all three turning heads at the sight of Malcolm being propelled backwards past them and track back to the Battle of the Crate now underway with Konrad swinging out wild and crazed but not hitting anyone. The sailors swarm, taking him down amidst a sea of elbows and legs flailing until the roar of a very large man peaks over the din of the music and behind Ben and Miri, Harry, Safa and Emily rush into the fray as more seamen from the culinary department arrive to assist their colleagues. US Navy ships are big; they have a lot of sailors and that means a lot of food to be cooked and served, which means a lot of sailors to cook and serve it.

'You don't think, do you?' Ben asks with a sudden thought, his back to the huge brawl going on behind.

'What?' Miri snaps in between swigging from her bottle of beer.

'Affa . . . You don't think it's like . . . You know . . . Alpha . . . affa . . . Alpha . . . Nah, haha . . . Silly . . . Ignore me.'

'Where's that damn rum?' Miri demands, spinning round to drunkenly view the mass fight underway. 'Mr Ryder . . .'

'What?'

'Mr Ryder, turnabout,' Miri orders.

'Fuck's sake,' Ben says, turning round. 'It could be Alpha . . . Affa and Alpha are . . . Oh hello, there's a big fight going on . . . Ooh, is that Harry? It is . . . He's got those two chaps in his hands . . . But what I'm saying, Miri, is Affa and Alpha sound the same . . . ish . . .' He trails off, realising Miri is no longer next to him, but is punching a man in the face.

'Oh,' Ben says, watching almost idly. He looks round to see everyone else has cleared away to stare at the bedlam with amused interest. Then he spots Safa in the middle, the love of his life battering everyone near to her. Even when drunk she moves faster than everyone else. He sighs happily, feeling his heart swell until E-3 rating Culinary Specialist Seaman Gibowski, having just got back up, takes a cheap shot at the back of Safa's head. 'OI, THAT'S MY GIRLFRIEND . . .'

Half an hour later the bar fills with the roar of a hundred voices joined in song and all of them surrounding a bearded giant of a man holding a beer bottle above his head while he leans back to sing.

'*Welcome to the Hotel California . . . such a lovely place . . .*'

It was a seething, brawling mess of floundering bodies and people rolling over each other until a quick-thinking young man from one of the local bars doused the fighters with a hose and within seconds, they were separated, soaking and looking round in a post-scrap daze wondering who started it and why.

It was Harry, with Emily at his side, who led them into the bar of the young man with the hose and decided he should buy everyone a beer. Miri paid, of course, in the way of quickly pushing banknotes into the hands of the bartenders and telling them, in part Spanish, part Portuguese and part Russian to keep them focussed on her instead of the money.

The song ends on the music system. A song that seems to have still happened despite the changes to the timeline.

'MORE,' Harry roars, holding his beer aloft.

'MORE,' everyone else roars, taking their cue from the epicentre of the party. All eyes on the big man. All eyes on his wide shoulders and the thickness of his neck glimpsed behind his beard and the whiteness of his teeth through those bushy dark hairs.

As the music starts again, so the people move and sway to sing and give voice and the compression of the crowd surrounding Harry closes in, pushing Emily further into his side.

Sometimes Edith looks like Emily. Sometimes, when Harry lies in his bed and tries hard to summon Edith's face he sees Emily's instead. He dreamt of Edith a few nights ago. They were walking on Blackpool seafront and stopped to kiss in the rain. It gave him a warm sensation inside but when he pulled back it was Emily instead and Harry woke up confused.

Now he drinks and sings but he still can't remember Edith's face. Even now, in the packed bar, he cannot summon the image of her face, so he sings the words of a song he just learnt as Emily loops her arm through his and leans back to glug from the bottle, showing the shape of her slender neck and her defined clavicle bones. She catches him staring and lowers the bottle to grin and laugh. 'Beardy,' she says, blinking heavy and slow.

'AYE,' Harry roars, holding his beer aloft.

'AYE,' everyone else roars, holding their beers aloft.

That makes Emily laugh again. Harry likes it when she laughs. He likes the sound of it and the way her cheeks blush when she's been giggling for a while. He likes the way the tip of her nose moves when she talks and the little lines around her eyes that crease deeper in mirth.

She slides her arm across his back and laughs at the difference in their sizes, and steps in front of him to feel his arm around her waist holding her tight. The man who took out Alpha and Bravo. The man she eats popcorn with on the big red sofa when they watch holo movies.

She lifts the bottle to her mouth and leans back, glugging deep and seeing him upside down. He looks down, smiling at her then planting a big kiss on her forehead that makes her choke and burst out laughing again.

'*Welcome to the Hotel California . . . such a lovely place . . .*'

They sing together with her looking up and him looking down. Both with flushed, ruddy faces glistening lightly with sweat. Both with wet clothes that cling to their frames in the steamy heat of the packed bar. She pushes her fingers to entwine in his, but it's not right, honour kicks in and Harry forces himself to look up and away. He is betrothed to Edith. He made a pledge. He can't remember Edith. He can't remember her. He tries hard and closes his eyes while singing to try with every ounce of effort to see her face, but it won't come. He is forgetting who he is. He is forgetting his loyalty and honour, but then he died in Norway. Edith will marry someone else and live a long happy life. She's already done it. She's now dead or she still has her life to live. She is neither the past nor the future but a singular reminder of a love he had that was true and pure, but that is now gone.

A hand on his neck and he opens his eyes to realise Emily is still clasped in his arms in front of him and reaching up to pull him down. He lowers gently, caught in the moment of feeling her body leaning back against him, of the shape and smell of her, of the tone of her skin and the feel of her hand on the back of his neck. If he turns his head a little he could kiss the soft tender skin of her inner forearm pressing against his jaw.

Emily saw Ben and Safa kissing off to one side and the image struck her. She wants to tell Harry to look, so he can see how cute it is and how well they suit each other. She wants to tell Harry that Safa said he might be horny and in her mind that joke will be funny and they'll both laugh and drink more beer.

She smiles up at him. The lighting low, the music blaring, the voices singing and her hand on the back of his neck and as he lowers so their eyes lock and her smile fades. His eases. Their eyes become focussed and serious. Breathing deepens. Hearts thunder. They are both young, fit, healthy and detached from everything they ever knew to do a thing of monumental meaning and in that second all those things can be seen and understood.

She pulls away, then pushes past him, aiming for the back of the bar. He watches her go, then feels the tug of her hand pulling him behind her.

She speeds up, heading through the dense bar to the doors at the back into a corridor leading to a storeroom filled with crates, barrels and bottles on shelves. Another door. A flight of stairs going up. Dark and gloomy with the neon lights outside the grimy windows filtering chemical illumination that mixes with the background noise of the bars surrounding them and the street outside. Not that they notice because she turned after climbing the first two stairs, grabbed her top and pulled it up over her head as Harry surged in to plant his mouth on hers.

Hands move with urgency. Fuelled by alcohol and lust. She feels his arms loop round her waist and lifts her legs to wrap round him. He climbs the stairs, carrying her easily while kissing hard. Both of them pushing into the other with weeks and months of tension bursting out from them. They cannot get close enough. They cannot move fast enough. She grunts as she kisses him, almost animalistic in her desire. Her hands pushing into his beard and the thrill inside at kissing Harry surges to give unabated pleasure. Mad Harry Madden. This is Mad Harry Madden. The thought of it. The thrill of it but more than that, this is the man who saved her, the man who refused to look at her nipples straining through the wet top that night, but now he is taking them in his mouth and feeling them stiffen on his tongue. She gasps at the sensation, at the bristles of his beard on her skin. He is safe. Whatever they do now is safe because he is Harry.

A battered old sofa once used in the main bar but taken upstairs for storage rather than paying the cost of dumping it. They sink down into the leather that creaks with the weight of their bodies kissing, searching, pushing and gasping for air.

The desire increases, becoming a craving, a need, an absolute necessity. She pulls his shirt overhead rather than waste time unbuttoning it. She kisses him while doing it, sitting astride his lap while his hands run and up and down her back. She feels his arms and shoulders then down his chest to fumble at the button and zipper on his shorts that she chose and bought for him while he does the same to her. Both of them getting in each other's way. Both trying to kiss and push and do everything all at the same time.

She grunts again in frustration and pulls away to stand up in front of him to yank her shorts and knickers off. He stands too, his shorts falling down. She places a hand on his chest, pushing him back onto the sofa, then stepping up to sink down all in one motion and the sensation of penetration makes them both gasp and hold still for a gloriously long beautiful second as her back arches and she faces up to the heavens.

She falls forward to kiss him while moving back and forth with Harry holding her hips, feeling the movement and the sensation of being inside her. Seeing her breasts sway and the touch of her lips on his and her tongue darting in and out.

Edith doesn't exist. Nothing exists. Not the bunker, not Safa or Ben, not Miri or anyone. Not the people they killed in any of the wars they have fought in. Only this matters; being here with Emily is his singular point of being and that absolute love, that hungry tenderness, extends out to envelop her. He becomes fascinated with the contours of her body, with the way the light shines on her hair hanging down her back. He slows his motion to savour every second, to search her eyes and smile when she grins at him, to laugh when she laughs at the delight they have together as she stares into his eyes, riding him with a pace that builds and grows.

'Oh my god,' she gasps, dropping forward to kiss his mouth while his hands move round to grasp her backside. The strength of him is immense, the pure ease in which he lifts her body in his hands and moves her back and forth with just the power of his arms and shoulders.

He is going to come, she can feel it with an instinct inside, but so is she and she gasps in disbelief at the ideology of synchronicity. It's building now, building faster and coming, coming now.

She throws her head back as the orgasm grips to surge up inside her whole body, sending electric currents that judder her muscles. At that same time so he grunts and moves faster. A feeling within both of a perfect moment gained and they both shake, move and gasp as the orgasms stretch on and hold for eternity until she finally sinks down to find his lips and kiss him with a tenderness that replaces the hunger she had but a second before.

Down the stairs, along the hallway, out into the packed bar and across the far side, Miri lowers the bottle from her mouth and shakes her head. She saw them going to the back. She saw the looks in their eyes too and felt, at that second, a contrasting range of reactions that spoke of jealousy, happiness, worry and just pure simple drunkenness.

'Damn it all to hell.' She grabs the arm of a young man with buzz-cut hair. 'Hey, sailor, bum a smoke?'

'Sure thing, ma'am.'

'Damn Harry. Damn Tango Two . . . Damn it all to hell . . . What's your rating?'

'E-3 Culinary Specialist, ma'am, we all are.'

'Cooks? Damn it. The navy's gotta eat though. What ship are you from? The only vessel near here is the USS *George Washington*. That your carrier, son?'

'I've not heard of that vessel, ma'am . . .'

'George Washington. The first goddam POTUS . . .'

'Say, you okay?' the sailor asks carefully. 'Where you from?'

'What's the name of your goddam ship, sailor?'

'The USS *John Adams* . . . You need me to get your friends, ma'am?'

'The *John Adams* submarine was decommissioned in nineteen eighty-nine . . . and it sure as shit didn't have E-3 rating culinary specialists on board. Who was the first POTUS? Was it Adams?'

The sailor nods, confusion in his expression. The older woman's manner screams officer. Hell, she could even be from his own ship. The USS *John Adams* is the largest aircraft carrier in the world and he only knows a fraction of the personnel on board.

She straightens up, bringing forth warmth and humour to her face, which transforms instantly to sober and sharp. 'Good work, son. Can never be too careful. Don't give your ship information away to strangers. I'll pass it on to your CO. Re-join your crew but don't be late back.'

'Ma'am, yes, ma'am,' he snaps, surging to stand properly with a smart salute and relief washing over his features without questioning that she never asked his name.

'First POTUS.' She laughs, shaking her head. 'Good line, huh?'

'Yes, ma'am.'

'Dismissed.'

'Thank you, ma'am.'

She waits as he rushes back inside, then sags against a wall to light another smoke from his packet, which she never gave back.

'Miri?' Ben calls, walking out to look round.

'Here,' she says.

'I asked someone inside . . . Affa is to do with a Roman patrol near Hadrian's Wall in one-two-six AD.'

'Good work,' she says, inhaling on the smoke. 'Got a starting point at least.'

'Yeah, have you seen Harry or Emily?'

'They're having sex out the back.'

'Are you taking the piss?'

'A very British saying, Mr Ryder, but no I am not taking the piss. You heard of the USS *George Washington*?'

'Yeah, big American carrier. Are you being serious about Harry and Emily?'

'Strange thing is, according the E-3 rating I just spoke with the *George Washington* doesn't exist and John Adams was the first POTUS.'

Ben stares, blinks and shakes his head. 'John Adams was?'

'Vice President to George Washington.'

'Yeah, right. How do you know Harry and Emily are shagging?'

'I think the whole bar just heard,' she says, as flat and hard as ever. 'Time has changed, Mr Ryder.'

'It has,' he says, nodding emphatically, trying to look and sound serious. 'Awful,' he tuts. 'Ah, well, we'll sort it . . . Fancy another beer?'

Thirteen

The Complex, one month later

She looks awful. Pale, drawn and haggard and sitting in her dark office with the screens glowing against her skin makes her look positively evil. Her behaviour is changing too. She's always been abrupt to the point of rudeness, but that acidic nature is now edged with barely concealed spite.

Alpha stands easy, his hands behind his back. Bravo at his side. Kate next to him. Gunjeep finishing the line. All of them silent.

'One month,' Mother says quietly in a voice like nails down a chalkboard. 'We've been here for ONE FUCKING MONTH!'

'Yes, ma'am,' Alpha says, the only one brave enough to speak.

'Yes, ma'am,' Mother mimics, slamming her hand down on the desk. Gunjeep and Kate flinch. Alpha and Bravo don't.

'Are you checking?' Mother asks, staring at Kate, who nods frantically. 'ANSWER ME!'

'Yes, ma'am! I'm checking. We're doing it several times a day.'

Mother purses her lips, scowling at them, at everything. 'Tell me again exactly what you are doing.'

Kate swallows, blinking a few times before drawing air. 'We're going into the history department of the university I used to work in to check for changes using the timeline comparison software program we developed to check for changes to the timeline . . . It's, er . . . It's what you told us to do.'

'Are you being flippant?'

'No,' Kate says urgently, shaking her head.

'It was too subtle,' Mother mutters, speaking to herself. 'Fuck off,' she snaps, nodding her head at them. 'Alpha can stay. The rest of you get back to work.'

The others leave quietly, closing the door behind them as Alpha remains standing easy in front of Mother's desk.

'Something has happened,' Mother says. 'There must be a reason we haven't seen a reaction.'

'Perhaps we need to do something else,' Alpha says carefully. 'One-two-six AD was a long time ago . . .'

'Was it?'

'Sorry,' he says at her biting tone.

'No, you're right,' she mutters. 'I can hear them all,' she adds after a pause.

'Hear them?' Alpha asks.

'Out there. The peasant cunts whispering about me. Saying Maggie Sanderson was a hero. Ben Ryder is a hero. Safa Patel is a hero . . .'

'I, er, I have not heard that,' he replies, feeling the urge to suggest she use the bloody portal to get some daylight and fresh air. She stalks the complex, slamming doors and screaming at anyone in her way. Striding into rooms to glower round when the conversations end suddenly, ordering everyone to work when there isn't much work to do and even the agents are getting twitchy at not being active. He also wants to suggest maybe she let the people in the complex use the portal to have some time away, even a few hours.

'Too long ago, too subtle,' Mother says, bringing Alpha's attention back to her mutterings. She looks up at him with a decisive glare. 'Go bigger.'

'Bigger?'

'We go bigger. We do something that will make them fucking pay attention.'

Alpha listens intently with that nugget of worry already growing roots in the back of his mind. He has heard what the people in the complex talk about. He has heard how the world was a different place after Cavendish Manor but that despite the cold war rushing in there was a bizarre world peace. Not one missile or bomb had been used. Not one invasion. Not even a threat. Just a deep paranoia that seemed to have oppressed governments while the masses rejoiced. He learnt about the names too: Ben Ryder, Safa Patel, Harry Madden, Emily Rose and Maggie Sanderson.

The concern is there. The worry that this isn't about protecting the timeline or anything else. This is about winning and not being beaten by an insurance investigator, a cop, an old spy, a World War Two soldier and a shit agent who would have never made it to a One.

'Are you listening?' she barks.

'Of course,' he says quickly, politely.

'Good. We'll get started immediately.'

Fourteen

The Bunker, Thursday morning

The first thing Harry does when he wakes is remind himself where he is. Years of missions, bases and waking to new sights have taught him well.

He does it now and within a split second he knows he is in his room on his bed and the time of day is early morning. He knows that because the shutter covering the window is jammed and he can see the sky outside. He knows it's raining because he can see it pattering against the window.

He also knows he was drinking heavily last night from the taste of gorilla shit in his mouth, the dull whump at the back of his head and the general feeling of dehydration that comes from a big session.

Harry also knows he was in a fight last night. He knows that because he is remembering it in a series of flashbacks. Those flashbacks also start to bring forth other memories, such as dancing with the men and women in the procession and carrying Emily and Safa about for a while. He remembers the bar after and learning a new song about a hotel in California and some grinning lad spraying him with a hose, or was that before they went into the bar? When was the fight? Who did they fight? Ah yes, it was the Yanks. Good lads as it turns out. Didn't mind a ruck and a pint after and no harm so no foul. He smiles at the memory.

Aye, that was a good night. Maybe one of the best, although there was that night in London when he was on leave and they had the brawl with the Canadians. Now they can fight and they're big lads too. Stout and solid.

Then he remembers the other bit in one solid flashback that makes his eyes widen and his heart thump while his already tender stomach flips over a few times. The bar, the lights, they were both wet, they went out the back, she took her top off on the stairs and they . . . they . . . Oh dear. Oh no. The sofa. On the sofa. They did it. Emily. With Emily. Flashes of her naked body strobe his mind.

'Bugger.' He surges up from the bed towards the door with a rush of guilt.

'You are so loud,' Emily grumbles, rolling onto her back with a groan as Harry's eyes widen at the sober sight of her breasts and other lady parts.

'Bugger.' He grabs a towel and grapples with the door, cursing under his breath until finally remembering he has to pull and not push.

'Harry,' Ben says, standing bleary-eyed in his doorway opposite.

'ABLUTIONS,' Harry bellows, trying to slam his door closed, cover his penis with the towel and run across the middle room all at the same time.

Harry seals himself in the bathroom and brushes his teeth like a man possessed. He turns the shower on and yelps at the near-freezing water hitting his body. He takes the cold in a manly fashion of rushing to wash while thinking of last night while trying *not* to think of last night and the sight of Emily's lady parts. What does he do now? She's in his room. What about Edith? 'Bugger . . .'

War is a funny thing. It brings out the best and worst in humanity. Some men use it to bend the rules of honour. Harry doesn't. He went to a brothel just once. It was after a brutal action that lasted weeks and only finished when it came down to hand-to-hand fighting, a thing Harry excels at, and the first time he earned the nickname *Mad Harry.* He killed more Germans than everyone else in his platoon combined. Later, on leave in whatever port they stopped at, he got drunk, got in a scrap and paid for sex. The woman was thin from rationing. Her bones showed through her skin, but she gave kindness and held him after, which was the thing he really wanted in the first place. She even let him stay the night. It was his aura of utter calmness that she felt, and she too slept the first full night in a long time.

The chaplain told him later that it was fine. That prostitution was the oldest trade in the world and a comfort given to warriors ever since time began. The chaplain said to do the things Harry does leaves a mark on the soul and to take comfort in the arms of a woman, even paid for, is sometimes a good thing and, besides, Harry is a decent chap and it's not like he roughed her up or anything.

So Harry got on with his war and held his honour intact. Until last night that is. He rushes from the shower and sets about drying himself off like a bear fighting with a rabid towel. He is betrothed, but then Edith isn't born yet or died years ago. Harry died in Norway. Is he still betrothed? Was it wrong? Is it wrong? It's Emily! Of course it's bloody wrong. She's a shipmate, a comrade-in-arms, one of the lads, one of the team. Oh dear. Oh no. This won't do. *You bloody fool, Harry.*

He has to apologise and report himself to the CO immediately and seek a redeployment to spare the girl's blushes. He stops fighting with the rabid towel to remember there is no redeployment. 'Bugger.'

He stops drying himself, wraps the towel round his waist and firms his resolve to do what must be done.

Harry throws open the bathroom door and marches into his room to see his bed neatly made and Emily's naked backside bending over as she stoops to pick up her clothes. A sight to see that renders him hopeless to cognitive thought, and with willpower dredged from the depths of his soul he forces himself to turn away to cease any vision of her lady parts.

'Morning,' she says in a husky sleep-filled voice. 'My head,' she groans.

'Aye, head.'

'What a night.'

'Aye, night . . .'

'You okay?'

'Aye.'

'Sure?'

'Aye,' he says, still facing away while listening to the rustle of clothes being pulled on behind him. He had a speech in his head. He had words ready and now fumbles to think clearly and know where to start. He wrings his hands in front of his waist and exhales noisily through his nose. 'Miss, I . . . It was . . . Ach, but the thing is . . . I'm not a rogue that . . .'

She smiles at his nerves with a glint of mischief in her eyes as she steals up behind him and moves in to press against his skin still cold from the shower. Her arms loop round his waist and she thinks back to last night, sighing softly and exhaling warm air over his back that makes him stand that bit taller and stiffer. She takes that as a sign of pleasure and presses her lips to kiss lightly as the magic of the night comes back. The same desire, the same urge, the same thing in sobriety as when drunk and her hand drops to move over the bulge in the towel but the enormous hand coming down to grip her wrist makes her realise she entirely misjudged the situation.

'I am not that man, miss . . .'

She hears the rebuke but doesn't see the wince on his face at the harshness of his words.

'You were last night,' she says in a tone equalling his.

'What I mean, miss . . .'

'So what was last night?' she asks, pulling away and feeling an ever so slight tug when he tries to draw her arm back as though he is reluctant to let go.

The words he had in the bathroom won't come and he flounders to try and think what to say, to form the words right and hold his honour and decency to do the right thing.

'It's fine,' she says lightly, patting his arm. 'We were drunk. Forget it. I'd better go.'

'Miss . . .'

'Emily. My name is Emily, Harry. I've earned my place here.'

'Miss . . . Emily.' He turns quickly, seeing her just in her bra and shorts with her top held in her hand.

'What?' she snaps, when he turns away. 'Oh, don't be so bloody prudish, Harry. You were all over them last night . . .'

'Ach, miss . . .'

'EMILY,' she shouts, pulling the door open, then instantly hating herself for shouting at him. She can see the nerves on his face and the complete lack of understanding at what to say. 'Please, my name is Emily,' she adds, forcing a softer tone.

'Emily,' he rumbles.

'Hot water still off? Great. Another day in the fucking bunker . . .' She walks briskly away as Ben opens his door to come out, but spots Emily and quickly pushes it closed. 'Morning, Ben,' she snaps, rushing faster out into the corridor with tears pricking her eyes.

'You okay, shithead?' Safa asks as Emily storms into their set of rooms.

'EMILY,' Emily shouts before moving back to the door to face out into the corridor. 'MY FUCKING NAME IS EMILY . . .'

'Hung over much?' Safa asks, then walks out and up into Ben's and Harry's rooms to see Harry still standing with his towel round his waist staring into space and Ben peeking out from his room. 'What's up with you lot?' she asks.

'She gone?' Ben asks through the gap in his door.

'Stop being a twat. Beardy, what's up?'

'Nowt,' Harry says, reaching out to slam his door closed.

'What the fuck?' Safa asks. 'What's going on?'

'Shush,' Ben says.

'Shush what? What's happened?'

Ben nods at Harry's room then nods at the main door while making his eyes wider.

'What?' Safa asks.

Harry, Ben mouths.

'What about him?' Safa asks.

'Emily and Harry last night,' Ben whispers.

'What? What last night? Last night what? Spit it out . . .'

'They had sex.'

'So?'

'Eh?'

'They're adults. They can do what they want. You coming for breakfast?'

'But . . .'

'But what?'

'But they had sex,' Ben exclaims quietly.

'So what? You're such a woman.'

'Are you hung over?' Ben asks, giving her a suspicious look.

'Nope, not at all. You?'

'God, yes. I feel like shit. Why aren't you?'

'Cos I'm special. Get dressed and come for breakfast . . . Unless you want sex now.'

'What?'

'Sex.'

'Sex?'

'Yes, sex. Would you like sex?'

Ben blinks and stares. His head hurts, his body hurts, he feels dehydrated, lethargic and slow-witted. 'Yeah, sure . . .'

At the other end of the bunker, Doctor Watson walks into the main room, crossing towards the big table laden with food and the smell of a freshly brewed pot of coffee. 'Morning . . .'

'Morning,' Miri replies curtly, looking up from the table.

'Good night?' he asks.

'Interesting to say the least,' she replies. 'Time has changed.'

'Changed? Changed how?'

'Something in Roman times.'

'Oh,' Doctor Watson says mildly, pouring a cup of coffee. That he doesn't feel an instant strong reaction to such news shows his absolute detachment to the former world he inhabited. 'Bad change?'

'No idea. Needs research.'

'Indeed. Yes. Well, just say if I can help . . . Have you got a minute?' he asks, easing down into chair as she watches him expectantly. 'It's about Ria.'

'What about her?'

'I'll have to bring her round today.'

'Do it.'

'She'll need help.'

'Help?'

'Psychological help. From someone that specialises in trauma and post-traumatic stress disorder. Without that she will be a significant suicide risk the minute she comes round. The sheer guilt she will face is . . .'

'Are you trained?'

'God no. I'm a medical doctor and a poor one at that.'

'Now is not a good time.'

'Miri, the poor girl was abandoned by her father, first as a child . . .'

'I am aware of Miss Cavendish's history, Doctor Watson.'

'Great, then I am sure you agree she needs therapy from an expert.'

'Get a book. Learn it.'

'Good god no. I am a medical doctor and a recovering alcoholic . . . I am the last person to administer therapy. Safa would be better at it than I would.'

'Give the book to Safa then.'

'Miri, not everything can be dealt with like that. Ria is here against her will. You owe it to her to do the very best you can . . .'

'Whole world to save.'

'And you're a hero and when we get medals I shall give you one.'

Miri stares devoid of expression while detecting the good doctor has a stubborn streak, which is about to reveal itself.

'Fine,' she says decisively.

'Pardon?' he asks.

'Do you have someone in mind?'

'Er . . .'

'Roland compiled a list of experts previously. Have a look at that. If not, I am sure we can pop back and ask Freud to help us out.'

'Right,' the doctor says, almost feeling a little dejected at not being able to use some of the points he had ready. 'Were you joking about Freud?'

'We're not extracting Sigmund Freud,' Miri says bluntly.

'No, of course. I was just checking you were joking . . . which you obviously were . . . Ah, Tango Two! A pleasant morning to you . . . Oh dear, whatever is that glare for?'

'Emily. My name is Emily.'

'Yes of course. It was just a joke . . . Er . . . Morning Harry.'

'Aye.'

Miri and the doctor watch as Harry nods curtly, then hesitates at seeing Emily ahead of him at the main table.

'Coffee, Harry?' Emily asks, turning round to offer him a forced cheery smile.

'Er . . .' he says, slowing down.

'Or do you only like coffee when you're drunk?'

'Ach . . .' Harry says deeply as Miri rolls her eyes.

'Eggs?' Emily asks him. 'Fruit?'

'Miss . . .'

'EMILY.'

'Emily . . .'

'What?'

'Nowt,' he says quickly.

'Morning,' Safa says, walking into the room while fanning her face with a hand. 'Is that coffee?' she asks, taking the mug in Emily's hand. 'Cheers. Morning, doc. You missed an awesome night. We got in a fight with some Yanks. Nice blokes actually. Fuck me it's hot in here . . .'

'Why are you so red?' Emily asks, watching Safa busy herself at the breakfast table.

'Just had sex.'

'What did she say?' the doctor asks, blinking in disbelief.

'Only a quick one, Ben's hung over . . . Whatever. You two okay?' Safa asks, shooting a glance from Harry to Emily.

'Going for a smoke,' Harry says, rushing towards the door.

'Wrong door,' Safa calls out.

'Aye,' Harry says, about-turning to rush towards the other door.

'Morning,' Ben says, pushing into the room and the frozen atmosphere. 'Er . . .' He hesitates, frowning and looking round.

'Morning, Ben!' the doctor calls out. 'Apparently you just had sex . . .'

'Safa,' he groans.

'What? They asked so I said,' she says.

'Sergeant,' Miri calls before Harry gets to the door. 'Briefing.'

'Yes, ma'am,' he says, about-turning again.

'Get food and sit down,' Miri orders everyone. 'We've got work to do.'

'Are we fit to work today?' Ben asks, joining the others at the food table. 'Bit of a heavy night . . . Where's Malc and Kon?'

'I'll get them,' Safa says, moving over to push the door open with her foot. 'GET UP YOU LAZY SHITS . . .'

'Safa shush,' Ben urges. 'Ria's down there . . .'

'Sorry,' Safa replies with a wince. 'Forgot . . .'

'We're up, we're up,' Konrad says quietly, waving a hand at Safa as he walks up the corridor. 'Is the doc in there?'

'Yeah. You two look like shit,' Safa says.

'Head hurts,' Malcolm mumbles.

'Everything hurts,' Konrad adds.

'Self-inflicted, no sympathy,' the doctor says brightly, pulling a face at the state of the two men walking in. Bleary red eyes, hair tussled, skin pale and bruised from the fight.

Miri taps the end of her pen on the notepad in front of her with a show of impatience as the others take their seats round the big table, placing mugs of coffee and bowls of food down in front of them, apart from Malcolm, who turns a shade of green at the sight of food and looks away for a few seconds.

'Do not vomit in here,' Miri orders, pointing her pen at him. 'To business. The timeline has changed . . .'

'Yolk,' Emily says, holding the small yellow portion of her boiled egg out for Harry.

'Ta,' Harry says, reaching out to take it at the very second Emily remembers she is upset with him.

'Oh, you want my eggs now . . .'

'What the fuck,' Safa sputters, covering her mouth to prevent the fruit coming out.

'Briefing,' Miri snaps.

'Sorry, ma'am,' Harry says dutifully, trying to take the yolk from Emily that she grips too hard, making it squish apart.

'The timeline has changed,' Miri says again. 'Early enquiries indicate a change to the Roman era in or around the time of Hadrian's Wall in . . . Give him the damn yolk,' she snaps at the squabble going on.

'He doesn't deserve the damn yolk,' Emily retorts.

'We. Are. Briefing,' Miri states, her voice dropping to a dangerous level.

'Yeah,' Safa says, tutting at the others. 'Briefing . . . fuck's sake. Carry on, Miri.'

'Get off!' Emily yelps, slapping at Harry's hand reaching for the last egg in her bowl.

'You only eat two,' Harry says.

'I want three today.'

A slam of a hand makes everyone jump as Miri brings order back to her breakfast briefing. 'The timeline has changed and appears to have originated in—' She cuts off as Malcolm suddenly heaves, covers his mouth and lurches from the table to run for the door. 'Jesus wept,' Miri mutters darkly.

'I am so sorry,' Malcolm says weakly, pushing back into the room. 'I just puked on that dead Nazi . . . He really smells, by the way.'

'Fine,' Miri snaps. 'Briefing is over.'

'That was quick,' Safa says. 'So what we doing then?'

'Get kitted. We're deploying to London twenty-one eleven in thirty minutes.' Miri stands up. 'And we will *not* let personal situations interfere with our work. Clear?'

'Yes, ma'am,' Harry says.

'I'm fine. I don't care,' Emily scoffs. 'I'm a professional.'

'I am pleased to hear that, Tango Two,' Miri says, striding out.

'MY BLOODY NAME IS EMILY . . .'

Fifteen

Berlin, Friday 2 February 1945

It's the noise of it. One thousand bombers accompanied by nearly six hundred fighters in the sky over Berlin. To see them is one thing, but to hear them is something else.

Hundreds of black shapes flying in strict formation overhead. American bombers: big, broad and distinct with smaller fighters zooming between them.

The Luftwaffe send what they have and the anti-aircraft guns fire with deep booming explosions and air-raid sirens still warble as the city fills with panic, but it's the noise that holds the five men still. The sound of the bombers, the lighter pitch of the fighters and the machine guns rattling out, the explosive AA fire and the bombs raining down that detonate and shake the ground as people run screaming for cover.

Berlin was evacuated early in the war, but the children crept back in to be with their mothers and it's those mothers now running the city. They operate the AA guns and the fire hoses to douse the flames. They are the search-and-rescue parties and they work in the factories making munitions or processing the food. They are the doctors and nurses. The gravediggers and cloth makers. The builders, the foragers, the backbone of a city from which all the men have been taken to fight.

Now the numbers in Berlin swell as millions flee the advancing Red Army and the carnage brought in brutal vengeance for the German invasion of Russia. Now the city infrastructure is the target of the Allies, who increasingly blur the justification for the targets they bomb, but then this is war and all is fair.

Within the chaos of that air raid, five men stand huddled together under the jutting curve of Arch 451. A disused storage shed fitted with a weathered but solid door behind which a green portal shimmers hidden from view. The portal they came through before stepping out to stare up in awe.

'DON'T STAND THERE,' a frantic man in the crowd calls out in German as he rushes past, pointing at the archway above their heads. His warning is obvious. The bombers are aiming for the railway lines running through the city, so to stand under the arch of a main track means several hundred tonnes of rubble coming down if a bomb hits. The five don't move because they know Arch 451 survives this bombing raid. In fact, Arch 451 survives all the bombing raids throughout the whole war and is still standing in 2062.

They know Arch 451 is safe in the same way they know which buildings located in Bundesstraße 2 are bombed and which remain intact.

'Arch four five one is located at the end of the street,' Kate told the five agents in her office two days ago. 'It's got a door too and what with the allies bombing all the railway lines we figured it would be safe to use. It actually became a bit of a thing for Berliners. Like a lucky charm thing . . .' She stopped to look round at the agents gathered in her office, lingering with her eyes on Alpha.

'I say, are you okay, my dear?' Bravo asked, bringing her back to reality with a rush of colour spreading through her cheeks.

'Um, yes, er . . . completely lost my train of thought then, haha! Oh gosh, I am embarrassing myself, aren't I . . . ?'

'It's fine,' Alpha said. 'What's the name of the street?'

'I can't read German but, er, Rodney and I have been calling it Bunder Street.'

'*Bundesstraße 2*,' Alpha said, reading the name from a map on a tablet on her desk.

'Oh wow, do you read German?' she asked, staring at him again.

'We all do,' he replied, studying the map for a minute before looking up at her. 'Kate?'

'That is so hot,' she whispered to herself, then winced at realising it came out loud. 'Rushing on! So Arch four five one on Bunder Street is the entry point . . .'

Now, two days later, the five agents stare out from underneath Arch 451 and view Bundesstraße 2 ahead of them. A wide road lined with high-fronted grand buildings. Gothic in style and once a grand, affluent typically German city street filled with offices, apartments and stores.

'Bunder Street,' Bravo quips, looking at Alpha. 'She's a nice girl,' he adds in fluent German.

'Lovely,' Charlie says in German.

'Very nice,' Echo says, also in German.

'Very pretty,' Delta says, also in German as all four stare at Alpha.

'Single too from what I hear,' Bravo says.

'Enough,' Alpha says, sharing the joke with a discreet smile. 'Bravo with me, you three stagger out behind us. German only from this point on.'

They step out in carefully chosen clothes that are slightly too big, to give the appearance of weight-loss to match that of the starving populace. They haven't shaved for two days either to aid that haggard, tired look.

Alpha and Bravo slow their pace as they near the target building while Charlie, Delta and Echo work to keep the specified distance.

The three behind see the reason for the slowdown. A unit of uniformed German soldiers running down the street. Old men and young boys pressed to serve their country. The rifles they carry seem too heavy for them and to the last they glance up at the sky made darker by the shadows of the warplanes and smoke billowing up from the bombs and fires.

The five adopt panicked expressions and flounder in the chaos. Echo staggers away. Delta runs a few metres in another direction. Charlie stands slack-jawed and stunned as he stares at the sky.

'DON'T STAND THERE GAWPING, YOU FOOL,' a hoarse voice screams as someone runs past. Charlie blinks and looks round to see the heavy-jowled face of an old German soldier. The man must be late fifties, maybe sixty. His nose streaked with red veins. His whiskers grey and wild. His eyes sunken and bloodshot. 'GET TO COVER . . .'

'Ja . . . ja . . .' Charlie gibbers as the unit runs past. Alpha and Bravo both turn to watch the interaction, their hands reaching for the pistols in the deep pockets of their overcoats. The officer of the unit of old men and boys slows his run and looks hard at Charlie. One arm missing and the empty sleeve tucked into his belt, but the free hand clutches a Luger pistol. A scar on his cheek and hard blue eyes that flicker from Charlie to Echo then to Delta. This man is switched on. He was on the front line. He commanded units of men in action and the loss of an arm has not dulled his senses. A suspicious look begins to form on his battle-hardened features.

'So loud,' Charlie says weakly, pretending to be terrified. 'It's so loud . . .'

'HALT,' the officer barks the order, bringing his men to a stop. They turn to look at their commanding officer with confusion. 'Papers,' the officer says, waving his Luger at Charlie. 'Watch them,' he adds, swinging the pistol towards Delta then Echo.

'It's so loud,' Charlie says again, as if he is so shell-shocked at the bombing raid underway his mind cannot process what is happening.

'Papers . . . NOW!' the officer roars, aiming at Charlie, his suspicions growing as he finally spots Alpha and Bravo. 'COVER THOSE TWO . . .'

An escalation from a chance interaction to a confrontation that can now only end one way. Alpha and Bravo look confused and alarmed as Delta and Echo watch the rifles being brought to aim while inside their pockets they start to apply the first bites of pressure on the triggers.

People stream past. Mothers and children crying out loud. Old men and women stunned to the core. A young girl carrying a baby. Blackened faces from smoke and filth. Explosions all around them.

Several hundred feet in the sky above them the US fighter flips and rolls down between the formation of bombers. The G force presses the pilot back into his seat as he dives the aircraft towards the ground. A hatred for the enemy shows in his eyes. His two brothers killed by the Nazi war machine, but this is war and all is fair so he aims for the wide street and increases the pressure on the trigger that feeds to the six wing-mounted heavy machine guns.

He pitches side to side, creating a swinging yawing target for the AA flak coming back. Details of the lives of those below start to show. The buildings reduced to rubble from previous bombing raids. The smoke and fire billowing up from fresh explosions. The vehicles, ambulances and fire trucks careering through the packed streets full of people. Old men and women. Mothers with children. All of them German and responsible for the death of his brothers. He presses to fire and brings the six machine guns to life to strafe the street in a roaring overhead pass and such is his speed he does not see the one-armed battle-hardened German officer obliterated by the large rounds shredding through his body and making his unit of boys and old men scatter screaming to find cover.

The fighter lifts to join the fight above. Alpha and Bravo step out into the street to stare in wonder at the aircraft as Charlie, Echo and Delta spin round to see the soldiers fleeing in all directions. A thing seen. A thing witnessed, and the fighter almost makes it back to the sky above before the AA round blows the canopy apart and sends it spinning to crash into the buildings below where it ignites a fresh ball of flame to scorch the sky.

The five press on. To be here is a thing indeed but this is not the first war for any of them and they have work to do.

The building is unmarked, save for a dust-covered brass plaque on the heavy wooden door. The front door was once guarded and secure but it's too late in the war to worry about such things now. Alpha and Bravo go in first. Alpha leading the way into the dark interior and the dust particles falling from the tremors running through the ground and walls.

A pretty woman with blonde-ringlet hair walks briskly from a room, rushing into the hallway to grab her heavy overcoat from the wooden stand. She barely glances at Alpha and Bravo but the bags under her eyes speak of the tension and stress.

'Closed,' she says firmly. 'Air raid . . . Can't you hear it?'

'Yes, miss,' Alpha says. 'We need to see Herr Weber . . .'

'Air raid,' she says emphatically as the building shakes from a nearby explosion.

'Is he here?' Alpha asks.

She tuts, huffs, puts her coat on and rushes past to the front door. 'Upstairs.' She falters as Charlie, Delta and Echo step inside then continues on with her head down. She doesn't care who they are. She doesn't care for anything other than taking her son to the shelter.

Alpha and Bravo share a look while Delta leans over to admire the woman's backside as she runs out. He nods as he looks back at the others. 'Nice,' he mutters.

'Skinny,' Charlie says.

'War on,' Delta says. 'Hadn't you noticed?'

'Delta, Echo, stay downstairs. Charlie, you come up and wait outside,' Alpha orders.

A swift climb to the top floor. A series of plain wooden doors each with a nameplate on the wall beside it. They pass several people running down the stairs while tugging on winter coats. Harassed, scared and rushing for the safety of the shelters. None of them ask who the three are.

'That one,' Bravo says, nodding ahead to the nameplate beside the closed door, which opens to a small bald-headed man bustling out, doing the same as everyone else and tugging a winter coat on as dust rains down amidst the cacophony of booms and bangs from outside.

'Herr Weber?' Alpha asks.

The small man barely glances at them. His face a mask of panic.

'Air raid. Get to shelter,' he says quickly.

'I need a moment of your time,' Alpha says, stepping in front of Herr Weber, blocking his path to the stairs.

'Who are you? There's an air raid on . . . Come on, move!'

'A moment, Herr Weber,' Alpha says as Bravo and Charlie close in from the sides.

That does it. That gets the small man's attention. He blinks up at Alpha, then across to Bravo and Charlie. Healthy strong men. Tall and broad-shouldered with intelligent eyes. 'What?' Herr Weber blurts. 'What do you want?'

'Something for you,' Alpha says, ushering the man back inside his office. Bravo goes in with them as Charlie closes the door and holds position outside, nodding politely to the other office dwellers rushing from their rooms.

A wooden desk piled with papers and books. Shelves filled with more reference material. Science journals. Physics. Chemistry. The walls filled with sheets of paper and chalkboards etched with equations. The building tremors again from a detonation too close for Herr Weber's comfort. He turns back to the door as Alpha pulls a folded clutch of papers from an inside pocket and holds them out. Herr Weber balks, blinking in confusion then flinching at another booming detonation.

'What is this?'

'Look,' Alpha says with a warm smile.

'Good god, man, we'll be bombed any minute,' Herr Weber says, snatching the papers away. 'What is it?' he asks impatiently, unfolding the sheets to read the front page. He glances quickly, tutting and becoming increasingly angry. Equations fill the sheets. Chemical compositions. Gobbledegook to most people, but Herr Weber is not most people, but, still, the panic of the air raid stops him from focussing.

'Slow down and read it properly now, old chap,' Bravo says in perfect English, which makes Herr Weber's head snap up as the blood drains from his face.

'English?'

'Oh, do read the bloody papers,' Bravo groans. 'There's a war on, don't you know.'

Herr Weber glances down to the front sheet. His heart hammering. He reads a few lines and blinks rapidly while wondering how to summon help. Then he stops wondering how to summon help and reads on. By the third page he looks up to the smiling face of Bravo and glances over to Alpha walking round his office and for a second the hope of victory shines in his eyes until he hears the bombers and fighters outside and feels the building shake.

'It's too late,' Herr Weber says sadly. 'The theory is clear, yes it can be done but . . . now? Even if I can convince the Führer that this is possible how do I convince him to allocate men and resources? The Russians are already in Germany . . . The war is over . . .'

'Thing is,' Bravo says, his cultured voice holding Herr Weber rapt and frozen, 'it's not just theory, old chap. We've got one.'

'You have one?' Herr Weber gasps in English, his accent thick.

'Oh, we do,' Bravo says. 'Would you like it?'

'Like it?' Herr Weber whispers.

'But of course,' Bravo says happily. 'Anything to help, old chap.'

'Tell you what,' Alpha says from the other side of the office, 'we'll trade it for this . . .'

◆ ◆ ◆

'Rodders? Is that you pissing about?'

'No, it's me,' Alpha says, pushing the door open. 'Just got back . . .'

'Oh my god,' Kate says, rushing up from behind her desk. 'So sorry, I thought it was Rodders, I mean Rodney . . .'

'It's fine,' Alpha says, taking another step into her office.

'Nice suit,' she scoffs before wincing yet again. 'Jesus. I get so nervous around you. It's like words just come out . . .'

'It's fine. Stop apologising,' he says.

'I'm not normally like this. No, well, I am. I mean I'm always like this but you make me worse . . . Oh my god, I can't stop talking. Er, so . . . How was it then? Did you get bombed?' She trails off, affecting a mock serious look that makes him smile.

'It's fine,' Alpha says. 'I found this.' He holds up the object in his hand.

'Oh my god . . .' Kate blurts, rushing out from behind the desk. 'Is that a Zeiss?'

'I think it is,' Alpha says, knowing fully well what it is.

'A Zeiss? Carl Zeiss? Can I see it? Oh my god, it is! It's a Carl Zeiss microscope . . .'

'I think it's old too.'

'Old? Are you taking the piss, Alpha? This is from the eighteen sixties . . . It's all brass and shiny.'

'Good,' Alpha says. 'Well, enjoy it.'

'Eh? You what? Is it for me?'

'I knew you liked the sword so . . .'

'Is this an integrity test? Because I will so fail if it is. Mother said nothing can come back and the whole cross-contamination thing and . . .'

'It's fine,' Alpha says casually as he walks to the door. 'I'm Alpha.'

'That's so hot,' she mumbles, then instantly squeezes her eyes closed in shame as he laughs and closes the door, before moving down the corridor to Mother's office.

'Well?' Mother asks, staring expectantly. 'Report.'

'Herr Weber accepts our kind offer,' Alpha says, the humour fading from his expression.

'I bet he fucking does,' Mother whispers, her eyes blazing in the gloom of her office.

'Have you made the announcement yet?' he asks.

'Are you questioning me, Alpha?'

'No, Mother. I am not.'

'I give orders. I do not make announcements and, no, I have not *given* my orders yet. Why? What have you heard?'

'I haven't heard anything. I was just asking, Mother.'

She holds the glare on him, suspicion etched on her face as she grabs a tablet from her desk, activates the screen and holds it close to her mouth.

'All personnel will report to the briefing room immediately.'

Her harsh voice blasts from speakers throughout the complex. An order given like she is making a statement to Alpha, who watches on impassively.

'I'll give them the good news now,' she tells him with a humourless grin.

A bare fifteen minutes later she stands on the stage and to say the silence in the room is heavy would be an understatement.

'It's gone very quiet in here.' Bravo's voice sails out from the front row as he turns to look behind him with a cheery nod that earns a few weak smiles. 'They're still there, Alpha . . . I thought they'd all snuck out.'

Mother acknowledges the perfect timing with a very discreet head dip to Bravo when he faces back to the front.

'Questions?' she snaps, bringing every head in the room looking back towards her. 'No? Good. You have your orders and instructions. Speak to your section heads if you have questions, section heads can report to Gunjeep. I do not want to be disturbed with petty queries. You *will* all work hard to achieve our objective. Are we clear? I said, are we clear?'

Nods and murmurs come back as her cold gaze sweeps the tiered audience. 'Good. Gunjeep?' She walks off and out, slamming the door as Gunjeep takes his place at the podium and allows a moment of pensive reflection before speaking.

'We must all do our bit,' he says with a serious expression. 'Terrorism cannot ever be allowed to, er . . . to win. We're here to save the world, which is no easy task . . . but . . . we have the best minds here and you've all been psychometrically tested to ensure you can cope . . . Apart from Kate, of course . . .' he adds with a weak grin. 'Mother has assured me that whatever we do can be reset after . . .' He pauses to nod, clearly unsure of his own words. 'So work hard, support each other and we'll get through it . . .' He trails off to a sudden awkward silence as Alpha reads the non-verbal tells coming from the chief technician that suggest the man had no idea what Mother's plan was until now. None of them did and the shock is palpable.

'How do we reset something like that?' someone asks from the tiered seats.

Alpha twists round to look. Everyone does. All of them looking to Doctor Holmes, who looks from Gunjeep to Alpha.

'We have a time machine, Doctor Holmes,' Bravo replies, his deep, rich voice so full of humour. 'We just go back and stop it.'

'It's that simple?' Doctor Holmes asks, and in that minute she speaks for everyone.

'Things are never that simple,' Bravo snorts with an endearing roll of his eyes. 'But do remember our dear Maggie Sanderson came here and happily slaughtered you all, eh? We can't let that happen, can we? No. Now, what's this I hear about an evening of themed entertainment?'

'Yes, yes,' Gunjeep says, rallying to project a greater air of confidence. 'We shall prevail. Now, I hope you're all coming to my *Star Trek* night? Yes? Yes? Nod at me then, you stupid bastards . . . haha! That's better.' He grins round at the wan faces nodding slowly with shock and worry. 'It's the original series and the chefs, well, I say chefs but more the people that burn our food . . . Oh, I am sorry, Janet. You are a wonderful cook . . .'

'Nicely done,' Alpha whispers, leaning towards Bravo as Gunjeep carries on.

'Happy to help,' Bravo whispers back.

'Right, get on with it then,' Gunjeep calls out, clapping his hands. 'Work hard, support each other and we'll get through it.'

'People are very odd,' Charlie murmurs a few moments later as the five agents stand together, listening to the chats around them that talk about the Star Trek night as much as about the mission defined by Mother.

'They are,' Delta replies softly.

'Hi!' Kate says, beaming at the five men and just about the only person now brave enough to approach them. 'Oh my god, Mother is sooo scary,' she whispers, then double takes at their serious expressions. 'Please don't say she's standing behind me.'

'She is,' Bravo says.

'I am so sorry,' Kate blurts, spinning round to apologise to thin air. 'Oh you,' she exclaims, slapping Bravo's shoulder. 'I thought some poo came out then . . . Are you all going to the *Star Trek* night?'

'I am sorry, my dear, are you asking the five most highly trained agents in the British Secret Service if they are going to a movie night?'

'Ooh, sounds really bad when you say it like that, Bravo,' she says, biting her bottom lip in instant angst.

'We're not going,' Alpha says.

'Apparently we are not going,' Bravo relays to Kate. 'Doesn't do for us to fraternise. Tends to lead to random heads of history departments walking up and punching us in the arms . . .'

'I get that,' Kate says seriously. 'I totally get that . . . Oh, that's me!'

'She's quick,' Charlie jokes.

'She is,' Delta says.

'So mean,' she says, still smiling at them all. 'But listen, I hate *Star Trek* . . . like totally hate it. What are you guys doing? Can we say we've got history stuff to do and I'll hang with you?'

Those five most highly trained agents in the British Secret Service find themselves rendered mute and stupid at such a question being asked of them.

'I'm researching bombs and things,' Echo says, looking at the other four.

'Bombs and things?' Delta asks.

'Yeah, the mission . . . bombs and things,' Echo says.

'Sure,' Alpha says to Kate. 'Come over. We've got work to do but it's fine.'

'Great! I'll keep it on the Q T too,' she whispers, winks, nods and pats the side of her nose before heading off.

'What?' Alpha asks as the other four look at him. 'I can't stand *Star Trek* either.'

'I quite like *Star Trek*,' Charlie says. 'Never seen the original on holo . . .'

'And to think we once trained armies in Africa,' Bravo says with a dramatic tut.

'Right, on with it,' Alpha says. 'Lot to do . . .'

An understatement if ever one was said. *A lot to do* does not cover it and every person in the complex is put to work.

It is an awful thing they plan for but, as they are often reminded, they were murdered in cold blood and anything changed can be reset, and so the horror of the thing they plan for lessens until it simply becomes the job at hand and the days soon start going by in a blur of activity.

Problems arise as they always will. The mission cannot go ahead without understanding weather patterns, but such things are the expertise of meteorologists, and with space at a premium within the complex none were selected for the project. Short straws are drawn and the bearded physics guys are tasked with learning the new subject, but that means close liaison with Rodney in the history department for the specified date and, in turn, the history department has to understand many things not related to history in order to choose that date, so they work with the engineers, physicists, chemists, biologists, doctors, IT specialists and programmers to start building an idea of just how they do what Mother ordered.

The *Star Trek* night soon comes and those attending, which equates to ninety-five per cent of the entire staff, soon gather in varying costumes in the briefing theatre for the buffet meal and a rare allowance of wine and beers with Gunjeep dressed as Captain Kirk proudly putting the holo series on.

It's that night that Kate is exposed to the true genius and utter capability of the agents with an outstanding foray into their world with an infiltration by the five agents and Kate into the theatre, to snaffle food and drinks while in a double disguise of *other* complex workers dressed outlandishly as characters from Star Trek. It works too. They go in, mingle, chat, steal food and drink then exfil back to the agents' quarters for their own mini party.

That the five men bond in such a way is unheard of within their world. That they share jokes is one thing, but the fact they adopt Kate into their fold as they work towards a thing of such magnitude is akin to Tango Two seeing the world through new eyes and choosing, of her own free will, to stay with Safa and the others.

Besides, Kate gets on with everyone and by the agents keeping her on side it means they have a steady flow of intelligence of the internal workings of the complex. They are agents after all.

They know, through Kate, that one of the physics guys is having sex with the redhead from the medical wing and that Gerry and one of the Portal Observation Specialists keep sneaking into each other's rooms at night. They learn that pretty much everyone is having sex with everyone else.

'Because, you know, we all got injected so no babies,' Kate told them one day over coffee while imparting a fresh round of delicious gossip. 'Ooh, anyway, so you know Jenny? Jenny? She's got the big boobs? You know Jenny . . . You do know her. She works in Gunjeep's department. Yes, her, so Roger, one of the technicians? He's got the little beard? Anyway, so he has this thing for her and keeps, like, appearing wherever she is, but she is totally smitten with Echo . . .'

'Oh, that one,' Echo said. 'I keep seeing her in the gym.'

'She is *so* into you,' Kate said. 'Like, oh my god, she hates that I'm friends with you all.'

'You're our informant, my dear, not our friend,' Bravo said.

'Oh, you sod,' she said, whacking him in the arm with a laugh.

Days turn into weeks and while Mother becomes increasingly hostile and overtly paranoid that the Roman Affa situation still hasn't gained a reaction, the mission starts taking shape, becoming defined with rules and established principles. Dates are chosen, disagreed on, scrapped and chosen again and Mother purveys all with an intrusive eye while Alpha grows closer to Kate, spending more time in her company.

'You like her?' Mother asked during a routine intelligence meeting with Mother during which they compared the intel received from Kate against that which Mother knows from her sources.

'Kate? She's okay,' Alpha said mildly. 'She could be a good cover. She's intelligent too underneath that excitability.'

'Good,' Mother said. 'Use her as you see fit.'

'. . . Oh my god, that's so good . . . say it . . . say it . . . please say it . . . come on, say it for me . . .'

'I'm Alpha,' Alpha said, gripping Kate's backside while thrusting at her bent over his bed in his private room the previous night.

'Oh my god, that's so hot,' she gasped, gripping the bedsheets in her hands. 'Say it again . . .'

'I'm not going to keep saying it . . .'

'SAY IT!'

'Fuck's sake . . . I'm Alpha . . .'

'So hot . . . Fuck me harder . . . Ooh, can you get me another one of those silk scarves for Jenny next time you go through . . . ? They're so pretty . . .'

'Come with me,' Alpha said, pausing mid-thrust as she looks over her shoulder at him.

'Can I?'

'Sure you can,' he said, holding her gaze. 'I'm Alpha . . .'

'Oh, you're good, you dirty, dirty man . . .'

Mother knew the answer before she asked Alpha if he liked Kate as she had watched them fucking on a glowing screen in the darkness of her office while all around her monitors showed feeds from cameras throughout the complex. She watched Delta in another room fucking one of the catering girls and Echo and Jenny lying in a post-coital embrace. She watched Bravo pushing one of the physics guys' head into a pillow while going at him from behind. She watched everyone fucking, living, eating and existing while only ever really thinking about Maggie Sanderson and that smug tone the bitch had when she claimed victory.

As time goes on, so a strange atmosphere grows within the complex. An excitement of shared endeavours mixed with a disharmony of mutterings and whispered comments, with quiet conversations snatched in the kitchens over steaming pots of food and in the gym when the treadmills and swimming pods are working. In the rooms at night in the hours of darkness with mouths pressed to ears. A thing that grows nearly unheard and undetected because those that talk are careful with whom they share.

Ben Ryder saved a woman and her child when he was seventeen, then later he saved hundreds of people in a terrorist attack. Ben Ryder stands for goodness and decency. Safa Patel was the last person alive to see Ben Ryder. She died saving the Prime Minister and killed scores of terrorists in Downing Street. And Harry Madden? Mad Harry Madden? The hero commando who served his country and took down a Nazi base single-handed.

Everyone in the complex also knows Emily Rose was an agent. It came out afterwards, when that image showing Emily giving the middle finger to the sky spread round the world. It was a symbolic gesture of modern times. An act of defiance against a government.

It was the act of a freedom fighter, not a fanatical terrorist, but those people came here and murdered them. Didn't they? They murdered the Prime Minister and members of parliament too. Didn't they? But the footage was wiped and Mother was the only person to have seen it, but they have a time machine, so why didn't the agents go back and stop it happening? Questions without answers, but questions whispered for fear of being asked out loud.

'I look so pretty,' Kate whispers, staring at her reflection in the full-length mirror. A black dress with white dots. Flared in the skirts and tight across her chest with one strap going up round her neck. A white belt cinched tight around her waist.

'It's too pretty,' Gerry grumbles. 'You'll draw attention.'

'It's fine,' Alpha says, earning a wry smile from Bravo in the process.

'If you say so,' Gerry mutters.

'Ready?' Alpha asks.

'God yes, this is so exciting and, like, totally beats Rodney going to Hadrian's Wall.'

'Remember what I said?' Alpha asks, walking her down the corridor towards the portal room.

'We're legends,' she says firmly.

'No,' Alpha says with a smile. 'We have a legend. The legend is our backstory.'

'Shit! Sorry. I'm so nervous,' she says, looping her arm through his. 'I am Mrs Alpha from England . . .'

'Kate . . .'

'I'm playing. I'm Mrs Kate Carter, married to Alfie Carter. We're on holiday.'

'Oh wow, now there is a rare beauty,' Gunjeep calls out as Kate walks into the portal room.

'Oh sod off,' she says with a self-deprecating laugh while glowing from the attention.

'Set and ready?' Alpha asks, pulling his sidearm from a holster attached to the back of his trousers and hidden under his black 1950s suit.

'Ready,' Gunjeep says, nodding at the shimmering green portal. 'Have fun, kids.'

◆ ◆ ◆

California. 1953. A husband and wife on vacation from England stroll hand in hand down a wide store-lined avenue to the target premises. A diner near the research campus on the right side. They take a table at the back. Smiling at the waiting staff and talking about their vacation while Kate makes eyes at Alpha.

'That was so hot,' she whispers when the waitress walks off. 'You're so good at this . . . Oh my god . . . have you seen that jukebox? Can we steal it? We're totally wearing these clothes tonight in your room . . . But seriously, steal that jukebox . . .'

Alpha listens intently as she chats away while also taking in the conversation of the scientists at the next table.

The food is incredible. Everything is incredible. The décor, the music in the background, the light bulbs, the tables, chairs, the menu, the font used on the menu, and Kate takes a last lingering look at the diner as they walk out with a polite thank you to the man holding the door open for her.

'You are most welcome, my dear,' Bravo says, winking while walking in as she and Alpha walk out.

'That was Bravo,' she whispers urgently tugging on Alpha's arm.

'Hi,' Echo says from the bench they walk past, looking up from his newspaper.

'Oh my god . . . Ooh look . . . there's Charlie . . . Shit, I almost waved.'

'So you didn't see Delta behind you in the diner then?' Alpha asks.

'No way! Was he really?' she asks, smiling at Alpha for a second, but the smile fades as a serious look creeps into her eyes. 'Can I ask a question?'

'Sure,' he says quietly, carefully.

'Do you believe in what you are doing?'

'Always,' he replies instantly. 'Why?'

'Just asking,' she says, smiling again. 'It's so pretty here. I love it . . .'

Sixteen

'Almost ready to go,' Ben calls out, passing Miri's office door.

She nods curtly, still simmering from the damned awful breakfast briefing and grimaces at the pervading stench of shit hanging in the air and steps back to the window, jabbing her thumb into the switch to make the shutter rise that clanks, whirrs and spits sparks from the box before slamming down to seal the room in darkness again.

'What was that?' Konrad asks, rushing in on hearing the noise with a sick-looking Malcolm behind him.

'Shutter,' Miri says. She fumbles for the switch to her desk lamp, clicking it on, then snatching her hand away from the spark coming out as a surge of power blows the bulb with a distinct crack.

'Water's got into the circuits,' Konrad says. 'We need to replace wiring, motors . . . put some vents and filters in. I said to Malc we should knock a door into the far end for circulation . . .'

'And?' Miri asks bluntly. 'Get it done today.'

'We've got nothing here. We need tools and . . .'

'Use Milwau . . .' She stops on remembering that staging area is now gone. 'Do what you can.'

'How?' Konrad asks.

'Use your imagination, Mr Johans,' Miri snaps. 'Improvise.'

'With what? Fresh air?' Konrad mutters, offering a weak smile at Miri before rushing after Malcolm.

'Jesus wept,' Miri mutters, striding into the portal room.

'Yours,' Safa says, handing her a pistol and holster. 'I guessed we're arming today.'

'You guessed correctly, Miss Patel.'

'So what's the plan?' Safa asks.

'We'll go up to Piccadilly,' Ben explains. 'See what's changed and make sure it's safe, then we'll bring Bertie through later and see if it matches what he saw. Then at some point we'll look at that Affa thing. Miri? Is that alright with you?'

'Affirmative.'

'If you eggheads are right,' Safa says, 'and someone is pissing about with a time machine, other than us pissing about with our time machine, that is . . . then we should put a guard on it. I'll go with Ben and Miri into Piccadilly. Harry and Emily stay near the Blue. If we get in trouble then Emily deploys to us and, Harry, your priority is protecting the device. Got it? Emily and Harry, you two might have shagged last night, but this is work now. It's time to switch on and get our heads in the game. Fair one?'

'Understood,' Emily says in a business-like fashion.

'Aye,' Harry says.

'Ben, you and Miri do what you need to do, but if I say we move then we move. I am team leader. Got it?'

'Good,' Miri says, pleasantly surprised at not having to say any of those things herself.

They deploy to the gloomy interior of the gardener's hut in Hyde Park, with Safa moving to the windows to spot the same people lying on the grass and sitting on the benches that she saw yesterday, but it was only an hour ago local time.

Harry and Emily slip out first, going down the bank and across the path to stand and look round as though deciding which way to go. Safa watches people walking past them without a flicker of a glance at the big man. Mind you, he's dressed normally this time and not in tight denim shorts.

'*Clear.*' Emily's voice comes through their discreet ear pieces with the signal given for Safa, Ben and Miri to move out.

The three do the same and slip out quietly while Ben considers the fact that history has changed but Hyde Park is still here and looking largely the same.

'*Safa to Emily and Harry. Comms check.*'

'*Emily to Safa. Receiving you loud and clear.*'

'The bandstand isn't there,' Ben says, motioning to the left. He's walked through Hyde Park many times but not enough to be overly familiar. There are still benches, verges and street lights. Then he remembers there should be a kiosk up ahead on the right. A wooden-framed thing with big lift-up shutters that were held in place by ornate poles. He scans ahead as they walk, straining to see it, then spotting the lights and queues of people on the other side of the path.

'That wasn't there,' Safa says, observing a completely different brick-built concessions outlet. 'It was on the other side and it didn't look like that,' she adds. 'Ben, you remember the statue that was over there?'

'Achilles,' Ben says, looking to where it should be and seeing a wide concrete plinth and an altogether different statue on the top. He looks for Apsley House, the former home of the Duke of Wellington. A house is there but it's bigger and grander than even the gorgeous Apsley House was. This one is sprawling and less Roman, but more Gothic in architecture. The colour is different too and the roof looks more castle-type with crenulations.

They pass the lee of the house and breach the exit road to stand where once Piccadilly met Knightsbridge and that jarring sensation comes swimming back as all three have the same feeling of seeing a place known to them that has changed.

The huge arch that once dominated the junction and bore the glory of the Duke of Wellington for his victories is not there. The road layout is different. The access point for Knightsbridge underground Tube station isn't there. The buildings are just as high, just as wide and just as imposing but they're not the buildings Ben or the others have seen from this point before.

Ben's mouth drops open as he finally takes in the traffic in front of him. His eyes saw it when he first looked, but his brain processed the images into a thing he expected to see instead of the reality. What he takes in now are cars similar to before with different colours, shapes and sizes. Two-seaters with sporty lines. Larger family-sized vehicles and up to bigger things carrying goods. Not one of them is touching the road but gliding a few inches above it. The noise isn't that of combustion engines either, but electric whines and motors that all mingle to give the impression of city noises.

'Piccadilly is that way,' Ben says, pointing down the main road. 'Or at least it was . . .'

'*Safa to Emily and Harry. We're out of the park, moving to Piccadilly.*'

'Received,' Emily says, dropping her head as though to inspect her shoes while speaking into the microphone under her top. She looks back up and round with years of training and experience to study the motion of people. The same with Harry, and they both reflect a relaxed, easy manner while watching everything and everyone. She looks down towards the café, half wishing they could get a cup of coffee and idly wondering if money is still used here. Harry looks the other way while half wishing he could smoke, but seeing no one else is smoking and guessing that it's either outlawed or hasn't been invented here. They both turn to look the other direction and meet eyes with polite smiles and facial expressions that only seem to make the silence between them heavier and more awkward.

'It's, er . . .' she says.

'Looks nice,' he says at the same time.

They both pause, waiting for the other to speak.

'You go,' she says.

'Ladies first,' he says.

'Why? Because you say so?' she asks in a biting tone she immediately regrets. She can't help it. He's so big and capable, but every nasty comment she makes prompts a fleeting look of hurt innocence in his eyes. She thinks to apologise, then remembers being rejected in his room, then remembers what Safa said about this being work and leads him to the tree they rested against yesterday, motioning for him to sit down before lowering to rest her head on his thighs like she did the last time they came here. He stiffens in surprise, blanching slightly at the contact.

'For our cover,' she says quietly, looking out at the world.

'Aye,' he says simply.

She lifts her hand and holds it over her head, wiggling her fingers until Harry takes it, then sighs and settles into the job at hand.

◆ ◆ ◆

'Feeling better?' Konrad asks in the main room of the bunker.

'Yeah, a bit,' Malcolm says, looking into the cup he just downed. 'What's in it?'

'No idea, Malc. The doc made it. Painkillers, glucose . . . some other stuff probably. What we going to do?' he asks, looking round while shaking his head. 'We need all sorts of stuff. We don't even have pliers here, Malc.'

'I know,' Malcolm says.

'She said she wants it all fixed. She said stay here and fix it. She said that. I said what with? I said we don't have anything. She said improvise.'

'I know,' Malcolm says.

'And they haven't sorted that dead bloke out yet. Bloody mess, Malc.'

'It is, Kon,' Malcolm says.

'Listen, we both know Berlin. We pop there and get a few bits, yeah? We can have it looking spick and span in no time . . .'

'Berlin? Are you joking? No. Just no, Kon.'

'Milwaukee then. We can go a couple of hours before they take the van away. Miri said she leaves gaps like that so it can be used. We'll pop in, get some gear, pop back and get on with it. She said to improvise, which basically means do what you think is right.'

'I'm not sure, Kon.'

'Ah, you're hung over, Malc. You leave it to me. Come on . . .'

◆ ◆ ◆

With evening slowly giving way to night, Miri, Ben and Safa walk a route that should have been straightforward and easy. The point they exited Hyde Park was known as Hyde Park Corner where the ultra-expensive quarters of Knightsbridge and Belgravia met the road to the famous circus junction.

That road also bordered Green Park, a much smaller expanse of rurality within the urban sprawl of London. The problem is that Green Park isn't there.

'It's not there,' Ben says again. 'Green Park surrounds Buckingham Palace . . . How can it not be there? And I'm sure that used to be the Japanese embassy . . .' He carries on pointing out things that were in a city that once was but is no more. Everything is different. The buildings, the side roads, the junctions, the road markings, the cars and vehicles on those roads. It's recognisably a city and the feel is that of London, but any familiarity ends there.

'Seen that?' Safa asks, pointing ahead.

'Jesus,' Ben whispers. There should be brick-and-stone buildings that reflect the centuries of change in London but what they see are modern, futuristic towers of dark glass and sleek design. Skyscrapers only became a feature in relatively modern life from the twentieth century onwards, and Ben's London had enough of them, but they were largely restricted to the financial sections. Here they are everywhere. A dizzying resemblance to a modern Dubai. A luxurious cityscape, which none of them recognise.

Hovering cars and vehicles whizz and move about the roads. Lights everywhere, but different to the lights they are used to. Not sodium or harsh or cheap-looking even, but these are smooth and natural.

As the journey on the road to Piccadilly progresses, so those changes become more absolute. Almost as though the fringes of this section were blended to meet the old styles of architecture whereas it now morphs into something from a science fiction movie, except this is real life and full of the grit of living without the gloss of a movie set.

Then it ends. It simply ends, and Miri, Ben and Safa come to a halt to stare in awe at the vast open expanse that was once Piccadilly.

People everywhere. Thousands of people walking, sitting, standing, resting. Some move with purpose in the manner of commuters. Others stroll and chat.

'Look at that,' Ben says at seeing a hovering narrow train moving through the crowd from right to left. A cross between a monorail and a theme park feature with dozens of carriages all covered with bright designs and vibrant colours. Men, women and children on board, some waving as they pass while others adopt that far-away look as they access whatever operating system only they can see.

Those ultra-modern buildings border the open area. Sentinels that stand proud and forever watchful. Screens on some that are big enough to be seen from any angle and crowds of people sitting in defined areas, laughing and cheering at the silent footage.

The whole thing, the whole of it, the sheer size makes the three grin and look at each other in wonder. Even Miri, who has mastered the overt show of facial expressions, now allows stunned surprise to reflect on her features.

Gardens here and there. Raised sections of greenery with lawns, ferns and willowing trees. Other statues, works of art and public interaction pieces dot the landscape, but of the old Piccadilly Circus there is no sign.

No grand old buildings. No graffiti-covered walls. No dirty roads contrasting against shiny sleek glass-fronted stores. No hawkers selling guides or pickpockets making the most of the bustling crowds.

'The size of it,' Ben says, looking ahead to the distant line of skyscrapers bordering the far end. He tries to calculate the distances involved and guesses the plaza area extends past where Leicester Square was, maybe all the way up to Covent Garden and across to where Tottenham Court Road was on the northern edge. A vast area that once contained millions of people crammed into the myriad of old buildings of London.

Not now though. Now only this massive place devoid of habitable structures. But how? From the thing called Affa? From something near Hadrian's Wall over two thousand years ago? Hyde Park was relatively the same, so how can this be so different?

'See that?' Miri asks, nodding ahead to a tall black obelisk statue. 'Must be the middle.'

It takes minutes of solid walking to reach it, and as they get closer they see the sheer size of it. A towering thing that looks ugly and unpleasant with nasty bulges and spokes jutting out at irregular angles.

An old-fashioned plaque is fitted to a stand on one side and it takes time for the crowds to move on so that Ben, Miri and Safa can edge close enough to read the words and as they do so a deep crawling horror flips their stomachs with a sickening realisation that this game just ramped exponentially.

◆ ◆ ◆

'Malc, grow some balls. The doc's here with Ria. Bertie's safe. We nip into Milwaukee, get to the depot, buy what we need and get on with it. Got the money? Good. On we go then.'

Konrad goes first, stepping through the portal to wait for Malcolm who comes through to blanch in fright.

'This isn't the van we used before, Kon . . . This is a motorhome . . .'

'It's fine. We're in the same place.'

'Kon, it's changed . . . We can't be here.'

'It's fine, Malc. Look outside . . . We're in a motorhome sales depot. Nobody is going to come inside this one . . . We're right at the back for a start.'

'Oh bloody hell, Kon. We shouldn't be doing this.'

'Come on, look . . . the door opens from the inside.'

'Kon, the mall isn't there . . . It's all different.'

'We'll find something; stop being a wimp. Roland always said you were a wimp.'

'Now, now, Kon, that's not nice, that isn't. I'm hung over and being the voice of reason.'

'The voice of a big girl more like. Look, you stay here then. I'll go and find what we need.'

'You aren't going alone!'

'I am,' Konrad says, jumping out the side door.

'Oh bloody hell,' Malcolm mumbles, following him out. 'Miri will go nuts.'

'She will applaud our ingenuity, Malc.'

'Yeah, with a hammer and nails on our bollocks.'

◆ ◆ ◆

'Just go and have one,' Emily says. She looks round again, staring at faces and people as the sensation of being watched comes back again. She shrugs it off, putting it down to an emotional reaction from last night and getting so drunk. Harry shifts his leg under her head, making her look up. 'Go on,' she sighs. 'It's fine.'

'Ach no.'

'It's fine. There's nothing happening and you'll only be over there.'

'I can wait,' Harry says, looking round at the people passing by.

'Go and have a cigarette. Blow the smoke through the portal though in case they've got a sensor in there. I'll go for a wee when you get back.'

'Sure?' he asks.

'Go on,' she says, pulling her hand free from his as she sits up. 'I'll be fine.'

◆ ◆ ◆

The greatest sense of detachment comes now in a wide-open plaza filled with thousands of people in a city of millions who have no idea they are pawns in a game.

Safa slides her hand to the back of her waistband to grip the pistol in readiness for anything that might happen. Her other hand gently holds the switch on her microphone, ready to transmit to Emily and Harry while moving closer to Ben as though expecting to be attacked now, as though this very thing is a trick to lure them to this point.

'Don't speak a word,' Miri says, tugging an old smartphone from her pocket to take a picture of the plaque while her mind processes what she is reading. She nods curtly for the other two to move away with her, then smiles a warm grin at the people waiting to read the plaque. 'Say, sorry for taking your time,' she tells them in a nasal American drawl.

'Oh, that's fine, me love,' a woman grins.

The night is here proper. An inky sky above them with flashing lights of airborne craft in every direction. The giant screens on the skyscrapers and the lights within the plaza all work to magnify that futuristic feel as they walk away from the obelisk and hear snatches of music coming from different directions.

Ben and Miri think hard and fast of all the things this could mean. Safa watches the crowd, checking the hands and eyes of anyone coming near them.

Halfway back to the exit they came in from and they see it at the same time. The red-and-blue strobing lights of a thing the size of a car wheel flying slowly over the plaza at a height of four metres with a shining red light glowing underneath that makes Ben think of the barcode scanners in supermarkets. The light turns as the drone flies, scanning the crowds below as the three walk faster, veering off to get out of the drone's flight path.

'Move faster,' Miri urges. They speed up, all of them feeling the urge to break into a jog as that red light moves over them and away, then spins back to stay fixed and glowing on Safa as the drone alters course and starts flying towards them.

'*FIREARM ALERT. FIREARM ALERT. UNKNOWN ADULT FEMALE. FIREARM ALERT . . .*'

'Fuck,' Safa snaps as everyone around them spins in alarm to see her torso peppered with red-dot lights.

'*FIREARM ALERT . . . DISARM NOW . . . DISARM NOW . . .*'

The voice booms louder and louder, growing in volume to fill the area as the people near them cry out as a second drone zooms into view, the red-and-blue lights strobing as it aims at the three now standing in an open patch of ground.

'*UNKNOWN ADULT MALE . . . UNKNOWN ADULT FEMALE . . . UNKNOWN ADULT FEMALE . . . FIREARMS ALERT . . . DISARM NOW . . . DISARM NOW . . .*'

The automated voices fall in sync with each other. Booming the orders to disarm as the second drone arrives to hover a few feet from the first with yet more coming through the air towards them.

'Shit,' Ben grunts as his torso lights up with multiple red-dot laser points holding steady on him. Safa spots the threat to Ben and draws instantly, bringing her pistol up to aim, and fires once with the pistol giving a sharp crack in the open space.

'*DISARM NOW . . . DISaaaarrrrsssszzzz . . .*' The drone slews to the side with the voice warping as it spins and skids across the ground.

'*SHOTS FIRED . . . MOVE AWAY NOW . . . MOVE AWAY NOW . . . DISARM NOW . . .*'

'Run,' Safa orders, aiming to fire at the next closest drone. She misses with the first shot as it takes evasive action and rocks quickly left to right. The second shot hits, making it flip upside down as it drops with a heavy thud to the hard surface of the plaza.

'*TERRORISTS. TERRORISTS. YOU WILL BE FIRED UPON. DISARM NOW . . .*'

The voices come from all directions, all in sync as the drones fly at speed towards the three now running as fast as they can.

◆ ◆ ◆

'See, what did I say?' Konrad says. 'Yeah, they've all got different names for things here, but we managed okay.'

'Yeah, maybe,' Malcolm grumbles.

'Stop sulking. Miri will be pleased as punch she will.'

Malcolm hefts one of his big black holdalls purchased in the hardware store to carry all the tools, wiring and supplies they needed. 'Bit funny about the money though,' he says at length. 'They didn't want the twenties . . . Fifties were okay though. Who's on the twenties?'

'Andrew Jackson,' Konrad says. 'Maybe they didn't have an Andrew Jackson here. We're lucky they didn't call the police.'

'It's not the bloody police I'm afraid of . . . Miri will kill us to death if we get arrested . . .'

'Ah, but we're fine,' Konrad says happily. 'And there's our motorhome all waiting for us, eh? We'll have a cuppa and you can cheer up a bit, you hung-over sulky twat.'

◆ ◆ ◆

She bellows as another one lunges in to bite her legs that already stream with blood. Her skin is thick and hard and the blood loss can be survived, but they'll keep coming and keep biting. They won't stop now. They can taste her and they are hungry.

◆ ◆ ◆

Doctor John Watson holds Ria's wrist and counts the beats before sighing deeply and gently lowering her arm. He can't keep her under sedation any longer. Not safely anyway. Her body needs motion, her limbs need to move and her mind needs to start functioning in order to heal. Not that anyone can ever truly heal from such a thing.

◆ ◆ ◆

Four feet support her weight. Each the size of a washing machine and from the tip of her nose to the end of her tail she measures over one hundred and twenty feet. Her weight is many, many tonnes and she only moved away from the other sauropods of her herd to follow the strange scents that carried up nasal passages big enough for a man to crawl through. Food, cigarette smoke, faeces, sweat and the dozens of odours brought with the arrival of humans into an environment that is not theirs to occupy.

◆ ◆ ◆

Doctor Watson smiles sadly at her sleeping form. Time for a cup of tea and maybe a nice sit down outside now that it's stopped raining. The lads will be back soon, then he can go and have a paddle and snooze in his hammock on the island.

◆ ◆ ◆

They are far smaller than her and they run on two powerful hind legs aided by a thick tail that gives balance. Feathered, leathered, over three metres high with mouths full of rows of teeth and over twenty of them hunt the big sauropod through the thick forest, which fills with the sounds of logs snapping, branches breaking and creatures screeching out in fear and alarm.

◆ ◆ ◆

He walks from Ria's room and pauses at the scuffling he heard coming from the armoury. He goes down, peering in to see it's all empty and tuts softly at his imagination before setting off, lost in his thoughts while humming to himself. He sets water to heat and carries on humming while preparing a cup and glancing to the window to see the overcast sky outside.

◆ ◆ ◆

She is tiring. She cannot run much longer and even her tiny brain knows the end will surely come. She still goes on, because the instinct of any creature is to survive, so she shifts her colossal bulk with her tail swishing left to right and snapping small trees as she goes. She has no idea she killed one of the predators by swishing her tail and slamming it into the base of a huge tree. If she knew that she might try to kill a few more and increase her chances, but alas she thinks only to keep moving and each thud of her feet drums the ground and each cry from her huge mouth fills the air with a pain-filled screech of terror.

◆ ◆ ◆

The gas burns in the hob, heating the water with a motion that sends a gentle vibration through the table and the doctor drums his hands lightly on the wooden top while waiting for it to boil. He taps a foot too and thinks to listen to some jazz while drinking his tea. Those things serve to cover the sounds and vibrations outside. He looks again at the window and misses the rippling tremor in the water on the stove. He drums a bit louder, hums a bit more and still does not hear it.

She screeches again, but each bite only seems to inject a fresh burst of power into her exhausted body. Her enormous heart booms so fast now and her lungs suck air in like the turbines on a jet aircraft. Her eyes are huge and filled with fear and her great head swishes side to side on top of the long neck. She pays no heed to the trees in front of her, but uses brute force to batter through and out into the clearing of the plateau once used as a training ground for the assault on Cavendish Manor.

'Dumdumdum de de de . . .' he sings softly, then spies the open packet of cakes on the table and considers, in the great scheme of things, whether he should eat one or not. He does eat one on the basis of the self-justification brought from the victory of not drinking alcohol and taking more exercise. 'Hmmm,' he says pleasantly, mouthing the whole thing to chew noisily while pouring the boiling water into the mug. A noise outside. A bang maybe? He pauses to listen, ceasing his chewing for a second, then shrugging and carrying on to make his tea and eat his cake.

She crosses the plateau in seconds with her huge feet crushing the speakers left there by Ria when she added sound effects. The predators burst from the tree line too. Ranged out in a horseshoe shape behind her and taking turns to run up to bite and scratch with the claws on their small but powerful forearms. She doesn't know the valley is below. She doesn't know anything other than to keep going. They don't know about the valley either. They've tracked and chased the big female diplodocus for many miles and this ground is not their ground. They too detect the odours in the air, but the frenzy of the chase is all they care about.

Doctor Watson sits down heavily at the big table in the main room, then groans at remembering he was going to go outside. He contemplates staying where he is out of pure laziness, then grimaces at that nasty smell still hanging in the air and slowly rises to head towards the door.

The gait of her motion swings her tail left to right and the flexibility of that long appendage is such that it curls inwards on the apex of each swing. Again she doesn't know or feel when the last few feet of her curling tail strike one of the attackers with enough force to send it screeching and flying past her body and head and over the edge of the plateau to plummet down onto the roof of the bunker.

The doctor walks down the corridor towards the back door left open to generate air flow and sniffs the air at smelling Harry's cigarette smoke. He even looks round as though expecting to see the big man, then hears the screech and comes to a sudden stop with his mouth dropping open as something slams into the roof above his head. He ducks and veers to the side, his tea spilling from the mug as he hears the creature scrabbling to get upright with claws that slash at the smooth concrete and smash through the array of solar panels fitted on the top.

◆ ◆ ◆

She goes over the edge. She only knows she goes over the edge when her feet lose purchase and start to slide down. She bellows again at the fright of it and the sensation of falling and her whole body drops tumbling down as the predator she flicked over finally stands upright to see the sauropod coming at him. She lands hard, killing him instantly and driving down through the roof of the bunker that collapses inwards from the tonnes of meat impacting on it.

Ben's room is destroyed instantly. Harry's too. The rooms at that end are obliterated, with chunks of concrete flying over the edge of the hill to roll down the valley side to the great distance below. She tries to get upright from landing on her side and her huge neck, legs and tail slam about as she bellows with a sound that fills the world of Doctor John Watson. He dives to the floor as the ground heaves and the walls buckle and the ceiling above him crumbles inwards with rays of daylight punching through.

The attackers follow, scrabbling and falling down the bank to jump into and onto the bunker to finish off their prey. As they land so the roof buckles and crashes in with those leathered and feathered creatures landing amongst the debris.

Doctor Watson screams out in absolute horror and starts crawling with an instinct to get to Ria. A huge foot the colour and texture of an elephant's, but the size of a washing machine and dripping thick red blood slams down next to his head. He screams out again, wilting back and feeling the hot spray coat his face.

The diplodocus flails about with wild frantic panic. Screeches and cries rip the air apart. The main room and the furniture Ria took so long to gather are destroyed.

The doctor gibbers in fright, but crawls down the broken corridor and into the doorway of Ria's rooms as the roof above him comes crashing in. Chunks of concrete hit his arms and hands, breaking several fingers on his left hand. His head is hit and he drops with waves of nausea pulsing up through his body and seeing stars behind his eyes. The attacking creatures continue on, devoid of care as to where they are and only seeing their prey trapped and struggling to break free.

One of the attacking dinosaurs falls through the ceiling onto the doctor's legs, snapping a bone with ease and scoring his flesh open with filthy talons as it fights to get up. He cries out, writhing in agony before summoning reserves from his inner soul that make him roar and crawl to Ria's bed. The walls crash in around him. His whole world heaving and bucking as he grabs Ria and pulls hard, ripping her from the bed and pulling, tugging and pushing to get her underneath the solid metal frame. He crawls in after her, his mind closing, but the doctor holds his oath dear and protects the patient with the only thing he has, his own broken body.

◆ ◆ ◆

Harry smokes in the hut. His right arm extended to hold the cigarette in the portal room in the bunker while his body remains in 2111. He ducks to see through the hut's window to Emily sitting with her back to the tree, then pulls his arm back and takes a drag before once again extending his arm to hold the smoke in the Cretaceous period where a falling chunk of masonry narrowly misses his hand.

Harry looks at Emily again, thinking of last night and realising, despite the angst of his loss of honour, that he actually feels better for the night out and such is his focus on staring out the window that he doesn't see the debris and dust pushing through the portal behind him and doesn't detect the change in air flow over his hand hovering in the portal room holding the lit cigarette. He doesn't know one of the feathered heads drops towards him then veers off at the last second from the foul stench of the cigarette smoke curling up its nose.

He only becomes aware when a foot the size of a washing machine slams into his back, sending him flying across the hut to crash through the doors and down the bank.

'Harry!' Emily calls out, on her feet and running flat out while drawing her pistol.

Harry rolls as he lands and comes up on one knee with his pistol out and aimed at the huge foot battering the portal that stretches wider and higher as the rest of the body on the other side knocks the poles aside in the portal room. More of the creature comes through, slamming into the walls of the hut, smashing them apart and making the people in the park cry out and stop to watch.

'Oh shit,' Emily says, getting to Harry's side.

'UNKNOWN ADULT FEMALE. THE USE OF REVOLTING, ABUSIVE OR INSULTING WORDS IS PROHIBITED IN THIS PUBLIC PLACE.'

One of the attacking dinosaurs falls through the portal to land heavily in the hut, screeching and getting back up and spotting the big foot waggling about. It takes a lunge and bites deep. The big female cries out with a sound unheard by Harry and Emily and draws the foot back, dragging the other creature with it. The portal stretches wider, making shapes that distort and change as the poles get kicked and pushed about. The foot comes back down with the creature still attached by the mouth. Then the big female's tail slashes through, smashing the walls of the hut down and sending chunks of machinery flying off through the park.

◆ ◆ ◆

Malcolm and Konrad run. They run at the sight of the motorhome being obliterated from the inside, glimpsing huge legs and creatures with tails. They hear the screeching and the metallic sides banging and the chassis creaking, then stop dead at the sight of a huge evil-looking feathered head dripping blood from rows of oversized teeth. An eye like a lizard, yellow and black, staring through the windscreen.

'MALC,' Konrad yells, ditching his bags to stop his friend charging in.

'Ria's in there . . . RIA'S IN THERE . . .'

'Hang on, you bloody idiot,' Konrad says, heaving him back. The windscreen blows out, the sides buckle and split with a noise so loud it will surely draw people here. As the sides break apart they see the Red distorting, seemingly bending and stretching with things coming through then going back and everything happening so fast the two men can only watch with hearts racing.

'WHAT THE HELL?' a deep American voice bellows from behind them. A red-faced overweight man waddling between the rows of parked motorhomes towards the devastation being wrought.

'RIA? RIA?' Malcolm lunges forward again with Konrad fighting to hold him back and seeing an elephant's foot the size of a washing machine suddenly yank back and away through the Red. The feathered creature goes after it as the Red ceases to be, severing the predator neatly in half with the arse, legs and tail falling in chunks on the ruined motorhome floor.

'RIA?' Malcolm roars.

'We gotta go,' Konrad says, snatching a glimpse of people running towards them. 'Malc . . . we gotta go . . .'

◆ ◆ ◆

'*COMING IN HOT . . . BE READY TO GO . . .*' Safa shouts into the radio, running behind Ben down the path in Hyde Park towards the hut. 'POLICE . . . MOVE AWAY . . . POLICE MOVE AWAY.' She reverts to her training, shouting at people to move as yet more blue-and-red flashing lights come gliding towards them through the air.

More shots in the air and she spots the drones ahead over Harry and Emily and the hut smashed to bits.

'ARMED FEMALE. ARMED MALE. UNKNOWN SUBJECTS. DISARM NOW. DISARM NOW . . .'

A drone over Harry's head lights him up with red dots until Emily aims and fires with a double tap that makes it spin away and the crowd gathered to watch scream out and run while the gardener's hut obliterates from the frantic motions of the dinosaurs popping in and out of existence.

The Blue goes off. The poles crushed under the weight of the big female thrashing to stay alive. More drones come flying in. Sirens in the distance too with bigger vehicles aiming for the five staring in shock at the ruined hut.

A deeper siren fills the air, making them look up as larger manned craft come flying towards them with panels on their undersides sliding away as barrelled weapons drop down into view.

Emily looks down at her body, seeing the red lasers on her and Harry and the others. 'Targeting system,' she mutters. 'TARGETING SYSTEM . . .' She screams the warning as a deep boom comes from behind them. The unmistakable sound of a Barrett fifty-calibre rifle firing that sends a round into the manned craft, making it slew off into the park as it loses height, crashing down into trees and bushes with a deafening crash.

The five spin round to see the Blue portal shining in the night air a few metres away from the ruins of the hut. A lone figure standing silhouetted with a rifle braced in her shoulder that sends a recoil through her body as she fires at the drones.

'MOVE NOW . . . GET THROUGH.' A female voice, harsh and angry.

They run fast with Miri taken off her feet from being launched by Harry through the portal as the others crash into the silence of another world. Ben, Safa and Miri heaving for air from the run while Emily and Harry gather their wits and stare at the woman holding the Barrett, who comes in last to deactivate the portal.

'What the fuck?' Ben gasps, bent over with his hands on his knees.

'Wait here.' The woman who saved them thumbs the tablet, reactivating the light, then steps out of sight. A second or two of silence before Malcolm comes staggering through followed by Konrad, both gibbering and talking too fast and too rushed as the woman steps through after them and shuts the portal off once again. 'You're safe,' she says bluntly.

A tanned woman with dark hair held back by a strip of material tied round her head. Her frame lean and hard with defined muscles showing in her shoulders and white livid scars criss-crossing her tanned face and arms. Black combat boots scuffed and worn. Black combat trousers and a tight black vest patched with material sewn in and a German SS dagger tucked into a scabbard on her belt. A pistol on her hip and the look of a battle-hardened warrior. She lowers the Barrett, handling the heavy weight with ease as the others stare on in stunned silence.

'Jesus,' Malcolm whispers. 'Wh . . . what happened?'

The woman lifts her chin to show a complete lack of fear as she stares back without a flicker of a reaction. 'Happened?' Ria asks. 'Two years happened . . .'

Seventeen

The Complex

'Let me read it to you,' she says petulantly, adding a little foot stamp that makes her breasts jiggle enticingly. 'Stop gawping at my boobs.'

'Stamp your foot again,' Alpha says, smiling at her while lying back on his bed.

'Alpha!' she snaps, bursting out laughing halfway before suddenly deciding a new tactic is needed and drops to land with her hands on the edge of the bed, fluttering her eyelids seductively.

'Got something in your eye?' he asks.

'Idiot,' she snorts. 'I'm being seductive.' She straddles his thighs as his hands come up to gently stroke her legs. 'Please let me read it. It's for Mother . . . You know she scares the shit out of me.'

'Go for it,' Alpha says.

'Great!' She reaches back for the tablet she dropped on the bed, bringing it round while clearing her throat. 'Eyes up, buster . . .'

'Yep,' he says, looking up with a grin.

She clears her throat again, checks he is watching, swats his chest when he isn't and starts reading the report from the screen. '*My conclusion is that although I sanctioned the Affa mission in the first place, in hindsight it was a stupid thing to do. It had no real purpose and only served to confuse everything. I think we were all somewhat bedazzled by the prospect of having a time machine. We can, however, draw some positives from the exercise and I would suggest we treat it as such, an exercise, and . . .'*

Alpha watches her speaking, the way her mouth forms the words. He likes the tone of her voice and the intelligence that shines through her playful exterior. This is the longest time Alpha has spent with a member of the opposite sex since joining the British Secret Service. It's not even a secret within the complex that he is seeing Kate. Everyone knows it. She sleeps in his bed every night. Her company is so easy and relaxed and the wonder she shows at everything is captivating.

'Well?' she asks him, biting her bottom lip when she finishes.

'You've got a doctorate in history.'

'Yeah, I know, but this is Mother. She'll hang me upside down and whip me if it's bad . . .'

'Take out the bit where you said it was a stupid thing to do. It was Mother's idea to run that mission so don't call her stupid and re-word or remove the section where you say, "*I think we were all somewhat bedazzled by the prospect of having a time machine.*" Take that out. It's subjective and not necessary. Mother likes short reports as brief as possible. She processes a ton of data every day so yours will be one of many . . . but it's your report. Ignore me if you want . . . Now get up and dance for me, woman.'

'You sod,' she laughs, ditching the tablet to drop down and snuggle into him. 'How can you be so calm?'

He shrugs but doesn't answer.

'Can I ask a question?' she whispers into his ear.

'Sure.'

'Mother said we're not allowed to ask questions.'

'It's fine,' he replies quietly.

'Does this mission bother you?' she whispers, breathing hot air past his ear, which makes his skin prickle, but the sensation is pleasant and he turns his head to kiss her cheek.

'No.'

'None of it?' she asks.

'It's a mission.'

She goes quiet for a moment, her hand moving up to trace circles on his chest. 'It's weird being in here, like it's not real out there now. Like this is the only real life and everything else is . . . is unreal. You mind me asking more questions?'

'Are you a spy?' he asks.

'No, but I want to know the man I'm in love with.'

He turns to look at her, holding eye contact at the first subtle declaration of an emotional connection. She stares back with something close to defiance in her eyes that hides the fear of what she just said. 'Ask me anything,' he says softly, kissing her cheek again.

'You're going to kill so many people,' she whispers. 'British people . . . How do you cope with that?'

He doesn't reply at first, but reflects on the question as she studies his features. 'We're trained,' he says simply. 'We're experienced, we're capable and we're all psychologically tested to make sure we can cope, and we all have ways of dealing with stress. Bravo plays chess and finds an audience to make jokes with. Echo blows things up. Delta sleeps with as many women as he can find. Charlie works out and . . .'

'And?' she presses when he trails off.

'And I have you,' he whispers. 'Now sleep, busy day tomorrow . . .'

A touching moment. Trite and clichéd. Mother tuts in her office and reaches over to end the link to the listening device in Alpha's room. Listening to them fuck is one thing, but declarations of love make her want to puke. She switches the various tablets, screens and devices off and walks briskly from her office through to her private room because, as Alpha said, they have a busy day tomorrow.

Tomorrow comes as any other within the complex with a thick, palpable tension hanging in the air as the workers go through last-minute notes and plans.

Tension in the armoury too where Alpha meets the other four agents to get dressed and prepared in silence. Their minds now on the mission at hand.

They leave the armoury together, walking down the corridor towards the portal room. Five agents dressed in full black combat rig with their balaclavas rolled up. That image sears into the minds of the people they pass, who go quiet with sudden nerves at the reality of the mission. Pistols in holsters, grenades and magazines in pouches. Sub-machine guns fitted with suppressors slung to the rear. Menacing, capable and a stark reminder of who these men are.

'Ah,' Gunjeep states, taking them in as they enter the portal room. 'The men in black are here.' His joke falls flat in the nervous air.

'Any issues overnight?' Alpha asks.

'Negative,' Mother replies, standing with her arms folded watching the green shimmering light.

Alpha looks at his four colleagues, taking in the steady gazes and expressions of readiness. He doesn't need to ask if they are good to go. He nods once. They nod back. Enough said.

'Ready?' Gunjeep asks as the five walk to the portal. 'We'll be standing by to receive,' he adds with a look at the team of white-lab-coat-wearing workers at the side of the room. 'Activating . . .' The five reach up to roll their balaclavas down and bring the sub-machines ready in front. 'Go,' Gunjeep says.

Alpha leads from the brightly lit complex into another brightly lit complex. From a room full of white-lab-coat-wearing people into another room full of white-lab-coat-wearing people, but these cry out at the shock of the green light and the five men striding through it.

The five don't hesitate but open fire the second they come through. Delta and Echo turn to shoot down the armed guards on the large metal sliding door. Charlie and Bravo take out the scientists and workers clustered in the middle while Alpha aims for those running for the other door.

Screams and yells of pain and terror mix with the soft sounds of the modern suppressors and within seconds over twenty people lie dead and bleeding.

'Echo, on you,' Alpha says.

'On it.' Echo strides to the big bulging object in the middle of the room while the others range out and hold position, aiming at the sliding door, which grinds with gears as it starts opening. The four fire at the soldiers the second the door opens while Echo focuses on checking the mechanics and electrics. 'Yep, it's set,' he reports. 'Delta, get them through . . .'

'Roger,' Delta says. He walks to the portal, leans through and points at the team of workers waiting in the room. They burst forward, all of them clearly nervous with worried expressions, but they do as drilled and go through to flinch and blanch at the bodies in the room and the dead soldiers slumped in the open doorway. 'Get it through,' Delta orders calmly. The men and women rush to heave the huge object on the wheeled platform towards the portal, which widens in size. The agents fall back as they go through, stepping one by one into the complex.

'Shut it down,' Alpha orders.

'De-activating,' Gunjeep announces, shutting the portal off.

Everyone stares at it. The size, the shape, the weirdness of it. The technology it's made from is so old and dangerous that the prospect of it being in the complex is terrifying.

The agents change clothing. Removing the black combat gear and getting into new uniforms and boots. Within minutes they step out and only have to wait a short time for a bearded technician to step back with a thumbs up. 'Ready,' he declares.

'Activating,' Gunjeep says. The green light comes back on. Alpha goes forward, checking the destination is clear before leaning back out.

'Clear.' He moves out of the way, going further into the truck as the workers wheel in the sliding trolley, making the truck sink on its springs. The workers fasten it in place with straps while the agents come through and make ready with Alpha and Bravo taking position in the cab of the truck and the other three staying in the back.

The workers go back, the green light goes off and Charlie bangs on the bulkhead. Alpha starts the engine and drives the heavy diesel truck out of the disused barn and down a wide lane threading between bare winter trees and snow-covered banks.

'It's bloody cold,' Bravo says, rubbing his hands together.

'Very cold,' Alpha replies, manhandling the steering wheel to keep the truck on course.

'Having fun?' Bravo asks, glancing across.

'Like driving a bloody tank,' Alpha says.

'We've driven tanks – this is worse than a tank,' Bravo observes.

'Just watch out for potholes,' Alpha says.

'How's Kate?' Bravo asks after another few minutes of silence broken by the dull roar of the engine.

'Good,' Alpha says, glancing across. Before this mission, he and Bravo would never have shared a question about their private lives or their personal business. 'She read a report to me last night that Mother asked her to prepare.'

'She read it to the rest of us this morning over breakfast while you were with Mother,' Bravo says. 'She said to tell you she took out the *stupid* comment.'

In the back of the truck, Charlie and Delta share glances at being so close to the object in the back of a bouncing truck.

'Don't look so worried,' Echo tells them. 'If it goes pop we won't know a thing.'

'That's reassuring,' Charlie replies.

Alpha eases the speed down as they near the barrier and watches the sentries stride out with their machine guns held ready. The soldiers

look drained and gaunt, but then almost six years of war will do that
to anyone.

'You have it?' the German officer asks, stopping at the side of the
truck to look up at Alpha.

'Oh yes,' Alpha replies in German. 'Open the barrier.'

'OPEN,' the officer calls out.

The truck goes through, snaking between buildings and vehicles
to the edge of the runway and the single heavy bomber waiting there.
The Affa effect shows in everything from the names of the guns to the
aircraft. The Nazi heavy bombers in their timeline were Heinkels, but
are now something else. Nearly everything is jarred and off-centre. Not
that it matters. Not after today. They pull up and wait for the German
workers to operate winches and machinery to lift the contents from the
truck and into the aircraft.

'You did it,' Herr Weber says, calling out as he rushes over from
the closest building. 'You actually did it . . . You have it . . . That's it?'

'There it is,' Bravo says.

'The Führer doesn't know,' Herr Weber blurts, looking at the five
men. 'He won't talk to anyone . . .'

'Well, maybe this will bring him out,' Alpha says. 'The plane is
adapted and ready?'

'It is! Yes, it is. Exactly as you said. It's ready and, look, it fits like a
glove. My god, this is a thing. I said we should have done it, but they
didn't listen. Wait and see. Just wait and see. We can win this yet.'

'Sure you can,' Bravo says.

Weeks in the planning made harder and longer by the Affa affect.
They had to find where they were being developed. They had to find
the places and the people and work out the dates one would be ready.
They had to understand the principles, the shape, the size and how
it was used in order to feed that information to Herr Weber, and all
without him getting overly suspicious. That he didn't believe it until
seeing it was obvious.

With the heavy bomber loaded, the five agents climb up into the newly adapted rear, receiving smiles and nods from the German airmen so thrilled at the turn of events. Everything goes smoothly but then this is why they put the effort in, to make sure this happens properly.

Herr Weber joins them. The aircraft taxis and very shortly later, and without any form of ceremony, the engines roar to pull it down the runway and up into the air. A small group of fighters take off after it, but even they have been scavenged, begged, borrowed and even stolen to support the bomber. Such is the systematic destruction of Germany by the Allies that there is hardly anything left of the Third Reich. The Russians are advancing. The bombs fall more each day.

The Affa effect had no bearing on the course of the war. Hitler still rose to seize power and unleash hell with his hatred of Jews. He still caused the deaths of millions and brought the globe into the biggest conflict ever known. The sides stayed the same. The machinery, the weapons, the battles, victories and losses too. Only the names and some of the dates. Only the tiny things that seem not to matter.

Alpha reflects on it all and the weeks this has taken and for a fleeting second he gains an overwhelming feeling of utter insignificance. That what they are doing has no reason or purpose. Life will continue one way or the other and, in that second, predestiny means everything and what they do will make no difference because they would have always done it and suddenly he wants nothing more than to stop this mission and to return to the complex and go back to bed with Kate.

I always believed in them. Kate's soft voice in his ear late last night as they lay entwined in the darkness of his room. *Didn't you?* He never replied, but that lack of reply seemed to give the answer he couldn't vocalise. *I studied all of them: Maggie Sanderson, Ben Ryder, Safa Patel and Harry Madden.*

Alpha looks round and marvels at how something so old and ancient as this bomber gets off the ground in the first place. The aircraft is rattling like it's ready to fall apart. He turns to Charlie and

Delta goofing around, telling jokes and laughing. They've become good mates and Charlie is getting plenty of sex by being Delta's wingman as they work through the ladies in the complex. Even Echo looks in bliss, tinkering about with a fucking nuclear bomb on a shitty old German war plane flanked by a half score of misfiring fighter planes piloted by boys or shell-shocked men.

I even had that image of Emily Rose printed out and framed in my office. She looked so cool. Sticking a finger up at the governments of the world.

Go big. That's what Mother said and there's nothing bigger than a nuke. The physical size of the bloody thing is just monstrous. The Americans dropped two at the end of the Second World War. The first bomb was called Little Boy and was dropped on Hiroshima. The second bomb was a plutonium implosion device, significantly more powerful than the first, and was called Fat Boy. That was dropped on Nagasaki.

They chose the Fat Boy because the Affa effect meant the Little Boy was never developed and the tweaked timeline saw two Fat Boys dropped, and in the few years that followed the end of the war, the Americans refined and worked to make it better, bigger, stronger and more powerful.

Not that it matters what nuclear bomb they use, Alpha reflects bitterly. This is a statement. That was what the whole Affa thing was about. A statement to cause confusion. A thing done for Mother to tell Maggie Sanderson she also has a time machine. That they can go back and beat the shit out of the Romans and then do something as big as this.

Uncertainty hits Alpha. A fleeting rush of pre-emptive guilt that he has never ever experienced before. He drops his head and rubs his face.

'We're all feeling it, old chap.' Bravo's voice as the second in command leans in to make himself heard over the roar of the engines. 'We're dropping a nuke on London. Who wouldn't feel bad?'

Alpha looks up sharply with a rebuke ready to put Bravo back in his place. Who the hell does he think he is, talking to him like that? Bravo pulls a face and blows air out with an expression that matches the guilt Alpha just felt and that surge of anger slides away.

Surprisingly, the flight is easy and smooth. They're not picked up or attacked, but then it's broad daylight and the last thing the allies are expecting now is a single rogue bomber taking a pot shot at England and it's not long before the fighters reach their maximum range and drop away, ready to turn back.

So much planning has gone into this. Every detail thought about. Every action that could cause a reaction. Every possibility discussed and worked out. He is Alpha. He could cancel the mission now. He could return, make the bomb safe, go into the complex and kill Mother.

A tap on his arm. He turns to see Bravo motioning for him to look out the window to the white cliffs of Dover and the green lands of England and time goes on as every passing minute takes them closer to London. The Anti-Aircraft fire still doesn't come and they slip through unnoticed.

Then it's time and Echo announces the bomb is armed and ready. The German airmen open the doors, filling the plane with a louder rush of air. The greenery below gives way to streets and towns as they venture closer to the capital and the mood in the plane lifts as the Germans realise they are actually going to do it. Herr Weber just stares at the bomb, shaking his head and muttering with an expression of abject glee.

The AA fire finally comes. A sudden booming in the skies around them, but the pilots have been told to hold a steady course. The tension mounts. The grins and laughs fade and Echo stares hard at Alpha, waiting for the order.

'LAUNCH IT,' Herr Weber shouts. He looks to the strange men who came to him with a promise of a way to win the war and spots the hesitancy etched on their faces. He sees the sudden uncertainty in the glances between Alpha and Bravo and the way Charlie and Delta simply wait for instructions. 'LAUNCH IT,' he shouts again. They are over London. Now is the time to drop it. The AA flak is getting closer.

They need to launch it now. 'DROP IT . . .' he screams. Still Echo waits for the order from his commanding officer. Bravo stares at him too, everyone does.

Then Herr Weber makes a mistake with the arrogance that comes from his belief in an Aryan race. He reaches to pull his Luger, intending to order them at gunpoint but Delta and Charlie draw faster and the airman around them cry out in surprise as Bravo and Echo whip modern pistols from old holsters specially adapted to hold them.

'WHAT ARE WE DOING, ALPHA?' Echo shouts.

Alpha blinks. What *is* he doing? This is a mission. This is his job. He nods at Echo then smiles at Herr Weber. 'LAUNCH IT . . .'

The bomb drops.

The plane flies on. The motorised doors close and the AA fire continues to rock the plane as it gains height and pushes the speed to make as much distance as possible.

Fifty-one seconds after launch and at a height of five hundred and twenty-three metres over Piccadilly, the nuclear bomb detonates with a flash of lightning and a mushroom cloud pluming high into the heavens as the heavy German bomber heads for home.

Eighteen

'Where are we?' Safa asks, scanning the room. A low ceiling of natural rock above their heads. The walls the same. Rugs and mats on the floor with hard compacted earth showing between the gaps. Safa recognises the mats and other furnishings from the bunker but they look old and faded now, worn and broken.

Ria doesn't reply, but kicks the lid open on a now gouged and battered white shabby chic chest and tugs a magazine from the Barret, then props the rifle against the wall and pulls a box of big fifty-calibre rounds from the chest that she starts pushing into the magazine.

'Where are we?' Safa asks again, her tone harder from her blood still being up.

'Caves,' Ria says bluntly. 'My rooms are through there.' She nods to one end. 'Way out is through that gap.' She nods in the other direction.

'Where's the bunker?' Ben asks.

Ria reloads the magazine, hefts the rifle and makes it ready before slinging it on her back with a crude strap crafted from two leather belts fastened together. Pictures on the walls from the bunker. The same pictures Ria bought from Milwaukee, but they look dented, buckled, split and torn. Items and objects the same everywhere. Small tables that what seemed like an hour ago held vases of flowers now hold pistols and knives with spare magazines loaded and lying nearby.

'Ria?' Malcolm says softly. Konrad nudges his arm, nodding at a large drawing on the wall. Malcolm blinks and mutters under his breath at the sight of it. Ria always was good at art and the two figures drawn on the paper resemble him and Konrad. The wording underneath is the thing that catches them both; *Ria Ria Smelly Dear* written in bold, flowing script.

When they turn back they see her staring at them, studying the details of their faces and features. 'Needed to remember you,' she says quietly.

'What happened, Ria?' Konrad asks. He takes in the livid white scars running down her cheeks and across her nose. More down her arms. Old and faded, but smaller, fresher cuts show here and there.

The question seems to jar her and she moves back a step to purse her lips then cocks her head as though straining to listen.

'Ria?' Konrad asks.

She waves a hand at him with a clear signal to be quiet. The others hear it. A soft snuffling sound coming from the direction she said was the way out. Feet scratching the earth. A blast of air. Ria smiles sudden and bright. 'Hang on,' she calls out.

'What's that?' Safa asks. Ria doesn't reply but walks past them out of sight round a curve in the wall. 'Asked you a question,' Safa snaps.

'Easy,' Ben says. He sets off after Ria with the rest following suit and mutters in shock at sight of the solid metal riveted door marked with Harry's name held in place against one wall with the locking bar taken from the rear exit of the bunker wedged in crevices in the natural rock next to an assault rifle and a small bag holding magazines and grenades.

With a grunt, Ria yanks the locking bar out, drops it down, then grips the edges of the door with her bare hands and steps back, lifting it away with the muscles bulging in her arms, shoulders and back.

Daylight floods through a natural gap in the wall as Ria rushes quickly to intercept the big leathery head looming in.

'WATCH OUT,' Ben shouts, snatching to draw his pistol.

'Shush!' Ria hisses at him, glaring balefully as the head pushes deeper through the gap to see what made the new noise. Everyone freezes with breaths held as Ria murmurs softly and strokes the head of the bipedal creature that shuffles in on two strong back legs and a thick tail stretching out behind.

'We've seen it before,' Harry says, his voice deep and low. The creature turns the lizard head to look at Harry through intelligent, cunning eyes.

'Can't be,' Ben whispers. It looks like the one they saw in the forest when they first got here except this is bigger and taller, it's head at Ria's shoulder height. It moves towards the group without a flicker of fear as it snorts the air, blasting the scents in and out like a dog.

'He's friendly,' Ria says, rubbing the dinosaur's head vigorously. It rests back on its haunches, sinking lower with eyes rolling back in obvious pleasure at the fuss being given.

'That is a baby T-rex,' Emily states. 'Why the hell are you fussing a baby T-rex? Can someone tell me what's going on, please?'

'When we first got here,' Ben says. He reaches up to wipe the sweat off his forehead with a motion the small dinosaur spots and tracks. 'We went into the wooded area and saw one of those eating spiders . . . but it was smaller . . . like up to Safa's waist.'

'He's growing,' Ria says, staring only at the creature. 'Eats too much . . .' She steps back, grabbing a big metal tin from the floor. The dinosaur goes with her, pushing deeper into the cave entrance to sniff at the tin in Ria's hand. She pushes him back in the same way someone would do with a hungry dog. 'Wait.' She pulls the lid off as the creature starts making deep keening noises with obvious excitement as those eyes watch her pull a huge dead bug from the tin. 'Go on.' She throws it past his head, smiling like a parent as the dinosaur whips round and runs off.

'Ria?' Malcolm asks, moving out from the others. 'What's happened?'

Again she doesn't reply, but puts the tin back and walks out. The others follow her into bright daylight and a view that once more makes them become silent in awe.

'The valley,' Ben says, recognising it instantly. He moves out to look up above the cave at the hillside, tracking the way the land slopes backwards as it climbs.

'Dear god,' Emily murmurs. Malcolm and Konrad glance at each other. Miri taking it in the same as Ben.

The herds they all saw from the ledge outside the bunker are right there. Huge numbers of long-necked, long-tailed enormous dinosaurs.

'Can smell them,' Harry says, sniffing the air. 'Smells like Africa.'

'Safer down here,' Ria says. They all look as one to the captivating young woman standing next to the baby T-rex. The rifle on her back. Her hand on the creature's head. 'He smells them when they come,' she says without looking at anyone.

'Smells what?' Ben asks, realising Ria isn't talking about the herding creatures on the plains in front of them.

'Bad ones,' Ria says without further explanation. Her pet stands fully upright as though to stretch and sets off to sniff the newcomers in search of food or treats.

'What happened, Ria?' Ben asks. 'Where's the doctor?'

'Dead.' Ria shrugs. 'He was on top of me when I woke up.'

Ben looks up at her, seeing that distant expression but also the energy rippling inside her. Like a cornered animal that is debating whether to strike or not. Her eyes dart to the sides and behind to the hillside and her hand constantly moves back to feel the rifle hanging down her back as though needing the reassurance that it's still there.

'Have we been gone for two years?' Miri asks, speaking for the first time since coming from Hyde Park. 'Asked you a question, Miss Cavendish . . .'

Ria stares at her and for that one second the young woman matches the old spy for lack of emotion.

'You've been gone about six weeks.'

'You said two years,' Ben says.

'It took my brother a month to realise you weren't coming back. Then, being the genius that he is, he built another time machine and went to the bunker to look for everyone, except the bloody idiot put the date in wrong and went there two years after you went to London . . .'

'Shit,' Safa mutters.

'Two years?' Emily asks.

'He rushed putting the dates in,' Ria says with a humourless smile. 'Know what he said when he realised? He said it doesn't matter and he'll just go and get me from the right date . . . He also said he ran out of toilet paper and the leaves he was using were giving him a rash.'

'I'll kill him,' Malcolm whispers. 'I will. I'll bloody kill him.'

'Okay,' Ben says gently.

She looks at him and in that second Ben sees an altogether different woman than the one they left sedated in bed an hour ago. Miri has seen that look before too when working with hunters in Africa and South America and in the eyes of mercenaries. Haunted, driven, but with an inner core that radiates the complete opposite of fear.

'I forgot your names,' Ria says casually as though discussing something of no importance. 'All of you. I forgot you. I drew that picture but . . .' She goes quiet at hearing something and turns as the bipedal dinosaur lifts his head from sniffing Harry's boots. Both stare off to the side, waiting to see if the noise is something that poses a risk or something they can eat. A dull thud sounds out that makes Ria relax and the creature resume his sniffing.

Then it comes into view round a section of the hill, pushing out further into the valley and everyone else takes an involuntary step back at the sight of it. One of the huge long-necked, long-tailed dinosaurs from the plain, but close now. Only a few dozen metres away and the sheer size boggles their minds. The big female walks slowly, her body over a hundred and twenty feet in length, her head bobbing up and down with one leg landing harder than the others.

'She's a bit lame now,' Ria says, making them snap from looking at the enormous animal to her. The big female pauses in her walk too and swings her head towards the cave entrance. Huge nostrils flare as she sucks in gallons of air that inflate lungs that expand her torso with a noise like a gust of wind when she exhales. Her eyes are huge and soft, almost expressive. Scars on her legs and flanks. Old wounds now healed. She takes in the group, then lowers her head while changing direction to walk closer towards them. She goes slowly, ponderously and with movements that make her look lazy and slow, but each step takes seconds to complete and that back leg thumps down hard with enough force for the others to feel it through their feet.

'Jesus,' Malcolm says. His protective instinct towards Ria is still strong and he moves out to intercept, to pull Ria back, to do the job her father should have done and protect the woman he sees as a daughter.

'It's fine,' Ria says. She looks up at the head looming towards her and only then does she smile and that smile radiates through her face, bringing life and warmth where previously there was none. She stands her ground too, smiling up as the head swooshes down through the air on the end of that thick neck. Blasts of air come from the nose, pushing Ria's hair out behind her. The young woman reaches up, laying a hand on the point of the nose and that simple touch gives instant scale to the staggering bulk and size. That it moves so gently makes the breath catch in Ben's throat and he doesn't notice that Safa, Emily and Harry are each holding pistols at their sides. Not that pistols would do a thing against something that big.

'Go on, go eat,' Ria says, patting the nose. The creature blasts air at her again, then pushes a tiny fraction, but with enough force to make Ria step back with a laugh. Then it's off, swinging the head away to resume that slow walk past with the dull thud of the weak back leg and while the small bipedal pet slinks into the cave to claw at the tin and gobble the bugs held within.

'I'll show you the bunker,' Ria says suddenly with an instant transformation back to the hard face and even harder tone. 'Then you can go to Bertie . . .'

'Can we talk?' Ben asks.

'No,' Ria says, striding past them towards the cave. 'Hey! Stop eating that, you greedy guts,' she calls out, clapping her hands.

'Where are you going?' Ben asks. 'The bunker's up there, isn't it?' he adds, pointing up the hillside.

'Takes a day to walk up,' Ria says bluntly. 'We'll use the portal.'

'Fuck me,' Safa mutters. 'This is seriously messed up . . .'

They follow her back into the cave to watch as she takes up a battered-looking tablet that she operates to bring the Blue back to life and it's only then that Ben and Miri observe the poles of the device show dents and knocks from where they've been buckled then straightened. Even the speaker objects look scuffed and dented.

'Hello,' Harry says, grinning happily as he rubs the dinosaur's head. Everyone else stays quiet and watchful, not knowing quite what to say or how to react.

Without a word, Ria turns the Blue on and steps through out of sight. The creature follows her instantly, not reacting in the slightest to the shimmering light but instead running after Ria.

'Messed up,' Safa mutters again, going ahead to follow Ria.

They traipse through in silence to take in the remains of what was once the bunker.

Some walls still stand in semi-isolation and even one tiny patch of ceiling remains in the corner of one set of unused rooms. Weeds and plants now grow through the broken concrete and the remains scattered here and there. Old solar panels smashed and broken. Furniture faded, busted and destroyed. They can still see the basic layout from where the rear door once was, which gave way to the first corridor. Miri's office.

Malcolm's and Konrad's rooms. The armoury section. The bigger main room, then off to the other rooms and any doubt of Ria's claim that it's been exposed to the elements for two years vanishes instantly.

Ria's pet snuffles on, bounding into the remains with a confidence that speaks of them having been here many times before. It sniffs the ground, grunting noisily as it aims straight for the main room where the food was once held. A bug the size of a fist bursts out from under a chunk of concrete, making a dash for safety, but the dinosaur leaps and takes it underfoot with a crunch of bone and shell, then flicks it up to catch and chew noisily.

Everywhere they look they have the jarring sensation of coming back to a place many years after being here before. Like going to a childhood home as an adult, except they were here an hour ago, maybe less.

'Ben,' Emily says. He looks to see her pointing off towards the area where the shooting range once was and a grassed mound of earth bulging up. A basic wooden cross driven into the ground with the name *Doctor John Watson* scored into the wood.

'Bloody hell,' he says, taking it all in. Processing it all and what it means.

'What's that smell?' Harry asks, sniffing the air.

'Up there,' Ria says, nodding up towards the plateau above their heads.

'What is?' Ben asks.

That she decides not to reply indicates the control she is exerting over this situation, either that or she has absolutely no care for what any of them think.

Ben sets off with deliberate steps to scale the bank he's been up and down many times. Harry starts after him, then the others, all of them clambering to reach the top.

'Fuck me,' Ben says. 'Any more surprises, Ria?' he asks at last, earning a wan smile.

The bodies are everywhere and in varying states of decay. Bipedal dinosaurs, leathered and feathered, three metres tall with thick back legs and thick tails but that's where the similarity ends to the appearance with Ria's pet. He is a classic mini T-rex in shape and style. These are different, with oversized rows of teeth pushing out of mouths and stunted little arms like wings but with vicious claws at the end. Every one of them is either tied or fixed to a length of wood driven into the ground. A morbid, macabre graveyard of decaying corpses.

'You do this?' Miri asks.

'Yes,' Ria replies, the Barrett now brought round and held across her body. 'They keep coming . . .'

Ben drops his head to scratch his jaw then his forehead. A wry smile of thought etched on his face. 'That big one? She landed on the roof, right?'

'Yep,' Ria says, showing no reaction to Ben's deductive ability.

'What big one?' Safa asks, looking round.

'The big one that sniffed Ria. Her legs and sides were all scarred. It'd take something of that size to get through the roof . . . I'm guessing these chased her over the side and she went through the bunker.'

'How the fuck did you work that out?' Safa asks.

'Obvious really,' Emily says.

'Obvious my arse. You didn't work it out,' Safa says. 'Beardy? Did you work it out?'

'Nope.'

'Miri?'

'Negative.'

'No, I mean it's obvious now Ben has explained it,' Emily adds quickly.

'How did it get down to the bottom?' Ben asks Ria.

She takes her time in responding, as though thinking of what to say and the whole time her eyes never leave the tree line. 'Slowly,' she says at last.

'Right,' Ben says. 'Makes sense I guess. Er . . . Ria? How long ago did Bertie come for you?'

'Few weeks.'

'A few weeks!' Konrad exclaims. 'A few bloody weeks? What is it with you lot leaving people dead . . .'

'You,' Ria says, still not looking away from the tree line, 'are not my priority. I didn't ask for this. My father . . . you . . . all of what you do . . . I had nothing to do with it.' She speaks flat and hard with no undulation of emotion that gives her words even more impact. 'You've seen it. The bunker's ruined. Go to Bertie.' She turns away.

'Ria,' Ben says, making her pause in step. 'What about . . .'

She walks on, slinging the rifle as she drops down the bank to land deftly next to the portal, striding through without looking back.

'Hang on a minute,' Emily says. 'What happened in Piccadilly? Why were you running?'

'Someone nuked it,' Safa says.

'What?!' Emily snaps as Harry, Malcolm and Konrad stop to gawp. 'While you were there?'

'No! You twat,' Safa says.

'Did you really just ask that?' Ben asks.

'Er, excuse me, had a long day thank you,' Emily says primly.

'Dropped a nuclear bomb on Piccadilly in nineteen forty-five,' Safa says. 'Wiped it out . . . That plaza we saw is where it went bang.'

'Killed nearly two hundred thousand people,' Ben says. 'Had a big statue thing in the middle with a plaque at the base . . . Miri, you took a picture.'

Miri pulls out her smartphone, keys the screen and shows it to the others, who crowd round to read the words inscribed on the plaque.

Upon this site on 12 February 1945, the first detonation
of a nuclear weapon used in war took place.

The failing Nazi war machine, in the final throes of defeat,
sought to kill as many innocent British people as possible.

We, the survivors, dedicate this monument and this space
to the fallen men, women and children of London.

25,367 people died in the initial blast.

127,458 people died in the days, weeks and months that
followed.

Lives lost in the stand against tyranny and evil.

We shall always prevail . . .

'Oh my god,' Emily whispers. 'London?'

'Who did that then?' Malcolm asks.

'One thing at a time,' Miri says, pushing the camera back into her
pocket. 'Miss Cavendish. Your intentions, please?'

Ria stares at her, a mirror image of each for the lack of expression.
She simply turns and walks back through the portal with her pet running behind her.

'She's not right, Kon,' Malcolm says with a worried shake of his
head.

'You think?' Konrad asks him. 'What gave you that impression?'

'Well, living in a cave and all those dead . . .'

'I was being sarcastic, you bloody idiot,' Konrad snaps. 'Of course
she's not right. She's been living here for two years on her own. I think
anyone would go potty gaga after two years here . . .'

'Ria cannot be left with a device,' Miri says, cutting in.

'I think we can come back to that rule a bit later, Miri,' Ben says.

'What rule?' Safa asks.

'The no-one-else-can-have-a-time-machine rule,' Ben says.

'Oh, that rule,' Safa says. 'So?'

'Um, she's not exactly bloody stable, is she,' Ben whispers, glancing at the Blue to make sure Ria's gone through.

'She seems alright,' Safa says.

'Did you not just see the dead things tied to sticks?' Ben asks.

'So what? Fuck 'em. They're obviously hunting her and she's obviously kicking the shit out of them. Leave her to it.'

'We are making too many assumptions,' Miri says. 'Deploy to Bertie and assess. We need to ensure he has a second device before we allow Ria to shut hers off.'

'He does have a second device,' Ben says. 'Ria said he made another one and used it to come here.'

'You clever sod,' Safa says, staring at him.

'You're on fire today, Ben,' Emily says.

'Cheers,' Ben mumbles. 'Let's go to Bertie.'

'Nice chat?' Ria asks Ben as he steps into the cave.

'Can't blame us, Ria,' he replies.

'I am staying here. Do not ask me to leave,' she states as the rest file in behind Ben. 'If I change my mind, I have that,' she adds, nodding at the portal.

'Miss Cavendish . . .'

'I am staying here. I have work to do.'

'What work?' Ben asks.

'Killing those crocodile bird things by the looks of it,' Safa says. 'Fair one,' she says to Ria. 'You got ammunition?'

'I do,' Ria says tightly.

'Cleaning it?' Safa asks, looking at the Barrett.

'Every day. I saw Ben doing it . . . before,' Ria replies.

'Need food?'

'No.'

'Fine, sorted,' Safa says. 'Don't leave the magazine in the assault rifle by that door for too long.'

'I check it daily . . . Is that enough?'

'Best to take it out. Leave it by the side and check the magazine is working properly. Want me to stay here and show you?'

'I'll be fine.'

'Awesome,' Safa says. 'Well done you. We going then? I need a wee. I keep on needing a wee today. Maybe I'm pregnant. We should get a piss-test. Change the portal thingy then so we can see Bertie?'

'Ria, come with us,' Malcolm says, rushing in after Safa stops talking.

'Sweetie,' Konrad says softly.

'Done,' Ria says. The Blue blinks off then back on as she reaches out to stop her pet rushing towards it.

'Ria,' Malcolm says, clearly upset. 'Come with us for a bit so we can talk . . .'

She doesn't reply, but waits with her hand on the dinosaur's head, rubbing lightly.

'Can we come back and see you?' Konrad asks gently.

'I will come to you,' Ria says.

'But . . .' Malcolm says.

'Come on, Malc. We've got to respect what she wants. We're back now, Ria. We're here,' he says.

She doesn't reply, but watches as they go through the light until only Safa remains.

'Pain is a mindset,' Ria says quietly, earning a smile from Safa.

'Yeah, something like that,' Safa says. 'You've done well.'

'Thanks,' Ria says.

'Come get me if you need a hand killing evil-looking dinosaurs.'

'I will.'

'Laters.'

Ria stares for a second before swiping her thumb to end the Blue, which blinks out, and finally lets her breath go to sigh long and deep while rubbing her face with a shaky hand.

Nineteen

The Complex

It brings forth a sense of panic inside. Like a feeling you've done something very, very wrong, but if you don't react then no one else will. A bad thing done. A most evil act perpetrated and Mother watches the footage on the screen recorded by a small camera carried by Bravo and calmly sips from her teacup.

The footage is shaky in places and filmed through a scratched window of a German heavy bomber while behind and below them the plutonium implosion nuclear bomb detonates. A bomb taken from a Californian nuclear research facility in the 1950s from a timeline that had already been changed by the Affa effect. A bomb taken back to 1945 and dropped on London, and now they watch as the mushroom cloud plumes up and the sheer bright light of the flash seems to turn day into night.

That mushroom cloud grows taller and wider and the spreading smoke at the base speaks of the destruction underway.

'It's a very similar device as was used on Nagasaki,' Echo says into the near silence of the briefing room as the others watch the two-dimensional footage on a large screen. 'But the difference between London and Nagasaki is vast. Nagasaki had a lot of wooden-framed buildings, whereas London has brick- and stone-constructed buildings, which means a greater amount will withstand the blast, or crumble and fall but still create pockets of places for survivors . . . which is pretty much the same with any massive aerial bombing campaign on a city.' Echo stops talking to watch the footage for a second before continuing. 'But it will still have the same firestorms as Nagasaki with temperatures near-ing four thousand degrees Celsius and winds over six hundred miles an hour . . . Those not killed instantly within the hypo-centre of the blast will suffer flash burns with line-of-sight phenomena . . . Having said that, it's winter, so people with thick coats or clothes may have greater protection . . .' He trails off, caught in the replay and that sickening feeling inside they all feel. That their adherence to duty has taken them in a direction that is very, very wrong.

'That's enough,' Mother says abruptly, coldly. 'How many people did it kill?'

Everyone apart from Mother looks to Kate who clears her throat and swipes the screen of her tablet. 'Er, 25,367 were killed in the initial blast and, er . . . 127, 458 are said to have perished later as a direct result and then of course there are the birth defects and all sorts of awful things that . . .' she trails off as the shocked mutterings spreading through the room die off the second Mother clears her throat while still watching the footage on the screen as the camera moves to sweep round the inside of the aircraft, catching a glimpse of the stricken faces of the agents before going back to the window.

'Good,' Mother states. 'Switch it off.' She finally stands to address the rest of the room, withering in her contempt at their shock. 'Do not let the concept of time travel confuse you. We are immune to changes in the timeline of the world. I could go back into the timeline and kill you all as children and you would still be here. Not that we exist in that timeline now, of course, nor does anyone you ever knew . . .' She smiles coldly, letting her words sink in. 'We are detached from the timeline. Is that clear? I said, is that clear?' Murmurs sound out, heads nod, weak and wan, and she reads the fear in their faces. 'Now we wait. At some point, Maggie Sanderson will react and we *will* be ready. Kate, you will continue to monitor and look for changes in the timeline . . . Do you have a problem?' Mother snaps, fixing those cold grey eyes on the historian.

'No, Mother,' Kate says quickly. 'I, er . . .' She swallows and goes quiet.

'What?' Mother demands.

'How do we reset that?' Kate blurts. 'I mean . . . How do you stop the agents dropping that bomb and . . . and stop them doing that thing in one-two-six AD? I'm so sorry.' She rushes the words out, wringing her hands as she speaks. 'I just got confused. I shouldn't have asked . . . My apologies.'

Mother glares round the room. 'That,' she hisses, pointing at the screen to where the footage was showing a moment ago, 'was necessary and proportionate to ensure our mission objectives. Does anyone have a problem with it? SPEAK UP?' she shouts, making several people flinch. 'Do your fucking jobs and do not ever question me again. Insubordination will not be tolerated.'

She storms out, slamming the door to stalk back to her office, rushing to the desk to activate the camera feed from the briefing room, smiling to herself at the heavy stunned silence and the sight of Kate wiping the tears from her eyes as those closest lean over to rub her arm and ask if she is okay while the agents share glances.

A rush inside. A thrill at sensing the game is underway and the pieces of the board are moving into place. Maggie fucking Sanderson thinks she is the hero of this game. The weary warrior defending the world from the evils of power and that is the advantage Mother will play.

That is the ace up her sleeve.

Twenty

The Island

Hot sunshine beats down from a deep blue sky above gorgeous turquoise waters lapping at the shore. Trees, bushes and ferns dapple the island. They shield their eyes from the glare and adjust as they emerge from the cave.

'BERTIE!' Malcolm shouts with an edge to his voice that most of the others haven't heard before.

'Don't be cross with him, Malc,' Konrad says, still squinting. 'It's not his fault.'

'He left his sister for two bloody years, Kon.'

'He's autistic,' Konrad says in explanation. 'And Ria said he put the date in wrong.'

'BERTIE . . .' Malcolm shouts again.

'MALC . . . KON . . . BENHARRYSAFAEMILYMIRI . . .' The voice comes from behind them, making them turn to see Bertie standing on a raft waving like crazy with his hands above his head a few dozen metres out to sea.

'BERTIE, YOU NEED TO COME HERE RIGHT NOW,' Malcolm shouts.

'There's no point, Malc,' Konrad says. 'He won't understand what he's being told off for.'

'He will bloody understand. He'll understand he needs to get his head out of his backside . . .'

'COMING, MALC AND KON AND BEN AND SAFA AND HARRY AND EMILY AND MIRI . . . DOCTOR JOHN WATSON IS DEAD BUT RIA SAID I'M NOT ALLOWED TO GO AND GET HIM BACK . . .'

'How's that raft moving?' Harry asks. 'Tide is going out but he's coming in.'

'No idea,' Ben says as the others watch Bertie on the flat raft moving towards them through the water, but without any obvious signs of propulsion. 'Probably sellotaped it to a bloody dolphin,' Ben says.

Bertie dives into the sea, going deep and long before surfacing to swim easily across the last expanse of water, then surging upright to his feet and running through the shallows with water pouring from his tanned and toned body and a huge grin spreading across his face. He hasn't seen them for ages and ages. Like ages. He has so much to tell them. Like, so many things he has thought about and new ideas and fresh ideas about old ideas. Then he spots something in the long grass bordering the shore and all thoughts of everyone are gone in an instant.

'ISAAC!' he cries out and veers off, laughing with glee while grabbing something to lift that he turns and brings closer to his face. 'Look!' he says, showing the others. 'Tortoise . . . I called him Isaac Asimov.'

'See?' Konrad says to Malcolm. 'There's no point telling him off, Malc.'

'Well,' Malcolm huffs.

'You're still hung over, you grumpy sod . . . Ah, shit . . . we left the bags of kit in Milwaukee . . .'

'Milwaukee?' Miri asks.

'His idea,' Malcolm blurts, pointing at Konrad while stepping away.

'How did that raft move, Bertie?' Ben asks, strolling over to look at the tortoise.

'Haha, like, totally . . . OHMYGOD, I've got to show you this . . . come see . . . er . . . Hang on, I'll just put Isaac Asimov down over here, no over here . . . Um, no . . . he can go here . . .' The child in him shows as Bertie bends forward at the waist and gets caught in a loop of trying to decide where to put the tortoise down until Ben intervenes gently.

'That'll do, mate,' Ben says, helping him lower the animal, who seems nonplussed about being hefted and shown about, but then tortoises aren't known for their complex facial expressions.

'So cool,' Bertie says, standing up to grin at Ben.

'What did you want to show me?' Ben asks.

'What?' Bertie asks.

'You just said,' Ben says. 'You said "I've got to show you this . . ."'

'What?' Bertie asks. 'Isaac Asimov?'

'No, after that. You said . . . Never mind. How are you?'

'Fine, thank you, Ben Ryder. How are you? Ria always told me to ask the other person how they are.'

'You've been alone for a month,' Ben says. 'Have you . . .'

'No.'

'Pardon?'

'No.'

'No what, Bertie?'

'No, Ben Ryder.'

'No, I mean what are you saying no to?'

'One month.'

'Right. Ria said you were here for a month before you went to find her.'

'Seven weeks, two days and' – he pauses to squint at the sky – 'thirteen and a half hours . . .'

'Right,' Ben says, rubbing his face. 'Bertie, I'm going to ask you a question.'

'Totally,' Bertie says, nodding quickly.

'How did you get the date wrong? You left your sister at the bunker for two years.'

'So, like, you know, I was working the date out when Isaac started eating my fish I caught and I was, like, "*Hey, stop eating my fish, Isaac*" and he was, like, totally eating it and I smudged my writing so, like, when I made the new portal and I was, like, totally going to get Ria, but I couldn't read what I had written because Isaac had eaten the fish so . . .' He stops to blink, then smiles.

'Okay,' Ben says wearily.

'Did I do something wrong?'

'No, no you didn't, mate. You did well,' Ben says, offering him a tight smile.

A day of jarring sights and weird things that tax their already tender heads made sore from the heavy night's drinking and they traipse with a heavy tread to the shack in the clearing as Bertie chatters on at top speed, his arm looped through Emily's.

'. . . and, like, I was totally thinking it needs an upstairs because what if someone wants to stay the night and Doctor John Watson was always sleeping here but in the hammock so I made a new level, but Doctor John Watson is dead now, but when he comes back he can see the . . .'

'Jesus,' Emily whispers at the sight of it. A whole new level built on the shack with a rough-hewn staircase fitted to the side of the building going up to a new door. Shutters on the glassless windows and an apex roof covered in a dark, even coating of what looks like sun-baked mud.

'Do you like it, Emily? You can use it too,' he says earnestly, his attention solely on her and her alone, but Bertie does that. He pours everything into the person he is talking to, as though their very opinion means life or death for him.

'I, er . . . I love it,' she says, trying to sound eager and happy, but looking as jarred as everyone else.

'Bertie?' Konrad asks. 'Where did you get the wood from to build that?' He points at the new level in the shack as Bertie grins at him.

'Trees.'

'What trees? The trees here are . . . Well, they're still here . . .'

'Mainland,' Bertie says, pointing off towards the west without looking.

'Did you use that raft to get the wood here?' Konrad asks.

'Oh, totally,' Bertie says. 'S'anti . . . haha! Isaac Asimov mated with a lady tortoise, but the gestation period takes, like, forever.'

'What?' Konrad asks as Bertie rushes off into the shack.

'He meant anti-grav,' Safa says. 'That lawnmower engine Konrad nicked from London. I bet he used that.'

'Jesus, Safa,' Ben says. 'How did you work that out?'

'Cos I don't overthink stuff like you eggheads do. Bertie, where are the drinks?' she asks, striding into the shack.

'Jesus, is anyone else's head spinning a bit?' Ben asks.

'Just a bit,' Emily says.

'We need to talk,' Miri says, pulling a packet of cigarettes from a pocket.

'Ben!' Safa calls from the shack. 'Come here . . .'

'What's up?' Ben asks, walking in to see Safa rubbing her shin while playfully swiping at Bertie with her other hand.

'I walked into that,' she says.

'What?' Ben asks as Malcolm and Konrad walk in behind him.

'Look properly,' Safa says.

'At what?' Ben asks, then finally sees it. Two black objects hanging just below head height from the ceiling and two more poking up from the floor.

No strings. No rope. Nothing. Ben pushes his hand over the top through where the string should be but there's nothing. The other one is the same too. Two small black round things, each a quarter the size of tennis balls, weirdly shaped and made from either moulded plastic or some kind of resin. He looks down to examine the other two of the same size and design, then steps back to see that the way they hang forms the shape of a doorway. 'Fuck . . .' He reaches out to touch one and finds it holding position. He tries to push it gently, but it doesn't move. He pushes harder, but still it doesn't move.

A shadow falls in the room as Harry looms in the doorway, then steps aside to let Miri in.

'What are they?' Safa asks Bertie, flashing a hand out to tweak his nose, making him giggle and laugh like a child. 'Tell me before I do it again,' she says, hovering her hand in front of his face.

'Portal,' he laughs.

'Tell me properly,' she warns with a smile.

'It's a portal . . . I made it for Miri . . . Do you want to see it?' he asks eagerly.

'Better be interesting,' she warns, letting go of his hands. 'If I yawn you're getting it . . .'

'Okay, okay . . . look . . .' He grabs a tablet from his desk, pressing the screen, which makes a shimmering blue light form instantly between the four objects hanging in the air.

'So?' Safa says, starting a mock yawn. 'We've got one of them. Boring!'

'No, Safa! I'll show you . . .' He presses the tablet to end the blue light. Another press and the four objects collapse towards each other where they come together as one round object that makes Ben realise why they were shaped so weirdly. A perfect ball now hangs in the air and he snaps his head to Bertie's desk and the other identical round black balls being used as paperweights.

'See?!' Bertie tells Safa. 'And look . . . I can do this . . .' He thumbs the tablet, which makes the ball fly at him as he reaches out to catch it, but Safa moves faster, grabbing it quickly and bringing it into her hand to stare at. She holds it as though examining it, glancing at Bertie, who gives fresh giggles each time she looks at him. She can feel the weight of it and gently tosses it into the air to see gravity now working as it goes up, then comes back down in the way a ball should.

'It's just a ball,' she says, throwing it up in the air again.

'It's not . . . Throw it.' Bertie giggles like a child, enraptured by Safa and completely unaware of everyone else watching with intense focus.

'Fine.' Safa chucks it lightly towards the back of the room. The ball moves as it should do: sailing up with the momentum of the throw, then reaching the apex of the climb before starting to plummet. Bertie presses the tablet and the ball splits into the four parts that shoot out to form the same size and shape as before. A second later and the Blue comes back on. Hanging in the air and bathing them all in the light.

'Where is it open to?' Safa asks. 'BORING,' she shouts when he starts to answer, making everyone else laugh at the sight. Miri thinks back to the grav boards and the things they saw hovering in London and suspects that what Bertie has done is way beyond even that technology.

'It's not live,' Bertie says quickly. Ben pushes his hands through while leaning round the edge of the sliver of thin light to see his hand coming out the rear.

'Enough?' Safa murmurs quietly.

'Yeah,' Ben says. He glances at Miri, who stares back with a strange expression. 'At least we know how to ask him stuff now,' he adds. 'Deploy the Patel.'

'Deploy the Patel.' Safa laughs. 'I like that . . . Did you hear that, Bertie? Eh? Deploy the Patel on your nose. What now anyway? We might as well get the doc back.'

'Not yet,' Ben says.

'Oh god,' Safa groans. 'Not this again . . . We're not leaving him for a month so you can have a poo and think about it.'

'Twat,' Ben chuckles. 'Emily, chuck us a bottle, please. Cheers . . . Where did these come from anyway?'

'Ria must have got them,' Safa says. 'Loads of stuff in the back but all the labels are different. It's really weird. Like seeing something you should recognise but it's not the same.'

'Rio was like that,' Emily says. 'All the beers behind the bar and the other drinks, then upstairs they had old posters and signs for drinks and things . . . Didn't recognise any of them.'

'Upstairs?' Safa asks. 'What were you doing up upstairs?'

'When me and Harry . . . Oh piss off,' she snaps at Safa, who's bursting out laughing.

'How's your eggs?' Safa asks.

'I don't know,' Emily says icily. 'How are my eggs, Harry?'

'Ach,' the big man says deeply with a blush spreading across his face.

'Ben, find out where Ria got the supplies from,' Miri says. 'Everyone else get a drink. We have a lot to go through.' She walks out and finally lights the cigarette she was holding in her hand and after decades of service in the most extreme of situations even she feels the shock of it. It's too big. Way too big. Dropping a nuclear bomb on London is a statement of intent and Miri knows in her gut exactly who did it and why.

In the shack, the Blue comes on, shimmering into existence as Ben passes the controller to Safa and steps into the cave to see daylight pouring in through the opening and moves down and through the gap to look at that amazing view stretching out.

'I said don't come here.' A dull voice from above and behind him makes Ben spin to see Ria perched on the top of a big flat rock above the cave opening, the rifle across her lap and that same passive-aggressive expression etched on her face.

'How did you buy Bertie's food?'

'Trade.'

'What? Where from? When from?'

'Don't question me, Ben.'

'Sorry, Ria. Been a long day . . .'

She stays quiet, staring out across the vista and showing no signs of being interested in anything he has to say. 'There was a dead guy in the bunker wearing Nazi clothes. I traded the jacket.'

'When, Ria? Where?'

She looks down at him, holding that impenetrable gaze for several long seconds. 'Twenty-one eleven . . .'

'What!? Ria, what are you doing?' he asks in alarm as Ria stands up, yanks the bolt back and aims down the scope into the vast plains.

'I made Bertie recover the co-ordinates you used for Hyde Park. I went to the far end and walked down.' Her voice comes out flat and dull with statements made instead of conversation given. 'I saw Emily by a tree and Harry in that hut smoking . . .' She goes quiet, still as rock and holding position for what seems an eternity. The shot, when it comes, makes Ben flinch. The noise is immense. A solid boom of a fifty-calibre round being fired at high velocity, which spins away through the gaps in the herd to slam into a leathered and feathered predator leading a pack towards an errant youngster left isolated by its mother. The creature screeches in alarm at the sudden pain. Ria adjusts the aim and fires again, killing another one before the pack burst away in fright and the air starts to fill with the deep brays of alarmed herbivores calling out. Ria studies the area, seeing the things filter back into the dense undergrowth at the edge of the plain and out of sight. Only when she is sure they are gone does she lower the rifle and look down at Ben. 'The cops came and killed you all. I saw you all die . . . so I came back, got my rifle and got you out before that happened. Happy now? Or is that misusing the device? Is Miri going to execute me now?'

'Shit,' Ben whispers to himself at the thought of what she saw. 'You saw us die?'

'Yep.'

'Thank you,' he says simply, not knowing what else he *can* say to such a thing. 'I, er . . .'

'There's an antique shop across the river in what used to be Lambeth. The settings are in Bertie's device. The guy who owns it paid good money for that Nazi gear. I used the credit chip to get Bertie what he needed.'

'Credit chip?' Ben asks.

Ria lifts the rifle to view through the scope, sweeping from far left to far right before slinging it to the rear and jumping lithely from her rock to a path that winds down the side of the hill. Every movement is assured and confident and she leaps the last few feet to land easily on the hard earth in front of the cave.

'I need to go now. Don't come back.' She sets off towards the herds still braying in alarm.

'Ria, please,' Ben says.

'What?' Ria snaps, turning to glare at him.

'What's a credit chip? How did you . . . ?'

'If I tell you, will you go away?' she asks, striding back at him. Not towards him, but at him. Aggression rippling from her whole manner. Her hard eyes seemingly blazing with energy, with a look so similar to Safa when she's been fighting that it makes Ben gawp in silence. 'Deal?' she demands.

'Deal,' he says.

'Don't come back here.'

'Not unless we absolutely need to.'

'By twenty-one eleven the advanced countries of the world use a credit system.' She speaks clearly but in a hard voice. 'People get credits for work. Same as money, except it doesn't exist. It's virtual. The problem is those countries still want tourists from other countries to visit so they use credit chips. Like currency exchanging. Tourists pre-load a credit chip to use in places that have the shared credit system. The guy in the antique shop gave me a credit chip. It's unregistered, which means it can be used by anyone. Some of them are linked biometrically and can only be used by the person they were assigned to . . . but black markets still exist. The world will always have fucking bastards in it . . .' She stops talking as though aiming the accusation at him. 'Someone dropped a nuke on London in nineteen forty-five. Did you know?'

'We just found out,' Ben replies, stunned to the core by the woman talking to him.

'Affa. That's new too,' Ria says. 'A Roman army patrol near Hadrian's Wall in one-two-six AD was killed by a small group of locals led by a man called Affa. It caused a mass civil uprising and changed the course of history. Affa became famous . . . like Spartacus was in our time . . .' She stops talking and waits, but Ben holds off the urge to fill the silence to see if Ria will continue. She smiles instead. 'That's why I don't want you here . . . This place is lethal, but it doesn't manipulate . . .'

'Ria,' Ben calls as she turns to walk off.

'Do not come back.' She tugs something from her pocket and turns as she walks to throw it at Ben, who catches it from the air. 'The credit system is confusing, but think of it as money and that has about a grand on it . . .'

Ben looks at the small flat card. Half the size of a credit card and matt black with delicate golden lines criss-crossing the centre. A logo in the corner with the words London Tourist Credit Chip printed in clear letters.

'Oh, and if you go back to London don't take a weapon with you because I won't save you again . . . The drones scan everyone and mark their targets with lasers. Even if you shoot them down you're still marked.' She walks off, leaving Ben as stunned as before.

Twenty-One

Bertie's Island

'I know we're all tired, but this has to be done now,' Miri says in the shack on Bertie's island an hour after coming back from Hyde Park. 'There are two changes to the timeline that we are aware of. The Affa incident in one-two-six AD and a nuclear bomb dropped on London in nineteen forty-five. We need information on those incidents to find out where we can deploy to monitor them and establish who caused them.'

'I think it's bloody obvious who caused them,' Emily says. 'You said it yourself, Ben. Affa must be Alpha . . .'

'We will investigate and draw conclusions from fact in place of guesswork, Tango Two.'

Emily bridles, ready to snap back, but swallows the rebuke and stays silent.

'Why are we rushing?' Safa asks, clocking the look between Miri and Ben.

'We're detached from the timeline,' Ben explains. 'And if we are then whoever else has a time machine is also detached . . . and there's a risk we're both now on our own timeline and we just lost two months. Why make two changes to the timeline? Miri and I discussed it and one of our theories is that they dropped the nuke because we failed to react to the changes in Roman times . . .'

'Because we were gone for two months?' Safa asks.

'Possibly,' Ben says. 'We need to find out. Hence going into the place Ria used.'

'Ready?' Miri asks, not waiting for a response as she activates the portal that comes to life with the blue doorway shining between the floating devices.

The settings were stored in Bertie's controller as *Lambeth-not-Lambeth*, with an entry point at the end of a deep dog-legged alley and they go through to venture out with Safa in the lead.

'Harry, Emily . . . you two hold the alley,' Safa says. 'This our fall-back position. If it goes bent we do the same as before . . . Emily, you come to us if we need you. Harry, you protect the Blue. I am team leader. I have control on the ground.'

'Give me a minute,' Ben says quietly, sweeping his eyes over the street, the buildings, the people, the forms, structures, noises, sights, smells and a thousand other things all at the same time. Miri does the same, examining and assessing to absorb and understand the new environment.

'You and me again then, Harry,' Emily says from behind him.

'Aye,' the big man says.

'Bring your smokes this time?' she asks lightly.

'Aye,' he says, eyeing her suspiciously at the good-natured question that seems to be lacking any dig at their increasingly confusing situation.

'Good,' she says, nodding at him. Ben de-tunes from studying the area, waiting for the dig. Safa too. Miri just tuts to herself.

'Nothing?' Ben asks, turning to glance at Emily when no comment is forthcoming.

'Nope,' she says, looping her arm through Harry's. 'We're all good today.'

'Right,' Ben says. 'Great.'

'All good,' Emily says.

'Awesome,' Ben says.

'Unless, you know, Harry gets drunk and wants to have sex with someone . . .'

'And there it is,' Ben says, facing back round to carry on studying the area.

'Ach,' Harry says. 'You've said it enough now.'

'Nowhere near enough,' Emily replies sweetly. 'My big handsome lover . . .'

'Yeah, that's just creepy,' Safa says.

'I meant it sarcastically,' Emily says quickly.

'It didn't sound sarcastic,' Ben says, looking back round at her.

'Well, I meant it sarcastically. I did! I was being mean, not creepy . . . It came out wrong . . .'

'What like it went in wrong?' Safa asks as Ben bursts out laughing.

'I don't get it,' Emily says primly.

'You got it the other night . . .'

'Safa!' Ben says. 'Right . . . ready?'

'That's what she said,' Safa says.

'Fuck off, Patel . . .' Emily says.

'UNKNOWN ADULT FEMALE. THE USE OF REVOLTING, ABUSIVE OR INSULTING WORDS IS PROHIBITED IN THIS PUBLIC PLACE.'

'Fucking awesome . . .' Safa adds with a laugh as the others wait for the automated voice that still doesn't come. 'I think it likes me.'

'This is not the time for a test,' Miri snaps.

Ben smiles and looks on in awe at Lambeth-not-Lambeth and the wide road running through made to feel narrower by the towering architecture. *Not towering*, he corrects himself. *More imploding, or exploding*. A riot of colours and noise. A futuristic film set of Oriental-pagoda-style houses with tiered roofs built in amongst concrete, glass, steel and sleek modern things and those buildings seem to grow out as they rise with what look like bolt-ons and additional structures fitted to the sides. Vehicles glide here and there in the chaos of a long thoroughfare packed with people. Gliding food stalls hover next to shouting merchants. Fronts of shops stand wide open with retractable concertina walls pulled back.

Music everywhere, people shouting to buy, to sell, calling names and every few seconds the automated voice booms out telling someone the use of revolting, abusive or insulting words is prohibited. Drones swoosh and glide overhead. Some at ten feet high, others at fifteen, more at twenty feet high and yet more above them. Some hold payloads, clutching parcels and packages. Others are small and veer faster through the busy sky-lanes with what must be connectivity to an interface that plots courses, speeds, trajectories, angles and take-off and landing points with a processing power far beyond anything a human mind could do.

Ben spots a heavyset bearded guy wearing a canary-yellow sarong and a blue vest with tattoos covering his upper body leaning over a hovering stall bearing stacks of brightly coloured fruit. He laughs and chats with a woman, selecting huge red tomatoes that he puts in her open bag. She laughs back, joking in a way of familiarity born from years of cohabitation.

A drone holding position over the woman lowers down as she lifts the bag to a metallic-looking arm fitted with gripping claws extending from the underside. She carries on chatting and laughing while the drone lifts back to where it was.

'Best go then,' Ben says, leading the way out into the street.

'Bye, my big handsome lovers,' Safa says.

'Seriously, Safa. It was sarcastic.'

'Sure,' Safa laughs.

'It was! Harry, it was sarcastic,' Emily tells him. 'Whatever, give me my arm back . . .' She goes to tug it free, glaring at him when he presses his arm closer to his body, trapping it in place. 'Harry! Give me my arm back . . .'

'Ach, stop going on,' he says with a deep sigh.

'Fine.' She stops squirming to stand with her arm still looped in his. 'Could have let me sleep on you last night though. I've got a stiff neck now.'

'I said you could,' he retorts.

'You didn't mean it,' she says. 'Whatever. I don't want to talk about it.'

'Hope so,' he mumbles.

'I heard that,' she snaps.

Safa grins, seeing them bickering as she walks up the street with Ben and Miri. What she also notices is the way Emily and Harry have their eyes up, watching every angle and studying every person that passes by and that squabbling by no means detracts from their ability to work.

'This is nuts,' Ben says, marvelling as they pass the mouths of junctions and see the same thing in the side streets. The same packed environment of stalls, drones, people and colours. Music playing from shops and even from some of the drones moving slowly over their owners. Old tunes he recognises mixed in with ultra-fast synthetic beats. Opera blasts from a storefront that he peers into to see a bald man using an old-style cut-throat razor over the stubbled head of a beautiful woman. Men in make-up, the same dark eyes they saw in Hyde Park. Men with breasts, women with luxurious facial hair. Children with tattooed faces and bodies running through the crowds with parents yelling for them to slow down.

Scents of herbs and spices hang in the air. Aromatic and enticing. The smells of Chinese, Indian, Asian and Mexican foods. They pass vendors with floating stalls filled with sizzling woks, pots and pans, which give steam and smoke into the air.

Everywhere he looks there is something new to see. Something uniquely different. Something captivating that makes him want to stop and stare and understand and seek knowledge on how the intricacies of this world take place.

'Look for a bookstore,' Miri says, bringing Ben's focus back to the job and mission at hand, having already discussed that trying to access whatever internet system or interface in place might leave them open to tracking.

'Course,' Ben says.

'Try down here,' Miri says, spotting a side street. 'Looks less crowded.'

'Safa to Emily and Harry . . . We're going down a side street . . . Fourth on the right from your position . . .'

'Received. Harry said bring some food back. He said it smells nice. I said he should only try new things when he's drunk in case he doesn't like them . . .'

Safa bursts out laughing, shaking her head as they stroll into the junction to see chairs and tables set outside cafes and restaurants. Ben notices people eating and drinking in the same way with an equal split between the use of cutlery and chopsticks.

'You wanna table? Table for three? Yeah?' A waiter steps out to block their path with an action that makes Ben think of European city centre cafés and their staff vying for the lucrative passing tourist trade. 'Come on, Affas! Have a table, yeah? Best locusts in London . . .'

'Locusts?' Ben asks.

'Yeah,' the man laughs. 'Table for three.' He ushers them with the expert precision of a guidance missile. Swarming round like a sheepdog to herd them to his establishment. 'Best fried locusts in London . . . All in the sauce, yeah? Family secret though so don't get all Affa about it, haha! Oleg? Oleg? These are my new friends . . . You want locusts? Three for locusts? Oleg! Three for locusts for my new best friends. On holiday, yeah? Got your two beautiful sisters with you, eh, Affa?' He nudges Ben, winking with an infectious laugh while nodding at Safa and Miri. 'Eh? Beautiful ladies. Oleg? We've got two beautiful ladies here. Mind you,

you're a handsome Affa too, eh?' He winks at Ben again, pulling chairs out, then pushing them back in as they sit down. 'What you want to drink? My name is Jerry and I'll be your waiter today, haha! Bit early for a beer if you ask me, but I can get them in for you. Three beers? Want beer? On holiday so have a beer . . .'

'Er, have you got coffee?'

'Coffee! Oleg? Affa wants to know if we've got coffee! Have we got coffee? Actually, no, mate. We don't have coffee.'

'Oh,' Ben says.

'Haha! Course we got coffee. Best coffee in London . . . Well, I say London, but the best coffee this side of the river . . . or in this street anyway . . . Well, let's just say it's the best coffee in this café, haha! Only joking, Affa. Three coffees. Three fried locusts. You'll love it! Oleg? Three coffees and three fried locusts for my best friends here . . .'

'Say, honey,' Miri drawls, her accent nasal and thickly American. 'Where do we get local history here, huh?'

'History, love? What you wanna know about? Just ask! Oleg? We got an American wants to know about history. They love their history the Yanks do.'

Safa leans over, trying to see anyone called Oleg in the café.

'We wanna read up on the local stuff,' Miri says. 'London is so small. I love that about it here. I love your history and I promised the girls back home I'd take them a book. You got books here?'

'Books! Oleg? She wants a book!'

'Hard to get, huh?' Miri asks, taking her cue from his reaction.

'Hard to get! Nah, just pricey. Know what I mean? Download it. What you want? I can do it while you eat.'

'Ah, that's very kind of you,' Ben says, smiling at Jerry as he bustles back and forth bringing cups and jugs to the table. 'We promised my aunt we'd try and get a proper book.'

'Know what you mean. Say no more,' Jerry says. 'Hope you got deep pockets though, Affa . . . haha! Oleg . . . is old Ruben still trading, is he?'

'YES,' a thunderous voice roars from the depths of the building.

'Fuck me,' Safa says. 'Was that Oleg?'

Jerry pauses, looking round in obvious surprise. 'Eh, you don't set it off.' He grins, winking at Safa. 'One in a million can do that. Cor, got a rare one there, Affa,' he adds with a grin at Ben. 'Oleg? She doesn't set it off when she swears . . . Anyway, so you want old Ruben. Back on the main road. Go down to Slatty the fishmonger's, but then come back cos you gone too far! Haha! Nah, but seriously, Ruben's got a bookshop down on the right side. Can't miss it, but the greedy sod'll take a kidney for a book. You sure you don't want a download? While you're down there have a look at Mishka's Antiques if you like old stuff. They got a genuine Nazi uniform in there. Ain't seen nothing like it. Pristine it is. Still got the blood stains on it. Mishka's got folk coming from all over the world to see it. Be able to retire on that he will.'

'Ria,' Ben says under his breath.

'You know her?' Jerry asks, snapping his attention to Ben on hearing the comment. 'You know Ria, do you? Oleg? This Affa knows Ria so he does. How do you know her? Where is she then? Ain't seen her for a few days. She tell you to try our locusts, did she? She likes them she does. She loves them! Ria, eh? Love that girl.'

'Holy shit,' Safa says at the man mountain coming from the café door. Seven feet tall and with shoulders that make Harry look like an underdeveloped schoolboy.

'Locusts?' the man rumbles.

'Oleg! Over here for my new best friends. Just telling 'em about that Nazi stuff. They know Ria they do.'

'You talk too much,' Oleg grumbles, putting the plates down. 'He doesn't talk to me that much at home, you know. Goes all quiet he does. How do you know Ria?'

'Oh, here we go,' Jerry huffs, throwing his arms in the air. 'Don't be telling 'em our domestic situations now.'

Oleg waits for an answer in the way of a mountain waiting for passage of millennia.

'Erm, she, er . . .' Ben thinks fast, showing surprise at the plate of locusts to buy time.

'Niece,' Miri drawls. 'Gotta love that girl.'

'No way,' Jerry whispers. 'She's your niece? Like family, yeah? Holy Affa. You hear that, Oleg. We got Ria's family here. Ria's family! Eating here! Ere, don't suppose you can get your hands on any more of those dinosaur claws she sells?'

'We'll ask her,' Miri says as Ben chokes on his coffee.

'Enjoy your food,' Oleg says, giving Ben a strange look. 'I shall take my husband away to give you some peace.'

'Did that just happen?' Ben asks, wiping his chin.

'What the fuck?' Safa asks, staring at her plate. She lowers her head to sniff a few times, peering at the insects arranged on her plate with salad and dressings. 'Smells nice . . . Fuck it . . .' She grabs one, mouths it and starts chewing, slowly at first then faster as the taste hits. 'Best locusts in London . . . seriously . . . Ria, eh? She's a sod.'

◆ ◆ ◆

'Oh no, he's seen us,' Emily groans. 'Just don't talk to him.' She rolls her eyes as the man starts making his way over. It might be the future and a landscape shaped and changed from anything she ever knew, but one thing apparently remains the same.

'Hello,' the man says sincerely. Small build, short, neatly cropped hair and dressed in an off-white flowing robe.

'Hello,' Harry says as Emily groans inwardly.

'Have you heard the word of our Lord?' the man asks, staring up at Harry with that clean-living, slightly feverish aura that Emily, and anyone with half a brain, can spot a mile away.

'God?' Harry asks. 'Aye.'

'You are a believer?' the man asks hopefully.

'No,' Emily says. 'He's not. We're atheists.'

'What now?' the man asks.

'Atheists.'

The man frowns gently, adopting a reflective manner. 'Forgive me, I am not familiar with that religion? Are you of Christ our Lord and Saviour?'

'Aye.'

'No! We're non-believers. Atheists.'

'Oh, my child,' the man says softly. 'There is only one path to redemption.'

'Tell him,' she says, nodding at Harry. 'He needs bloody redeeming.'

'*UNKNOWN ADULT FEMALE. THE USE OF REVOLTING, ABUSIVE OR INSULTING WORDS IS PROHIBITED IN THIS PUBLIC PLACE.*'

'Oh now, such strong words from one of Christ's own children.'

'We're busy. Go away.'

'We are all busy, my child. We are all rushing to gather possessions and baubles that glitter to fill our empty voids where there should be only love and the word of our Lord Christ the Saviour . . .'

'No, we're actually busy guarding our time machine.'

Harry tuts, shaking his head at Emily.

'We all need time. Yes. Yes, we all need a time machine to give us more, when all we really need is love in our hearts to hear the word of God our Saviour. They say Affa himself was a believer. They say Affa himself met our Lord and took that word to overthrow the oppressors and lead us to righteous—'

'He didn't.'

'What now?'

'He really didn't,' Emily says. 'He was the lead agent from the British Secret Service that Harry and I killed in one-two-six, but we think they went back and got him again.'

The man blinks, confusion spreading over his face as he refocusses to bring the conversation back. 'Yes, my child. We all want Affa to come back. Affa is in all our hearts for following the word of God our Saviour who he met on the mound and they broke bread to pray together and—'

'Have you met him? I've met him. Alpha's a good agent but he's not God and Harry kicked the shit out of him so . . .'

'UNKNOWN ADULT FEMALE. THE USE OF REVOLTING, ABUSIVE OR INSULTING WORDS IS PROHIBITED IN THIS PUBLIC PLACE.'

'You are right, my child. Affa is not God. God is God. God is love and forgiveness. God is within us all . . .'

'Okay,' Emily says, 'can I ask you a question?'

'But of course,' the man says piously, bobbing his head at Emily.

'So let's say two friends get drunk together one night, right?'

'Ach, Emily.'

'And they have a bit too much to drink and they end up going upstairs and having just the best sex ever. Like, imagine the best sex ever, but better than that. I mean steamy, really steamy, like clothes off, kissing, licking . . . hot hands and sweating bodies all grinding and . . .'

The man coughs into his hand, listening intently. 'I understand. Go on, my child.'

'I mean this is the best sex you could imagine. His hands are all over her body. He's strong but gentle and she's so turned on, really, really turned on . . . Can you imagine that?'

'I can, my child,' he whispers earnestly, leaning in to listen.

'And they even orgasm at the same time. Imagine that? Then they go back to his room and they do it again.'

'Again?' the man asks.

'Again?' Harry asks, staring at Emily.

'Two more times,' Emily says, holding two fingers up.

'Two more times you say,' the man asks breathlessly.

'Two?' Harry asks, rubbing a hand through his beard. 'I remember the first but not the other two . . .'

'Oh, you should remember,' she says, not looking away from the man. 'Can you imagine all of that?'

'I can,' the man says.

'Then what happens the next day when the man is a total dick?'

'*UNKNOWN ADULT FEMALE. THE USE OF REVOLTING, ABUSIVE OR INSULTING WORDS IS PROHIBITED IN THIS PUBLIC PLACE.*'

'Seriously? Dick isn't swearing.'

'*UNKNOWN ADULT FEMALE. THE USE OF REVOLTING, ABUSIVE OR INSULTING WORDS IS PROHIBITED IN THIS PUBLIC PLACE.*'

'It is,' the man says.

'Wow, strict times,' Emily says. 'Anyway, that's my story. What about it?'

'Well now,' the man says. 'Three times you say?'

'Three times,' Emily says.

'Drunk you say?'

'Drunk,' Emily says.

'I'd say the man must show honour and decency. These are modern times and promiscuity is rife, but the sin is in the intent, my child. Does the man have genuine regard for the woman?'

'Er . . .' Emily says, not expecting the answer.

'Aye, he does,' Harry says.

'Would the man ever harm the woman?'

'Not a hair on her head.'

'Would the man stand by the woman in times of peril and darkness?'

225

'Aye, he has and he would.'

'Does the man love the woman . . .'

Harry stares down at Emily, seeing her blush.

'Look just sod off,' Emily snaps.

'I will pray for you both,' the man says, making the sign of the cross while backing away with a little bow.

Emily stares out at the street. Watching. Assessing. Scanning and looking for threat and risk while her cheeks burn and her hands feel strange hanging down at her sides. She goes to fold her arms and stops midway, not knowing what to do with them.

'Emily . . .'

'Don't,' she snaps. 'Watch your side.'

◆　◆　◆

'So nice,' Safa says. 'Harry will love these. Coffee's a bit shit though. Got a weird taste, like chemicals or something . . .'

'I'm guessing it's probably synthetic,' Ben says. 'It feels hot here and I noticed yesterday in Hyde Park and the plaza that the heat is more like Italy, which I'm guessing is global warming. Beef cattle was said to be a major contributor to global warming and if locusts are being served then it suggests either a cessation of meat-eating or a viable alternative to a sustainable source of protein. They were talking about locusts and insects as food in our time, and if it's getting hotter this far north of the equator then maybe something messed up the plantations growing the coffee beans. A lack of water or a change in environmental conditions could do it. Plants get diseases too – could be anything – so a synthetic derivative would plug the gap in the market . . . Either that or it's just cheap coffee.'

Miri sips from her cup, watching him intently while inwardly admiring the ease with which he connects the dots.

'How was it?' Jerry asks, sweeping from the building with the well-practised air of making sure people don't leg it without paying while pretending to be concerned over their enjoyment of the food. 'Enjoy it, did you? Like the locusts?'

'Very nice,' Ben says. 'Is that coffee synthetic?'

'Eh?' Jerry asks, blanching in response. 'Where you from then? Course it's synthetic. What are you, the coffee police? Haha! We don't touch the natural stuff here. Oh no. No, no, Affa. No natural coffee here. Oleg? We don't do natural here, do we?'

'NO.'

'I was just asking,' Ben says quickly. 'It was very nice . . .'

'I got's to say that,' Jerry says, sidling closer to Ben with a hushed tone. 'You want some of the real stuff, do you? How much you want? Enough for a cup in the morning? We roasted them last night. Gorgeous they are. Proper Arabica. Got a source from a mate. Know what I mean? Tell you what. You get Ria to drop me a couple of them claws in and you can have a half kilo. How about that?' He steps away to the table, grabbing the plates and cups to load onto a large hovering tray. 'Natural coffee! Cor, do me a favour, Affa. We don't peddle that stuff here . . . How you paying today, Affa? Got a tourist chip, have ya?'

'Er, yeah, a credit chip . . .'

'Lovely stuff,' Jerry says, whipping it from Ben's hand and holding it up to his eye. He takes on that far-away look they saw so many times yesterday then blinks back to focus. 'All done,' he beams, handing the card back. 'Hang on here,' he whispers, rushing out of sight into the building.

'We know how the credit chip works then . . .' Ben starts to say as the waiter bustles back out, grinning and laughing. 'So you follow the road and find old Ruben up the way.' He stops next to Ben, placing one hand on his shoulder and leaning close as though to explain directions while pressing a small paper bag into Ben's hand. 'Enough for the morning,' he whispers. 'Little taster, yeah? Get me some claws and I'll get half a K . . . Give Ria our regards. Bye then, Affas! Best locusts in London, yeah? All in the sauce . . .'

He walks off, striding out into the street to intercept the next potential customers as Ben, Miri and Safa head back up towards the junction, with Ben looking round guiltily while pushing the baggie into his pocket. 'Did we just do a drug deal?' he whispers.

'Feels like it,' Safa says, glancing back to wave at the waiter. 'Ria's selling claws? That's funny as anything.'

'It is not funny, Miss Patel. It is a misuse of the device and something that will be stopped.'

'Why?' Ben asks, seeing the grim expression on Miri's face.

'The girl is accessing points of time for her own use,' Miri says tightly. 'What if someone carbon dates those claws?'

'Or,' Ben says in a voice dropping several notches, 'she was getting by and using what she had to survive . . . This isn't our history, Miri. This isn't our timeline.'

'Discuss later,' Miri says, ending the conversation abruptly as they walk back into the bedlam of the main road.

There is a crowd ahead, blocking the side of the road as people stop and gather to look inside one of the stores: the Nazi jacket on proud display in the window. It looks surreal. They only saw it a few days ago. The same jacket that Harry ripped open to pull the papers from. The same blood stains from the bullet entry wounds from Emily shooting him.

'Misuse,' Miri states firmly.

'Sure,' Ben says, shaking his head. 'Good luck to her.'

'At least we didn't have to worry about the body,' Safa muses, going ahead of the other two to push through the door into the book store.

◆ ◆ ◆

Silence in the alley. Harry leaning on one side. Emily on the other. Nobody pays them any attention. This is a city full of weird and wonderful folk, so two more only add to the backdrop of chaos.

Harry thinks back, trying to remember the other two times. She said three times. He could remember the first above the bar but not the other two, but now she's said it, and now he thinks about it, so he gains flashes of memory, of sensations, sounds, feelings and things happening in his room in the bunker. Emily on top. Him on top. Against the door? Did that happen? Something in his mind about being outside too on the grass. When did they go outside?

'Did we go outside?'

'I'm not talking to you,' she replies stiffly.

He rubs a hand through his beard, watching people as they pass by and trying to remember while glancing, every now and then, at Emily as though to try and jog his memory.

'Yes,' she says after a few minutes of silence. 'On the grass.'

'Oh.'

The silence comes back and he frowns, still thinking hard and not seeing the glances, every now and then, from Emily as she looks at him.

'And in the portal room.'

'Eh?' he asks.

'The portal room,' she says without looking at him. 'Our legs were in the bunker but our heads were in Rio.'

'Oh.'

'It was funny at the time.'

He thinks harder. Sighing and shaking his head.

'And the main room on the big table.'

'The big table, you say?'

'Then in your room against the door.'

'Ach.'

'Then in your bed.'

'I see.'

'Then again in your bed.'

'Ach.'

'But, hey, forget it. Just a bad night, yeah?'

'Ah now, miss.'

'They're back,' Emily says, pushing off the wall at the sight of Safa, Ben and Miri coming through the crowd. 'And my name is Emily.'

'Thousand quid,' Safa says, looking at them both. 'Thousand quid for two books. Unbelievable. We had locusts and this weird crappy coffee. Harry, you'll love locusts. Anything here?'

'Nowt,' Harry says. 'A religious man talking about god.'

'An agent?' Miri asks sharply.

'No, Miri, just a weirdo,' Emily says quietly.

'Everything okay?' Ben asks, detecting the atmosphere between them.

'Aye,' Harry says, avoiding looking at him.

'Fine,' Emily says. 'Er, did you get food and clothes?' She spots their empty hands and looks quizzically from one to the next.

'I just said,' Safa replies. 'We spent all the money on two bloody books.'

'We need supplies,' Emily says.

'We've got the sword and helmet. We'll bring them back and trade,' Ben says.

'Or a book . . . or a claw . . . or maybe a dinosaur,' Safa says with a grin. 'Ria's been selling our bunker off bit by bit . . .'

Twenty-Two

Bertie's Island

A gorgeous warm evening and Ben looks up at Miri lighting a cigarette, then goes back to the book open on the table in front of him. A quiet afternoon of reading the history books. Drinking coffee, eating fruit and stopping now and then to look out at Safa, Emily and Harry swimming in the sea with Malcolm and Konrad fishing on the shore.

'Stop bloody smoking!' the doctor shouts from his hammock.

'Go back to being dead,' Miri mutters, making Ben snort a laugh. It was the first thing they did on returning from Lambeth-not-Lambeth. An application of thought given to resolve a problem because Safa told them, very clearly and very honestly, that she would be extracting Doctor John Watson and there was no hope in hell anyone would be stopping her.

Ben explained his thoughts to Miri. 'Bertie went from the island timeline to the bunker timeline to extract Ria and brought her back into the island timeline. If we extracted the doc before Bertie got Ria then there wouldn't be a Ria, but we're not. We're extracting the doc *after* Ria was extracted. She's now detached from the original bunker timeline.

The fact she chose to go back there isn't relevant. So yes, it's safe to get the doc back and it will not make Ria cease to exist.'

Even Miri struggled on that one for a few minutes, which resulted in a whiteboard from Bertie's shack being brought out to help give visual aid as Ben explained it again.

It was during that lengthy and very in-depth discussion that Safa snuck into the shack, set the portal, went into the bunker, rescued the doctor just seconds before the big female Diplodocus crashed through the roof and brought the confused chap back to the island still holding the tea he had just made.

'So there,' Ben said, prodding the whiteboard full of diagrams.

'Evening,' the doc said, strolling over.

'Evening,' Ben said in greeting before turning back to Miri for a full five seconds before the penny dropped. 'What the fuck, Safa!'

Now they read the history books to understand the changes made and how they altered the world they knew. It's all there too. Laid out in the succinct way of fact and proven conjecture that history books have, and as Ben reaches the last few pages of the second book so a cold drip on the back of his neck makes him yelp and twist round to a soaking wet Safa fresh from the sea standing behind him and he finds himself captivated by the way the water runs over her skin, made darker from the sun, and between the mounds of her breasts hidden under her sports bra.

She plonks down next to him, sending a shower of seawater over Miri's history book. 'I want to go to Paris.'

'What?' Ben asks, blinking at her.

'Paris. It's meant to be romantic.'

'What the fuck? Are you Safa?'

'I'm still a woman, Ben,' she says as Emily and Harry walk over from swimming. 'Ben's taking me to Paris later for kissing and hand holding.'

'Am I?' Ben asks.

'That's nice,' Emily says, flopping down next to Safa and sending another shower of seawater over Miri's book. 'Make sure you don't get drunk and end up . . .'

'Oh, give it a rest, Emily,' Ben groans.

'How is it?' Harry asks, looking from Ben to Miri. 'Read it all?'

'Yeah, I think so,' Ben says.

'And?' Safa asks. 'No, hang on . . . whatever you're going to say, cut it in half then half again then say it . . .'

'I don't overexplain things.'

'You do,' Emily says.

'Aye.'

'Well, sod off then. Ask Miri.'

'One twenty-six AD. Romans got killed. Bad guys did it. Changed stuff but mostly it was okay,' Miri says with the perfect timing of a rare joke.

'See!' Safa says, all of them laughing as Ben huffs. 'What about the other bit?'

'Nineteen forty-five. Bad guys drop a nuclear bomb on London,' Miri says.

'Bit more to it than that,' Ben says. 'For instance, a chap called Herr Weber was in charge of Nazi Germany's nuclear programme . . .'

'Did Hitler still happen then?' Emily asks.

'Don't ask questions,' Safa groans.

'Yeah, it's weird because by then it's really close to our own history. Like, for instance, some of our Prime Ministers didn't happen but some did. Churchill still happened, Stalin . . . Roosevelt . . . Anyway, the Nazis ditched the nuclear programme early on. They didn't see it had any worth, plus they killed nearly all of their Jewish physicists and in the first few years of the war they're pretty much winning . . .'

'Were they?'

'Sorry, Harry, but they were. Point is they don't build a nuclear bomb. By nineteen forty-five the Germans are losing badly. Russia are pounding them, the allies are bombing the shit out of Berlin, Hitler is hiding in his bunker, then a physicist called Herr Weber, who was on the original Nazi nuclear programme or whatever they called it, gets a visit from five men who *give him* an atomic bomb. There's a bit more to it than that obviously. He never learns who they are, but pretty much acts on his own volition with a few fervent Nazi units still committed to the cause. Five visits are made by these mysterious men and on the last visit they deliver the bomb, which is dropped on London. Now this is where it gets interesting . . . Later, when the war is over, everyone points the finger at America because they were the only country developing nuclear bombs at that time. America obviously deny it. They only had two operational bombs at that point. One was dropped on Hiroshima, but no second bomb was dropped on Nagasaki in their time. That means it was still *only* two nuclear bombs used during the Second World War: Hiroshima and London. I'm guessing that Alpha and his lot used their device to nick one from America after the war and used that. Long story short, they never actually prove or work out who did it. America deny ever losing a nuclear bomb, but then as the historians point out, which country in their right mind would ever admit to losing one? Herr Weber was killed on returning to the airfield after the bombing raid. So were all his men, apparently by a surprise Allied attack that was later confirmed by the Allies, who said they were given a tip-off about a high-ranking German official or something. Lots of conspiracy theories all over the place. Think nine eleven but with a nuclear bomb. Who really did it? That sort of thing.'

'Nine eleven?' Harry asks.

'Terrorist attack in New York,' Emily says. 'Brought down two famous buildings and everyone later thought it was the American government that did it.'

'Not everyone,' Safa says. 'I didn't.'

'Point right there,' Ben says. 'It created enough of a conspiracy theory to become a thing in history. Who did it and why? Not that any of it actually matters because the world gets on with living.'

'Germany still lost though, right?' Emily asks.

'God, yes,' Ben says enthusiastically. 'They could have dropped five nuclear bombs by then and they'd still lose, but what's really interesting when you read the books is the concept of . . .'

'Oh god, please stop, my ears are bleeding. What Miri said was all we needed. Nuclear bomb. Bad guys. Nineteen forty-five. Easy. So where do we start?' Safa asks.

'Dunno, ask Miri,' Ben says sulkily.

'We start at one twenty-six AD first thing in the morning,' Miri says.

'Bingo,' Safa says, pointing at Miri. 'I'm liking you more and more. Cheer up, egghead, you're still sexy,' she says, kissing Ben's cheek before pushing off. 'Come for a swim you nerd . . .'

◆　◆　◆

126 AD

'Bit bloody cold on the old chap though,' Bravo says, rubbing his hands together while Charlie, Echo and Delta snort quiet laughs that blast mists of air from their mouths and noses . 'I think he might withdraw inside like a tortoise,' Bravo adds, reaching down theatrically to check his penis is still there.

'When do they invent trousers?' Charlie asks Rodney.

'Good question,' Bravo says. 'We should ask that nice filly Rodney works with in the history department. Eh, Delta? Mission for you, that is. Infiltrate the trouser secrets of the history department.'

'I knew it,' Emily whispers, nodding down the line at everyone else. 'I said it was them.'

'Ssshhhh,' Ben says.

'I said it,' Emily whispers, nudging Harry. 'I said it would be them.'

'Who's that other one with them?' Safa whispers.

'I don't bloody know, Safa,' Ben whispers. 'I'm watching the same thing as you . . .'

'Wish they'd hurry up. I hate the cold,' Safa says.

'When you've been in a war with cold.'

'Shush,' Ben says again. 'They'll hear us.'

'So?' Safa asks. 'Why don't we just go round and get in their portal to their base and . . .'

'Because we're gathering information for now,' Ben groans softly, dropping his face into his hands while lying prone on the freezing snow-covered ground on a bank a hundred metres into the thicket of trees. 'And this is them in the past, not the them now.'

'Confusing,' Safa mumbles.

'It is cold though,' Emily whispers, leaning forward to look past Harry at Ben and Safa.

'Oh my god,' Ben groans again. 'Go back then . . . Me and Harry will watch.'

'Harry and I,' Emily says.

'Me and you?' Harry asks her.

'No, I was correcting Ben's English,' Emily whispers. 'I'm not watching with you. You'll just get me drunk and have sex with me again and . . .'

'Ach, enough now,' Harry says as Ben drops his face into the snow.

'Joking,' Emily says, nudging Harry with her elbow, then looking down the bank to the six men grouped together on the path below them. 'Not joking,' she whispers a few seconds later.

'Stop it,' Ben whispers at her.

'Don't tell me to stop it,' she whispers back at him. 'Why isn't Miri here anyway?'

'I told you,' Ben whispers, rubbing the snow from his face. 'The cold hurts her shrapnel wounds . . . Alpha's moving out,' he says quickly, pointing down to the men on the path.

'Marching,' Harry whispers knowingly at the sound coming through the trees. 'Marching that is . . . Ben, that's marching . . .'

'I think we've got that now,' Emily whispers.

They stay silent, craning necks to try and glimpse through the trees to the path and gaining snatches of views of men walking in formation.

'I was expecting a bit more, to be honest,' Emily whispers.

'Me too,' Safa says. 'Not like the movies, are they? Bit shit really.'

'That's what I think,' Emily whispers back agreeably.

Ben and Harry don't think so. What they see are Roman soldiers. Real Roman soldiers. They look a bit grotty and grim but still, it's an actual Roman army unit with shields.

The four watch the action play out, with two soldiers running at Alpha and Bravo, and each feels the tightening in their guts at seeing a dozen people die in front of them. The detachment from reality is one thing, but these are still real men suffering awful injuries. They see Charlie, Delta and Echo swarm in from the sides and rear and, despite the Roman unit having superior numbers, they are taken down quickly and brutally until one remains.

'ALPHA . . .' Echo shouts. 'Last one.'

'There it is,' Ben whispers to himself. He watches as Alpha shouts and motions for the last soldier to go.

They stay hidden as the agents walk down the bank to the younger one who ran off before the killing started now bent over and puking. A glint of a green shimmering light further back in the tree line that the men walk towards and a minute later the green shuts off.

'That was grim,' Safa says, getting to her feet. The others rise up, shivering and cold from only wearing the clothes they went to London in. 'You need to go down?' she asks Ben.

'Yeah,' he says. 'Quick look?'

They head down the bank, slipping and sliding through the snow until they reach the path, with pistols held ready in double-handed grips.

Ben drops to pick a fallen sword up in the same way Bravo did a few minutes ago. 'Fuck me . . .' He hefts it a few times, partly disgusted by the loss of life and partly in awe at handling a real Roman sword. 'Grab a helmet, Harry . . .'

'We're not nicking stuff,' Safa says firmly, turning from her position of watching the direction the agents went.

'We can trade it and get a credit chip.'

'I said no,' Safa says, her tone hardening. 'There's a word for people who nick from war dead.'

'What word?' Emily asks.

'Fucking arseholes,' Safa says.

'Um, so that's, like, two words . . . Actually it's more like three . . .' Emily points out.

'Ben, I said we're not . . .'

'We need money, a sword and a helmet. That's it. We're not touching personal effects . . . I don't like doing it, Safa,' Ben says, looking across to a grim-faced Harry holding one of the dull metal helmets. 'Ah, you know what, fair one . . . we'll leave it then,' he adds at seeing Safa's expression.

'No,' she says slowly, quietly. 'No, I get it . . .'

'If it means that much to you,' Ben says, lowering the sword down to rest next to the fallen soldier.

'Just a sword and helmet,' Harry says. 'We took from the Germans . . . They took from us . . . It's war.'

A groan silences them. A low throaty noise from a throat struggling to draw air.

'Blimey,' Harry says, striding over to a Roman soldier. 'He's alive . . .'

'Shit.' Ben rushes over with the other two as the soldier opens his eyes to stare up. He doesn't focus on them, he doesn't even seem to see them, but blinks and gargles with frothy pink saliva spilling from his mouth as his life blood seeps from the slashes on his body made by surgically sharp blades.

'He's done for,' Harry says quietly, lowering to the man's side. 'Got minutes at the most . . .' He reaches out to draw the man up onto his lap. Cradling his head, then reaching over to grasp his hand. 'Eh, son, you're okay now . . . shush . . . easy now . . .'

The soldier finally blinks to see Harry smiling down at him with warmth in his eyes. He tries to speak, sounding lost words from a language unknown in a voice rasping and broken.

'I know,' Harry says deeply, wiping blood from the man's face and squeezing his hand. 'Emily? You'll be saying nice words to the wee man now.'

'God, yeah, of course,' Emily says, dropping at the soldier's side. She smiles at him, seeing the focus when he looks at her, and pushes a hand across his brow as he murmurs with tears falling down his cheeks. 'It's okay, you'll be okay . . . shush now . . .'

'Aye, there's a good lad,' Harry rumbles. Emily sees the calmness spread through the soldier as that aura from Harry she knows so well reaches out. Everything is okay when Harry says it is. The whole world is okay. Death is okay. There is no pain now, no suffering. 'Good lad. You say your prayers now, son . . .'

'It's okay,' Emily says, smoothing her hand over his cheeks. The soldier looks at her. Pain in his eyes and he's young too. Maybe twenty-two, twenty-three at the most. Stubble on his jaw and his skin tone and hair colour speak of heritage from a Mediterranean country. He must be far from home in a cold, unforgiving place and now dying for something he doesn't understand. She smiles softly, stroking his cheeks as his eyes start to flutter heavily.

'Go in peace, lad . . . You've done your bit now . . .' Harry speaks gently, using the back of his hand to wipe the blood from the dying man's lips.

Safa watches the tree line, but listens intently while Ben holds back out of sight from the dying man and looks down at the sword in his hand.

It takes another few minutes, but the soldier slips away cradled and held by strangers who give warmth and comfort in his passing.

'Done,' Harry says, gently lowering the soldier down. He sighs heavily, grabs the helmet he was holding and rises to his feet. 'Thank you,' he says to Emily.

'No, it's . . . it's fine,' Emily says.

A moment of silence hangs between them.

'Harry, leave the helmet,' Ben says, dropping the sword. 'Safa's right . . .'

'She's not,' Harry says, stooping to grab the sword. 'The lad's dead . . . These are things . . . They're not life . . . You got enough information?'

'Yeah,' Ben says quietly. 'We'll go back.'

◆ ◆ ◆

Alpha watches them go. The pistol held down at his right side and not a sound he makes as the four clamber back up the bank. He searches again for sight of their portal, but sees none, but then he didn't see them either until they broke cover and came down.

He waits for several minutes until the winter air takes on that utter silence of deep cold where there is a void of life and nature in the frozen landscape. Then he waits minutes longer because he is an agent and this is the level he works at. To wait and watch. To see and not be seen.

Alpha finally moves out from his position and walks silently through the undergrowth to once more climb up and onto the track. It felt very strange watching himself and the others, and it felt stranger still seeing himself in action like that. He almost became lost in the technical details of the kills.

He looks at the soldiers as though seeing them for the first time, taking in their youth and the blueness already creeping into their skin from the loss of blood and heat from their rapidly cooling corpses.

He stops at the one they cradled and holds still while thinking. Sound travels well in the silence of winter and he heard every word they said. He goes over it now, processing the new information gained.

Emily Rose. He shakes his head at the thought of it. Tango Two was one of them, but she is very clearly holding her own position in their team.

He has to go. He knows that, and he takes a last slow look round before setting off down the bank and back through the undergrowth to the green light that he steps through to see Mother walking through the door of the darkened portal room bathed only by the shimmering green and the low lights of the complex at night.

'Mother,' he says, nodding a respectful greeting without showing a flicker of surprise.

'On your own?' she asks.

'Wanted to check something,' he says in a business-like fashion.

She folds her arms with a projection of expectation.

'Would you like me to say what?' he asks, moving past her to the control panel to switch off the portal, aware of her rotating to track him and even more aware that every setting put into the system is stored. 'I went back to the Roman patrol . . . I wanted to see the positions and actions of Charlie, Delta and Echo when they split from Bravo and me on the track and before we commenced the attack.' The green portal shuts off as he works the controls.

'You have concerns?' she asks.

'None,' he says instantly. 'But it never hurts to be sure . . . They stayed silent, no conversations, no concerns at all. I know they're sleeping or in their quarters now so I took the chance to go and see without them knowing.'

'Good,' she says, staring at him. 'Any sign of our friends yet?'

'Not yet,' he says, only now aware of the fact he knew he was going to lie the second he saw her in the portal room. He stays calm and controlled, shifting into work-mode, of hiding every reaction, of showing only what needs to be shown.

'You don't seem yourself,' she says suddenly, with a reminder who he is dealing with and that her instincts are dangerously sharp.

'I'm fine,' he says carefully, offering a quick glance. 'I think we're all feeling the strain of waiting.'

She walks closer, examining his features closely. 'You should be fine, Alpha. You're getting fucked every night by our historian. How is that for you anyway? Hmmm? Enjoying it, are you?'

'Do you want me to stop seeing her?' he asks plainly.

'God no, you carry on your sordid little affair. I don't care what you do. I only care about winning. This is a mission, Alpha. This is a job.'

'Yes, Mother.'

'Goodnight.' She turns to walk off. 'Have fun with your little slut . . .' she adds before pushing through the door.

He fights to keep a neutral manner because he knows she will check the camera feed. He completes the checks once again to show what a thorough and methodical agent he is. He walks out into the corridor and walks slowly through to the large mess room and pauses to look round then on to the briefing room, peering inside as though to check. He goes on through the complex, visually examining rooms and showing Mother what a thorough and methodical agent he is.

He walks slowly through the corridor feeding to the living quarters, hearing the voices of people talking in their rooms. Holo movies playing, music and even the rhythmic grunt of sexual intercourse underway. People living lives. People existing.

'I'm awake,' Kate says sleepily, sitting up to try and look awake while peering out through half-asleep eyes. 'I'm not.' She waves a hand and crumples back down into his bed. 'You were gone for ages,' she murmurs. 'Come to bed now and stop being all agenty . . .'

'I am,' he says, undressing quickly. He climbs in to feel the warmth made by her body within the sheets, the pressure of her form, and inhales the scent of her hair and body.

'Do you like it?' she asks, peering up at him. 'It's the perfume you got from that store in America.'

'It's nice,' he says.

'It's divine,' she says, rolling onto her back to stretch her arms above her head with a languorous groan. 'You okay?' she asks, seeing his quiet, pensive look.

'Fine,' he says, easing down to curl into her as she rolls over.

'Where did you go?' she asks. 'Spoon me properly . . .'

'I'm trying . . .'

'Try harder. That's better . . . What were you saying?'

'You asked me where I went.'

'Did I? That's nice,' she murmurs. 'Do tell me . . .'

He wants to tell her. He wants to tell her what he saw and the kindness Harry and Emily showed to the young soldier. He wants to tell her he lied to Mother and something is changing inside him and they should go and just disappear into time, because everything they are doing is flawed and broken and wrong. It can't be fixed. None of it can be fixed. Maggie Sanderson can stop them detonating that bomb, but Mother will escalate and on it will go until either one side is caught and trapped or everyone is dead. He wants to ask her what the song was he heard playing as he walked through the complex because he never really had an interest in music before. He wants to say many things and tell her his real name, but he stares into the darkness of his room and listens with an expert ear to the changes in her breathing that tell him she is asleep and so he says nothing because to say anything would be dangerous for both of them.

Instead, he wonders where in time and space Maggie and her team are, what they are doing and if the lives they have are so much different, and he wonders why the hell he didn't tell Mother he saw them.

Twenty-Three

The Complex

Alpha walks out from his private quarters and through the corridors, thinking of last night and seeing Ben, Emily, Safa and Harry on the track, then after and the way Mother spoke to him.

Why did he lie? He had the element of surprise too; he could have attacked them when they were giving aid to the Roman soldier and stood a strong chance of taking them out. He could have got through their portal to Maggie. He felt sure it was them now and not a memory of them, so why didn't he react? Why did he lie?

'Morning.' A worker passes him in the corridor. He lifts his chin in greeting, noting the dull eyes of the people he passes and the awful, heavy mood now permeating the place. It's like a pressure cooker in here and getting worse by the day.

It's over seven weeks since they arrived and two weeks since they dropped the bomb in London, but if Maggie's team have now seen 126 AD then they'll be moving on to investigating the next change. Time is running out. They'll show soon and if they don't then Mother will do something else.

He knocks on her door to report for the day, pausing for her awful biting voice telling him to enter and goes in, nodding a respectful greeting at the cold bitch already parked behind her desk; either that or she's been there all night.

'Good night?' she asks in a light tone that doesn't match the seething violence behind her eyes. 'Have a nice fuck?'

'Any changes?' he asks politely.

'Oh my,' Mother says with ice dripping from her tongue. 'Did I just offend the great Alpha? Are you grumpy today? What happened? Did she spit instead of swallow?'

A switch in his head with a smooth transition and he smiles with humour, chuckling at her words. 'She was asleep when I went in,' he says ruefully. This is a part now. This is a role. This is Siberia or one of the countless other legends he has held. Be the legend. Live it. Believe it and give nothing away.

'So? You're Alpha. Wake her up. Who is she going to complain to? Me?'

'I'll keep that in mind,' he says with a glint in his eye. 'I'll go over the footage for Cavendish Manor with my team today. We need to push this I think. It's taking too long.'

'It was taking too long six fucking weeks ago,' she says, spitting the words out as her face contorts with barely suppressed rage that she struggles to control. 'I've got a plan,' she says, giving him a sudden ice-cold smile.

'Plan?' he asks.

'Something bigger,' she whispers. 'Now fuck off,' she snaps, instantly losing interest.

He goes out as he entered, professionally and showing no response to her increasingly hostile tone.

He doesn't wait for a reply at the next door he knocks on. He is Alpha. Only Mother is above him in this place. He walks in, nodding once to the team of the IT department, who fall silent as he enters. 'Do you have it ready?'

'Sir.' A technician rushes forward holding a tablet. 'All on there, sir.'

'Alpha, not sir.'

'Sorry, Alpha . . . sir . . .'

He walks out as he entered. Professionally and like the leader of men that he is. With the tablet in hand he heads through to the next door and again knocks and walks in.

'Well hello, sailor.' Kate beams, spinning round in her chair to look at him.

'Morning,' he says, glancing round. 'Rodney?'

'Gone to the gym. He wants to get all buffed up like you . . . Erm . . . have you seen Mother yet?'

'Just saw her. Why?' he asks, narrowing his eyes as a signal for her to be careful what she says.

'She asked for hourly checks,' she says plainly.

'Hourly?' Alpha asks.

'Hourly,' she says. 'Mother has requested we undertake hourly checks on the timeline comparison software to ensure we have early identification of any changes.' She reels off the order from memory.

'Right, that's a good idea,' Alpha says.

'Absolutely,' she replies, holding his eye contact. 'Meet for lunch?'

'Lunch will be great,' he says, still holding that eye contact.

He leans in to kiss her cheek with an action that makes her balk in response. He never shows affection outside of his room. 'Talk later,' he whispers.

He walks out as he entered. Professionally and like the leader of men that he is with Kate staring after him.

'Aha, our leader doth enter. Good morning,' Bravo says in his rich voice as Alpha walks through into their work room.

'Anything going on?'

'Alas nothing, unless you count my impending chess game with Gunjeep as intelligence worthy of note.'

'I don't,' Alpha says bluntly. 'Mother has ordered hourly timeline comparison checks.'

'A grand idea,' Bravo booms as the other three look on in silence.

Alpha goes into his small office to sit down at the desk and thumbs the screen on the tablet. The first time he saw the footage from Cavendish Manor, it invoked a reaction and made him want to exact personal revenge, but something is changing within him that gives him the ability to peer in from the outside and gain a new perspective.

He finds a start point, presses an icon and places the tablet down to let the holo bloom out in the air, and there she is. Emily Rose, or Tango Two as she was then. In the chopper on the way to the deployment. He spots Bravo, Charlie, Delta and Echo from the camera mounted on his own tac-vest. Except the Alpha in this footage is not the Alpha who watches now.

'That bored, eh?' Bravo asks, strolling in through the door to see the footage, with that laconic relaxed air he always has and therein is the exact reason Alpha must hide his thoughts because if Mother knew he lied Bravo would execute him instantly, especially if he thought it would further his own career.

'Beats paperwork,' Alpha replies without looking up.

'Oh my, we look so young and carefree,' Bravo quips.

Alpha wants to watch it privately. He has purpose and a new view-point from which to see it, but he must be the legend. He must live it and believe it. 'Lads, if you're bored come and watch this. Might be something we've missed we can use,' he calls out. He is Alpha. He is the leader of men who is dedicated to his mission and his role.

Echo walks in. The quietest of the five but quietness is often linked with intelligence, and Alpha senses there might be a connection he can exploit with him. Charlie and Delta behind him, hovering by the door and sharing glances with a hint of humour in their eyes. They're becoming good mates, those two.

'What?' Alpha asks them both.

'We were thinking of going to the gym,' Delta says, eyeing the foot-age with an expression that suggests the last thing he wants to do is sit down and watch it all. 'If you don't need us, that is,' he adds quickly.

The instinct makes him want to agree and say *sure, go train*. He is Alpha though. He has to be the leader of men. 'We'll go through this first. Train after.'

'Sure,' Delta says, quickly masking any hint of disappointment.

Alpha waits for them to find perches and seats, then swipes to restart the footage, going back to the camera activation in the chopper and Tango Two staring back at him.

◆ ◆ ◆

'Everything okay?' Kate asks over the table in the canteen at lunch.

'Fine. You?'

'Fine.' She chews thoughtfully for a second. 'Got some gossip if you want it? Or should I say *intelligence*,' she adds with a wink.

'Yeah, sure.'

'What's wrong?'

'Nothing.'

'Doesn't look like it,' she says quietly, staring down at her food. 'Is it me?'

'No,' he says quickly, forcing himself to sit up straight and be Alpha. He looks round, spotting the quiet conversations going on, the whispered talks, the heads lowered and huddled together and the urge to leave comes back. The need to be away from here. This place is making his skin crawl. He clears his mind, focussing on the now. He has to maintain cover until he figures a way out. 'You go to twenty ninety-five every hour?' he asks in an attempt to make conversation.

'Oh, don't,' she says with a groan. 'Might as well stay there. I don't mind and Rodney's okay with it but what a ball-ache going every hour.'

'Where do you go?'

'University in London. Come and see,' she says quietly.

'See what?'

'How we do it. You should really, you're Alpha. You should, like, know everything . . . and, er . . . we go at night too. I mean it's night there when we go . . .'

'Yeah, I get it,' he says with a smile.

'So,' she says, letting the word hang. 'Dark offices . . . desks . . . nudge nudge, wink wink, say no more, Mr Alpha, sir . . . not having sex on a desk at all. Oh no . . .' Something in her eyes catches his attention more than the offer of sex, a seriousness hidden behind the playful manner.

'You're right,' he says officiously. 'I am Alpha. I should know these things.'

'Totally,' she says, nodding eagerly at him. 'Finished?' she asks, looking at his still full plate of food.

'Yes,' he says.

'Me too,' she says, putting her cutlery down next to her own still full plate. 'Oh wow, lunch goes fast . . . We should totally go and do the hourly check that is required for the safety of the world.'

'Agreed,' he says. 'Portal room, two minutes?'

'Make it one,' she says, grabbing his plate to take back as he walks off.

'Set the portal for the hourly check,' he orders, walking into the portal room.

'Umpghgh,' the duty technician says, trying to hide the sandwich behind her back.

'Don't eat in here,' Alpha says, giving her a look. 'Go outside and finish it, I can set up.'

'Shorry, Alpha,' she says, covering her mouth. 'Wash sshho hungry.'

'Out,' he orders, 'before Gunjeep catches you.'

'Yesh, Alpha . . . Shorry, Alpha . . .' She rushes out as Kate comes in, staring at the technician covering her mouth.

'Did you punch her in the gob?'

'What? No! She was trying to hide the food in her mouth.'

'Oh . . . oh, I thought . . . Haha! I'm such a twat.'

'Done,' he says.

The green light shimmers into existence as he draws a pistol from his holster, checking the magazine and making the sidearm ready.

'So hot when you do that.'

'I am the lead agent for the British Secret Service. Your familiarity is not appropriate.'

'You should, like, spank me for it . . .'

'I'll go first,' he says, walking towards the portal.

'I'm coming right behind you . . . Get it? Cumming?'

'Jesus,' he mutters, and steps through into the dark interior of a large office filled with wooden desks and lined with bookshelves. A place of study and learning. A place of advanced education and his mouth finds hers the second she comes through with a raw hunger that makes her flinch for the most fleeting of seconds before she pushes into him. It can't happen fast enough. He lifts her up onto one of the desks, then tugs down her trousers and knickers, while she works his zipper.

'Your gun's in my hip,' she gasps.

'That's not my gun . . .'

'You dirty man.' She snorts a laugh as he slides the pistol out to lay on the desk and keeps on thrusting. 'Kiss me . . .'

It's raw, hard and with an explosion of emotional need. A desire that overcomes and makes him take a risk he would never have contemplated before and it only makes his feelings for her grow deeper. He comes hard, thrusting into her as she gasps and bites his ear lobe.

'I love you,' she whispers. 'Oh my god. I love you . . . Say it back . . . Say it back . . .'

'I love you . . .'

'You'd better mean it . . . Keep going, I'm coming . . . oh god . . . oh god . . . Say it again . . .'

He does say it again. He says it again while she orgasms and clings on to his hard body. Then it's done. Over. And the emotions morph and transmute from lust to care and gentle love, to kissing and holding and breathing in each other.

'What's going on?' she whispers, her mouth pressed to his ear.

'You tell me,' he whispers back. 'What are people whispering about?'

'Don't ask me that.'

'Tell me.'

'No.'

'Kate, tell me.'

'Tell me your name. Tell me who you are.'

'Joe Edwards. My name is Joe Edwards. I'm forty-one years old.'

'Are you?' she asks, pulling back to look at him. 'You really don't look forty-one.'

'Tell me,' he says, staring into her eyes.

'Why? So you can kill them? I'm not doing that, Alpha . . . Joe . . . Alpha . . . Joe sounds wrong.'

He smiles, chuckling at the way she speaks and the expressions that flitter across her face. 'I'm called Alfie during missions sometimes.'

'Alfie? I like Alfie. I can do Alfie.'

'Tell me.'

She bites her bottom lip, fear in her eyes as she searches his. 'They're bloody heroes,' she blurts quietly. 'None of us can understand it. Ben Ryder? Harry Madden? Are you joking? Safa Patel? They're not terrorists. Emily Rose gave the entire world the finger and chose to go over to their side. We don't understand it . . .' She trails off quickly, suddenly fearful and worried as she pushes him away and drops from the desk to start pulling her clothes back on. 'I didn't say that.'

'Kate, it's . . .'

'We're all committed to the cause. Some just . . . just have a few questions, but it's fine. Everyone is working and . . .'

He lifts her head to look at him, holding the eye contact. 'It's okay. I won't do anything.'

'You're Alpha,' she says. 'I'm just a source for you, yeah? Get the gossip and a fuck on the side? It's fine. I love you. Do what you want to me.'

'Kate, I said I won't do anything. Is that what people are talking about?'

She hesitates again, glancing at the shimmering green light. 'None of it makes sense. Why would Maggie Sanderson kill us? We didn't do anything to her and the security footage in the complex being wiped doesn't make sense either. None of it does and none of us believe Mother will reset it all either. She's mad, like . . . like demented and screaming at everyone all the time . . . like paranoid and . . .' She goes suddenly quiet.

'I saw them,' he says, not knowing he was going to say it until the words came out.

'Who?' she asks.

'Them. Ben, Safa . . . I went back to one twenty-six AD last night.'

'Did you see Maggie?' she asks urgently.

'No, just Ben, Harry, Safa and Emily . . .'

'Oh my god. You saw them? They know about what we did? There's no changes though. I mean . . . the software system hasn't detected any . . . You've got to tell Moth— You've not told her, have you?'

He picks up the pistol from the desk, sliding it back into the holster while cursing himself for opening his mouth.

'Alpha? Alfie,' she says, trying to smile. 'What's going on? What did they do?'

'Nothing. They watched us killing those soldiers, then came down to look and I heard them talking. They looked sickened at what we'd done. One of the soldiers was still alive . . . They comforted him while he died. Harry Madden held him in his arms while Emily Rose stroked his face . . .'

'Oh my—' she holds a hand to her mouth, staring in horror.

'I don't think they attacked the complex and killed you all,' he says honestly, feeling wretched at voicing the thing he's held inside. He bites it down, forcing himself to be Alpha. 'I watched the footage of Cavendish Manor. The first time I saw it I only looked for what they did to us. I saw Bravo die, Charlie, Delta, Echo . . . I died. It's on camera. I saw Emily Rose shoot me through the head after Harry beat the shit out of me and Bravo.'

'Oh no, don't say that, don't you say that.' She cups his face, tears pushing out from her eyes.

'That's all I saw. Them winning and that wasn't right. We had to win. We're the British Secret Service. We're the good guys.'

'So they are bad then, they're terrorists . . .'

'No. No, they're not. They were doing all of that to get an autistic man and his family out of the house. They were losing but they used the time machine to come back and help themselves. They did all of that to get Bertram out, and his sister and family too. That's it. We had gunships and the army . . . I watched it again today, the footage I mean. You can see them doing everything possible to give Bertram a chance to get out. Sacrificing themselves . . . Putting themselves into harm's way again and again. Maggie Sanderson used her body to cover him. I've done my job a long time, I've killed many and the only people that do things like that are the ones that have a cause and a belief, and people like that don't storm into government facilities and kill innocent, unarmed scientists.'

'They're terrorists,' she asserts, trying to make the words sound forceful.

He shakes his head. 'One man's terrorist . . .'

'Is another's freedom fighter.' She finishes the words and closes her eyes.

'This is a vendetta for Mother to win against Maggie Sanderson. That's all it is,' he says, staring into the gloom of the room. 'She won't stop . . . Mother won't stop . . .' He sighs deeply, blowing air from his nose. 'You'd better run the check.'

'Yeah, of course.' She picks the tablet up from the side with shaky hands.

RR Haywood

'What does that do?' he asks.

'Accesses the interface here and downloads the entire history data to compare against our own . . . Any changes are flagged immediately.'

He watches her work, eyeing the tremble in her fingers. 'Don't be scared,' he says gently.

'I just orgasmed,' she quips, smiling at him. 'My legs are like rubber. It's downloading . . . So what now? I mean . . .'

'Nothing. Do nothing. I need to think.'

'About what? Er . . .' She looks at the portal again, then bites her lip while wincing. 'We can just go? You and me . . .'

'We'll have the other four best agents in the world coming after us.'

'Maybe they won't.'

'Bravo will. We do nothing for now.'

'Alpha, Maggie and her team will react soon. This software will pick it up. They already know about the Affa situation. Did you know the full extent of the Affa thing? I don't think I've told you all of it.'

'You said it became famous.'

'You did,' she says softly. 'Affa in this time is like Ben Ryder was in our time but multiplied by a thousand or a million.'

'Ironic,' he says bitterly.

'I don't think so.' She leans in to kiss his lips as the tablet vibrates. 'Done. We'll put it into our system and check. What do you want me to do? I'm with you, Alfie.'

'Do nothing. If they suspect anything we'll be executed. Bravo won't hesitate. Not a word. Don't act differently. Not even at night in our bed. Nothing.'

'Okay,' she says. 'Our bed? I like that. We'll have our own bed one day. Me and you somewhere in history . . . I'm with you, Alfie. No, Alfie doesn't sound right either. Alpha. You're Alpha.'

'I'm Alpha.'

'Oh wow, fancy another quickie?'

Twenty-Four

Berlin, Bundesstraße 2, 2 February 1945

'RUN . . . GET TO COVER . . . GET TO COVER.' The words are shouted all around him and he runs with his heart jack-hammering in his chest and adrenaline coursing through his veins and looks up at the hundreds of silhouetted planes in the sky and the puffs of smoke coming from the AA guns. He can even see small black objects falling from the planes that seem to tumble gently through the sky to hit the ground, which heaves and shakes from the constant detonations. A hand on his collar yanks him along and the face of an older man screams at him. 'DON'T GAWP . . . GET TO COVER . . .'

'Yes, sir,' Konrad mumbles, nodding in panic. He runs with the crowd down the street and, like them, he covers his head with his hands to protect it from flying debris, dodging and weaving through the old men and women, through the mothers clutching babies and the women running from the buildings.

'IDIOTS,' the old man shouts, making Konrad look over to see five men huddled under the archway of a railway line and to the last they adopt expressions of worry and angst. 'DON'T STAND THERE.' The man points at the archway above their heads as he runs past. 'THEY'RE BOMBING THE TRACKS . . .'

Konrad veers off quickly, weaving to get to the edge of the running crowd while turning to snatch more glimpses of the five men. He pretends to stumble and cries out in pain at his twisted ankle. He half expects someone to stop and try to help, but there are a thousand USAAF planes over Berlin and right now it's every person for themselves. A few seconds go by and through the running crowds he sees them. Then he sets off, running back the way he came, against the flow of people heading for the shelter at the end of the road.

Time and again he whacks into shoulders, trips and stumbles, but keeps going while constantly looking back at the five figures and also up at the hundreds of aircraft in the sky. The noise is terrible. The explosions are terrible. Everything is terrible. A bomb hits a building on his left side, blowing masonry and debris across the street. Women scream out in pain with shrill voices heard over the drone of the planes and the solid rattling of the distant AA guns.

He spots the uniforms coming towards him. A unit of German soldiers consisting of old men and young boys with a one-armed hard-faced leader in front clutching a Luger. His instinct is to hide or run the other way, but he rushes on and doesn't have to fake the fear on his face.

'GET TO COVER . . . GET TO COVER . . .' The soldiers shout the words over and over. The high-pitched tones of teenage boys and the hoarse voices of old men with red faces and grey whiskers. 'WRONG WAY,' one shouts at Konrad.

'YOU.' The one-armed officer points the Luger at Konrad. 'WRONG WAY . . . GET TO COVER . . .'

'My unit,' Konrad shouts, pulling papers from his pocket. 'MY UNIT IS THAT WAY . . . I HAD LEAVE FOR A DAY . . .'

The officer glances at Konrad, seeing the Germanic features and hearing the accent that is pure Berlin. The papers he waves are the right colour too. Bought from Mishka's store in Lambeth-not-Lambeth, although they detail that Heinrich Schmidt was declared deceased in 1944. That glance is enough, though, and the officer leaves, instantly forgetting about Konrad, who waits for a second before running on.

At the end of the street he turns sharply, ramming into a wooden door that yields to let him stagger into the darkened hallway. A flight of wooden stairs that he runs up and the muffled sounds from outside now seem sinister for the drop in volume. He goes up and up, panting harder and harder until finally reaching the top floor and staggering down the hallway to the end door that he bangs on and tries to call through while gasping for air.

The door opens. A big hairy hand comes out, grips his collar and takes him off his feet through the opening.

'It's . . . I . . . it . . . Oh my god . . .'

'Slow down,' Harry says gently, holding Konrad up. 'Take a breath.'

'You need to do some phys,' Safa tells him. 'How unfit are you?'

'Report,' Miri orders.

'Them,' Konrad blurts, sucking a huge lungful of air while grateful that Harry is still holding him up. 'Saw them . . . at the end . . . Arch . . .'

'Fucking hell, Kon,' Safa says. 'Breathe, for god's sake.'

'I saw them . . . at the end of the street under an arch. Alpha and the others.'

'Are you sure?' Miri asks.

'Yes, them,' Konrad says. 'Same men that surrounded me and Malc outside the warehouse . . . They're dressed like locals, old clothes . . .'

Ben moves to the window, angling to stare through the grimy glass and down the street. 'Show me,' he says.

'It's not safe,' Konrad says. 'There's, like, a thousand planes dropping . . .'

'This building is fine,' Ben cuts in. 'We checked it.'

Konrad wipes the sweat from his eyes and takes in the street below him, the people running and the smoke billowing across it from the blown-out building he ran past. Something catches his eye. The German soldiers all coming to a stop as the one-armed leader speaks to a man. 'There . . . that's one of them!'

'Where?' Ben asks as the others crowd forward to look.

'See the soldiers? That officer is talking to one of them . . .'

'That's Charlie,' Emily says, recognising him even from this distance. 'Alpha and Bravo are to the side, Delta . . . and there's Echo.'

'Can I go now?' Konrad asks.

'Hang on,' Ben says. 'Might need you.'

'What for? Emily and Miri speak German . . .'

'Yes, but they're women,' Ben says. 'We've been through this, Kon.'

'They're asking for papers,' Harry says. 'The officer doesn't like the look of them . . . Bloody Nazis are switched on. See, he's ordering his men to cover them. Men? Old men and boys by the look of it. Bloody Nazis. Excusing my French, but I fucking hate Nazis.'

'Harry,' Emily says in shock as everyone looks at the huge man glowering out the window.

'SHIT,' Ben cries out as a Mustang fighter roars down the street with the wing-mounted machine guns spewing flame as it weaves and bobs. It goes past at their height, close enough for them to see the pilot screaming out in victory as he lifts the aircraft up into the sky straight into the AA fire that blows it apart. When they look back to the street the officer is dead, gunned down by the plane, and his old men and young boys are now running with everyone in complete fear, but they see the last British agent going into a doorway and a few seconds later a slim woman rushing out.

◆ ◆ ◆

'And there he is,' Bravo says. 'The one-armed Kraut challenging our dear Charlie . . . We all look very scared and suitably worried.'

Alpha watches out the window, seeing the same thing.

'Any second now,' Bravo says, leaning over to look for the Mustang. 'Oh, there he is, swooshing down to strafe the whole bloody street. Watch out for civilian casualties, eh? And a rat-a-tat-tat and . . .' His voice drowns out as the Mustang roars past outside, the machine guns booming to kill the German officer and anyone else caught by the bullets. '. . . and up into the sky and puff . . . there he was dead.' Bravo sighs, finishing his commentary. 'How's the filly?'

'Kate? She's okay,' Alpha says, scanning the street. He'd suggested they commence counter-surveillance as soon as he got back to the complex after visiting 2095 with Kate.

'We undertake four visits to Herr Weber in Bundesstraße 2 before we deliver the bomb, so it makes sense Maggie will conduct surveillance,' he said to Mother, but she barely glanced at him and seemed entirely focussed on the tablets and screens glowing all around her. 'Is that okay?' he asked when she didn't reply.

She looked up sharply then, fixing him with her now bloodshot grey eyes. 'Are you a fucking child? You don't need consent. You're Alpha. You're getting soft . . .'

Alpha then told the agents, but made it clear there was no point in all of them going.

'I'll take Bravo for the first one. We'll stay dressed in period clothing – the rest of you stay kitted and ready for immediate deployment.'

He wasn't sure how they would react, but if anything they seemed relieved at finally having something to do.

'Still no changes to the old timeline, eh?' Bravo asks.

'Nope,' Alpha says.

'They must know by now; Maggie Sanderson was a bloody good agent in her day.'

'Maybe they do,' Alpha says. 'Maybe they are behind us now holding guns to the backs of our heads . . .' A second's worth of silence before they slowly look at each other and turn to check behind them and smile at the absence of anyone pointing guns at their heads.

'Time travel,' Bravo says, looking back out the window. 'The mind boggles. Here we are watching the old us, while looking for them watching the old us, so we can see them . . .'

Alpha shakes his head, blinking in response as though struggling to take it in. 'When you put it like that . . .'

'Still, better than sitting round that complex with our thumbs up our arses. Having said that, I think our Delta has shoved his thumbs up a few arses by now, and a few other digits into orifices too.'

Alpha wants to see the others, but he doesn't want to see them. He wants to know they are doing something and reacting, but he doesn't want Bravo to see it. He scans and stares, taking in the people as they run by while glancing frequently at Herr Weber's building.

'Old Charlie's getting in on the action too,' Bravo says conversationally. 'I don't think we've ever been together in one place for this long, have we?'

'No, we haven't,' Alpha says. 'I did a course with Echo for a week; he was instructing on explosives.'

'I did that course after you,' Bravo says. 'Good course.'

'Was a good course,' Alpha says. 'Come on. They must be reacting by now.' Every rule in the book tells him Maggie will deploy to here first to determine who organised the bomb being dropped on London. She will insist they start at the beginning and work from there, but then she is Maggie Sanderson and she could be any of the women he has seen run past in the street. The woman was a master at her trade.

'Not long now,' Bravo says, nodding at Herr Weber's building.

Alpha scans harder, willing them to show, while not knowing how he will react if they do. The best thing is for them to show another day when he isn't with Bravo. Echo will be the best one. Echo is the quietest and Alpha knows he stands the best chance of getting Echo on side. Charlie and Delta he isn't sure about. They're brilliant agents, exceptional really, but he just doesn't know if they are dedicated to the service, to Mother or to him. The British Secret Service doesn't promote allegiance to individuals, but then Emily Rose turned and if she did it then there might be some hope. Not that Alpha has a plan. He doesn't have a plan. He has no idea of what he is doing other than the fact that he must be Alpha.

'There we are,' Bravo says, spotting the old them coming out of Herr Weber's building. 'And there you are holding that microscope to woo young Kate.'

Alpha smiles at the way Bravo says it and the view of himself holding the shiny brass implement to his side.

'I am a handsome chap you know,' Bravo quips, watching himself go down the street.

Alpha snorts a dry laugh and turns to look up the other way and only the combined years of his training and skills prevent him from showing a visible reaction to the glow of a blue light shining from a room on the top floor of a building at the far end.

His mind immediately recalls the street layout from the maps they used in planning their incursions. A bird's eye view looking down with Arch 451 at the far end facing the opening to the street, which uses the European method of house numbering with odd numbers one side and even numbers on the other.

His own position now, their *OP*, or observation point, is in building number eight on the left side, more or less opposite Herr Weber's building, number thirteen, on the other side. He calculates quickly, counting up the street to work out that Maggie's *OP* must be in number twenty-five on the same side of the street as thirteen, but when he looks up to the window on the top floor the glow is gone.

'Got something?' Bravo asks, seeing Alpha staring up.

'Negative,' Alpha says, sighing as though frustrated. 'Where are the old us?'

'Down at the arch,' Bravo says. 'We're just going into the dingy little room in the arch.'

Alpha checks the view, seeing himself bringing up the rear, then going through the weathered door into Arch 451.

'Right,' Bravo says. 'Jolly great shame, but I declare that a no-show.'

'Looks that way,' Alpha says. He wants to stay. He wants to reset the device and come back a few minutes ago to be sure of what he saw, except he can't. He can't do anything, but he knows what he saw. Maggie's team is reacting and that means they have very little time left before Mother becomes aware.

'Are we going back?' Bravo asks, seeing Alpha staring up the street.

'Affirmative,' Alpha says smartly. He is Alpha. Believe it. Be Alpha.

They step from building eight Bundesstraße 2, Berlin, into the portal room of the complex and a noticeably charged atmosphere of heads down and people working in silence.

'Mother wants to see you,' Gunjeep tells Alpha, his tone low, his face betraying none of the usual humour the man has.

The two agents walk through the complex, both sensing a change in the air. The workers they see don't smile or say hi. They pass offices full of people looking tight-lipped and grim-faced.

'See you in a minute,' Alpha tells Bravo, stopping at the door to Mother's office. He knocks and waits, hears the call to enter and pushes on to see her rising from the desk with a look of expectancy.

'Nothing yet.' He shakes his head and walks deeper into the room that smells of coffee and a lack of ventilation. Musty almost.

She slams her hands down on the desk and kicks back at the chair, sending it wheeling away into the wall. She doesn't say anything, but her whole body tenses, trembling with rage while the veins in her head protrude through her thin grey skin.

With what seems a great effort she pulls composure into her features and addresses him formally. 'Check the comparison software. If there are no changes then deploy for the second visit to Berlin . . . If there are no changes after that then keep going. In the meantime, I have ordered for preliminary plans on the extraction of a hydrogen bomb.'

His heart misses a beat, his mouth goes dry and his vision threatens to close in at the sides, but he suppresses any visible reaction. 'I see,' he says mildly.

'We go bigger,' she says, staring at him, into him, through him. To the depths of his soul where she can see the lies and the doubts and the changes within. She sees it all laid bare because she knows the secrets of humanity and will use them to destroy everything to win.

'Okay,' he replies dispassionately.

'We'll also consider a release of anthrax in a major population zone: New York or Mumbai, London, Paris . . . Tokyo . . .' She throws her hands up and smiles. 'All of them.'

'Good idea. That'll certainly draw them out,' he says firmly.

'Good,' she says lightly. 'On you go then, chop chop. Good luck.'

'Echo, get ready. We're deploying,' Alpha orders, walking through their room to his office.

'On it,' Echo says smartly, rushing off.

Charlie and Delta exchange a look while Bravo idly tracks the lead agent across the room. 'All well?' he calls out as though only mildly interested.

'Yep,' Alpha says. 'Have you heard?'

'Just did, old chap. H-bomb, eh? Anthrax too.'

'That's the plan,' Alpha says.

'I see,' Bravo says deeply, drawing the words out.

'Stay ready to respond,' Alpha says, marching back into the main room to address the others. He didn't need to go into the office at all, but such is the worry and anger that he is already doing things without thinking. He has to be calm, be Alpha and show that distinct lack of reaction he would normally adopt. 'Getting a bit claustrophobic in here,' he remarks under his breath.

'Fucking right,' Delta murmurs.

'You feeling it too?' Alpha asks him.

'Just a bit,' Delta replies. 'Never been in one place for so long, not like this I mean.'

'The only reason you are whining is you have exhausted your supply of available women,' Bravo says, giving Delta a wry smile. 'You'll be starting from the beginning again soon.'

'Are you enjoying it then, Bravo?' Charlie asks.

'My dear boy, I enjoy all of our work.'

'Get it done, get it reset, then we can go back to our day jobs,' Delta says.

'Amen,' Charlie adds.

'Reset?' Bravo enquiries lightly.

'That's the plan,' Delta says.

'Of course,' Bravo says. 'Of course it is.'

'Isn't it?' Delta asks, sitting up straighter and looking at Alpha. 'We catch them, reset what we've changed and go back, right?'

'Affirmative,' Alpha says firmly. 'Echo?'

'Almost ready.'

'You understand that resetting means stopping the old us, don't you, old chap?' Bravo asks Delta. 'And by stopping I mean killing. We have to kill ourselves . . .' He says the words slowly, staring hard at Delta as though looking for a reaction.

'Yes,' Delta says. 'But we're not dying, are we? It's the old us.'

'Clever and good-looking,' Bravo says, offering a huge humourless smile.

Alpha detects the tension between them. The smug posh manner Bravo has that is normally so funny and witty is starting to grate. The agents aren't used to being cooped up.

'Echo, meet me in the portal room.'

'Roger that.'

Alpha goes out, marching down the corridor to the history department to see Kate and Rodney in deep conversation, which ends as he walks in.

'We need to check the software,' Alpha says, maintaining a business-like manner that makes Rodney briskly walk off and Kate nod smartly as she grabs the download tool.

They walk silently to the portal room and through to the darkened interior of the university.

'What's happened?' Kate asks, programming the device to start working. 'Mother held a meeting. She wants a hydrogen bomb extracted and said we're to start researching anthrax.'

'She wants results,' Alpha says darkly. 'Listen, I saw a flash of blue in Berlin.'

'Okay,' she says quietly, widening her eyes. 'Them?'

'Got to be . . . Far end of the street. They've got an OP in . . .'

'What's an OP again?' she asks with a wince. 'Sorry, I can't remember all the terms for things.'

'Observation point. Top floor of number twenty-five.'

She frowns as though thinking. 'Far end on the right side? Yes, yes, I remember it. Twenty-seven is hit by a bomb but twenty-five stays intact . . . Would Mother do it? An H-bomb. Would she use one?'

'She won't stop . . . Unless I told her I saw them, of course.'

'No, you can't. She'll make you kill them or . . . I don't know. What can we do?'

'I'll keep thinking. I'm going back in with Echo to monitor our second visit.'

'Do you trust Echo?'

'Maybe,' he says. 'It's impossible to know. We're meant to catch them, reset everything we did, then go back to our lives, but . . .'

She listens intently, her eyes searching his face. 'We can't let it happen. It's not right. It's not. Resetting doesn't stop millions dying . . .'

'You said the timeline wants to cling to a set course . . . Maybe whatever we do is pre-destiny.'

'No.' She shakes her head with all the sadness of the world in her eyes. 'She's planning an extinction-level event . . . You've got to reach out to them,' she says, looking up into his eyes, holding his gaze trapped in her blue eyes.

'How? Echo is with me, then one of the others will be with me, and I can't do every observation deployment without them getting suspicious. We don't work like that . . .'

'Take me with you,' she jokes. 'I'll just go over and say hi and ask them what they want.'

He snorts a grim laugh. 'That would probably work.'

'Well, why not then? I'll tell them what Mother is doing and say we want out.'

'God, no. Jesus, Kate, we don't know anything about them . . . I'm not putting you at risk.'

'But—'

'No,' he says firmly. 'I'll think of something.'

The tablet vibrates, signalling the download is complete. 'Reach out to them,' she whispers. 'You've got to. Mother will kill everyone.'

Twenty-Five

Bertie's Island

'How was it?' Malcolm asks, rushing over on seeing a very pale and shaken Konrad coming out of the shack.

'Bloody awful, Malc. Worse than Norway when we got Harry.'

'Worse than that, was it?'

'Much worse. Never heard anything like it . . . Eh, look at that, you got the tents up then.'

'They went up themselves, Kon. Just open the case, press a button and they self-erect.'

'Do they really? That's good, that is, Malc.'

'Wow,' Emily says, stopping with the others to look at the row of green walk-in-sized army tents arranged in a line next to the shack. 'We're reduced to this. Sleeping in tents.'

'A temporary measure,' Miri says curtly, walking past. 'Until we have time for an assessment of a permanent HB.'

Turns out you can pretty much buy anything in Lambeth-not-Lambeth, or the streets and areas surrounding it anyway, which are just as chaotic and packed. It also turns out the trade in ex and surplus military gear is as high in the future as it was in their times. Six tents purchased along with anti-grav hovering collapsible cots, bedrolls, boots and even down to basic hygiene kits of good old-fashioned toothbrushes and safety razors.

'Aye,' Harry says, nodding happily as he looks round the inside of the closest one. 'Good kit, this.'

'Is it?' Emily asks, arching an eyebrow at him.

'We slept in muddy puddles in my time. It's got a roof and walls, bed, kit. What more do you want?'

'Oh, I don't know, say a cupboard, some shelves, maybe a hanging rail, holo-player, music-system, hot running water . . .'

'Ignore her,' Harry says to Malcolm, whacking him on the arm. 'She moans a lot. Done a great job.'

'What did you say?' Emily asks, folding her arms to glare at Harry. 'I moan a lot?'

'Aye. All the time.'

'And time for a brew,' Ben says. 'Nicely done, Malc.'

'What about me?' Konrad asks, following Ben, Safa and Miri back round to the front. 'I risked my life.'

'Well done you too,' Ben says.

'I'm not a super-soldier, you know. I'm an engineer and general expert on . . .'

'He's not an expert on anything.'

'Shut up, Malc. You weren't there. I was there— Hey, I can say it.'

'Say what?' Malcolm asks.

'When you've been in a war,' Konrad says, looking round proudly at the eye rolls and tuts.

'Oh god, you sound like Harry,' Emily says, staring at the tents. 'Which one is mine?'

'Er . . .' Malcolm says.

'I want that one,' she says, pointing at the far end. 'And Harry wants that one,' she adds, pointing to the other end. 'So I can't hear him snoring.'

'Right,' Malcolm says quickly, nodding in agreement as she walks over to claim the end tent.

'I like this one,' Harry says, walking into the one next to Emily's, who hears the proximity of his voice and rushes out.

'What are you doing? Yours is at the end.'

'I like this one.'

'You are so annoying today!'

'Debrief,' Miri calls out.

Ben sits down at the table as the others make their way over, Emily giving Harry loaded looks while the big man smiles and nods happily at her.

Miri clears her throat, waiting for them to pay attention. 'The Affa and London changes were both done by British secret service agents. This suggests the British Government have a device and used it to extract the agents from before Cavendish Manor. There are five dates in February nineteen forty-five when Herr Weber is visited by the agents. We'll continue the observations and . . .'

'Pardon?' Ben asks, cutting across her.

'We've got enough now,' Emily says. 'We've got the element of surprise so we can stop them easily . . . Oh, hang on.' She frowns and shakes her head. 'It's not them we need, is it . . . not them in Berlin, I mean . . . That will be the old them . . . so even if we find their portal it'll be the memory of the portal and not the live one . . . as it is now? Bloody hell, this is confusing.'

'Lay a trap,' Harry says, making them all turn to look at him. 'We need them now. Like we are now. Anything behind us is a memory. We need to do something to change what they did and when they come out to look that's when we strike.'

'What Harry said,' Ben says.

'That's what I said,' Emily says.

'Bloody wasn't,' Safa scoffs.

'That's it then,' Ben says to Miri. 'Lay a trap and wait for them to pop up, then we get into their base . . . Obviously it'll take some more planning but . . .' He stops talking when she shakes her head.

'Observe for now. Run the OP and gain intel,' Miri says.

'Why? We know it's them,' Ben says as the others murmur agreement while Malcolm, Konrad and the doctor listen intently.

'Fools rush, Mr Ryder. We are not fools. They will be watching for us so this is not the time for rash decisions . . .' She holds her hand up at the voices disagreeing with her. 'You are all good at what you do, exceptional in some cases, but this is what I do. This is my expertise. We run the OP and gain intel.'

A begrudging silence settles in response to her words. Harry nods, lifting a hand in a show of compliance.

'Okay,' Emily says.

'Fair enough,' Safa adds.

'Take refs. We'll deploy for the second Berlin visit in twenty minutes,' Miri says, pushing up from the table to pull a pack of cigarettes from her pocket as she walks off towards the shore.

Ben watches her go, something in her words, the nuances, the tells, the tone of her voice. 'Can someone make me and Miri a coffee, please?' He walks off, following behind Miri and watching as she stops on the edge of the soft sand to smoke and stare out across the blue waters. She shows no reaction when he falls in at her side, standing quietly.

'Why aren't we responding now, Miri?'

She sucks on the cigarette, pulling the smoke into her lungs before blasting it out through her nose. 'Diligence,' she says bluntly.

He nods, folding his arms. 'True, but isn't there a risk of escalation? We didn't respond to the Affa thing so maybe that's what made them drop a nuke. What if we don't respond now? They might drop a bigger nuke . . .'

She smokes again and he finally turns to see that her normally cold grey eyes now look more blue. Stress in her features, her lips pursed with a bare hint of worry.

'Never use a nuke,' she says, shaking her head. 'Even we never used one after Japan. Even Russia in the cold war never used them. We had them to make sure no one used them . . . It wouldn't be sanctioned.'

'What?'

'The Brits would not sanction the use of a nuclear weapon on their own country, Ben.'

He almost flinches at her using his first name and the real emotion showing in her voice, then her words hit, the realisation of what she means. 'Oh,' he says.

'Yeah,' she says bitterly. 'Oh.'

'Right, well, that's us between a rock and a hard place.'

'Damn right. Now you can see why I'm hesitating. No government would sanction the use of a nuke on their own people. Not even for this. It changes their own history, it stops them existing . . .'

'And if the government didn't sanction it then it means whoever is running that show did it themselves.'

'They killed twenty-five thousand people like that to get at us, Mr Ryder.' She snaps her fingers as she says it, ramming the point home. 'Hundreds of thousands then suffered the worst kind of injuries you can imagine . . . just to get at us.' She stops to smoke, shaking her head again. 'That's a cost too high to pay.' She looks stricken for a second at allowing the thought that so many died because of her actions, that she didn't make enough effort to ensure no blueprints or plans survived Cavendish Manor, that this is her fault – her ego and desire to be back in the game made this happen. Agents and operatives have to separate emotion from duty, but after that? After seeing that someone dropped a nuke just to get their attention?

'Okay,' Ben says, bringing her mind back. 'So maybe they're thinking they can make changes and then reset it once we're caught. Like, go back and tell the old them not to kill the Romans or drop the nuke . . . But that could have dire consequences depending on if the old them was in the same timeline they are in now as that goes back to the whole killing-yourself-as-a-baby thing. Bloody hell. Right . . . we need to think about this.'

'I want you focussed on this situation,' she says firmly. 'We can run the OP. Stay here and work out a solution.'

'What? Me?'

'As much as I hate to admit it, and trust me, Mr Ryder, it gives me great pains, you are smarter than me . . .'

'Really?' he asks, smiling at her.

'Don't get cocky,' she says flatly, easing back into normal Miri-mode.

'I'll come with you to Berlin,' he says casually, casting her a look. 'Geniuses can multi-task.'

She snorts a rare laugh and drops to stub the smoke out.

'We'll sort it,' he says with a confidence reserved for the young, foolish and brave.

Twenty-Six

Berlin, Bundesstraße 2, 3 February 1945

Berlin. The day after the mass bombing raid and still the fires burn with black smoke choking the air. This isn't earth. This is hell. A place forsaken by a God who turned his back on the evils of mankind. This is a city on its knees, suffering for the years of horror it unleashed on everyone else. This is punishment on a scale unwitnessed in the history of this planet.

Over a thousand USAAF heavy bombers dropped payloads to decimate the infrastructure and make the giant die a death of a thousand cuts. To weaken the might of the Third Reich and bring its people to the brink of annihilation and yet it's not over. The Führer cowers in his bunker and those of his high command who can sniff the wind and see the coming armies bolt for South America to new identities and new lives.

To see that day, the day of the bombing, was a thing indeed, but to see this now, the aftermath and the horror of human suffering, is something else.

It's freezing cold, it stinks and dead bodies are everywhere – mangled corpses that lie half-covered by whatever burnt and smouldering material could be found. The buildings stand like broken skeletons. Walls here and there tower over rubble. Mounds of brick and masonry still too hot to search for bodies or even hope of survivors.

There are no young men now. Not here. They're all away fighting a war and so women and the old and infirm carry the stretchers to the broken ambulances. They hold the hoses to spray water on fires. They tear down walls to make fire-breaks. They drag the bodies into the street so the survivors can try to name the fallen. Clothing and faces are blackened from the grime, soot and smoke. There is no valour here, no hope that it will get better. The Russians are coming closer, and everyone knows those heavy bombers will return to punish them more.

They thread a slow route through the street. Clambering over chunks of buildings and round piles of corpses waiting to be taken away. They cover their mouths and noses in a vain attempt to prevent the putrid stench seeping through. Emily has seen death. She has given death many times, but this is beyond anything and she grips Konrad's hand as he takes the lead over a pile of bricks. Konrad has a sepia photograph of a smiling child, cherubic and angelic. The clothes they wear were once tailored and expensive but are now as ripped, torn and stained as everyone else's. They pretend to have been searching all night with filth rubbed on their faces to hide the healthy glow of their sun-kissed skin.

Konrad stops at a pile of bodies, his stomach heaving. His eyes fill with tears and at that second he detests Roland Cavendish with every ounce of his being. For taking him away from his death to be a part of this. To be here in this place.

'Who?' an old man asks, his voice broken and low. He nods at the photograph in their hands.

'Our boy,' Konrad says, his voice cracking with emotion.

The old man limps over to them, his sore red eyes squinting as he studies the photograph. 'Not here,' he says, motioning the pile of bodies. 'Try further down.'

'*Danke*,' Konrad says quietly.

'*Danke*,' Emily says, following her husband down the street. She might have been a Two, but she is a trained agent and this is where she excels. To blend, to assume the cover needed to become a part of the scenery. She clocks the railway arch at the end of the street and looks back to the third building from the end on the right side from where Ben and the others are watching. She takes in the remaining buildings in the street, any one of which could be used by Alpha and his team to conduct surveillance now. She drops her head, pretending to be distraught and heart-broken, without hope of finding her son and she walks on with her husband through the broken lives and broken buildings.

They go slow. They are tired, weary to the bone, but they will search every street in Berlin for him. They'll not stop until they know. It's an awful thing to do, to borrow grief from those suffering to blend in, while holding a picture of a child bought from a shop in Lambeth-not-Lambeth. It feels wrong, like voyeurism, like fraud of the soul.

More bodies laid out in a neat row. Mostly adults but the smaller covered mounds at the end mean they must stop and check. Konrad falters, his heart breaking into a million pieces at the thought of looking at dead children. Emily squeezes his hand, sensing his fear. 'It's okay,' she whispers in German. 'I'll do it. Watch the arch.'

'I can't,' he says, the emotion clear in his voice. Tears track down his cheeks, scoring marks through the grime. 'I can't . . . not children . . .'

'Let me see,' a woman walks over to them. She looks exhausted, drained to the point of passing out, and Emily can see it's pure grit and nothing more keeping her up.

'My husband,' Emily says, her voice quavering. 'He can't look . . .'

The woman nods once, glaring balefully at Konrad as though the whole of this war is his fault, the fault of man, the greed and ego of man. She studies the photograph and nods once again. 'We might have him.' When she speaks she does so softly, kindly, and sets off to the end of the row and the small mounds with Emily following and Konrad weeping as he tries to watch the arch.

The woman looks at Emily, lowers to her knees and gently pulls a single rose-patterned curtain back from the body of the child. Blond-haired, small and so fragile. Emily feels the reality of it, the trueness of it and the tears that come are not faked at all. 'No,' she says hoarsely.

'Are you sure?' the woman asks.

'I'm sure.'

The woman covers the boy and rises stiffly to rest a hand on Emily's shoulder. 'Down the street, there's more . . . I'll pray for you.'

'*Danke.*' Emily moves off, her hand finding Konrad's as they once more set off in their search.

'I can't do this,' Konrad whispers. 'I'm not one of you . . .'

She looks past Konrad to Arch 451 at the end of the street and the door opening with a hint of a green glow shining behind the five men coming out and pulls on Konrad's hand to guide him over to the side of the street. 'Face me,' she whispers urgently.

'I can't do this, Emily . . .' He turns to look at her, his face in abject misery.

'*It's Emily, they're coming out of a doorway underneath the arch. Five of them. Distance too great to confirm. Standby . . .*'

'*Standing by.*' Ben's soft voice in her ear.

'*Ben, there's a green light behind the door – only saw a glimpse.*'

'*Understood.*'

Emily holds the photograph in her right hand that rests on her husband's shoulder. It makes sure anyone passing will see the image of the child and complete the mental picture of two grieving adults. She leans in closer, pressing her cheek to Konrad's as the tears fall.

'*Emily to Ben. Confirmed . . . It's them.*' She whispers the words softly as though praying with Konrad. '*Alpha and Bravo in the lead, Charlie behind them. Delta and Echo at the rear . . .*'

'*Thanks, Emily,*' Ben replies, his voice as soft as hers. He stays at the window on the top floor of building twenty-five, his view fixed down the street as he waits for them to come into view.

◆ ◆ ◆

Further down and on the other side of the street in building number eight, Alpha and Echo stand quietly in the front room on the top floor.

They deployed two hours early, to watch and *study the street*. To buy time for Alpha to be out of the complex and away from Mother and Bravo. To buy time with Echo. To buy time to think.

'It's not pretty,' Alpha remarks quietly, taking in the destruction of the street below them.

'They did it first,' Echo replies. He shifts position, looking left and right up and down the street. 'And the Holocaust.'

A light bulb moment. Ian Isaacs. Echo is Ian Isaacs. Alpha has access to all of their personnel files. Ian's heritage is Jewish. Does it give leverage? If anything it makes him realise Echo is committed to his role. He has worked to give the Nazis a nuclear bomb.

'Your family are Jewish, aren't they?' Alpha asks as though making conversation to pass the time.

'Non-practising,' Echo says. 'We're from Germany actually.'

'Are you?'

Echo nods, maintaining his vigil at the window. 'They got out in nineteen thirty-eight . . . Some did anyway. We lost people in the camps.'

'Jesus,' Alpha says, gently humanising himself and the conversation. 'You could have said.'

'Said what?' Echo asks.

'Your heritage. You've just helped us give the Nazis a nuclear bomb.'

'It's a mission,' Echo says quickly. 'I'm an agent, Alpha . . . My commitment is to the service.'

'Take it easy. I wasn't questioning your loyalty.'

Echo glances at him, his face as impassive as ever, but then he is highly trained to suppress any reaction. 'I'm loyal.'

'I know,' Alpha says, looking back at him. 'I know you are.'

'But, yeah, it sucks,' Echo says, turning to face the window again.

Tread carefully. Was Echo testing Alpha by saying that? Has Mother spoken to him and asked him to probe Alpha's loyalty or is it simply a passing remark?

Echo inhales deeply and releases the air slowly, studying the people below as Alpha looks up at the top floor of building number twenty-five where he saw the flash of blue light before. Are they there now? Is Maggie Sanderson staring out of that window looking for them?

'It's going to be hard to steal a modern nuclear bomb,' Echo says.

'You think?' Alpha asks drily.

'Missiles are built into entire systems. We'd need that entire system to launch one of the biggest. We can take a smaller one to plant and detonate from a distance, but the yield won't be as great . . .'

'She'll want the biggest,' Alpha says.

'Can't be done,' Echo says. 'The biggest is ten thousand times more powerful than the one we dropped in London . . . but they're launched from those systems. We'd have to take over a whole launch facility while holding whatever country's head of state hostage to get the launch codes. We're good, but there's only five of us . . .' He pauses to look at Alpha. 'And if we did launch one, everyone else will detect that launch and start throwing theirs about . . . It's an extinction level event, Alpha . . .'

It hangs in the air. An instinct in Alpha that they are two men who want to say the same thing but are holding back through fear of the repercussions of being wrong. He watches a man and woman threading a route through the street. Clambering and slipping over piles of bricks and broken buildings. They stop at every row of corpses, checking the smaller ones as they go. Something in the woman's hand, maybe a picture of someone they lost.

'We're coming out,' Echo says, looking down at the arch at the end of the street.

'Got it,' Alpha says, seeing the five coming from the doorway. He remembers seeing this street. He remembers all of it. His memory is highly trained to retain sights and information. He remembers the shape of the ruined buildings and looking up at the undamaged buildings and picking this one out to use as an observation point in the future. He remembers the rows of bodies. The old men and young women working to clear the area, the broken ambulances, the smoke coming from the fires, the tiny details that make this scene up.

He doesn't remember that man and woman. They were not here. They are new.

He looks at Echo, trying to see what the other agent is looking at, but it's impossible to tell. Alpha glances up to building twenty-five, then back down to the man and woman now moving over to the side of the road. They appear devastated and filthy. Their clothing is the same as everyone else's, torn and stained with grime. Their faces are pale and drawn, smeared with black streaks. He can see the man is crying and the way the woman holds her hand on his shoulder giving comfort while clutching a picture that is angled out for anyone passing to see, and his heart thumps louder because the skin of her hand is tanned and stark against the skin on her face. She's taken an effort to disguise her features but not her hand. She's one of them.

'Look at that,' Echo says, making Alpha snap his head over. 'At us. I mean, weird seeing us . . .'

'Yeah,' Alpha says, forcing a hint of humour in his voice. 'Bravo said the same thing . . . along with a running commentary of everything he saw.'

◆　◆　◆

Emily holds her husband in his grief. Whispering words of comfort while snatching glances past Konrad's head to Alpha and Bravo walking up the street. Charlie behind them. Delta and Echo a short distance away. She nestles further into Konrad, hiding her own features while making sure the picture of the child can be seen. She wants to change hands and hold the picture in her left so her right can go into the pocket of her filthy overcoat to grip the butt of the pistol. Her senses ramp, her heart beats harder and the agents pass on by as she notices her suntanned hand holding the photograph that shines like a beacon in the desolation of this place. Instinct tells her to pull it back now, but a rapid movement will be detected so she forces herself to move slowly and pull the hand down to the gap between her body and Konrad's. She glances down to Konrad's hands, seeing them the same, suntanned and healthy. She drags at his wrist, pulling his arm up to smother it between them in the desperate actions of a grief-stricken wife clutching at her husband.

◆ ◆ ◆

Don't see them. Don't see them. Alpha pleads silently from the top floor of building number eight that neither the agents walking through nor Echo next to him at the window see the man and woman. He spots her bringing her suntanned hand down, then a few seconds later she paws at the man's arm, dragging it between them. His hand is also tanned, but the movements look natural to the situation. The woman is trained in covert behaviours. His mind flashes back to the track and watching them give comfort to the dying Roman soldier. He matches the body shapes of the two women to the woman in the street. It's not Safa Patel. Her skin is darker, her hair is black, she's a bit shorter and slimmer. It must be Tango Two. Emily Rose.

'I don't remember those two,' Echo says quietly.

'Which two?' Alpha asks.

'Man and woman over there, see them? They look upset . . .'

'They were here before,' Alpha says, glancing away to track the five agents moving up the street.

'Yeah?' Echo asks, scratching the side of his head. 'You sure?'

'I'm sure. They had a picture of someone. I saw them and figured they were looking for a body.'

'Christ,' Echo says. 'I'm so sorry, Alpha . . . I didn't see them.'

'Lot going on.'

'Yeah, but that's basic stuff.'

'You know what,' Alpha says. 'I'll go and take a closer look at them . . .'

'I can do it. It's my error if I didn't see them.'

'It's fine. I'll go and have a walk up and down the street. You keep watch on Herr Weber's building in case anyone goes in after us.'

'We can both go,' Echo says, displaying a tone and manner that suggests he feels bad at not spotting something.

'Stay here and watch that door. Radio me if anyone goes in.'

'Roger that. Alpha, don't forget the air-raid siren goes off before we come out . . .'

◆ ◆ ◆

'Konrad, look past me . . . Tell me when they go in,' Emily whispers into his ear. 'Slowly,' she hisses when he jerks his head up too fast.

'Crossing the road now,' he says. 'I don't want to do this. I'm an engineer . . .'

'Just watch,' she says calmly. 'It's okay . . . We're just watching . . .'

'They're going in now,' Konrad whispers. 'One . . . two . . . three . . . four and five . . . They're all inside. Can we go now?'

'It's Emily. They've gone inside.'

'Okay. Keep your eyes on that arch to see if they come from there again. They'll be here somewhere watching for us.'

'Understood. Emily out.'

'This isn't fair . . . I'm an engineer, not a spy . . .'

'Shush, we're fine. We need to go down a bit further, okay?'

'No! It's not okay. I don't want to look at dead kids or dead anybody . . .'

'I'll do it. Just hold my hand and look upset.'

'I am upset. I'm very upset.'

They set off with a visibly shaken Konrad trudging on slowly with his head down in abject misery while Emily scans everything and constantly flicks her gaze to the door in the arch, but worries there are too many points from which they could be observed.

She guides Konrad on towards the next row of bodies dragged, carried and pulled from the bombed buildings. Smoke wafts across the street and fires burn and crackle with orange flames still licking at the wooden frames. People move around them, lost in their own grief and shock. They go past a woman sitting with her back against a wall holding the body of a child clasped to her chest. Her eyes unblinking as she stares up at the heavens.

◆ ◆ ◆

Alpha descends the stairs. Moving swiftly down the flights until he reaches the ground floor. A long, narrow hallway with a once tiled and polished floor now tracked in dirt. The walls, which were cream, now smudged and tinged with the same soot that seems to coat every surface.

Every turn of events can be manipulated to an advantage. Echo saw them, but Alpha can use that to get closer. Not that he has a plan yet. He has no plan. He has nothing except wits and instinct that propel him on and out into the street.

He walks slowly with his head down and his hands tucked into the pockets of his dark-grey overcoat. These are the same clothes he wore during the visits to Herr Weber so it poses a risk of someone spotting the same man twice in a few minutes, but it's a risk he has to take.

Within a few seconds, he gains sight of the man and woman ahead on the left side. They've moved off to continue searching for whoever they are looking for, but Alpha can see they are heading closer to the archway and keeping it in their line of sight. He goes slowly, carefully, blending into the background and adopting his own expression of anguish and grief to match those around him.

◆ ◆ ◆

Another row of bodes laid out neatly, covered by scraps of material. There isn't anyone here. No old man or woman willing to look at the picture. That means Emily has to examine the corpses herself to maintain their cover, but her sixth sense is going nuts. That feeling of being watched. She wants to look up and round to try and spot if anyone is staring from a window, but resists.

'Oh god no . . . please no,' Konrad says, seeing the covered mounds.

'I'll look. Just stay close.'

She moves away from him, stepping over the broken bricks and burnt chunks of furniture to reach the bodies. She lowers down, grips a sheet and gently lifts it to see the awful injuries of the child that make her tense and squeeze her eyes closed, but to anyone observing they will see an entirely human reaction.

She looks up as though summoning courage to keep going, blinking rapidly while quickly scanning the windows and doorways as the air-raid siren fills the air. Everyone bursts to action, abandoning whatever they are doing to run down the street for the safety of the shelter at the far end. The horror of yesterday drives them on, the knowledge of another coming air raid and within seconds people are streaming past, screaming out and barging into a terrified looking Konrad.

'*Emily . . . can you hear me? Get back now . . . air raid . . . can . . . me . . .*'

She rises and runs to Konrad, grabbing his wrist to drag him on as she catches sight of a man in a grey overcoat also pushing against the flow of people. Something jars in her mind. Recognition of the coat, the build of the man and the way he walks. It's Alpha. She looks for the other agents and realises it's too quick for them to have come out. He's on his own. This is Alpha now and not the memory of him. She heaves on with Konrad in her grasp, her head down as she pushes through the people running past.

'GET TO COVER . . . GET TO COVER . . . WRONG WAY, YOU'RE GOING THE WRONG WAY . . .' A woman grabs at Emily, screaming in her face.

'MY SON,' Emily shouts back, showing the picture of the child. She jerks her arm free and keeps going, then spots that Alpha has turned to walk away from her and goes after him.

The noise is immense. A solid wall of sound made by people screaming in fear and the air-raid siren. Distant booms soon join the noise as the bombers start dropping their loads and the AA guns add their bass-filled sounds to the cacophony.

She tries to transmit to Ben, but she can't hear her own voice let alone anything coming back. Still, she is an agent, trained to respond to live events in the field, and the chance of capturing Alpha now is too great to pass up.

She starts weaving across the street, over the rubble and round the people going past. Running now with Konrad behind her, not having a clue what is going on. She spots the grey overcoat go hard left towards a row of intact buildings and aims after him, grim-faced and leaning left and right to keep him in sight. A doorway ahead of him. She sees him go for it, speeding up over the last few metres to push inside.

'GET TO BEN,' she screams at Konrad and then runs on, faster now she is free of his hand. She grabs at the pistol in her coat pocket, flicking the safety off as she covers those last few metres to burst through the door, yanking the pistol to hold it up and aimed as she transitions from the bedlam of the street to the muted interior of the long, narrow hallway.

The pressure comes fast. The feel of a barrel pushing against the back of her head followed swiftly by his hand clamping on her shoulder to prevent her launching back into him.

'Don't move . . .' Alpha's voice. The best agent in the British Secret Service. In a heartbeat she is outwitted and out-manoeuvred.

'Fuck you,' she says, and starts to turn to fight and show she isn't afraid. Harry will come for her. Her team will use the device and Harry will tear Alpha apart again.

'Stop,' Alpha whispers. He moves in fast, wrapping an arm round to clamp over her mouth while bringing the pistol to jab under her chin. 'I won't kill you . . . Listen, Emily . . .'

She stiffens in readiness for the shot and waits for the Blue to show and for Harry to come. She waits for the roar of his bellow and the cessation of pressure on her mouth and in the heat of that second she realises he called her Emily and not Tango Two.

'Echo is on the top floor. If you scream he will hear you and come down, then I'll have to kill you and I do not want to kill you. Nod.'

She nods once. Breathing hard through her nose while gently pushing back to test his weight and centre of mass.

'No.' He pushes into her, sensing the test. 'Why did you join them? I'll take my hand away . . . Just tell me . . . why did you join them?' He eases the hand away a fraction, ready to clamp it back while holding her tight.

'Fuck you.' She tries to shout out, but the hand comes back.

'Please,' he whispers into her ear. 'Why did you join them?'

'They're good people,' she whispers angrily when his hand lifts away. 'Not murdering fucking bastards . . . Kill me and Harry won't stop until you're dead.'

He thinks hard and he thinks fast. His hand still holding away from her mouth. So many questions run through his mind, but he has only a few seconds. 'You chose to go with them.' He didn't know he was going to say that, but the words come out. 'They're good, right? Tell me they're good . . .'

'They're good,' she says, wincing at the pistol jabbing under her chin. 'Better than you . . . better than that evil bitch . . .'

'Mother won't stop. She wants Maggie . . . She's planning an extinction level event.'

Emily freezes any tiny motion she had. Listening hard and taking it in.

'Hydrogen bomb and anthrax. Tell Maggie to react and do something small to buy time. We'll see the change in the timeline. I want out . . .'

'Fuck you . . . I saw you in Cavendish Manor, Alpha. I was there . . .'

'That was a different me. I'll try and find a way to get a message to you . . . Is Maggie in charge?'

She hesitates, not wanting to give any information.

'Tell Maggie to react. Do something to make us know you are aware of us . . .' He moves fast and swift. Yanking her shoulder to make her pivot while spinning round to ease back down the hallway towards the stairs. 'Your hand,' he says quietly.

'I know,' she says without looking at it.

'Poor skills,' he says, still backing away towards the stairs. 'Don't let that happen again, seven Ps, Tango Two . . .'

'My name is Emily now.'

'I need tonight to think. Tell Maggie to meet me on our third visit to Herr Weber. I'll be alone . . .'

She watches him back away to the stairs and only then does he lower the pistol, but pauses as though waiting to see if she will aim and fire.

She doesn't.

◆ ◆ ◆

Alpha goes fast up the stairs, pushing his sidearm into the holster while thinking of things he should have said and done. He reaches the top floor and slows his motion to ease his breathing before tapping lightly three times on the door and pushing in.

'Anything?' he asks Echo standing side at the window.

'Negative. You?' Echo replies, staring at his leader.

'Nothing,' Alpha says. 'That couple lost a child.'

'Okay,' Echo says, turning back to face the window.

He saw the woman and the man pushing to run against the flow of people. He saw her staring at Alpha and he saw her veer off towards the building. He also noted the point Alpha went out of view below and the time it took to reach this room, which was too long, but he stays quiet and stares out of the window.

Alpha falls in at his side, resuming the observations and realising just what a view it is from up here. Echo would have seen the man and woman pushing through the people. He would have seen her coming after Alpha and he would know the time between entering the building and arriving in this room is too long.

Neither move. Neither say or do anything, but nerves and sinew bunch and gather and adrenaline starts to dump. Senses become heightened. They both watch her running up the street, tracking her progress and Alpha's heart sinks when she goes inside the ground floor door to building number twenty-five. She should have deviated the route or waited. She's just shown them where her point of entry is.

'Everything okay?' Echo asks, his voice soft and quiet. A personal question almost, from one man to another.

'Fine,' Alpha whispers. They don't look at each other. They don't move for fear of making the other react faster.

'Tango Two,' Echo whispers.

Everything poised on this second. Everything weighted on this second now. Alpha's instincts tell him to take a chance on Echo. To at least try.

'Yes.'

Echo says nothing and both men stare ahead and slightly lower their heads to increase their peripheral vision. Both with hands loose at their sides ready to reach for sidearms. Tension mounts. Neither willing to take the next step without knowing which way it will end. Both trained. Both professional. Both calculating every possible outcome that holds them in a stalemate.

Echo moves first and he's fast, but the mistake he makes is going for his pistol while turning and moving back to clear space to draw and fire. Alpha doesn't try to outdraw him, but simply steps in and kicks hard at Echo's stomach, sending the agent smashing into the wall.

'Fuck,' Echo gasps, bending double as he slides down the wall clutching his stomach.

'Don't,' Alpha says, pulling his gun to aim at Echo's head and seeing the other agent's hand moving towards his belt line. 'I said don't.' Alpha lashes out, slamming his foot into Echo's shin to make him topple down. 'Hands out . . . OUT . . .'

'What did they do?' Echo gasps, twisting his neck to look up at Alpha. 'What? What did they do?'

'Who?'

'Them. I don't get it . . .'

'Get what?' Alpha demands, pressing his gun to Echo's temple.

'The others! We saw it on that footage . . . They saved an autistic kid from us, Alpha . . . People like that don't murder. They didn't kill everyone in the complex . . . They're not fucking terrorists so why are we going after them?'

Alpha holds still, thinking hard with the gun aimed at Echo's head.

'Kill me,' Echo says in disgust. 'I'm not part of this. I didn't sign up for this shit . . .'

'Why did you try and pull your gun?' Alpha asks.

'To warn them,' Echo snarls. 'It's Tango Two . . . She's with them . . . Go on. Mother's lost the plot. She's fucking crazy so you'd better kill me because I swear the second you lower that gun I'm going for you . . .'

288

'Shut up,' Alpha snaps, trying to think.

'Alpha, I swear to god you'd better shoot me now. I dropped a nuke for this . . . You kill me now because I'm not going back to that sick bitch . . .'

'Shut up.'

'I can't sleep at night . . . We killed thousands for nothing. I dropped a fucking nuclear bomb for revenge . . .'

'Christ, Ian, shut the fuck up and let me think . . .'

'PULL THE . . .' Echo's voice drops out midway as Alpha's words sink into his head.

'Who else?' Alpha asks quickly, his voice soft and urgent. 'You spoke to Charlie and Delta about this?'

'No one else,' Echo replies instantly. 'Just me . . .'

Alpha rolls his eyes at the reply, realising the stupidity of the question and wondering what he expected Echo to say. This could be a trap. This could be a test, but his instincts tell him to take a punt. 'I've warned them. I told Tango Two they need to react, to slow Mother down . . . I spoke to her downstairs.'

Echo stares at him, trying to read every muscle twitch and facial expression in Alpha's face and posture.

'Don't shoot me,' Alpha says, lowering his gun as he rises and steps back. He sweeps his overcoat back to holster his weapon and rubs the tension from his face with the first human gesture Echo has ever seen him make. The other agent stays on the floor, watching Alpha as he goes to the window and stares out with a look of intense worry showing.

'What's going on?' Echo asks.

'You tell me,' Alpha whispers.

Echo rises slowly, wincing at the pain in his gut from the hard kick. A few steps and he joins Alpha at the window, both staring out in silence.

'It's not right,' Echo finally says. 'What we're doing . . . It's not right . . .'

'I know.'

'Bravo?' Echo asks.

'Don't trust him.'

Echo shakes his head while rubbing at his stomach with another grimace. 'Charlie and Delta, they don't like the mission, but I think they're just bored. This a trap, Alpha?'

Alpha looks at him, lifting his eyebrows in question. 'Seriously?'

'Gotta ask,' Echo says with a shrug.

'Yeah, like I'd admit it.'

'You might.'

'I wouldn't. Would you?'

'No.'

'Then don't ask stupid questions.'

'Sorry, Alpha. What now?'

◆ ◆ ◆

Emily runs down the ground floor hallway to the stairs and starts going up as she hears footsteps coming down. 'Coming up,' she shouts in German, drawing her pistol.

'Emily? It's us,' Safa calls out, running down with the others, all of them holding weapons ready. 'What happened?'

'I spoke to Alpha,' she whispers urgently.

'Not here,' Miri says. 'Fall back to the island.'

She follows them through to the instant warmth and golden light of the shack and out into the bright sunshine to see Konrad sitting on the floor with his knees to his chest, weeping hard as Malcolm and the doctor give comfort.

'I'm not going back,' Konrad says, hearing them coming out. He rises to his feet, glaring at them all through red eyes and tear-soaked cheeks. 'I'm an engineer . . . not a bloody spy . . .'

'It's okay, Kon,' Malcolm says softly.

'It's not okay, Malc. I saw dead kiddies. I don't want to see that. I'm not one of you . . .'

Emily tugs at her overcoat, suddenly stifling in the heat. A presence behind her and Harry's big hands come to her shoulders, helping her from the coat.

'Report,' Miri orders.

Emily relays the details, keeping it succinct and to the point while everyone listens, and spots the nod passing between Miri and Ben. 'That's it,' she finishes off. 'What's going on?'

'Do you trust him?' Ben asks.

'Alpha? Not a chance but . . . there was something about the way he spoke. Having said that he *is* Alpha and very bloody good at what he does . . . and he gave me a chance to shoot him.'

'Should have done,' Safa mutters.

'Ben? Miri?' Emily asks. 'What's going on?'

'We thought about it earlier,' Ben says, thinking hard as he talks. 'Miri said the UK government wouldn't have sanctioned the use of a nuke, especially on their own people . . . And it fits what Alpha told Emily . . . We were gone for nearly two months, remember. They did the Roman thing and we didn't react so she escalated up to dropping a nuke and now we're still not reacting . . . This isn't the government coming after us. It's just Mother.'

'He said she's planning an extinction level event,' Emily says, repeating what she said before.

'How does dropping one H-bomb cause an extinction?' Safa asks. 'I know they're big but . . .'

'It doesn't work like that,' Ben says. 'A big modern nuke needs a launch facility and if Mother launches one then everyone launches theirs . . . If she does that *and* releases anthrax then . . .' He trails off with a shrug.

'Yeah, that's bad,' Safa says mildly. 'Right, better fix it.' She looks round at the others, at the stress showing, even on Miri and Ben. 'It'll be fine. Worrying doesn't get things fixed. We've got a time machine. Plus we've got Miri and Ben, who are a hundred times smarter than they are, plus we've got Harry and me . . . and Malcolm, and Konrad . . . and the doc . . .' She stops to smile as everyone looks at Emily. 'Oh, and Emily too, who will be making everyone a nice drink.'

'I beg your pardon? I just risked my life for . . .'

'You got caught by Alpha is what you just did,' Safa cuts in. 'Only a twat runs after someone like that on their own. You're on brew duty. We'll have a drink and go back for the third visit.'

'Alpha said he needs time to think tonight,' Emily says.

'I'm going to regret asking this,' Safa says, more to herself, 'but what difference does that make? We've got time machines. We can go now and he can go next bloody year but we'll still be there at the same time . . .'

'They noticed our two-month gap,' Ben says. 'Which means our time is synched to theirs.'

'So . . .' Safa says slowly. 'Does that mean we've got the night off? Yes? Awesome. Paris it is then.'

'What?' Ben asks.

'I am going to see Paris before we get made extinct. Get brewing, Rose . . . Mine's a tea.'

Twenty-Seven

The Complex

'Shut it down,' Alpha orders in the portal room.

'Gasping for a coffee,' Echo says lightly. 'Alpha? Want one?'

'Er, yeah, sure,' Alpha replies as though distracted and in deep thought. He looks round the room, seeing the pensive expressions on the faces of the workers. 'Plans going okay?' he asks Gunjeep.

'They are,' the man replies without any trace of humour. 'Turns out it's far easier to steal a hydrogen bomb than we thought.' He busies himself at the portal terminal, jabbing and swiping at the screen.

'We've got our own,' Echo says, making the connection.

'We certainly do,' Gunjeep says. 'The UK nuclear arsenal is fully equipped. Using a big one is out of the question because of the codes and launch protocols . . .' He trails off, glancing at the two men with a neutral expression. 'However, and as Mother pointed out, we don't have to launch a big one at all. Lots of smaller ones all in one place will do the job . . . or, as she suggested, lots of small ones in *lots* of places . . .'

A look between Alpha and Echo and both men nod as though impressed.

'Lots of big bangs and everyone dies.' Gunjeep beams at them, forcing the smile. 'Then we catch the bad guys, reset and go home for our dinners, eh?'

'Shouldn't be doing it.' A voice behind them makes Alpha and Echo spin round to see Roger, one of the technicians glaring at them both.

'What did you say?' Alpha demands, striding to the man to grab him by the collar and drag him several feet across the room. 'Say it again . . . SAY IT AGAIN . . .'

'We shouldn't be doing it,' Roger shouts. 'It's wrong . . . It's genocide . . .' His head snaps back from the punch delivered by Alpha that breaks his nose, sending a spray of blood over the man's white lab coat.

'This is our mission,' Alpha says through gritted teeth. 'You signed up for it. YOU ALL SIGNED UP FOR IT . . .' He shoves the man to the ground, watching with distaste as he curls up into a ball while clutching his face. 'You two, get him to the infirmary . . .' he shouts at two men. 'We will not have insubordination here. This is a disciplined mission. Do you understand? DO YOU UNDERSTAND?'

Murmurs come back, scared nods and low voices from people who can't look him in the eye.

The two agents walk through the complex, unable to speak or share words on what they just learnt or what just happened. An act to maintain. A cover to hold, but it's shared now and there is strength in that unity and a glance between them tells both that Alpha had to hit the man. Mother watches everything, she hears everything, and a broken nose is a small price to pay to save the world.

Alpha stops at Mother's door, knocking once and waiting as Echo walks on.

'Enter.'

Alpha pushes in and stops with one foot over the threshold, turning to call out to Echo, 'Stand down for tonight. Be ready to deploy in the morning.'

'Roger,' Echo says smartly.

Extinct

'Mother,' Alpha says, coming to a stop in front of her desk.

She carries on working with a show of power at making him wait. It stinks in here. Pungent and unhealthy and he notices her hair looks greasy too, unwashed, and the array of coffee cups and plates tell him she's hardly leaving her office.

'Nice punch,' she remarks quietly, not bothering to look at him.

'I was . . .'

'Report,' she orders, speaking over him.

'Nothing.'

'Nothing?' she asks as if it's his fault.

'Not yet. We'll pick it up tomorrow . . .'

'You'll go now,' she says.

'Tomorrow,' he says firmly, at last making her head jerk up. 'I want to get my head round your plans.'

A pause, a look from her to him and for a second he fears she will launch into another fit of rage, but she just nods. 'Basic plan is on that. Smaller warheads with . . .'

'Gunjeep just said—'

'I don't care what GUNJEEP JUST FUCKING SAID . . .' she screeches. 'Don't ever interrupt me again or it will be Bravo standing in front of me as the lead agent.'

The temptation is right there. The urge to pull his gun and shoot her through the head, but that leaves Bravo, Charlie and Delta plus a facility full of innocent people.

'Apologies,' he says calmly.

'Go away,' she snaps.

He goes out, heading for the canteen, which falls silent as he walks through. He stops at the food bar, grabbing pieces of fruit and shoving a mug under the coffee dispenser before glaring round enough to make people carry on talking, albeit quietly and in hushed tones. At Kate's door he strides in, ignoring Rodney, who was in the middle of saying something before rushing off with a muttered excuse.

'Ooh, fruit,' Kate says. 'Is that a banana in your pocket or have you just got a big willy?'

He forces a smile before bending to kiss her cheek. 'We need to talk.' The risk of a whisper, but his breath is barely more than warm air.

'Can I have your apple?' she asks as he pulls back.

'Sure.'

'Thanks, so hungry,' she says, biting into it. 'Bad atmos today,' she adds with a roll of her eyes. 'Everyone's a bit grumpy.'

'I noticed.'

'Would be nice to get out,' she says, holding eye contact on him for a second. 'I'm doing the hourly check if you fancy it?'

'Er, yeah, yeah, sure. Few minutes wouldn't hurt. I'll meet you in the portal room.'

'Okay . . . and I know you have a big willy! Not as big as a banana, but then that would hurt so . . .'

'Bye, Kate,' he says, giving her a quick grin at the door.

He walks on, thinking a thousand thoughts with an urge inside to go back and shoot Mother, then find Bravo and shoot him. Sometimes the simplest method is the best. Negate both threats, take over the mission and establish a line of dialogue with Maggie Sanderson. They can agree to reset the changes and Alpha can report back to the government. Will that work?

'What ho,' Bravo booms as he enters their section. 'Fruit, eh? Nice and healthy.'

'Something like that,' Alpha replies, nodding at Charlie and Delta. 'Echo give you the news?'

'We're standing down for tonight?' Charlie asks.

Alpha nods. 'I want to look at Mother's plans for the extinct— For the next phase . . .' He covers the slip of the tongue but knows they noticed.

'Oops,' Bravo laughs, waggling a finger at Alpha. 'You almost said extinction then, old chap.'

'Almost,' Alpha says quietly, staring at the man, who beams at him while sitting back, as laconic as ever with his hands interlaced behind his head. 'But I didn't say it,' he adds.

'Good for you,' Bravo says, holding his eye contact as Charlie, Delta and Echo look over, sensing the atmosphere like dogs in a pack seeing the leader being challenged for dominance.

Alpha holds position, staring at the unmoving and still smiling Bravo. 'Problem, Bravo?'

'None at all, old chap,' Bravo replies with humour, but the eye contact holds and the edge shows in his voice.

Alpha should address it now. His professional response should be to take Bravo aside and speak to him privately, addressing the tone and way of speech while his gut instinct tells him to kill the man now and take his chances with Charlie and Delta, but the doubt is there. The worry that Kate will be left isolated and a target if it doesn't work so he smiles instead, flooding his features with warmth.

'I think we're all getting on each other's nerves a bit, eh? Come on, Bravo. Get rid of the glare . . . Go and beat someone at chess. I'll be glad when this mission is done, lads.'

An easing back of the tension, not a great deal, but enough for the others to chuckle while sharing glances.

Alpha heads for the door, pausing at the side of Bravo to lay a hand on his shoulder. 'Take it easy,' he says softly.

'Always do, old chap, always do.'

They barely look at him in the portal room and the blood still shows wet and crimson on the floor from Roger's broken nose. 'Get that cleaned up,' Alpha snaps.

'Will do,' Gunjeep says, bringing the portal to life. 'All yours.'

Kate stays silent, staring at the blood before walking after Alpha into the darkened office in 2095 and to Alpha standing with his hands on his head exhaling deeply with a look of intense worry etched on his features.

'What happened?' she asks.

He moves in close, pulling her in to press his mouth to her ear, not trusting that there isn't a listening device somewhere, not trusting anything. He whispers the explanation as quickly as possible, telling Kate about Tango Two, about Echo and coming back through the portal and punching the technician.

'Forget about Roger,' she whispers, her arms wrapped round his neck to hold him close. 'He's a twat anyway, but wow on everything else. You did it . . . You made contact.'

'She said they're good people.'

'They are,' Kate asserts. 'Everyone knows it.'

'I'm going back to our third visit tomorrow . . .'

'Why tomorrow? Why wait?'

'I need time to think, Kate. I need to show Mother I'm not rushing or worried . . .'

'Take me with you. We'll tell Mother it's a field trip and I'll help convince Maggie . . . She'll see I'm not an agent or anything.'

'Not yet, it's not safe . . . We've got to do this right, and what about everyone else in the complex? And that still leaves Bravo and Mother . . . These are dangerous people, Kate.'

'Okay, it was just an idea . . . Whatever you think is right. Just tell me what you need and I'll do it.'

'We'd better get back. I've got an extinction plan to read.'

Twenty-Eight

Lambeth-not-Lambeth, 2111

They walk slowly through the early-morning chaos of a busy street getting ready for the day. A street full of noise and life with vendors guiding their floating stalls to position while calling out to each other and the store owners operating switches to draw their shopfronts back. The amplified sound of a radio DJ's voice sounding in the air. Smells of cooking, of fried locusts and synthetic coffee wafting here and there.

'An incredible place,' Doctor John Watson says, marvelling at the sights. 'Did you ever visit New Orleans?'

'I did,' Miri says, walking at his side. 'And, yes, there is a similarity.'

'In mood I'd say, in vibe, yes. The atmosphere . . . that community feel of the place.'

'Morning!' a vendor calls over. 'Beautiful day again, Affas . . .'

'Good morning,' the doctor calls out, waving a cheery hand. 'I say, old chap, where can we get some pastries and coffee to take away?'

'Up the road, Affa. Stall on the right, big fella with huge boobs, best pastries in London! His coffee's shit though . . .'

'*UNKNOWN ADULT MALE. THE USE OF REVOLTING, ABUSIVE OR INSULTING WORDS IS PROHIBITED IN THIS PUBLIC PLACE.*'

'Ah, piss off,' the man laughs, setting it off again as a chorus of swear words are shouted up and down the street by vendors and hawkers.

They walk on with Doctor Watson chuckling at the sights and sounds while Miri stays mostly quiet as she works the problems in her mind. She thinks of Mother, of Alpha, of nuclear bombs and 25,000 people dying and how many more will perish or suffer before it ends, of how to reset it all and fix what Mother's done.

The offer from Alpha to switch sides seems too good to be true and feels like a trap, like a hand is being played, but is it something she can use? They must stop Mother. That is the primary objective, but then they must also reset the changes made by Mother and stop them killing the Romans and dropping the nuclear bomb on London.

'It was a grand evening though,' the doctor remarks, drawing her attention. 'And getting Bertie off the island for a few hours was very healthy for him.'

She nods, lending half an ear to his conversation. Safa was right yesterday; they needed that downtime and Paris was a good evening. Even if Emily did show off by ordering everyone's food in fluent French. Miri did order her own at the very end, also in fluent French, which made Emily smart and everyone else laugh.

'Good lord, is that our Ria?' the doctor asks, stopping as they cross the mouth of a side street. Miri looks down to Jerry's café and Ria sitting with a small group eating food at one of the tables.

'It is,' Miri says, her voice hardening.

'And you can stop that look,' the doctor tells her. 'She's young, let her live . . .'

'She should not be using the device for . . .'

'Miri, my dear, we dined in Paris, then slept on an island in the distant Mediterranean past and now we're in London getting pastries and coffee for everyone else still asleep in the Parisian hotel we left them in last night . . . and by all accounts I have died twice, yet here I am. How is any of that *not* misusing the device?'

'A good point succinctly made,' she remarks with a respectful dip of her head. She stares again at Ria, watching the young woman laugh. She looks hard now, tough and lean and the survival instincts Ria learnt to stay alive for two years in the Cretaceous period show as she seems to feel the eyes watching her and turns to look up. The laughter fading from her face as she rises to her feet on seeing Miri and the doctor watching her.

'Morning, Ria!' the doctor calls out. 'We're just getting some pastries. Everything okay?'

'Fine,' Ria says curtly.

'Great stuff. Come along now, Miri.' He loops his arm through hers, leading her on and away up the bustling street so full of noise and colour and life. They stop at the stall to buy coffees and pastries, the doctor chatting away to the vendor while Miri watches and listens and thinks. They need a plan and they need one fast.

'Be a shame to see this go,' the doctor remarks, looking round with a heavy sigh as they walk back. 'Still, can't have despots changing time all over the place now, can we?'

◆ ◆ ◆

Paris, France

The first thing Harry does when he wakes is remind himself where he is. He does it now and within a split second he knows he is stark naked in a four-poster bed in a sumptuous hotel room in Paris.

He knows it's morning by the sunlight coming through the windows and he also knows he was drinking heavily last night from the taste of gorilla shit in his mouth. He knows they ate a lovely meal last night in a big fancy restaurant where Emily showed off by ordering everything in fluent French. He remembers walking under what used to be called the Eiffel Tower, which is now called the Paris Tower and is a bit taller and in a different place. He knows all those things because they pass through his mind in a pleasant series of memories as he stretches languidly.

Then he remembers the other bit in one solid flashback as a graceful feminine hand gropes up his chest to his beard with an action that makes his eyes widen and his heart thump as he sits bolt upright.

'Harry!' Emily yelps, sliding off his chest.

'Bugger . . .'

She snaps her eyes open to stare up at him staring down. 'Oh shit . . . not again . . .'

'Bugger.' He lurches up and away as she groans and rolls on her back covering her face with her hands.

'Shit . . . shit, shit, shit . . .'

'Bugger . . .' Harry grabs a door handle and walks into a closet.

'Harry bloody Madden,' she snaps, sitting up to glare at him backing out of the closet.

'Eh, now,' he says, holding his hands out to placate the angry look on her face.

'Don't you bloody "*eh now*" me, Harry bloody Madden . . .'

He backs towards the door, trying ever so hard not to look at her boobs jiggling as she rolls from the bed and comes up holding a shoe.

'Oh blimey.' He runs for the door, deciding, at that point, that escape and evasion are the best thing to do.

'HARRY BLOODY MADDEN,' she yells, running after him.

Malcolm stirs on the chaise longue in the sumptuous middle room of the suite, lifting his head to stare bleary-eyed at a naked Harry being chased by an angry naked Emily clutching a shoe. 'Crikey,' he mumbles, blinking himself awake.

'Eh, now, you put that down,' Harry says, running behind a large sofa.

'You sod . . . you did it again,' she yells, running after him.

'Eh, now, miss,' he says, going round one end of the sofa while she goes round the other.

'Stop saying that and let me hit you . . .'

'Crikey,' Malcolm says, now sitting up on the chaise longue to watch them running naked circles round the sofa.

'Ach, just put the shoe down.'

'You seduced me again.'

'No, miss . . . I did . . .'

'You bloody did! You and your big manliness and hairy chest and beard . . . Stop running away, you shit . . .'

'You seduced me,' Harry bleats, scarpering out of arm's reach.

'What?! I did no such thing . . .'

'You did,' Malcolm says, watching the show with interest.

'You did,' Safa calls out from somewhere.

'We all heard it,' Malcolm says. 'You said "*Come on, Harry, I want you to sex me three times again*" . . .'

'I did not!'

'You did,' Safa calls from somewhere.

'Aye,' Harry says. 'That's what happened . . .'

'That's not the point and you lot can butt out . . .' She realises the folly of running round the sofa and decides, being the highly trained agent that she is, to go over it instead and launches deftly, while naked, over the back to land on the cushions with shoe in hand.

'Bugger,' Harry says, running for the bathroom door and deciding, being the highly trained commando that he is, to go for the island and maybe swim out a mile from the shore until she has calmed down. He goes in fast with Emily right behind him and aims for the portal that was a few inches off the wall and bounces back with a yelp into Emily with a slap of skin on skin.

'Crikey,' Konrad says, blinking awake in the large sumptuous bathtub to see a naked Harry and Emily collide and fall to the floor in a tangle of limbs while a shoe sails through the air to land in the toilet.

'Harry bloody Madden . . .' she says, writhing underneath his body. 'Get off me . . .'

'I'm trying,' he says deeply, floundering to get up with a face full of soft womanly bits.

'Eh,' Konrad says, looking at the wall. 'Where's the portal gone?'

'Where's my shoe?'

'In the toilet . . . Er . . . the portal's not there.'

'Now, miss . . . let me get up.'

'I'm not bloody stopping you. It's not like you actually want to cuddle the morning after, is it?'

'Ben?' Konrad calls out.

'What?'

'The portal's not there . . .'

Harry freezes, still on top of Emily as she goes still beneath him with her hands pressed to his chest and slowly they both look round to where the Blue should be.

'Fuck,' Ben says, running in to see the bare wall and the distinct lack of a shimmering blue light.

'What's happened?' Safa asks, pushing in next to him in bra and knickers. She looks down at Emily and Harry as though it's the most natural thing in the world to see them naked and virtually coupled on the floor of a sumptuous hotel bathroom. 'Morning.'

'Morning, Safa,' Emily says, taking one hand from Harry's chest to push stray hairs from her eyes.

'Morning,' Harry says.

Ben blinks at the wall, then at Harry and Emily, then at the shoe in the toilet and finally at a fully clothed Konrad lying in an empty bath.

'No beds,' Konrad says.

'Oh,' Ben says. 'Why is there a shoe in the toilet?'

'That's my shoe,' Emily says.

'Oh,' Ben says as the room bathes in blue from the portal blinking to existence like it was always there.

'Morning, morning,' the doctor calls out, bustling through it with a tray of drinks and a large paper bag. 'Queue for the toilet, is it?' he asks looking down at Harry's bare backside in between Emily's legs. 'Croissant?'

'Ooh, me please,' Emily says, stretching an arm up. 'Harry can't have one. He seduced me again.'

'He didn't,' Ben says, taking a croissant. 'He really didn't.'

'Did,' Emily says, blithely ignoring everyone saying otherwise while she bites into the pastry. 'Share?' she says, offering it up to Harry.

'Yeah, this is just wrong now,' Safa says, screwing her face up at the sight of them sharing food while naked on the bathroom floor.

'We saw young Ria,' the doctor says, covering his mouth with a hand while chewing. 'Seemed very happy, until she saw us, that is, then she didn't look so happy.' He pauses to turn as Miri comes through the portal, a coffee in her hand and an unlit cigarette between her lips. A glance round then down to Harry and Emily on the floor and everyone else in underwear eating croissants.

'Ah, well,' the doctor says sadly. 'Just be sure you get Ria out of there before you reset it. Shame though. World seems a nice place now. Still, I'm sure you chaps know what you're doing.'

A look between Miri and Ben, a meeting of eyes and the worry is there, the fear that they are being equalled by an opponent who has as much skill and experience as them, one who has a time machine and one who is prepared to kill the world.

Twenty-Nine

Berlin, Bundesstraße 2, 5 February 1945

Neither side have anything that could be called a plan. There's no precedent for something like this. There's no guidebook or rules for what happens when two opposing sides, both highly trained, highly skilled and highly experienced and both with time machines meet in a changed timeline with a heightened sense of distrust.

In building number twenty-five at one end of the street, Miri and her team gather to stare out of the grimy windows at the destruction below and down to building number eight where Alpha and Echo stand ready. Both sides also watch Arch 451 because in approximately one hour the five agents will be coming through for their third visit to Herr Weber.

The tension mounts. All of them feeling the stress of it. One side took a night off and had fun in Paris, but that is now pushed to the backs of minds.

Alpha and Echo read through Mother's notes on preparing for the use of modern thermonuclear warheads, combined with a release of anthrax in several high-density population zones, and the ease at which it can be done staggered both of them. Whatever they are going to do has to be done now because Mother needs just days to be able to carry out her extinction level event.

The immediate problem is that neither side can see the other due to the reflection of the glass and the light of the cold February day falling just so.

Who makes the first move? Who needs it most?

'What now?' Ben asks quietly, standing next to Miri at the window while the others hold back. 'Should we signal?'

She shakes her head, winging it and feeling the rules of the game play out in real time. 'Let them show first.'

In the complex, in the dark gloom of her office with her face reflecting the glow of the screens, Mother sits with her fingers steepled in front of her because she *does* have a plan. Mother has had a plan since this began and is feeling the thrill as the endgame now comes into view.

A knock at the door. She calls out to enter.

'You wanted an update?' the person asks politely.

'Don't fucking stand there gawping. Close the door and get on with it.'

The door closes and the figure strolls over to stand with hands in pockets and an eyebrow arched. 'You look like shit.'

'Is he ready?'

'Alpha thinks he's a hero and you're a mad crazy bitch who is losing the plot.'

'Is he ready?' Mother asks again.

'He's ready alright. He'll switch sides the second he gets the chance.'

'Good. Make it happen.'

'Now?'

'Yes, now. It has to be now. The only option left is for Alpha and Echo to join forces with Maggie and use them for a combined attack on this complex. Do it now. We cannot delay any further and I want you there when it happens . . .'

◆ ◆ ◆

In building number eight, Echo watches Arch 451, while Alpha watches building twenty-five. More than an hour has passed since they arrived. Time enough for the old them to complete their third visit and the tension mounts with still no sign of Maggie or her team.

'The old us are going back into the arch,' Echo says.

'Okay,' Alpha mutters, staring up the street. 'Where are they?'

'We'll run out of time,' Echo says. 'We have to take the risk – it's the only option we've got now.'

Alpha nods. 'I know.'

'There's only two of us, Alpha. We can't take on three other agents *and* Mother in a complex full of innocent civilians. We join forces with Maggie and we all attack the complex. Maggie can use their device to arrive in our quarters to negate Bravo and the other two if need be while we go back in through the portal room.'

'That means we hand our device over to Maggie Sanderson,' Alpha says.

'So what? Listen, Maggie could have used her device to come back to Cavendish Manor and kill every single soldier and operative there, but she didn't. They only did what they needed to do to get the inventor and his family away.'

Alpha nods. It makes sense and it really is the only option now. 'How do we convince Maggie?'

'Fuck knows,' Echo says. 'You can work that one out . . . You get paid more than me.'

Alpha snorts at the joke, sharing a look with Echo, who offers a wry smile. 'Nothing like winging it, eh?' Alpha says.

Echo checks his watch. 'We've got just under an hour,' he says with a glance down to the arch. 'We need to make a move.'

Alpha looks at the arch, staring hard while thinking. 'Got a torch?' he asks.

'I'm an agent,' Echo says, pulling a small flashlight from his pocket. 'Of course I've got a torch . . . Want me to signal?'

'Do it . . .'

◆ ◆ ◆

'Signal!' Ben says quickly, seeing the single flash of light coming from the window on the top floor of the house down the street. 'There. See it?'

'Got it,' Miri says.

'About bloody time,' Safa says.

'We need to signal back,' Miri says. 'Someone pass me a flashlight . . .' Silence in the room. 'I need a flashlight,' she says, holding her hand out while keeping her eyes on the window down the street. Safa and Emily shrug at each other and look at Harry, who lifts his hands a few inches. 'Seriously?' Miri asks, looking round.

'Have you got a torch?' Safa asks her.

'Can't think of everything,' she mumbles.

'Lighter?' Harry asks, offering his cigarette lighter.

'We can try it,' Ben says. 'Wave it at the window.'

◆ ◆ ◆

'Still nothing,' Echo says. 'I'll give it another single flash.'

'Roger,' Alpha says.

'Flash done,' Echo reports, his eyes fixed.

◆ ◆ ◆

'They flashed again,' Ben says. 'Did you see it?'

'Aye,' Harry says, leaning closer to look while holding the lighter against the pane of glass and waving his hand a few inches side to side.

'Was that in response to us?' Ben asks.

'Must have been,' Harry says.

'Do Morse code,' Ben urges with a sudden idea.

'With a cigarette lighter?' Harry asks, watching down the street and not the flame from the lighter that heats the old paintwork on the dry wooden frame on the inside of the window. A singe, a blister, a flame and a thick tendril of acrid smoke curls up as the wood catches alight. 'Oops,' Harry says, moving his other hand in to pat the flames down in the manner of a gorilla smashing his hand through a window with a loud crack of glass that makes people in the street look up.

◆ ◆ ◆

'Er . . . one of them just punched the glass out,' Echo says.

'What are they doing?'

'No idea,' Echo says.

◆ ◆ ◆

'Harry!' Ben says, trying to pat out the flames creeping along the wooden frame.

'Thin glass,' Harry says, slamming his enormous hands down again.

'Unbelievable,' Safa says, leaning between them both to pour a bottle of water over the burning wood. 'Are we sending smoke signals . . . ?'

'Ah well, at least they know we're here,' Ben says. 'Right, better go down then.'

'I'll stay up here,' Safa says. 'Harry, you stay by the ground floor door with Konrad . . .'

'I really don't think I'm cut out for this,' Konrad says, looking sick to the stomach with nerves.

'We've been over this,' Safa says. 'Miri, Ben and Emily will go out. You're on standby for a distraction if it goes wrong. Deploy now.'

'You'll be fine,' Harry rumbles, clamping a hand on the poor man's shoulder to guide him out the room.

◆ ◆ ◆

'Movement,' Echo says urgently, leaning closer to the window.

'Got them,' Alpha says, watching three figures move out from the doorway at street level. 'Male and two females in period clothing . . . That's Tango Two. It's her . . . That's Maggie Sanderson and Ben Ryder.'

'Okay,' Echo says. 'Let me go down.'

'No, I'll do it,' Alpha replies.

'Let me. You're Alpha. I should go. Stay here in case it's a trap.'

'No, mate,' Alpha says. 'But thanks, Ian . . . I appreciate that.'

'I'm right here,' Echo says, nodding as Alpha moves to the door. 'Listen, want me to run back and draw a sniper rifle? I can give you overwatch . . .'

'It'll draw suspicion . . . but thanks.'

Alpha goes down the stairs and steps into the street to a view worse than ever before. Bodies everywhere and the buildings surrounding them in an even worse state. Smoke in the near distance from fires burning uncontrolled and he spots the shapes of aircraft in the sky from bombing raids underway on different parts of the city. People are still here though, dragging bodies out of the rubble and trying to scrape order from the destruction and chaos.

All of that is taken in within a glance as he looks round and settles his view on the three figures further up the street. He looks up to the window of the building the others came from and guesses they'll have someone on overwatch in radio contact. He spots Tango Two moving with Maggie and Ben across the street and sets off towards them, his hands tucked in the pockets of his coat and his head down to blend in.

Safa stares from the top floor of building number eight, taking in the solitary figure coming, then glances back up to the window, trying to see if he has left anyone on overwatch.

'It's just him coming out,' she says into her radio. 'Walking up the street towards you now.'

Harry stays next to Konrad inside the ground floor door, ready to respond and react if needed.

Alpha closes the distance, his eyes scanning everything in front of him. A group of German women clutching clipboards and wearing Nazi armbands to mark their authority move slowly through the street and he spots the way they point out the worst mounds of rubble and piles of bodies stacked and waiting to be taken away.

He has to take his hands out of his pockets to show trust. He has to show open hands. He does it now, taking them slowly out to hang at his sides while he walks.

'*Got you covered . . .*' Echo holds his pistol, aiming up the street. The distance for a pistol is huge, but by the grace of God he'll do what he can to cover Alpha.

Alpha walks on, feeling a strange surge of warmth at the gesture from Echo.

'*He's taken his hands out of his pockets,*' Safa transmits. '*Empty hands, but he'll have a weapon somewhere.*'

'Do the same,' Miri says, drawing her hands out to show they're empty.

'*I'm on pistol but I've got you covered,*' Safa says from the top floor, holding her own gun aimed at Alpha.

They come in sight of each other. All of them tense. All unblinking. The distance reduces, the space between them growing less. Miri tries reading his face, but the man is impassive. Alpha does the same, trying to see inflections.

'What are you doing?' a woman from the group wearing armbands shouts in German, her voice harsh and commanding.

Alpha stops walking, his hands at his sides. Miri, Ben and Emily watching him closely and none of them responding to the woman.

'You . . . Who are you?' the woman demands, moving at the head of her group of women, striding towards the three facing off in tense silence against Alpha.

'*Someone better answer her,*' Safa transmits. '*Konrad, be ready to go out and distract . . .*'

'I said who are you?' the German woman shouts angrily, tired, filthy and sick of the death and destruction in her home city.

'He's my brother,' Emily says, instantly morphing into a sickened and terrified German woman. She waves a tired hand at Alpha and closes her eyes at the horror of it all.

'Emily,' Alpha says in true sorrow, closing the last few feet with a look of intense worry. 'Have you found him?'

'Not yet,' Emily says, her lip trembling with emotion.

'Oh god,' Alpha whispers. He can see the scowl on the woman's face and the looks of suspicion from her cohorts. He closes in, taking his sister in his arms. 'We'll find him . . .' he says sincerely. 'Have hope . . .' He pulls back to shake his head sadly at Ben, patting him on the shoulder in a manly display of affection in this awful time, and steps to embrace Miri. 'Don't fret, we'll find him . . .' He takes in the group of women, observing the Nazi armbands on their arms, which signal they have taken authority to try and keep the city running. He spots the clipboards in their hands that hold lists of the dead and injured and where needs attention the most.

'Who?' the woman demands.

'My son,' Emily says, casting about with a wild look.

'My nephew,' Alpha says.

'Name?' the woman barks, reaching back to take a clipboard from another woman. 'Name!' she shouts.

'Hans,' Emily says weakly. 'I had a picture . . .' She puts her hand in her pocket as though searching for the photograph, but presses the button on her radio. 'I had a picture . . . I can't find it . . .'

'Hans what?' the woman asks.

'Johanns,' Emily says.

'Poor Hans,' Alpha says wretchedly, rubbing his face while Ben listens on. He doesn't speak German but guesses the conversation underway and adopts an expression of great worry.

'You the father?' the woman asks Ben.

'He is,' Alpha cuts in. 'His hearing has suffered from the bombing . . . We're trying to . . .'

'Why aren't you fighting?' the woman asks, glaring from Alpha to Ben.

'Please,' Alpha says. 'We're trying to . . .'

'My son,' Emily says. 'We'll look for him . . . I have to find him . . .'

'You're both young. You should be fighting,' the woman says angrily.

'Emily!' Konrad staggers from the door, running across the road, clutching the photograph they used last time. 'Have you found him?' He aims for the group of women wearing Nazi armbands, pushing through to show them the picture. 'Hans . . . Have you seen him? You must have seen him . . . Look again, look . . .'

'Another one!' the woman shouts. 'Who are you . . . ? Why aren't you fighting? Three men here looking for one child while the Russians and the damn Americans are killing us while we sleep . . .'

'I AM CAPTAIN SCHMIDT OF THE FIRST INFANTRY . . .' Alpha roars. 'My nephew is missing. My family are searching. I have been fighting for six years and I *will* have one day to search for him . . . DO YOU UNDERSTAND!'

'Yes, sir.' The woman backs down, showing instant supplication at the authority pouring from the man.

'Now unless you know where Hans is I suggest you move on and do your jobs. Emily . . . I am sorry you had to hear that . . .' He turns to Emily, showing his back to the women, who start moving off, but Ben spots the wary glances they cast towards them as they go.

Konrad stands seemingly lost as to what to do, holding the photograph while staring at Alpha, the man who tried to kill him and Malcolm outside the warehouse.

'My friend, we'll find him,' Alpha tells Ben, staying in role and noticing the glances of the women as they walk away. He turns back to Emily, distraught and wishing only to help her find Hans. 'They're suspicious,' he says quietly in German. 'We don't have long.' He motions to the side, indicating they should move away as though they are a family taking time during their search to stop and talk earnestly.

'In English now,' Miri says quietly. 'Ben doesn't speak German.'

Ben and Alpha stare at each other, standing face-to-face amidst the ruins. Ben remembers Alpha from Cavendish Manor. The viciousness of the man and what he did to Ria's mother.

'You dropped a nuke on London, you evil prick,' Ben hisses, stepping closer to Alpha as Emily reaches out to pull him back.

'The Roman patrol? What was that for?' Miri asks.

'Maggie, it's an honour to meet . . .'

'Shut up,' Miri snaps, surpassing the power of authority Mother has. 'Answer the question or I will kill you right now.'

'To draw you out,' Alpha replies instantly. 'You didn't react so Mother escalated . . . I know what we've done isn't right, but . . .'

'Report,' Miri orders.

Alpha glances round and draws breath. 'They found a blueprint in the remains of Cavendish Manor and used it to build a time machine in a purpose-built complex. Mother was disgraced after what happened, but she now claims she sanctioned the whole project. She also said everyone in the complex was murdered by you. She said you found out, got in and slaughtered innocent people, then wiped the footage. She said you also killed the PM . . . She then tasked us to extract those same scientists back into that complex, then sent the whole thing fifty million years into the past. Now she won't stop. She wants you dead . . . I saw her plans last night. She's planning to detonate modern thermonuclear warheads and release anthrax . . .'

'So?' Miri says flatly. 'You're an agent. Negate her and go back to your superiors.'

'There's only two of us – me and Echo, that's it . . . Bravo, Charlie and Delta are still in the complex . . .'

'Your problem, not ours. Was there anything else?' she asks, showing a hint of boredom. 'What? You want us to storm your complex? Is that right? We get filmed killing you, we're the bad guys or, worse, we walk into a pinchpoint trap and get killed. Yeah, sure, you think this is my first rodeo, son? This ain't my first rodeo . . . Go back and sort your own mess out.'

'We have to stop her,' Alpha says.

'*You* have to stop her,' Miri says.

'Maggie, listen . . . There's been enough killing. I can't risk the lives of the people in that complex.'

'You just dropped a nuclear bomb,' Emily says.

'I know, but . . .'

An idea comes. An idea that makes Ben drop his head and reach up to rub the side of his jaw with an action that makes Safa smile as she watches from the window as Alpha blinks in reaction. He saw the Ben Ryder movie and that same thing the actor playing Ben did to capture his essence.

Miri spots it too, and the wry smile on Ben's face. 'You got something?' she asks.

'I've got something,' he says.

'Go,' she says, giving her consent for him to say it.

'*Someone press a button so I can listen in,*' Safa says through their radio network.

'This is the you now, isn't it?' Ben says to Alpha, who frowns in response, unsure of the question. 'I mean we're all in the present . . .

and you're dressed in period clothing, which means you're conducting observations, right? Who else is up there?' he asks, motioning back down the street to the building Alpha came from.

'Just Echo.'

'Bravo, Charlie and Delta are on standby then?'

Alpha nods, his eyes showing understanding as Ben carries on.

'Order them out, then tell them to disarm. You're Alpha, they'll listen to you . . . Once they're out and safe then we'll discuss terms.'

Alpha thinks fast, seeing the sense in the idea. 'If I order them out Mother will want to know why. We'll have minutes to do something before she reacts.'

'And does what?' Ben asks. 'We've got a time machine. Once you five are out the way we'll take care of it.'

A pause, a beat of a heart, a blink of an eye, the air thick with tension as Alpha nods. 'Okay, I'll get them out, but then I go straight back in on my own to negate Mother.'

'How do we know you haven't got more agents or soldiers in there?' Emily asks.

'We'll cross that bridge when we come to it,' Ben says, looking at Miri who nods once.

'Run with that plan,' she says curtly.

'I go back straight back in,' Alpha says.

'We just said we'll deal with that bit when it happens,' Ben says.

'Negative. No deal. I'll order them to disarm and I'll even kill them for you if they don't, but I go straight back in.'

'You are in no position to dictate terms, mate,' Ben says.

Alpha tenses with stress showing in his features. 'There's a woman,' he says quickly, quietly, glancing down as he speaks. 'If Mother suspects anything she'll kill her.'

'Should have thought of that before you dropped a nuke. Call your agents out,' Ben says, rolling his eyes at the look Alpha gives him, the same look he would give if he was in that position. Emily sees it too.

An expression she never thought possible of the lead agent from the British Secret Service.

'*I'll go back in with him.*' Safa's voice in their ears. '*Accept the terms. I'll go back in with him . . . This is them live now, Ben. You just said it. If nothing else, we negate the threat from them. Miri can take them to the place she held Roland if need be.*'

Miri nods.

'Agreed,' Ben says. 'Call your agents out.'

'*Echo . . . go back in and get Bravo, Charlie and Delta through. Be discreet and if Mother asks say I've gone down into the street and you think I might have something.*'

'*Roger, doing it now.*'

'He's doing it now . . .' Alpha relays as the others stare on.

'Why don't you just get the girl out now?' Emily asks after a few seconds.

Why didn't he think of that? Alpha presses the button on his radio. '*Echo, Echo . . . are you receiving me?*'

◆ ◆ ◆

'*Echo . . . go back in and get Bravo, Charlie and Delta through. Be discreet and if Mother asks say I've gone down into the street and you think I might have something.*'

'*Roger, doing it now.*'

Echo moves swiftly across the room and out through the landing to the back room and through the green shimmering light to the portal room.

'Keep it open,' he orders, walking briskly out the room and down the corridor. He wants to run, but that will draw attention. He passes Mother's closed office door and moves on to the offices and canteen.

'Hey, are you both back?' Kate asks, seeing him rush past her office.

'Er, not yet,' he calls out. He walks on to their day room, pushing the door open to see Delta snapping awake and Charlie and Bravo looking up from a game of chess on a tablet resting on the table between them.

'Got something?' Charlie asks, seeing Echo's expression.

'Alpha ordered to be discreet, but he wants you out. He's down in the street and might have something.'

A glance between them as the three rise to follow Echo. Bravo, Charlie and Delta in combat tactical rig with pistols on hips following Echo in his 1940s suit.

'Did he say what?' Bravo asks, falling into step next to Echo as they pass Kate's office, who moves to the doorway to watch them go down the corridor.

'No, just said to be quiet,' Echo says.

'Have you told Mother?' Bravo asks.

'No time. He said to be quick.'

'Understood,' Bravo says, casting a look at Mother's office door as they march past.

They go into the portal room with Echo taking the lead through to the top floor of building number eight, moving straight back to the window to look down at Alpha still standing with Maggie, Ben and Emily. He glances behind, seeing that Bravo, Charlie and Delta are through.

'*Alpha, it's Echo . . . We're all here.*'

◆ ◆ ◆

In the complex, Kate watches the four agents go past her office and frowns lightly as she steps back, deep in thought with a small tablet held in her hand that she brings up to swipe the screen.

'Hey,' Rodney says, walking into the room red-faced and feeling pumped from his new gym regime.

'Howdy,' Kate says. 'Gym okay?'

'I love it,' the lad says happily. 'I'm huge now . . . Wanna see the gun show?'

She laughs and looks over, 'Go on then . . .' She smiles as he strikes a pose, tensing his thin arms as though she should be greatly impressed. 'Oh wow, you look so good now.'

'HUGE,' he says, laughing at himself. 'What you doing?'

'Choosing a song.'

'Song? What for?'

'Oh, I've got some work to do,' she says with a roll of her eyes. 'Music always helps it go quicker.'

He walks over to peer over her shoulder, seeing the names of the songs and artists as she scrolls through playlists. 'Queen,' he says quickly. 'I love Queen . . .'

'Er, no, it's not right,' she says. 'I want something a bit harder.'

'Guns N' Roses,' he says, pointing at the screen.

'Um, nope, not right . . . You know when you know . . . Does that make sense?'

'Oh, totally,' he says earnestly.

'Something a bit edgier . . .' She scrolls through.

'Those are all so old,' he remarks.

'Er, hello? We're historians.'

'Ha! Good one . . . Ooh, go back . . . Yeah, that one.'

'Nirvana? Good choice . . . Which one?'

'Which one,' he scoffs. 'There's only one . . .'

'"Smells Like Teen Spirit"?' she asks.

'Totally,' he says.

'Hmmm.' She takes the two tiny gel buds, pressing them into her ears and waiting till they expand out, filling the shape. A press of the screen and she stands upright, pushing the tablet into her pocket as the opening bars fill her ears.

'Good?' Rodney asks, looking at her expectantly.

'Brilliant!' she shouts.

He turns away, flexing his arms to see if his muscles are growing yet, while she opens the drawer of her desk, takes out the silenced pistol, aims and shoots him through the back of the head before stepping out of her office, humming to herself as the tones of Kurt Cobain belt the song out in her ears. Coreen walks into view, smiling weakly at seeing Kate and ready to stop and say she's considering telling Mother she wants out, they all are, even Gunjeep is ready to jack it in, and maybe Kate can talk to the agents, you know, seeing as she's so close to them.

Coreen doesn't get to say any of that. She doesn't get to say anything at all because the bullet enters her forehead and takes the back of her head off in a shower of gore that coats the wall behind her.

Kate sweeps into the canteen, striding to the mid-point as those eating glance up while absorbed in their hushed conversations as they build momentum to tell Gunjeep they want out. She gains the middle, lifts the pistol and starts firing. She's fast too. Incredibly fast, and each shot fired is a tiny noise of compressed air as the tables, chairs and floor run with blood. She hears the screams over the music, but it's done in seconds and she goes on, striding while changing magazine before knocking and entering the office of the bearded physics guys who look round, startled at being disturbed, to be shot and killed.

She walks through the complex, sending bullets through the air that slam into bodies and heads. She guns workers down in the corridors, in rooms, in doorways and not one sees it coming. Not one does anything other than show utter shock at the smiling woman they all know so well aiming a gun at them.

'Kate,' Gunjeep calls out as she strides into the portal room with the gun behind her back. Everyone already reacting to the screams they heard. 'What's going on?' the chief technician asks as she gauges the position of everyone in the room. She pulls the gun round and moves in a circle on the spot, firing quickly with deadly aim, humming to herself as she works, then it's done and everyone lies dead in pools of thick red blood.

She spins to aim as the door opens, the gun locked on with perfect sight as Mother walks in, taking care to move round the bodies while saying something.

'HANG ON,' Kate shouts. 'GOT MUSIC ON . . .' She pulls the buds out, shaking her head for a second. 'What did you say?'

'I said hurry up.'

'I am hurrying up,' Kate says. 'That was really quick.'

'Yes, great. Ready?'

'Er . . . need some blood on me. Hang on.' She ditches the pistol and drops at the side of Gunjeep's body, pushing her hands into the blood to flick it on her front and across her face, flinching as she does so. 'Urgh, hot blood is the worst.'

'You've had worse,' Mother mutters.

'That's disgusting,' Kate replies. 'And watching me having sex was just weird too. You didn't need to see that.'

'I will monitor whatever I need to . . .'

'I'm your bloody daughter,' Kate snaps, rising to her feet. 'It's gross.'

'This is the level we work at.'

'Oh my god, straight from the Maggie Sanderson big book of spy rules. Right, I'm off . . .' She moves to the portal while rapidly sucking air in and out.

'Kate?' Mother asks.

'What?' she gasps between breaths.

'Do you like him?'

'Alpha? Of course I do. He's an amazing man, but don't worry, Mother, I won't jeopardise your precious mission . . . See you soon.' She gulps air a few more times, waves, then runs flat out through the portal while screaming out as Mother draws the pistol she was carrying, stands off to the side, aims high through the portal and starts firing.

◆ ◆ ◆

'What's going on?' Bravo asks, moving to the window to look down at the street.

'Not sure,' Echo says, half lying.

'Oh my, is that Maggie Sanderson? Good lord . . . that's our Alpha talking to Maggie Sanderson . . .'

Charlie and Delta rush forward, peering up to see the small group standing together.

'Tango Two,' Charlie says.

'Ben Ryder,' Delta says. 'What the fuck? What's going on, Echo?'

'I don't know,' Echo says again.

'Charlie,' Bravo says. 'Run back and draw sniper rifles from the armoury, assault rifles too . . .'

'No!' Echo says as Charlie goes to move off. 'Alpha would have said if he wanted them . . .'

'I'm second in command, my dear chap. Charlie, go . . .'

The scream cuts them off as Kate runs flat out through the portal, diving to the ground as silent bullets whip after her, embedding in the walls with chunks of plaster smashing out.

The three react quickly with a glance at Kate to see her covered in blood and wild with panic. They draw fast, going low to aim back at the shimmering doorway.

'SHE'S KILLING EVERYONE!' Kate screams, scrabbling as though to crawl away in abject fear. More rounds come through. The noise of them taken away by the portal so just the hiss and ricochets of bullets hitting walls, but Bravo fires back, Charlie and Delta doing the same, with loud gunfire erupting in the rooms that is heard through the street. Alpha spins on the spot and Ben, Miri and Emily shove hands into pockets ready to draw while Harry braces at the ground floor door at building twenty-five, ready to run out, and Safa charges down the stairs.

'*Echo! Report. Report* . . .' Alpha orders.

The whole street can hear it. Sustained firing of pistols coming from the top floor of building number eight.

'*Kate . . . she got through . . . said Mother is killing everyone . . . We've got incoming fire through the portal at us . . .*'

The new noises come together. The warble of the air-raid siren screaming out from street to street as the air fills with the roar of heavy bombers, already thick in number, flying high overhead. The AA guns start up, drowning the sound of the pistol shots in building eight.

'Stand still.' Ben draws fast, aiming his pistol at Alpha as all around them people stream past, running and shouting in fear of the bombers coming and the late warning of the air raid. 'What's happening?'

'Kate got through . . .' Alpha blurts.

'Kate?' Ben asks, having to shout over the noise as Safa and Harry batter a path through the people to reach them.

'Go back,' Miri hisses at them.

'The girl,' Alpha says. 'She got through . . . She said Mother is killing everyone. I have to go *now* . . . Let me go now . . .'

In the complex, Mother fires into the portal, making sure her aim is high while counting seconds in her head.

On the other side, Kate crawls away, whimpering in fear, crying out, panicked and terrified, but also counting the seconds. She reaches Echo, who reaches out to yank her into the front room as Mother rolls a grenade through the portal.

'GRENADE!' Delta roars, diving away as all three launch themselves back into the room. The explosive detonates with a dull whump that starts collapsing the ceiling with scorching hot shards of metal embedding into walls, and a second later the portal goes off.

'*Alpha! It's Bravo . . . The portal is off. I repeat, the portal is off. Orders?*'

'Let me get to them,' Alpha says to Miri, Ben and the others in the panicked street. 'I'll disarm them and bring them to you . . .'

'Me and Harry will go with him,' Safa says. 'Rest of you draw back . . .'

The problem with time travel is that any incursion into a period, no matter how seemingly small, can cause a ripple effect. Building number twenty-five in Bundesstraße 2 is not meant to be hit by a bomb. In fact, this air raid was not meant to come until later, but Emily and Konrad were spotted in the street a few days ago. Their suntanned hands were seen and reported back and that report went through the channels, which resulted in a German battalion being diverted into the city with the possibility of spies operating. That report was picked up on by the allies, who decided to alter their air-raid plans and drop heavy ordnance with a view to disrupting that flow of troops, and so the heavy bombers unleash their payloads, which fall through the sky with one hitting the roof of building twenty-five and crashing through the attic to smash down through the ceiling and past the portal into the floor below and all the way down to the ground floor where it explodes with a roaring fireball that sends bricks flying out into the street.

'COVER.' Harry roars the words without thinking, barrelling into the others to take them down to avoid the debris flying at them. Alpha dives away, scrabbling to his feet amidst the dust and smoke to run down the street, his ears ringing from the noise.

So many things happening. So much noise and heat and smoke, but Harry rises first, the most used to this environment, and he spots the danger instantly. 'Ben! Get up . . .'

Ben shakes his head, rolling on his back in stunned shock. His ears are ringing, his senses feeling battered. Harry's above him, reaching down to drag him up, shouting about something and pointing. Ben shakes his head again, trying to understand, then snapping alert on seeing it.

Building twenty-five is now no more, with the roof gone, collapsed inwards as it fell in through the floors that blew out from the explosion, but there, hanging in the air where the top floor was, the blue portal shimmers and shines like a beacon.

'They'll aim for it,' Harry says. 'The bombers . . . they'll aim for it. We've got to get away . . .'

Time slows for Ben. Like it did before when he was seventeen and then when he was on the platform at Holborn. Everything in perfect clarity, everything understood in the blink of an eye. He looks up to the portal hanging in the air and knows instantly it is way too high to reach. He also knows there is nothing here they can use to get to it, certainly no ladders. He also understands exactly what Harry meant when he said the bombers will aim for it. The only option is the portal in building eight. They have to get through it now and take control so they can go to Bertie's island and switch their own portal off, and right then, in the midst of all that noise he also berates himself for not bringing one of Bertie's new mobile portals with him.

'Up. We've got to move,' he shouts over the bedlam, heaving Miri to her feet as Harry does the others, hefting Safa and Emily up, then planting a huge hand on Konrad's arm to lift him up too. 'Go . . . GO! That way . . . after Alpha . . .'

They set off, shielding their faces from the heat of the flames and the thick dust while coughing from the acrid smoke. Another bomb sails past the portal, hitting the remains of building twenty-five and sending more scorching debris out.

Alpha runs fast, sprinting down to building number eight and through the door to charge up the stairs. 'ECHO? ECHO?'

'ALPHA!' Bravo's voice. Alpha goes up, coughing on the smoke caused by the fires started by the grenade.

They meet on the landing to the first floor. Echo in his 1940s suit, the others in tactical rig with Kate held between them. 'Portal is off,' Echo reports. 'Mother's lost it. Killing everyone.'

'She was going mad,' Kate says, throwing herself into Alpha's arms. 'She killed Rodney and . . . She was going mad . . . Screaming and . . .'

'Exfil to building twenty-five,' Alpha orders. 'Go . . . GO!'

No time for explanations or reasons, no time to understand what is happening. They run down and out into a street given to chaos and the blue shimmering portal hanging in the air above the remains of building twenty-five, shining through the smoke and dust.

The blink of an eye, the beat of a heart and the two sides see each other. Alpha, Kate, Bravo, Charlie, Delta and Echo snapping their heads over to the sight of Maggie Sanderson running with her team towards them.

Bravo, Charlie and Delta spot the pistols held in the hands of Safa, Emily and Harry and draw fast.

Safa sees the threat of three agents reaching for weapons and raises her pistol, which in turn makes Emily and Harry lift to aim as Miri draws her gun.

'HALT!' A German voice, loud and deep coming from behind the agents and both sides snap their heads over to the scores of German soldiers pouring from the backs of trucks parked outside Arch 451 and running into the street. 'WEAPONS DOWN NOW.' The officer screams the words in German. 'PUT YOUR GUNS DOWN,' he adds in thickly accented English.

The blink of an eye, the beat of a heart and both sides, the agents and Miri's team, all turn, aim and fire their pistols at the charging German soldiers. A barrage of shots ringing out like fireworks sounding amidst the deeper explosions of heavy bombs and the roar of aircraft overhead.

German soldiers fall dead or fall screaming from the rounds hitting them while the rest dive for hard cover, dropping down behind piles of bricks and masonry.

'SCATTER,' Harry roars. This is his world now and he can see the immensity of the return fire that is about to come their way. They star-burst away, all of them running to the sides of the street as the Germans open up with sustained automatic gunfire that bounces off the walls and houses, smashing through windows and whizzing through the air and still more German soldiers jump from the trucks to pour into the street, joining in with returning fire.

It's carnage. Utter awful brutal carnage, with a noise so deafening it renders any communication between them impossible. Thoughts whirl in Alpha's mind that they should join forces now, but when he looks round he can't even see any of his own side, let alone Miri's team. The smoke is too thick. The dust and debris in the air. Kate at his side, who stays silent but takes it all in with a hidden expertise that matches his own.

Harry grabs Miri and his team, pulling them up to make them run. There's no way through the Germans so they have to go the other way. 'UP . . . RUN . . .' His enormous voice gets them moving and his huge arms and presence of mind keeps them together as they scrabble over piles of scorching bricks and leap over wooden window frames set alight lying in the street.

Their eyes sting and water, blurring their vision. Their throats hurt from the fumes, smoke and chemicals in the air, and visibility reduces to just feet in front, but still the rounds whizz past them and still the Germans fire.

Alpha and Kate run in the same way too. They all do. Echo, Bravo, Charlie and Delta, all with eyes watering, throats hurting, coughing and clambering over ruined buildings to get away. They can't see each other or anything other than the ground immediately in front of them.

Harry pushes them on, roaring at them to keep going, driving his unit forward, shooting a hand out to launch Konrad over a pile of bricks, then reaching back to do the same to Miri. An explosion somewhere near. A brick sails through the air, whacking into his side, but the big man doesn't flinch and carries on. A shadow on his left. Someone looming through the smoke. A figure dressed in modern black tactical combat clothes that Harry recognises from Cavendish Manor.

Charlie spots Harry too, the big man's face a mask of determination, and the agent swivels to aim his pistol. Harry glances at the pistol, then up to Charlie's eyes. The agent has the drop on him, has drawn faster and can now kill him, but Charlie doesn't fire. Delta runs in from his side, to see Charlie aiming at Harry, who simply turns his head and powers on to drive his team down the street, and when Harry glances back the two agents are gone from sight.

The German soldiers advance quickly, running after them with that sustained firing sending rounds flying past their heads. Safa lurches, a bullet grazing her left arm, but Emily is there, pulling her on, then screaming out when a bullet whispers past her leg drawing blood and giving immediate pain.

They're hit by splinters, by bricks and masonry. Cutting, bruising and hurting, but still they run with no idea where the end of the street is. It seems to take forever, every second now a minute, every minute feeling like an hour and then they break through to sweet clear air that they suck down, and suddenly the view ahead is open and they can run faster, sprinting into another road and down a side street. Charlie and Delta break free next, punching out from the cloying smoke and catching sight of the backs of Miri's team aiming for a side street and they go after them.

Alpha and Kate get through, but on the far side of the junction, and whereas the others before them went right, so they go left. Footsteps behind them. Alpha snatches a glance to see Echo running flat out to catch them up.

Bravo comes out last, his face streaked with grime, his eyes red. He looks left, then he looks right. Two paths to follow.

He makes his choice and sets off.

Thirty

Bertie's Island

'Dressings, morphine . . . sutures,' the doctor murmurs to himself, pottering about in his army-green medical tent pitched just outside the clearing near the shack. Birds singing in the air. The waves lapping the shore and a slight breeze whispering through the treetops.

In the shack, Bertie works at his desk, absorbed entirely in his own world and not seeing the single smouldering brick sailing out of the portal that flies out the open door to land outside. He doesn't notice the plumes of dust that come just after it as building number twenty-five collapses. After a few more seconds he coughs from the fumes hitting his throat, but still carries on working. Even when the smoke drifts in front of his eyes he carries on working and it's not until he coughs harder and finally turns round that he sees the shack full of thick black smoke billowing through the portal.

'MALCOLM AND DOCTOR JOHN WATSON!' he shouts out, hopping from foot to foot in front of the portal then grabs a glass of water from his desk and throws the glass through the portal. 'MALCOLM AND DOCTOR JOHN WATSON!'

'What!?' the doctor tuts and strides out to see the ground in front of the shack littered with smouldering bricks and chunks of masonry. 'What the . . .'

'Oh shit.' Malcolm spins from the shoreline, ditching his fishing rod to run into the clearing. 'BERTIE! Get out, get out!'

They rush in towards the shack, fearing the thing to be on fire, to see Bertie dancing in panic in front of the portal through which the smoke comes thick and fast.

'Oh blimey,' Malcolm says.

'I think there's a fire,' Bertie says.

'What do we do?' the doctor asks.

'I don't bloody know!' Malcolm says. 'We can't switch it off . . .'

'Bugger, bugger and bugger,' the doctor says. 'Have a look through it, Malc.'

'Me? Why me?'

'I'm the doctor. I'm essential staff . . .'

'You cheeky sod,' Malcolm says, edging closer to the portal. 'Cor, that stinks.' He wafts the air, trying to keep it clear of his face, then sucks a breath and bends forward through the portal, feeling instantly dizzy at the drop in front of him and the snatched view of the house in ruins beneath him. 'Switch it off!' he yelps, pulling back into the shack. 'The house is gone.'

'What house?' the doctor asks.

'The house, the place they went in . . .'

The doctor shakes his head in confusion and edges closer to lean in, instantly feeling the heat of the fires below and the smoke hitting his face, which makes his eyes water, but he risks a longer look, seeing German soldiers through the murky air running down a street while more stand and point up at him. Noise everywhere, planes overhead, fires burning but no sign of Miri or anyone else.

Someone shouts in German, screaming words out that the doctor doesn't understand and watches in confusion as several soldiers suddenly aim up at the blue portal and start firing.

'TURN IT OFF!' He pulls his upper body back into the shack, dropping quickly as bullets whizz through into the ceiling above them. 'OFF! BERTIE, turn the blasted thing off . . .'

Bertie grabs the controller, swiping the screen to kill the connection, and the portal winks out as Malcolm and the doctor stare at each other in horror.

Thirty-One

Berlin, 1945

Alpha runs on with Kate and Echo at his side, weaving through the mounds of rubble and skirting the edges of monstrous fires eating their way through the city. Smoke billows into their eyes, choking and stinging.

The air raid intensifies as they run through clouds of dust and smoke. Huge piles of rubble dotted with broken bodies speak of the carnage and that sight repeats in every direction they face. Burnt-out and bomb-damaged civilian and military vehicles lie amongst the skeletal buildings and blocked roadways.

With everyone hiding in bunkers and shelters they see very few people as they go. Some remain, still scrabbling in the broken ruins as they dig for loved ones, others walk shell-shocked and slack-jawed. Two small children cower underneath a fire-damaged truck bearing a virtually untouched swastika.

'Did you see the others?' Alpha asks Echo, speaking in German.

'Negative. Only just saw you when I got through the smoke.'

'What are you saying?' Kate whispers.

'We don't know where the others are,' Alpha says. 'We'll try down there . . .' He guides them towards the mouth of a side street in the hope of finding a basement or shelter in which to take cover.

The explosion behind blows them off their feet. A solid whoomph of bombs hitting buildings in the side street they almost went down. Flame scorches up. Debris flies out and the ground heaves as the air pressure around them changes with blasts of supercharged wind rushing past.

'Get up,' Alpha tries shouting, but he can't hear his own voice, only the roar of everything else. He grips Kate's shoulders, pulling her up while above them the bombers keep coming and the bombs keep falling. 'WE'VE GOT TO FIND COVER.' He screams the words out with his mouth next to her ear while Echo picks himself up to look back at the street now in ruins.

They run on for no other reason than they have to keep going and gain distance. Streets go by. Fires and noise, bombs and destruction. Bodies everywhere. Old dead from days ago and new ones broken and killed from this bombing raid. The sheer scale is beyond epic. This is destruction of a city street by street and Alpha knows these people have got the worse to come when the Red Army sweeps through bringing rape and murder in brutal revenge.

Alpha feels Kate's hand pulling on his and twists back to see her pointing down a crossroads to a large above-ground shelter built with a circular construction designed to deflect bomb damage.

'Shelter,' he shouts to Echo in German, who nods once, his face thick with grime and blood coming from his right ear from a burst drum. Pain everywhere. Lacerations, cuts and bruises all over his body, but he follows after them, knowing they have to find cover from the air raid and hoping the bombers will have instruction not to aim for the public shelters.

They spot the soldiers outside, urging stragglers to run faster. Old men and young boys in uniform. Women with armbands shouting and pushing people through the door. Alpha squeezes Kate's hand, making her look at him while he presses a finger to his mouth, signalling for her not to talk.

'HURRY,' a woman says in German as she runs out towards them, not noticing Kate's modern clothes in the dust and filth now covering them both. 'GET IN GET IN . . .'

'THANK YOU,' Alpha shouts back in German as he ushers Kate through the door to a packed interior and the wall of smell of unwashed bodies and the sound of children screaming in fear, of women sobbing, of people coughing from the dust and particles in the air, of people in pain from broken bones, lacerations and even a leg taken off at the knee that Alpha and Echo barely glance at as they flank Kate. They pass through the solid brick rooms, seeing faces staring up at the sky as though seeing the bombers through the walls. A quiet corner, a dark corner. The two agents guide Kate over, staying with her and helping her lower down to rest her back against the wall. Alpha remains close, wrapping his arm round her shoulders as she pushes into him, burying her head in his form while Echo sits down on her other side.

'Injuries? Injuries?' An old man walks slowly through, shining a torch into the sections. 'Any injuries?'

'No,' Alpha says.

'Just got in?' the man asks, shining the torch in Alpha and Echo's faces, making them turn away and hold hands up to shield their eyes.

'Yes,' Echo says quietly.

'Bad, is it?' the man asks.

'Very bad,' Echo says hoarsely.

The old man totters off, calling as he goes.

'Where you from, friend?'

Alpha curses inwardly at the male voice directing a question at him. He squints round, seeing another old man looking over.

'Otto, leave them alone.' An old woman next to him slaps at his arm.

'What? I was just asking a question.'

'There's an air raid on, you stupid old man. People don't want to chat with you.'

'Air raid,' the old man snorts. 'It'll get worse, you mark my words. By Affa, it will get worse.'

'Stop saying Affa. It's a British thing. We don't use it now, Otto. How many times do I have to tell you?'

'I've always said by Affa and I will always say by Affa . . . Affa wasn't British anyway. German, he was! Went over there to sort the English Romans out, he did . . .'

Alpha and Echo listen, sharing a look and a wry smile as Kate looks up at Alpha quizzically. She leans forward, pushing her mouth against his ear. 'Are they talking about you?'

'Shush,' he says quietly, turning to look at her. She smiles in the gloom, her face smeared in dirt and grime, her hair plastered down over her scalp, and never before has he seen someone more beautiful than at that second. His lips find hers, just a gentle kiss given in the chaos of the moment, but her hand moves up to cover his and they stay together with lips pressed and eyes closed as the building shakes from the bombs.

'You used to kiss me like that, Otto.'

'If you looked like her I'd do more than kiss you— Ow!'

Kate pulls back, looking round at the people in the room chuckling and the old man rubbing his arm.

'He said he'd kiss her if she looked like you,' Alpha whispers in her ear. She smiles softly, her eyes held on his.

The air raid passes, but the sirens keep on as the two agents deny the urge to leave now for fear of standing out. This is a city on high alert and people are wary of strangers.

The all-clear is eventually given, which stirs the occupants of the shelter to grumble and groan as they find their feet and start filing towards the exit. Alpha and Echo once again flank Kate and join the lines, trudging small steps in an oppressed, terrified atmosphere. Plans form in Alpha's mind, where to go, how to survive, priorities and objectives. Kate needs a change of clothing and something warmer to wear. They need water and food, they need to find Miri and the others. Will Miri have a way out if her portal was negated? Do they have someone else in their base to reset and find them?

They get closer to the door, Alpha and Echo with heads down appearing as scared and confused as everyone else, forced into single file as they move towards the cold bright daylight and a street filled with smoke from fresh fires and such is the press of bodies that all they can do is move with the crowd until they get through the doorway.

A commotion ahead. Alpha scans about, trying to see what's going on. His arms stretch behind him holding Kate's hands while Echo moves in close behind her.

'MOVE ASIDE . . .' A deep male voice shouts the order, forcing a ripple that spreads through the people in front of Alpha, who looks for an escape route but finds none. Such is the press on all sides.

Space opens in front of him and Alpha glances up to see a grey-uniformed German officer pushing towards him. 'THEM . . . THAT'S THEM . . .' a woman shouts, a voice that Alpha recognises and his mind matches the voice to the woman with the Nazi armband in the street when he met Miri, Ben and Emily. He spots her a second later, seeing her ruddy cheeks and the look of spite in her eyes as she points at Alpha. 'HIM . . . SAID HE WAS A CAPTAIN OF THE FIRST INFANTRY . . .'

'Halt,' the German officer commands, aiming a Luger at Alpha as Echo moves out a step.

'What's going on?' Alpha asks, looking round in confusion.

Echo spots the soldiers closing in through the crowd, mean-eyed, hard-looking and definitely not the young boys and old men they saw before. This is a fighting unit.

'Who are you?' the German officer demands.

'I'm Captain Schmidt . . .' Alpha replies with a blanch. 'What's going on? Has the raid passed? I'll need to get to my unit . . .'

'HANDS AWAY FROM YOUR BODY,' the officer shouts, seeing Alpha's hand moving towards his coat pocket.

Echo moves out another step towards a soldier aiming a submachine gun at Alpha.

'I have my papers,' Alpha says with disdain. 'What's this about?'

'I keep seeing him around,' the woman says. 'He's not right . . . I'm telling you he's not right . . .'

'Sir.' A soldier rushes in towards the officer, brushing past Echo. 'Report from Bundesstraße 2, sir. They had enemy contact and a blue light shining from the one of the buildings lighting a path for the bombers . . . Said the enemy were in civilian clothing, sir.'

'Spies!' the woman with the armband shouts, glaring at Alpha.

'Fool!' Alpha snaps. 'I'm no spy. I have family in Bundesstraße 2, as you well know. Check my papers. Inside left pocket . . .' He unbuttons his overcoat and pulls the left side out away from his body while walking towards the officer with a solid Aryan sneer as Kate scans for threat and risk and while Echo waits for the move.

Alpha's fast. Very fast. Faster than even Kate thought he would be. The officer reaches in towards Alpha's inside coat pocket as Alpha rolls his eyes, tuts, then strikes out, slamming the edge of his hand into the officer's wrist holding the Luger, dislodging his grip enough to pluck the weapon away, turn and fire it into the man's head, sending a shower of blood over the woman in the Nazi armband, who screams at the hot liquid spattering her face. Echo goes fast too, aiming at the closest soldier and stamping a foot into the side of his knee to make him drop and turn, snatching the sub-machine gun from his hands as he falls. He flips the weapon round and opens fire to send rounds into the soldier on the ground as the crowd around them scream and run in all directions.

Kate watches Alpha, seeing the hand change as he passes the Luger to his left and draws his modern pistol from his pocket with his right and knows that's a hard thing to do. To operate two pistols at the same time. He does it with skill though, spinning on the spot to pick his targets as Echo fires the sub-machine gun. She spots the closest dead soldiers, noting the positions of their weapons and preparing herself to run and grab one if the situation worsens.

'Run . . .' Alpha stays calm, he and Echo striding back to Kate and using their bodies to shield her as they start running down the street. She saw Alpha kill seven soldiers. Seven within a few seconds and while showing abject fear on the outside she gives respect internally for a very high standard of skill, but then he is Alpha.

Shots behind them from more soldiers running into the fray. Machine guns opening up and ricocheting bullets pinging off walls.

'Go,' Echo says, dropping to a knee to return fire.

Alpha and Kate run on, aiming for the mouth of a side street so Alpha can give covering fire for Echo.

'Now!' Alpha shouts, firing his pistol at the soldiers as Echo starts running backwards. The sub-machine gun clicks empty; he ditches it fast to pull his pistol, aiming for shots into the German soldiers. 'NOW, ECHO!' Alpha shouts. Echo turns on the move, running fast for the junction as a round slams into his shoulder, sending him staggering off to the side. 'ECHO!' Alpha screams out.

Echo rights himself, grimacing as he turns to shoot back, but another round strikes his chest, then one through his stomach and he falls backwards onto his arse with a stunned look on his face. 'Oh shit . . .' He glances at Alpha, who thinks to run out and drag Echo away, but the soldiers are advancing, pushing ahead with more fire-power and another round hits Echo, slamming him down onto his back to writhe in agony.

'Echo.' Alpha darts out, but the incoming fire drives him back.

'Go,' Echo whispers, blood coming from his mouth. 'GO!'

'I'm so sorry, Ian . . .'

They lock eyes for a fleeting second before Echo snarls. 'I'M A FUCKING JEW,' he screams in German, sitting up to fire back at the soldiers, killing three. 'HEAR THAT? A JEW IS KILLING YOU . . .'

Alpha doesn't flinch when Echo's head snaps back from the bullet going through his skull. He just stares for a brief second, grabs Kate's hand and runs. Dog-legging the pursuit and taking hard lefts and rights. Down alleys and smoke-filled side streets. Through ruined buildings showing obvious threat of collapse. His knowledge and instincts of escape and evasion are perfect, even showing the presence of mind when passing other people to tell them the Russians are coming. That word spreads like wildfire, forcing people out into the streets to run and scream and create more confusion for the chasing soldiers.

He stops to let Kate draw air, wiping the sweat from her brow and looking barely out of breath. He finds water, kicking in a back door after seeing a sink inside and twisting the tap to find it still working. He lets her drink first, protecting her while she does so. He takes his turn, gulping it down, then finds a clean cloth in a drawer that he soaks and uses to wipe her flushed face. He doesn't panic. He is the opposite of panic. He goes further into the building, leading her past the base of the stairs, now filled with a collapsed ceiling and the contents of the upstairs rooms.

An old winter coat is on the back of the front door. Big, heavy and warm. She might be hot and sweating now, but it's still February in northern Europe. He wraps it round her shoulders, then plucks a scarf from the hooks and drapes it over her head, securing the ends.

'Bend forward,' he whispers. 'Bit more . . .' He pushes her arse out and her shoulders down, making her adopt the stance and gait of an old woman. 'Good. Stay like that . . .' He ditches his overcoat and grabs a faded, worn checked thing that he tugs on and an old hat, changing their profile and appearance.

'Can't we stay here?' she asks, knowing the answer, but choosing to stay in role. He's good. She knows that and she still needs to find Maggie Sanderson and staying alive will be a whole lot easier with Alpha than on her own.

'It'll come down any second,' he says, turning to look at the already partially collapsed roof on the stairs. 'We'll go slow. We're old . . .

Remember we had legends before? I'm old Otto, you're my nagging wife, okay?'

In the street, they hold their legends true and shuffle on slowly. A bent old woman arm in arm with her husband.

'FIND THEM . . .' An officer runs past, leading a unit of soldiers.

Alpha and Kate enter a long street of heavily damaged buildings on both sides. Burnt-out vehicles here and there. Alpha clings to the right, scrutinising every building they pass until he spots it. A trapdoor to a cellar. The structure above looks stable, with most of the walls already down and those that might fall won't land on the trapdoor. It's the best they'll find. He looks round, checking the view before leading Kate in, helping his elderly wife up and over the rubble to slip and slide down into the depths of the destruction.

He pulls the door open and peers in, half-expecting to see refugees already taking cover, but it looks dark and empty.

They descend a flight of wooden stairs, descending into a near darkness that's warmer and quieter than the world outside.

He takes a small flashlight from his pocket with a bitter flash of memory at Echo and a surge of regret at not moving sooner to prevent all of this from happening.

'It'll do,' he says quietly, standing in front of her, his hands reaching out to push the scarf from her head. 'I'm so sorry this has—'

He doesn't get to finish the sentence as her mouth pushes into his with a raw hunger rushing through her. He freezes at her touch, instantly appalled at the thought of sex right now, but that fades in a heartbeat. A near-death experience will wake the thirst for life in many people. Adrenaline, fight or flight, the instincts to survive and procreate, the inner animal within the human that pushes out when the finer nuances of living are stripped away. His own hunger comes on. His hunger for her, to be with her, to taste and feel her, and in the dry darkness they fall into dusty old sheets and blankets with a yearning need pulsing through them both.

Thirty-Two

Hard lefts and hard rights. Through ruined buildings. Down a street with one side entirely engulfed in flame. With the air-raid sirens still sounding and the bombers overhead still dropping payloads, with the air full of the AA guns they run and run to keep up. Charlie and Delta staying side by side with Harry and Maggie's team continually glimpsed in the distance.

'There,' Delta says in German, pointing down a side street just in time to see Harry disappearing round the next corner. They set off again, running hard. Their combat black tactical clothes now covered in grey dust, their faces as grimy and marked as everyone else trying to survive the air raid.

They reach the junction, turning into a wide road once full of grand buildings, but now eerily silent with skeletal columns and walls standing erect within the hills of bricks and torn-down structures. A trick of the landscape and just by turning the corner the noise behind them lessens significantly, plunging them into an almost dystopian landscape where the city is crumbling and where no life lives.

'Where'd they go?' Charlie asks, breathing hard from the running.

'Didn't see,' Delta says. They jog on into the street, glimpsing staircases lying in the ruins and rubble. Bathtubs, furniture, pots and pans, the things people had in life now left to rot. They can see this area is not safe and the towering columns and walls around them might come down any second. The vibrations from a stray bomb hitting anywhere near here could do it. That's why it's deserted. It needs demolishing to be made safe.

'Where the hell did they go?' Charlie asks again.

A scuff behind them. They spin quickly as Delta flies off his feet from the punch given by Harry as Safa slams into Charlie, taking him down to land hard on his back with a pistol jabbed into his cheek. Delta lands hard too, grunting in pain and thinking to rise quickly as Ben drives him back down pushing a gun into his chest.

'No threat,' Charlie says urgently, holding his hands away from his body.

'Disarm them,' Miri orders. 'Check for secondary weapons.'

'Tac knives only,' Charlie says. 'No threat, no threat . . .'

'Clear,' Safa reports, taking Charlie's knife away.

'Done,' Harry reports, doing the same.

'What happened?' Miri asks them calmly.

'Our portal went off,' Charlie says quickly, lying on his back with his hands out to the side. 'Kate – she's the historian – she got away and said Mother was killing everyone . . .'

'Did you witness this attack?' Miri asks.

'No, but shots were coming through the portal, then she chucked a grenade in,' Delta says.

'You saw the grenade?' Miri asks.

'Affirmative,' Charlie answers while Delta nods.

Miri thinks for a second, glancing round at the deserted street. 'Why are you following us?'

A look between the agents, then both glance at Emily.

'I will shoot you now,' Miri says, aiming her gun at Charlie. 'Report!'

'No! Switch sides,' Charlie blurts.

'We want out,' Delta says at the same time.

'We don't believe her,' Charlie says, rushing the words out. 'Mother said you killed everyone. We don't buy it . . . Same with you killing the PM . . . We dropped that nuke, but . . . she's fucking nuts. She's getting ready for something bigger.'

'Extinction level event,' Delta says, taking over. 'Modern nukes and anthrax . . . Mother's lost the plot. Me and Charlie agreed days ago we wanted out.'

'We did,' Charlie says.

'You dropped a nuclear bomb on London,' Ben says.

'You don't know what it's like . . .' Charlie says. 'We can't say no to Mother and we didn't know what Alpha or Bravo thought . . .'

'We couldn't ask them – it's not like that,' Delta says.

'Your agents are making this a habit, Tango Two,' Miri says.

'Er, they're not my bloody agents and I was captured *before* I switched sides.'

'We're captured!' Charlie cuts in hopefully.

'Totally captured,' Delta says. 'Like really captured . . .'

'Emily,' Charlie says. 'You worked with Delta in China.'

'And?' Emily asks.

'We're not bad people,' Delta says. 'Tell Maggie we're good . . . We're good agents . . .'

'She's called Miri now,' Emily tells them. 'And, trust me, nobody *tells* her anything.'

'Permission to speak, ma'am,' Harry says.

'Go.'

'Saw that one when we were running,' he says, pointing at Charlie. 'Aimed at me, had the drop, but didn't fire, and his mate' – he points to Delta – 'got alongside, but didn't shoot either . . .'

'Understood. Cut 'em loose. Boys, you're on your own . . .'

'Ah, shit no,' Charlie says with a grimace. 'Don't cut us loose . . .'

'We want to switch sides,' Delta says.

'We're not a bloody country,' Safa says. 'You can't just defect to us . . . Is defect the right word, Ben?'

'It is,' Ben says.

'I'm clever,' Safa says. 'Now fuck off before I shoot you in the face.'

'Please,' Delta says. 'Not going back . . . No fucking way am I going back.'

'Piss off and live in Germany then,' Safa says.

'Hold us prisoner until you reset the changes,' Charlie says.

'Jesus, your agency is crap, Emily,' Safa says. 'You've got the least loyal people ever.'

'We need to get off the street,' Harry says. 'Sirens have stopped . . .' He looks up to a clear sky as the AA guns finally cease booming in the distance. Vehicle engines nearby. The heavy chug of diesel trucks, then deep male voices shouting orders in German.

Miri thinks fast, with every instinct telling her Charlie and Delta meant what they just said. There wasn't a hint of dishonesty within them and it matches what Alpha said too and the chance of two more highly trained agents switching sides is a big thing. The precedent set by Emily tells her these men, her team, are good people doing the right thing. She looks at Ben, seeing the tiny nod. A look to Harry, but he stays impassive. He's said his thoughts and that's that.

'Take them with us, but say a word or even glance in a way I don't like and I will slit your throats, gentlemen . . .'

'Roger that,' Charlie says.

'S'bit harsh, but fair enough,' Delta says.

Miri had stopped her team here on seeing the staircase going down into a basement and just as Alpha did with Kate, she leads them down into a gloomy darkness with Harry and Safa keeping their guns pressed into Charlie and Delta's backs.

'Torch in my pocket,' Charlie whispers.

A quick scout round to see empty shelves and anything usable already gone. No food, no drink, but it's hidden from view and quiet.

'Hunker down and rest,' Miri orders. 'Mr Ryder. We'll talk in a moment.'

'It's fine,' Safa says. 'Whatever we do will be fine. Know how I know? Because we haven't appeared to get us out the shit yet, which means we don't get in the shit enough to need us to come back and save us . . .'

'Or we all die here so we can't come back and save us,' Emily says after a brief silence of everyone trying to work out what Safa just said.

Safa nods. 'Good point.'

'When is the agents' next visit to Bundesstraße 2?' Emily asks.

'Tomorrow afternoon,' Charlie says, making everyone look at him. 'Last one before we take the bomb to the airfield but, er' – he pauses to swallow – 'the street wasn't that damaged when we came through on the fourth visit . . . I mean not so bomb damaged as it is now.'

'Will it stop you visiting Herr Weber?' Ben asks.

'I don't think so,' Charlie says, sharing a look with Delta, who shrugs and shakes his head.

'Confuses the hell out of me,' Delta mumbles.

'Not the only one,' Safa says.

Ben stays silent, frowning as he stares down at the dusty ground.

'What are you doing this for?' Delta asks, looking round at them.

'You'll not be asking questions now . . .'

'It's fine, Sergeant,' Miri says. 'They can know.'

Ben looks at her sharply as Safa speaks out. 'Basically, the world ends in twenty-one eleven. Inventor made the device, went forward and saw the world was ruined, panicked, extracted his dead dad, who first extracted two of his former employees, then extracted Ben, Harry and me, then Miri came on board and took over at the point Mother tracked us to the staging area in Berlin . . . That about right?' she asks, glancing round. 'I mean loads of other stuff happened, but . . .'

'Oh, and we had a night out in Rio, then in Paris,' Emily says, leaning over to rub Harry's arm. 'Isn't that right, dear?' she asks sweetly, smiling with too many teeth.

'Ach, don't start that again,' he rumbles.

'Idiots,' Safa snorts.

'Christ,' Charlie says. 'That's it?'

'Pretty much,' Safa says. 'We reacted to you lot at Cavendish Manor, then threatened all the governments so they wouldn't chuck nukes at each other . . .'

'So . . .' Delta says slowly. 'You didn't kill everyone in the complex and the PM then? What?' he asks when everyone glares at him. 'Was only asking.'

'How does the world end?' Charlie asks quickly, covering for the crass remark by his colleague.

'I don't think we ever worked that out, did we?' Emily asks.

'Seems fine now though,' Safa adds.

'You've seen it?' Charlie asks. 'What's it like?'

'Nice, actually. Bit weird and the coffee tastes like shit and everyone eats insects,' Safa says. 'But Piccadilly's gone from the massive nuclear bomb you dropped, of course.'

'And men have boobs,' Emily adds.

'And kids have tattoos,' Safa says.

'And they've got anti-grav tech,' Konrad says, joining in as the whispered chat goes on.

Ben listens intently, drawn from his thoughts about the problem to the surreal situation now of these people talking so casually, but then everyone here is used to combat and times of great stress so this is nothing new to them. This now is just downtime between whatever else they have to do and it's right then, at that point, that he snatches a glimpse of the world through Miri's eyes and sees the true genius of the woman. That even now she is cool and calm enough to manipulate and bend everyone else to her will. She appears gruff, angry and mean and has distanced herself from the others slightly as though to imbue the division between officers and soldiers, and by allowing Safa and Emily to chat normally she is humanising them and giving a positive reflection to the two captured agents. Exactly the same thing she did to Emily but compressed and done quicker. He looks up at her, seeing her face mostly hidden by shadow, but her eyes glint as she views the world around her. She detects his gaze and looks over. A nod from him to her, from the protégé to the master.

'I'm glad I'm on your side,' he says and in the darkness of the basement he sees her teeth as she gives a rare smile.

'So, what's your base like?' Safa asks the two men.

'The complex?' Charlie asks. 'It's purpose built so it is good but we've been there for too long . . .'

'Understatement,' Delta mumbles, earning a look from Charlie.

'But, er, yeah, I mean, we've got a medical centre, gym . . . swimming pods,' Charlie continues. 'Canteen is good . . .'

'I'll stay here in Berlin . . . Really not going back.'

'What's up with you?' Charlie asks as Delta mutters on.

'Just saying I'm not going back.'

'What the fuck?' Charlie says. 'Stop saying you're not going back . . .'

'I'm not going back.'

'Why not?'

'Just not,' Delta mumbles, looking away. 'Hanna found out I slept with Coreen . . .'

'Coreen?' Charlie asks. 'From IT?'

'Yeah, her, and Lena.'

'You slept with Lena?'

'Yes, and Petra . . . and Agnes and . . . some others. Point is they said they're going to cut my dick off.' Silence. Everyone listening while Delta shifts uncomfortably. 'I'm not going back,' he tells them all.

'Sounds like you deserve your dick being cut off,' Safa says.

'I hate it when men seduce women like that . . .' Emily says pointedly.

'Mr Ryder?' Miri cuts in. 'Word please. We'll go up . . . Stay focussed and watch the prisoners.'

'Dirty prisoners more like,' Emily says.

'Him, not me,' Charlie says, pointing at Delta.

Miri leads the way, moving slowly up the staircase to stare out into the rapidly dwindling light. Early evening in winter in northern Europe where the nights come early. Ben joins her, both of them standing still for long minutes to listen.

Engines in the distance. Deep and heavy that speak of military vehicles. The odd shout and the rumble of buildings falling. The smell of smoke and chemicals hang in the air with wafts of smoke pluming up into the darkening sky.

Nothing close though. Nothing moving near them, but Miri holds them for minutes longer until their eyes are fully adjusted to this light now and only then does she move him out and away from the staircase to hunker down in the shadows.

'Options?' she whispers.

'Our portal's out of reach. Hopefully Malcolm or the doc will turn it off, but even if they come looking they've got no chance of finding us so that rules out going back through our portal. Agreed?'

She nods once.

'The agents have got one more visit left to Herr Weber in that street . . .'

'Bundesstraβe 2,' Miri whispers.

'That one,' Ben says. 'They visit Herr Weber tomorrow, then after that they go to the airfield and take the bomb to London . . . That gives us two chances to get into their portal behind them and use their device to get back to—' He reels back with a yelp of pain from the chunk of brick flying into his face as Miri dives for cover.

'Shit,' Ben gasps, pulling his hand back to see dark patches of blood.

'Not a word,' Miri hisses.

Another ping sounds out from the ricochet of a bullet hitting a brick on the ground between them. Neither hear a shot fired or a sound made other than that ping. Ben rolls to his front to look out into the street as a bullet hits the ground a foot from his head, making him roll quickly deeper into the shadows as Miri scuttles back and away.

They both hold still, the darkness of the night now coming fast, and they barely breathe for fear of making noise, but stare towards the edge of the building and out into the street.

Seconds go by. Ben's face drips blood on the ground beneath his head. Miri slowly brings her hand up to her side, but she scuffs a tiny bit of debris that makes a scrape, and the shot comes, slamming into the ground by her hand and bouncing across her knuckles. She snatches her hand back, suppressing the urge to cry out at the pain and holds perfectly still.

Ben lifts his head a millimetre at a time, so slowly it makes his neck hurt, but gradually gains sight of the lip of the broken wall at the front of the ruined building. A snatched view of the ruins opposite and the ping comes again, whizzing past his ear to hit the debris behind and he hunkers down, hugging the ground.

Miri breathes slowly, easing her heart rate from the initial adrenaline dump that coursed through her body. Calm now. Easy. She starts moving her right arm, intending to draw her pistol, but slowly, so very slowly. Her arm lifts off the ground as she rotates her shoulder that starts to burn, but she gets her hand closer to the butt, stretching her fingers out, readying to grip and draw.

Ben glares across the ground, straining to see Miri in the shadows and just catching sight of her reaching for her sidearm. He starts doing the same, moving slowly to draw as the scuff sounds from the staircase from a foot pressing down.

'Ben?' Safa's voice whispering out and the shots come fast.

'Down,' Ben hisses.

'Contact,' Miri whispers across as the pings of bullets hit the staircase. A yelp, a thud from Safa falling down. More pings hitting the ground and walls surrounding them. Miri draws quickly, using the time to get her pistol in hand, but the shooter detects the noise and aims his fire at her.

'Safa?' Ben whispers, fearing she's been shot.

'I'm fine,' her voice whispers up as the bullets ping between them, sending chunks of wall and brick flying through the air. The pause comes with a faint click that Miri knows is the shooter changing magazines. She surges up, aiming out and trying to see where he could be positioned.

Ben goes up too, aiming his pistol and hearing the click of a fresh magazine going into the shooter's gun. He fires once at the sound, the noise from his gun a deafening boom in the near silence of the ruins.

'Don't shoot,' Miri hisses. The pings come back quickly, the shooter returning fire from a pistol fitted with a suppressor. She tries to run for it, intending to gain a better position in the distraction, but the round hits her stomach, sending her back against a wall with a grunt of agony.

'Miri!' Ben moves fast, breaking cover to dive for Miri. A bullet clips his arm, making him twist as he falls, grunting in pain while the wall above him pings from the rounds hitting it.

Miri gasps from the searing burning pain in her gut as Ben grabs her ankles to drag her across the ground behind a section of fallen chimney. She grunts again, wanting to scream at the pain, and looks down at her hands clutching her stomach now covered in blood and in the scrabbled panic of that second, in the darkness and while in utter agony she grabs Ben's hand and forces it over her own mouth, pushing it down to clamp hard.

He does as bid, holding down to stop the noises coming out, feeling her breath blasting from her nose over his knuckles as she gasps for air.

The pings stop coming and the world goes silent save for Miri breathing and Ben easing his hand a fraction from her mouth.

'Ben?' Safa's voice. The shots come again, only a few, but they hit the staircase, keeping Safa down.

'Miri's hit,' Ben whispers.

Safa hunkers on the stairs, her pistol in hand, her face smeared in blood from the round that glanced her scalp. Emily is at the base of the stairs, Harry in the basement covering Charlie and Delta. 'Miri's hit,' she whispers.

'Miri's hit.' Emily passes it on to Harry and Konrad.

'Must be Bravo,' Charlie says.

'Tell Ben not to shoot back without a suppressor,' Delta says. 'A gunshot will bring soldiers . . .'

'We don't have suppressors,' Emily says.

'We carry them,' Charlie says, pointing at his tac-vest.

'Quick, hand them over . . .' Emily says, moving to them.

'Let us take him,' Charlie says urgently. 'We'll crawl out and flank . . .'

'No,' Safa whispers firmly. 'Keep them covered. Give me the suppressors . . . Konrad, take this pistol and aim it at those two. They move then shoot them. Harry, take the other suppressor and come with me. Emily, stay here and watch them . . . Ben, do not shoot back.' She angles her head up as she whispers.

Ben holds Miri, feeling her body tense and tremble from the pain. He looks at the staircase, wishing he could get her down into the basement, but not daring to break cover.

'It'll be okay,' he whispers into Miri's ear.

'Don't shoot back.' She gasps the words out, bringing forth a volley of fire from the shooter.

'How many magazines do you lot carry?' Safa asks from the base of the staircase.

'Bravo carries loads,' Charlie says as Safa scowls, her hopes dashed that the shooter will run out of rounds. 'Okay. Harry . . . go slow and stay down.'

'Not my first war, Safa,' he whispers, easing past her.

'Where's she shot?' Charlie asks.

'Charlie's a medic,' Delta says.

'Ben? Where's Miri shot?' Safa whispers.

'Stomach,' he says softly, bringing more pings above his head.

'Stomach,' Safa relays.

'Just put pressure on the wound if it's bleeding heavily,' Charlie says. 'I've got morphine in my pocket . . . Reaching for it now . . .' He slowly reaches down to draw out a small tube fitted with a cap. 'In her thigh.' He throws it to Emily, who passes it up to Safa, to Harry, who risks the shots coming in to surge up and throw it to Ben.

'Morphia, in her leg,' Harry whispers, dropping back down.

Ben pulls the cap off and pushes the needle into her thigh, squeezing the tube to empty the contents. She goes limp in seconds, easing down into a drug-induced sleep as Ben pulls his 1940s suit jacket off and tears one of the sleeves away before bundling it together to put under Miri's head while he folds the sleeve to hold down on her stomach. She grunts at the motion that brings fresh waves of searing agony through her body. 'It'll be okay, just hold on . . .' He looks up, wondering why the hell none of them have appeared from the future to fix it and the first real fear hits that they die here and never get back.

A noise snaps his head up. A rhythmic sound of boots crunched from soldiers marching in step. A platoon walking into the street.

Harry lies flat on the stairs, easing up a fraction at a time to snake out. Safa behind him as the noise of the marching grows louder.

Ben feels the urge to call out and get medical aid for Miri, but they'll be shot as spies. There's nothing he can do so he holds Miri close and pushes his hand back over her mouth to keep her quiet.

Harry snakes out to the top of the stairs holding one of the agents' pistols now fitted with a suppressor. The marching comes closer. The crunch, crunch, crunch of booted feet and this isn't the first time Harry has used the passing of a German patrol to mask his noise and so he goes a bit faster, pushing out to crawl from the stairs into the ruined room with Safa coming behind him.

The soldiers reach the edge of the building. Torches shining, giving weak flashes of light as they look into the ruins on the left and right. Harry hugs the ground, waiting and knowing when to move. Safa copies him, going still when he does.

The platoon passes out front. Harry moves again, getting behind a broken wall as Safa stops a few metres to his side, both of them waiting as the crunch, crunch, crunch goes past. A glimpse up and Harry spots the last of the columns of men going by and lifts his pistol to aim across the street into the ruins on the other side. Safa the same, both of them settling into position to wait while they examine every shadow they can see for anything that looks other than how it should or anywhere big enough to hide a person.

The soldiers fade away, the noise easing. Everyone holds still, the only sound coming from Miri breathing fast and shallow while Ben feels her body temperature plummeting in the cold air. Still they hold. Breaths mist. Bodies start to tremble in the chill. Harry and Safa feeling the pain of holding position.

Minutes go by and the standoff continues as the moon rises to bathe their side of the street in a silvery glow with an unfair advantage given to the hidden shooter, who spots the barrel of Safa's gun and opens fire.

She drops fast at the bullet whizzing by while Harry sends return fire into a few of the deeper shadows before dropping down, and so they lie in the freezing cold, unable to speak, unable to move and unable to stop Miri slowly dying mere feet from them.

Then it comes. A thing that gives sudden hope. The air-raid siren spreading through the city in warning of the heavy bombers advancing slowly overhead.

Thirty-Three

Bertie's Island

'Okay,' Malcolm says, nodding at the portal. 'I'm ready.'

'I really don't think this is a good idea,' Doctor Watson says.

'We've got to do something,' Malcolm says. 'Turn it on, Bertie . . . Turn it on . . . Same date they had, the fifth of February nineteen forty-five but later, like . . . three, no, four . . . no, five hours later. Yes, do five hours later . . . and lower! Not in the same place . . . A few metres away and on the ground . . .'

'Malc,' the doctor says gently.

'No, doc, they came for me and Kon, they did. Albeit a few months later, but still . . . How do I look?' he asks, glancing down at the spare 1940s clothing he cobbled together from the bits lying around.

'Awful,' the doctor says honestly.

'You done it, Bertie?' Malcolm asks.

'S'just binary,' Bertie says, jabbing at the controller.

'Ere, gimme one of them new ones that you throw in the air,' Malcolm says. 'I'll take one just in case. Oh blimey,' he adds when the Blue comes on. 'That it, is it?'

'Yes, Malcolm,' Bertie says. 'Can I come?'

'No!' Malcolm and the doctor say together. 'Right, wish me luck . . .' Malcolm swallows, summons courage and leans in to look through the portal at a dark street seemingly deserted. He steps through, feeling the instant change from hot island weather to Berlin in February at night, his breath misting. His steps echo as he walks out and looks up and down the empty street. Nothing here. Smoke in the air and the glow from nearby fires left to burn out.

A few steps. A few steps more. He doesn't know where to look or even where to begin. He doesn't even know where Bertie placed the portal, what street this is or where it is in relation to the street Miri and the others used. He only knows he must do *something*. He bites his bottom lip, hesitating and feeling terrified, then setting off down the street to the junction at the end and the soldiers standing together smoking in the cold night air.

He stops dead and starts backing up into the street he came from with the instant realisation that this really is an awful idea and he lets the air go when he slides back into the shadows.

'What are you doing?' the soldier asks him from behind while doing his trousers up after taking a piss. Malcolm doesn't understand the question though; he just hears someone German speaking German and turns to stare.

'What was that?' he asks, then a second later realising he just spoke English in wartime Germany to a Nazi soldier. 'Oh, arse . . .' He runs away, sprinting as the soldier gives chase calling out for his comrades.

Malcolm goes left into an alley, then right into another one, then left again and remembers the new portal in his pocket and picks it up to throw ahead. It hits a wall and bounces off and he curses at remembering he has to use the controller at the same time as throwing it. He scoops it up as he runs, yelping on hearing the soldier behind and jabs at the screen of the controller while trying to hold the ball and then throw it. It works instantly, arcing into the air, then forming an instant shining doorway and in that split second he remembers that Emily said she saw him so he screams her name as he runs through into the main room of the bunker and a stunned Emily looking through the window.

'. . . ILY . . . EMILY . . . GET HIM . . .'

A few seconds later, and with one dead Nazi soldier shot by his own gun, Malcolm runs out from hiding. 'Oh my god . . . thank you, thank you.' He rushes over, aiming for the portal then veering off to her side. 'Emily, thank you . . . you're a bloody lifesaver.' He leans in fast to kiss her cheek with an action so natural and unexpected she doesn't even think to shoot him. 'I hate this bloody job . . . I'm Malc, by the way . . .'

He runs back out, knowing he has to turn this one off and get back to the first one. Jabbing the controller then catching the ball as it drops before running round the block a few times while panicking at being lost, then seeing his portal and diving through to a shocked John Watson and Bertie. 'Yeah, bad idea,' he says as Bertie turns it off. 'Really bad idea . . .'

'I think,' John says, rubbing his jaw. 'I think we'd better get young Ria . . .'

◆   ◆   ◆

'I don't care,' Ria says a little while later after being found in the café in Lambeth-not-Lambeth. She idly turns the pages of the history books open on the table in the clearing outside the shack on Bertie's island.

'Ria,' Malcolm says, looking wretched to the core. 'Konrad's there. We don't know what to do . . .'

'Sorry,' she says bluntly. 'I told you I want nothing to do with this now. What have they done for me? My mother is dead . . . My whole life was taken away from me . . .'

'You're being selfish and immature, Ria,' the doctor cuts in, speaking gravely. 'They saved me from drowning, Harry and Safa died doing it, then Ben came back for them. They saved your brother. They tried to save your mother . . . They're genuine people just trying to . . .'

She shrugs, zoning them out and looking back down to the pages of the book and the notes left in the margins by Ben. A series of five dates in 1945 and she knows enough to understand what they mean. Something gets her attention. The way Ben has written a note above the five dates in 1945. *The agents' visits to Herr Weber.* Her eyes narrow. Her lips purse in thought.

'How many visits have they made to Berlin?' she asks.

'Er . . . they were on the third one,' Malcolm says, exchanging a look with the doctor.

Ria reads the date of the third visit, *5 February 1945*, then looks at the fourth visit the day after, *6 February 1945. The agents' visits to Herr Weber.*

That's where Miri will aim for. She'll know the agents will have a portal open for that visit and she'll use it to get back here.

'No problem,' she murmurs, looking up at Malcolm and the doctor with a bright smile. 'Leave it with me . . .'

Thirty-Four

Berlin, 5 February 1945

They hold still in the ruins of the building while Ben keeps the pressure on Miri's stomach, feeling her body grow colder by the minute as she slips in and out of consciousness.

The air-raid sirens scream out and, in the distance, they hear the AA guns opening up and they wait for it to get closer. The noise will give them cover and distraction.

Emily hears it in the basement beneath the ruins. Wishing she could go up and give aid to the others, but that would leave just Konrad against two highly trained agents.

'We can help,' Charlie urges.

'Shut up,' she whispers angrily.

'Emily, we can help . . . Bravo's good . . .'

'Another word,' she says, aiming her gun at him while Konrad gulps.

It takes time for the bombers to get closer. Too much time and Ben frets, knowing that each minute takes Miri closer to death. 'You're going to be okay,' he whispers into her ear.

Her lips move, air comes out, a word, something said.

'Shush, just rest . . .' he whispers.

'Timelines,' she says, the word barely heard.

'Miri, just rest.'

'Think . . . Ben . . . time . . . timelines . . . you said . . .' She gabbles words, soft and missed, slurred and almost drunken in sound. 'Ria . . . he . . . extracted after Ria . . . doc . . .'

'Miri, shush now, just rest.'

'Listen to me!' she hisses, surging to wakefulness as Harry and Safa snaps their heads over at the noise and the ruins fill with the pings of shots fired. She tenses, then just as fast she fades away, her breathing coming fast and shallow. 'Timelines . . . Mother . . .'

He covers her body with his to protect her from chunks of brick and plaster and suddenly the bombers are overhead and the world fills with their deafening roar. Harry and Safa lift to fire back. Sending pings back into the ruins opposite as the rumble of nearby explosions reach them, quaking the buildings surrounding them with walls crashing down and chimneys falling. A bomb hits further down the street, sending flame into the air that gives light with noise and distraction.

'Go!' Safa urges, pushing forward with Harry.

'Keep them covered,' Emily orders Konrad, running up the stairs to peek out to see Harry and Safa moving to press the attack. She joins behind them, darting between broken walls to gain the edge of the building. She fires across, knowing the noise of the pistol will now be hidden in the chaos. Ben jerks up, hearing the louder gunfire, and sees the three moving forward and lifts to aim, sending shots into the shadows across the street as Safa, Harry and Emily break cover to run across.

'Move.' A voice at his side, and he flinches at being shoved by Charlie, who drops to Miri's side as Ben spots Delta holding the pistol taken with ease from Konrad and aims at him.

'Go,' Charlie says, pushing his hands into Miri's stomach. 'GO! Help them . . .'

A look from Ben to Delta and sometimes in life you have to take that chance and Ben takes it now, rising to leap over the downed chimney with Delta to run across the street firing rounds into the shadows on the other side.

'What the . . .' Safa spins, seeing Delta running with Ben.

Delta surges past her, his pistol held double-handed as he breaches the building line. 'Cover me . . .'

'Covering.' Safa spits the word, firing past him with Emily while Harry and Delta push in.

Delta brings his flashlight out, giving light to the shadows as they sweep through and the seconds go by as the net closes. 'Here!' Delta calls out. The others rush in to see a pile of spent casings forming a smiley face on the ground in a set of shadows further back in the building but no sign of Bravo.

'Fuck it,' Safa hisses. 'Fall back . . . but eyes up.'

A careful withdrawal back across the street, all of them aiming as they go in case Bravo starts firing again, but no shots come so they get back into their side to take cover while Safa and Emily glare at Konrad.

'I'm an engineer,' he says weakly.

'She's bad,' Charlie says, kneeling at Miri's side. 'No exit point so the bullet is still in there. Internal bleeding . . . organs could be damaged . . . She needs a hospital. Who is the OIC now?' he asks as everyone looks at Ben. 'Orders?' Charlie asks him.

'We need to move,' Harry says. 'Shooter knows our position; he could send soldiers here.'

Everyone looks at Ben, waiting for orders, waiting to be told what to do as he stares down to the near-silent form of Miri and suddenly he is but an insurance investigator surrounded by highly trained professionals and feeling way out of his depth. It's like he's been caught out, that up until now he's been hanging on Miri's coat-tails, knowing she was there to guide them, but now it's down to him. He should tell them he can't do this. One of them should take over. Safa or Charlie maybe. Harry was a sergeant; he could do it.

'Ben?' Safa asks softly.

'Okay.' Ben swallows and backs away into the shadow of a wall to stare out into the street.

Options, Mr Ryder? Ben can hear Miri's voice in his head. The expectation in her voice that his intelligence is right there with the answers. She'd tell him to think clearly and make an informed decision based on all the information they have. To know all the pieces on the board and out-think everyone. *The mission comes first.* She'd say that too.

'We need to exfil,' Delta whispers urgently.

Ben blows air from his cheeks and focusses on the problems facing them. Miri is injured and needs urgent medical attention. They have to stop Mother and reset the changes.

A flash of an idea forms that brings hope surging into his heart. The first available portal out of here comes from the agents visiting Herr Weber in Bundesstraße 2 in a few hours. They can get through that portal and take the complex with ease because the agents aren't in it. They can kill the agents before they return through the portal, which stops them dropping the nuclear bomb on London, which means they could reset the changes at the same time as getting Miri medical help. There it is. The solution.

So why isn't he giving the orders? Why isn't he telling them to move out to find somewhere to hole up for a few hours until they head back to Bundesstraße 2 and Arch 451.

A niggle. A voice in the back of his head that grows louder as he connects the dots from the very start to the now. From the time he was extracted and through everything that has happened in a stream of images and each image in his mind carries the emotions and feelings, the reasons for why it all happened and the realisation comes that makes him sag back into the wall. The realisation that brings forth an awful, terrible horror.

'Mother saves the world,' he whispers, and every head snaps to stare at him.

'What?' Emily asks, shock in her voice.

'The world was over,' he says. 'Then Mother made the changes in one-two-six AD and dropped that nuclear bomb and now it's not over . . .'

'Jesus,' Safa whispers, closing her eyes.

'I don't get it,' Delta says, looking from Safa to Ben.

'Bertie saw the world was over in twenty-one eleven,' Ben says. 'We did Cavendish Manor and all those things happened, then we checked the future and twenty-one eleven was fine . . . But the twenty-one eleven we saw has the changes from one-two-six AD and the nuclear bomb dropping in London . . . which means if those things *don't* happen then it goes back to the world being over . . . We can't reset it . . . We can't stop the agents dropping that bomb . . .'

The shock hits. The simple reasoning of it. The clarity that Ben gives as he explains it. The chain of events that happens that now cannot be touched.

'The portal opens again,' Safa says. 'When they deliver the bomb, when is that?'

'Day after tomorrow,' Charlie says. 'Seventh February, but we deployed into a barn about ten kilometres from here near an airfield . . .' He trails off as they look to Miri's unconscious form.

'Can we get her to a hospital here?' Emily asks.

'She needs specialist care,' Charlie says. 'A field hospital here won't save her . . . We've got a combat surgeon in our complex, but she won't last twelve hours, let alone a couple of days.'

'Those are the options,' Ben says. 'We can try and get Miri through the agents' portal in a few hours, but we risk killing the world, or we get through the portal in two days near the airfield by which time Miri will be dead . . .'

A heavy silence settles over them that touches even Charlie and Delta, not for the personal connection to the woman, but simply for the fact she is Maggie Sanderson. Everyone in their world knows who Maggie Sanderson is.

'I'm sorry,' Charlie whispers. 'For what it's worth, I doubt we'd even get through to Bundesstraße 2. They'll have a ring of steel round it after today . . .'

Thirty-Five

Berlin, 6 February 1945

Alpha comes to in a surge of adrenaline. Opening his eyes and staring round to a room full of noise and smells. People screaming. Men crying out in agony. People in blood-stained white coats rushing past. Old men and young boys dressed in grey uniforms hurrying past the end of his bed carrying stretchers laden with injured men, women and children.

It takes seconds to understand where he is and seconds longer for the pain to sweep through him. A crushing agony in the back of his head that makes him sink down and squeeze his eyes closed while his hands reach up to finger the dressing wound tightly round his skull.

Kate.

Alpha sits up, ignoring the pain and sickness to look round the huge room filled with beds and blood and screams. A makeshift field hospital. Exhausted-looking doctors and nurses flitting from bed to bed. A surgeon sawing at a leg while other men hold the screaming patient down.

Kate.

No sign of her. She's not next to him. He clambers up, swaying from the dizziness that he knows comes from concussion, but still he can't see her.

'Lie back down,' a brusque female voice orders behind him. Hands on his shoulders pulling him back towards the bed.

'A woman,' he says in German, pulling away and turning to look at the hooded eyes of a young nurse. 'There was a woman with me . . .'

'Lie down. You'll pass out.'

'The woman,' he snaps, earning glances from orderlies and doctors.

'I don't know,' the nurse says. She's too tired to care, too tired to keep moving.

'How long have I been here?'

'Yesterday, in the evening . . .'

He forces himself to be calm, resisting the urge to snap and demand answers. 'Thank you. Please, my wife . . . she was with me . . .'

She glances at his hand, seeing the lack of a ring on his fingers. 'They take women to the old schoolhouse sometimes . . . You didn't have any papers,' she says. 'They'll want to talk to you. I'll tell them you're awake now, shall I?' She walks off through the maze of beds with a flick of her hand at the glass-lined cubicle at one end and the hard-faced men wearing black uniforms smoking inside it. He casts round for his coat, not seeing it anywhere and guessing it was taken. His sidearm and the Luger were in it. He has to go. He has to find Kate and get to Bundesstraße 2. He starts to move, walking briskly to a wide aisle, aiming for the doors at the end.

'YOU THERE . . . STOP!'

He runs.

◆ ◆ ◆

A night in the basement under the bombed-out house. They made love several times. Buried in the warmth of the blankets, and while the bombers passed overhead, making the shelves in the basement rattle and dust fall from the beams, so they fucked slowly, exploring each other and feeling a strange rush of freedom at knowing there were no cameras or listening devices.

They found old jars filled with water and left in an obvious stockpile by whoever once lived above them. They drank deeply and washed each other, they spoke quietly of former lives, things they had seen and done, places they had been. Kate ad-libbed where needed, but stayed largely honest. Such is the skill required when inventing a past life. They held hands, stroked each other's heads, cuddled, dozed and grew as human beings.

She didn't have to fake any of it and that's the basis of a true legend; to be the person and allow real emotions to come out and react as they would normally. To laugh when something is funny and make sad noises when something is bad. Show empathy, but be selfish. Be selfish, but show a giving nature that seeks only to care and love. To embed in a situation and act with absolute confidence means allowing human nature to show and to be a real person.

Real people have hopes and desires too and she wasn't lying about the dreams she conjured with him. To have a device and spend their lives together going from era to era to see, study and live.

Their basement, for that night, became a kind of paradise.

'It's like that line from Charles Dickens,' Kate said into the darkness.

'Which one?' Alpha asked, lying on his back with her draped over his chest.

'*It was the best of times, it was the worst of times* . . . that one. From *A Tale of Two Cities*? Do you know it?'

'I think so,' he said softly, staring off to nothing while looping a strand of her hair round his thumb. '*It was the best of times, it was the worst of times, it was the age of wisdom, it was the age of foolishness, it was the epoch of belief, it was the epoch of incredulity . . .*' She sat up, listening in stunned awe. '*. . . it was the season of light, it was the season of darkness,* *it was the spring of hope, it was the winter of despair, we had everything before us, we had nothing before us, we were all going direct to heaven, we were all going direct the other way . . .'*

A moment in time that seared into her memory. A thing felt inside at the depths of a man she thought she had the measure of, who spoke so quietly, without a hint of boast or brag. Even when he finished and when most people would seek the acknowledgement of their audience he simply stared, listening intently with a mind constantly working while his fingers pushed into hers with raw vulnerability. She felt an urge at that point, a need to tell him who she really was and what she had done. To seek openness and honesty and with it, forgiveness.

'Sorry,' he whispered, finally looking at her with a rueful smile. 'Wasn't showing off . . .'

'God no, not at all,' she replied. 'I didn't think that . . . You're a strange man.'

'Not really,' he said, shifting position. 'We're all what we're told to be in a lot of ways . . .' She blinked at the resonance of his words, her heart thumping harder and her mouth suddenly dry. 'We get trained, we get told, we see goals and we work to be what we think we should be.' He gave a dry laugh, smiling to himself, at her, at all of it while she felt a growing sickness building up inside. 'Look at Emily Rose . . . She was trained and told to be one of us . . . She got through, maybe captured or escaping as Cavendish Manor went down, then she switched sides. She saw it. She saw what we see now . . . that we're told to act in the service of the good and to do the bad things for the service of the good . . .' He smiled again, exhaling slowly. 'Ignore me. I'm being melancholy.'

'You're not . . . I like it.'

'How about you? Ever do something you regret?'

Kate closed her eyes, feeling a sudden strange weight lifting from her shoulders and in that second she knew, she truly knew in the depths of her being that if she spoke now in honesty it would be okay and as she drew breath to form words to give sound to tell him so the bomb landed above them with a deafening, roaring, ear-splitting boom that brought down beams to flood their dark dry place with light and fire, with choking dust and falling chunks of masonry.

They reacted quickly, with reflexes honed over years of training. Both rolling from the beams, which thudded down from the ceiling. Everything shaking and heaving. The very ground trembling, but Alpha gained his feet and lifted her up, seeing the path ahead that they either took now or remained and died.

He didn't speak, but pulled her round to go in front, propelling her from behind over and under the falling beams and the awful, terrible noise above them. He got her to the stairs and pulled her back to charge up and ram his head and shoulder into the trapdoor, pushing and straining against the rocks and bricks piling up on top of it. He gritted his teeth, grunting with effort while bracing his legs to lock out and heave, but felt the immovable weight above him while behind the basement was filling with fire, wood and bricks.

This was it. He could see it and sense it. He knew it. This was the point they died, that it would all be over and at some point two bodies would be pulled from the rubble that would be forever nameless and unknown. In that choking moment, in that second before the world crashed through the ceiling and buried them forever, she squeezed in at the top of the stairs and braced her head and shoulder next to his. Both crammed, facing each other with barely an inch to move, but they pushed together, grunting and crying out with eyes locked as the heat grew and the noise got worse. As the building came down so the veins pushed from their foreheads as they surged up, pushing the trapdoor open by degrees that shifted the bricks piled on top.

They gained freedom with a cry of pain and victory, falling out to roll together amidst the masonry raining down that hit their backs and legs and one solid chunk that slammed into the rear of Kate's skull, making her sink with sudden nausea and an agony blooming in her head. She heard a sound like his voice and blinked in between the blackness to see his face smeared with blood and watched with almost idle detachment as she slid upside down with his hands gripping her wrists. She didn't feel the drop from the building to the street but opened her eyes a moment later to see flames and smoke and hear the deep avalanche sound of buildings coming down and engines roaring overhead.

'WAIT THERE . . .'

She heard his voice again, feeling his hands on her cheeks, but then he was gone and she blinked in the blackness that took her away only to bring her back so she could open her eyes and see Alpha walking from a burning building, a child held in one arm and his hand pulling an unconscious woman behind him. She slept. She woke. She puked and gasped for air and her head hurt and her vision swam and she saw him framed by fire with children in his arms, then a woman over his shoulder, then another child, but Kate could see the head was gone from the tiny body.

'ARE YOU OKAY?' She blinked back to life, sucking in air and feeling the burn of vomit in her throat. Her head hurt, everything hurt. 'ARE YOU OKAY?' She looked up at the face of a woman.

'Ja . . . ja,' she stammered with the sense to answer in German, scrabbling to her feet and looking round at a scene far worse than anything witnessed so far. Mass casualties everywhere. Hundreds killed and maimed instantly. Buildings blazing with flames scorching dozens of feet into the sky and yet more bombers overhead continuing the punishment. She looked round, desperately seeking Alpha. Then she saw him kneeling in the road and ran staggering towards him, seeing his hands pushing on the chest of a child, trying to get air into the broken body. She dropped at his side, instantly going to work to pull the chin back and clear the airways before bending down to give her breath into the lungs of another. They worked together, compressions given and breaths administered for long minutes until the tears pricked her eyes with the hopeless realisation it was too late.

370

They stopped together. No words were needed, no signals passed that told the other to cease, but an understanding that continuing was hopeless.

'We have to go,' Alpha said quietly, his voice almost lost in the chaos.

'Help this one,' the gruff voice of a man said, lowering a screaming child down next to Alpha before rushing off. A kid, maybe seven or eight, his arm broken and his face twisted in utter agony. Alpha looked round, his face a mask of conflict. They had to go and hide; this was not their war or their place to be.

'Hold him,' Kate said, grabbing the boy's broken arm. 'Alfie . . . hold him . . .'

He blinked once and reached out to hold the boy tight, seeing her hands work down his arm to grip double-handed on his wrist.

'The shock will kill him if it's left,' she said. 'Hold him tight . . .'

Alpha didn't question how she knew to do such a thing, but he held the boy tight, speaking soft words while the child screamed and Kate yanked to crunch the bone back into position. That it hurt was obvious, that it pinched nerves and gave the boy untold pain was also obvious, but within seconds that pain was less. They found a length of wood and tore material from the shirt on a corpse to wrap a splint on the boy's arm. Crude and awful, but effective and with luck the boy would feel his fingers again one day.

They stopped wounds from bleeding out and he saw the change in Kate. The confidence of her movements. The way she pressed her fingers to the boy's neck to check for pulse and life and the brutal ease of the professionally trained to know when life is gone and to move on to help the living. The firmness of her voice and the lack of fear she had before and they worked side by side, applying pressure with tourniquets and dressings made from filthy scraps of material ripped from bodies. They pulled the alive away from the dead and placed children into the arms of women to hold and soothe. They became blackened of face and hands, stinking of smoke, blood and soot.

They became absorbed and lost in the immediacy of giving aid to other human beings in peril, cleansing their souls of the foul things both had done in their lives.

Then, as the night started to wane and the first hint of daylight crept into the sky on the sixth day of February 1945 so they moved back to slip away into the city, to get closer to Bundesstraβe 2 and the chance of meeting back up with Maggie and getting out of here, to find somewhere to talk about what Alpha had just seen her do and neither saw the bomb hit the nearest building that blew the structure out in a thousand pieces that slammed into their heads and bodies rendering them, and everyone else, either dead or unconscious.

Thirty-Six

Berlin, Bundesstraße 2, 6 February 1945

Time has changed, but then time is not fixed.

The agents came to Bundesstraße 2 on 6 February for their last visit to Herr Weber before they delivered the nuclear bomb, but on that visit building twenty-five was still standing and the street was nowhere as damaged as it is now, and Charlie was right, soldiers now flood that area with a ring of steel around that street. Trucks of battle-hardened front-line troops born of the true Aryan race, who wear their Nazi swastikas with pride.

Herr Weber, with what weight he still carries, has ordered the soldiers out of the street and given strict instructions that five men seen together coming from the direction of Arch 451 must be allowed to proceed unhindered, because Herr Weber wants that bomb. He doesn't care what happens outside of Bundesstraße 2, but those five men *will* be left to visit him untouched.

Herr Weber isn't stupid and knows the five men come and go from Arch 451, but he suspects a tunnel giving access to somewhere that holds a radio system that the men use to communicate and receive orders. He could order an inspection of Arch 451, but he doesn't because he wants that bomb. He wants to hurt the enemy and so life in Bundesstraße 2 on 6 February appears as it did before, with people digging through remains for loved ones, with dead bodies piled up and fires still licking while others smoulder with thick black smoke curling up.

◆ ◆ ◆

Time has changed, but then time is not fixed.

Escape and evasion again. Run fast, but run smart and Alpha does that now. Sprinting from the makeshift field hospital into the streets of war-torn inner-city Berlin, taking hard turns left and right to lose the Gestapo-esque figures running behind him taking pot shots from Lugers with no regard to collateral damage of stray bullets hitting innocent bystanders.

He has to find Kate, then get to the portal appearing in Arch 451. He knows that the agents will be out of the complex visiting Herr Weber and he can get through, kill Mother and use the device to get away with Kate. It will change time, but to hell with it. To hell with the mission and everyone else. Only this matters now. Only Kate matters now.

◆ ◆ ◆

Time has changed, but then time is not fixed.

In the clearing outside the shack on Bertie's island, Ria makes ready. Pushing fifty-calibre rounds into the magazines for the Barrett rifle while the others do the same. Loading weapons and preparing their minds for what will come. That the two with Ria are somewhat stunned at the turn of events doesn't show because they have a job to do.

Time has changed, but then time is not fixed.

A kilometre from Bundesstraße 2, they get ready with what little they have. Checking pistols and sharing magazines out. Charlie tests the makeshift stretcher he fashioned from timber and cloth scavenged from ruined buildings and with Harry and Konrad's help they lift a silent and very pale Miri onto it.

Miri bent time to suit her will. She took a thing of immeasurable power that would corrupt the hearts of saints and she made it fit what she wanted.

Charlie told them in the shadows of the ruins that they wouldn't get near Arch 451 because the Germans will put a ring of steel on that area.

That comment made Ben think. It made him think hard, with ideas and images racing through his mind.

'We didn't see any soldiers when we came through on the sixth Feb,' Delta said.

'No, but we've changed time, haven't we?' Charlie said. 'Oh, hang on, how does that work then? Bloody hell, this is confusing.'

'How the hell do you work all this out?' Delta asked the others, shaking his head in confusion.

'We don't,' Emily said with a humourless snort. 'They do,' she added with a nod at Miri, then at Ben.

Safa saw it first and nudged Harry, making him look at Ben.

'Aye,' Harry whispered.

'What?' Emily asked, frowning at Safa then looking at Ben. 'Oh,' she said quietly, 'he's doing that thing.'

Ben stood with his head lowered, staring at the ground. His feet planted apart and his right hand rubbing the side of his jaw.

'Here it comes,' Safa whispered.

Ben's head lifted a fraction, his eyes looked up at them and gave that wry smile. 'Change of plan . . .'

◆ ◆ ◆

Alpha's head hurts like hell, a dull thumping ache that sends waves of nausea through his gut, but he suppresses the pain and sickness to push on, running through filthy broken streets and hearing the shots slowly dropping away as the distance increases and he loses the Gestapo officers who chased him from the hospital.

He slows down a little, easing his frantic breathing to blend in with the crowds of refugees and survivors. He has to switch on and think. Find Kate. Get to the Arch. Kill Mother and disappear somewhere.

A small crowd stand gathered round a line of dead bodies laid out and he approaches carefully, looking stricken and wretched. 'Can you help me?' he asks, some of them look at him with exhausted expressions. 'I'm looking for the old schoolhouse hospital . . . My wife . . . she . . .'

'Few streets away,' someone mutters.

'Which way?' Alpha asks, trying to identify who spoke.

'That way,' a woman says, flicking a tired hand. 'Round the corner from Bundesstraße 2 . . .'

He starts running with fresh hope in his heart. He can find Kate, get her out and reach the portal. He checks his watch, seeing he just has time if he runs hard.

In the darkness of Arch 451 a green shimmering doorway forms through which Alpha steps to pause and listen before sticking a hand through to the complex with a thumbs up for the others to follow. Bravo comes through, followed by Charlie, Delta and Echo. All of them in 1940s period clothing given to them by Gerry.

Alpha moves to the door, peering through the cracks to check the view. No soldiers, nothing obvious. Smoke coming from ruins.

'Looks like a bad air raid overnight,' he says quietly.

'How bad?' Bravo asks from behind. 'Do we need to redeploy?'

'No, I don't think so. Ready?'

They step out to do as before and huddle together as though frightened and weary for a few minutes before moving on and proceeding into the street proper.

'It was a bad raid,' Bravo says in German, looking at the ruined buildings. 'I'm sure Kate said some of these buildings remain intact . . .'

'We'll check when we get back,' Alpha replies in German as Charlie and Delta share a glance. 'Keep your eyes up . . .'

◆ ◆ ◆

One kilometre away from Bundesstraβe 2. A big man walks down the centre of the road. Broad and thick-limbed with a bushy black beard and black hair. He wears an old overcoat and keeps his head lowered and his eyes staring ahead.

The size of him draws attention. The way he walks too, with a confident stride and a strange glimmer in his eyes. He doesn't look German either, but then he isn't German. He is English.

He is Sergeant Harry Madden.

'We're going for the portal in that arch,' Ben said last night.

'You just said it will kill the world,' Delta said.

'Time isn't fixed . . .' Ben said in explanation.

'Er, sorry, but I'm lost,' Charlie said, cutting in.

'Just go with it,' Emily said. 'Trust me . . . it's easier than trying to figure it out.'

'Right,' Ben said. 'How the hell do we get through a shit ton of German soldiers?'

'Put me down for that one, Ben.'

'Jesus, Harry. You're not even joking,' Ben said as everyone stared at the big man. 'Mate, it could be hundreds . . . I know you're good, but . . .'

'Ach, you're probably right. Might be best to use a bit of caution on this one then.'

'Yeah, definitely . . . We'll think of something.'

'I'll take Safa and them two new lads with me.'

'What?' Ben asked.

'Oi,' Emily said.

'Fuck yes! I'm with beardy killing Nazis,' Safa said.

'What the . . .' Charlie said.

'I'm in,' Delta said, nodding eagerly.

'Oi,' Emily said again. 'What about me . . .'

'Protect Ben and Konrad carrying Miri,' Harry said.

'Right,' Emily said, clearly affronted. 'And why am I doing that specifically? Maybe I want to kill Nazis too.'

'We can't all kill Nazis,' Safa said. 'And you got one in the bunker anyway.'

'This is because we had sex, isn't it,' Emily said, glaring at Harry as Safa and Ben groaned.

Sergeant Harry Madden strides down the centre of the road to draw attention from the dark-haired woman of mixed race walking on one side with an old scarf tied round her head and the two men in filthy, torn coats walking with her while several metres behind them, Ben and Konrad carry the stretcher with Emily at Miri's side.

'Open it,' Ria tells her brother. 'Then get out and stay out until one of us comes back.'

'Okay, Ria,' Bertie mumbles, holding the controller.

'Bertie! What did I just say?'

'Um, so you, like, totally said to get out.'

'I mean it. If you come back I'll know and I'll kick your arse . . .' She glares at him, from a sister to a brother, and the only one who can justifiably use the threat of violence to make Bertie listen. 'Ready?' she asks the other two. 'Let's go . . .'

◆ ◆ ◆

Find Kate. Get to the Arch. A mantra in his mind pushing Alpha on and he makes good distance as he starts to recognise certain features of the landscape that tell him he is close to Bundesstraße 2.

He rounds a corner and comes to a sudden stop at the solid masses of grey German uniforms on high alert, who spot him running and the fleeting look of panic on his face that he is too slow to hide. They react fast, shouting out while lifting rifles and sub-machine guns, but Alpha reacts faster. A door to the right, wooden and intact, that he slams into, smashing it from the old worn hinges to stagger through a dusty hallway amid the screams of women and children crying out in fear at him, running to smash through the back door and out into a brick-walled yard. He runs to the end, leaping to scrabble over the wall that crumbles as he hits it, the weak mortar breaking apart into a heap that sees him rolling over bricks that cut into his knees, hands and elbows. Shots come through the house, slamming into the walls and fences surrounding him. He crawls first, then rises up to sprint on down the narrow alley running at the back of the street while all around the shouts of German soldiers fill the air.

◆ ◆ ◆

Shots in the air. Shouts too, and Harry feels the thrum of excitement building as he walks out of one road and crosses the junction towards the next. Bundesstraße 2 is close now. Only a few streets away and so he walks on, dominating that road, filling it with his presence as the menace of the man starts rippling out. The intent in his unblinking eyes. The sheer ferocity of his gaze that seems to increase with every step he takes, and he finally sees them at the end of the next street. A sea of grey uniforms and grey helmets. The enemy is there. His sworn enemy.

He starts unbuttoning the old coat as he walks, his eyes fixed on them and nothing else, counting heads, looking for officers, seeing positions.

The first German soldier casually looks up the road, double-taking with a bemused frown at the sight of the man striding towards them. A big man too. Big and angry-looking.

'What's his problem?' he asks, making several more soldiers turn to look and chuckle and smile.

'*Kampf mich*,' Harry mutters. Seeing them. Staring at them. '*Kampf mich* . . .'

'Get ready,' Safa says urgently.

Harry yanks the coat away from his body with an action that makes more German soldiers turn and look, and now they see him properly: a big man in black combat trousers and a black top in 1943 boots. And Harry stops walking to stand massive with his arms down at his sides and his head up. Seconds go by. His hands come out from his body, beckoning the soldiers, goading them to come. 'DIRTY BOCHE BASTARDS . . . *KAMPF MICH* . . .'

They hear the English voice and more turn and weapons are gripped as they start moving out and forward, still hardly believing that one man is telling them to fight him.

Then Harry smiles and stands fully upright, knowing his final words will ignite the touch paper. '*FICK . . . DEINE . . . MUTTER . . .*' His voice fills the street, booming out, and that does it. Tell any soldier in the world to fuck his mother and watch what happens.

The Germans react but so do Safa, Charlie and Delta, shredding their old clothes to run out from the sides towards Harry as the big man draws and starts firing as he goes, right with the other three, and the air fills with pistols firing. Germans drop fast, shot dead or spinning away screaming out, and as the rest aim to fire so Harry bursts into the alley he stopped adjacent to and runs like the clappers with Safa, Charlie and Delta hot on his heels.

'We're up,' Ben says, further down the street and kneeling with his back to the stretcher. 'Konrad . . . we can't stop, okay . . . No stopping . . . GO!'

◆ ◆ ◆

Alpha runs, feeling time ticking on and the pressure growing. There's too many soldiers behind him now. He has to break free. Tactics and strategies run through his mind, ideas and plans that flicker until he gains the essence of a way out, but first he has to draw them in.

He slows his run, easing down to recover his breath and let his heart rate settle. His head is pounding, his mouth and throat so dry and thirsty, but he studies the ends of the street and waits for the first soldiers to appear. He double-takes, showing fear and surprise before darting off towards the row of houses with bomb-damaged roofs. He goes in through an open back door to a kitchen and searches quickly for a knife, cursing his luck at choosing a house that has been stripped and emptied. A fork in the back of a drawer. Solid and heavy, but still just a three-pronged dining fork. It'll have to do.

The first soldier runs at the house, spraying bullets from his machine gun through the door and window. Sixteen years old, given a uniform and told how to fire a gun in his old school playing field before being told to go and hold the Russians back. A wispy hint of a moustache on his upper lip and the fear he feels is twisted to rage as he fires the gun without heed to over-heating, jamming or even aiming properly. He strides in, assuming the weapon has done the work and killed the spy they are hunting, but Alpha waits in the space behind the open front door, holding position until the soldier steps through, then coming up behind to wrap his arms round the young lad's head and drive the fork into his eye. The soldier screams in agony, thrashing while his finger squeezes the trigger as Alpha twists him round to fire into his comrades coming in through the door.

He lets the soldier drop the second the machine gun clicks empty, gripping the weapon hard to break the strap, then wrenching a magazine from the soldier's belt and lurching away to swap over, cursing at the hot barrel and the bloody idiot firing it on full. Movement from the back of the house; the sound of boots crunching.

'IN HERE, IN HERE,' Alpha screams in German, forcing his voice to break with tension and fear. He snatches a view, seeing several dead by the front door and more writhing and crying out from gunshots.

'I'VE GOT HIM . . . IN HERE, IN HERE . . .'

'HE'S GOT HIM,' the voices shout, screaming in panic, joy, worry and terror. They come quickly through the door, charging into the narrow hallway.

Alpha leans out low from a doorway to gun them down. He aims for legs first, burst firing to make them scream to give more noise to create more confusion. He drops his machine gun, grabs a body and heaves it into his room, quickly snapping the neck to give death before working fast to strip the big grey uniform jacket from the corpse. 'UPSTAIRS, UPSTAIRS . . .' he screams out while tugging hard to get the coat free and pulling it on.

More come in and he guns them down too. As soon as that wave is down he staggers out to drop and crawl, smearing blood over his face, then screaming out in pain while pretending to scrabble away. More soldiers come, seeing the awful slaughter and the blood spatters over the walls and floor.

'Where is he?' one asks, grabbing to heave Alpha across the floor towards the door.

Alpha screams and pretends to cry at the pain caused by being dragged, his face covered in blood, twisted in agony.

'He's in there . . . get in . . .' a voice orders, the hard voice of an officer. 'My god.' He balks at the sight of Alpha, shaking his head in anger. 'Where is he?'

'Sir . . . I don't know . . . I don't . . . I'm sorry . . .'

'It's okay, get him back . . .' the officer orders, patting Alpha's shoulder. 'Damn war . . . GET GRENADES IN THERE . . .'

'Our men are injured in there . . .' someone shouts back.

Alpha rises heroically to his feet, staggering and confused, crying and weak, but shuffling down the street as more soldiers run past him. Explosions behind. Grenades being thrown about. Gunshots, shouts, confusion and chaos. A battered old tank chugs into view, trundling over rubble and debris as the officer orders his men to make clear so the tank can join in with the absurd level of overkill.

'I WANT HIM ALIVE . . .' a man in black uniform with a peaked cap bellows while striding past Alpha. 'I SAID ALIVE,' he roars, setting off at a run when the tank booms a shot at the house, blowing chunks of masonry and brick out that pepper the soldiers nearby. He aims for a junction, running out to gawp in horror at a heavy truck trying to turn at speed as a grenade explodes, sending the truck slamming onto its side at Alpha, who vaults a wall to get clear.

◆ ◆ ◆

If they survive they will speak of this for years to come. That they, two agents in the British Secret Service, defected to the enemy and ended up in a firefight against Nazis in Berlin with Mad Harry Madden and Safa Patel.

'Drop,' Harry orders as they reach the end of an alley. They go flat, scooting over out of sight and waiting for the first soldiers to go sprinting past. Safa aims to fire, but Harry lifts a hand, telling her to wait and letting more come because this is what Harry does. This is where the big man made his name, by using the size of overwhelming forces against themselves.

'Now.' He fires into them as Charlie, Delta and Safa do the same. Sending rounds into bodies. 'INTO THEM . . .' Harry roars, surging up to go in deep to the ranks of men compressing as they come to a stop. Turning into each other, fumbling in the tight space while their mates scream in agony from the shots given, and if that wasn't bad enough they then see the legend of Mad Harry Madden coming to life before their eyes.

The wildness of him. The sheer bloodlust that takes over with a brutality that surpasses the refined skills of Safa, Charlie and Delta. A genial man by nature. A gentle giant who nurtures those around him. Who smiles slowly and keeps his thoughts in his head. A man of honour and principle, of integrity and a depth of courage that knows no bounds, that right now is a thing of seething violence erupting to decimate anything close to him wearing the grey of his enemy.

A foot to the stomach takes the first one off his feet and flying back, then Harry wades in with his mighty fists clenched and swinging. Downing man after man. Bang, bang, bang. They fall like dominos. One comes in from his left with a knife drawn, but Harry grabs the hand, twists, breaks the wrist and headbutts down before snatching the blade to stick in the soldier's chest. He pulls it free, twists and stabs another in the neck, then ducks to stab legs while gripping ankles to wrench them off their feet so he can stamp down in his sturdy 1943 boots.

He times it to perfection, grabbing a sub-machine gun from a body and turning it to fire at the next section coming into the alley. They fall screaming, torn down by the barrage of fire as Charlie, Delta and Safa do the same and grab sub-machine guns.

'Grenades . . . ON!' Harry roars, scooping to grab the stick grenades from bodies as they go, and he moves fast, sprinting with a speed even Safa didn't know he had, his jaw clenched, his face a mask of aggression. Harry knows they have to make distance and lead the soldiers on to give Ben space to get through.

'*FICK DEINE MUTTER,*' he roars, and lobs a grenade at a unit running into the road they sprint across. The four leap into the ruins opposite as the grenade detonates with a solid whump, then follow

Harry back out into the street to charge at the scattered enemy, pressing the attack with a withering aggression that sends those men fleeing for cover.

The four burst out into a wide crossroads and a heavy truck coming at them filled with soldiers.

'DOWN, DOWN.' Charlie reacts fast, throwing a grenade at the front of the truck as it slews to the side, trying to veer away. He opens fire, strafing the back with Delta as the grenade blows at the point of the truck turning sharply, the explosive giving enough lift for the truck to flip over on its side to slide down the road spilling broken bodies from the back, and they catch a glimpse of a man vaulting a wall to get clear as the truck slams into the side of a ruined house, but still they fire their guns, then run to the fallen to grab fresh weapons and more grenades.

The four go left, running mere feet from Alpha hunkering down and into the street Alpha came from, with Harry spotting the mass melee going on with a battered old tank laying waste to a house while scores of men gather around it, pouring fire into the doors and windows. A temptation too great to pass. A target too good, and the four come to a stop, setting their grenades ready and throwing at the same time into the men gathered by the tank.

The four explosions come near on together. Four percussive bangs that send men flying off their feet while others spin away screaming from the fragments slicing them deep.

Harry snarls, striding out to fire the sub-machine gun as he walks down the road. Safa gains his side, shooting at the men as Charlie and Delta rush out to join the line and as one they spot the officer in the black uniform and peaked cap trying to run away and as one they twitch their aim to gun him down.

'COVER!' Delta roars on seeing the top of the tank swivel the barrel from firing at the house to aim at them.

Safa and Delta go left. Charlie goes right, but Harry goes straight at it with fury in his eyes as the men inside panic and try to force their last shell into the tube. Harry moves faster. Snarling as the tank loads and side-stepping smartly when the thing goes bang and the shell flies past, whizzing down the road to hit the truck on its side, blowing it back across the junction through the lines of injured soldiers screaming in pain.

Harry vaults onto the track, then up onto the roof as the hatch opens with a leather-headset-wearing officer surging up with a Luger, who finds his face filled with a 1943 boot. Harry kicks hard, then ducks to wrench the man out, flinging him aside, then dropping into the hatch as the other three stare on, listening to the screams until it goes silent. A body comes flying out the top, pushed by Harry underneath, who sends it falling to the ground.

'Either of you drive a tank?' Harry shouts, jumping down and shooting a writhing man in the head as he walks calmly by.

'Delta did a tank course,' Charlie blurts, pointing at Delta.

'I didn't do a World War Two tank course, you twat,' Delta says.

'Don't stand there, lad, get in it . . . No shells left and the machine guns are broken so just drive it at the Boche . . . We'll be behind you.' Harry pauses mid-step with a glance up at the sudden roar of engines overhead as the air-raid sirens come to life across the city and once again the black silhouettes of the allied bombers fill the clear blue sky.

Miri isn't big at all, but an inert human form of any size is called a dead weight for a reason, and the lack of food, water and a night of being awake in the freezing cold soon take their toll as Ben and Konrad run hard with Emily trying to hold Miri on the stretcher.

They go into the road where Harry, Safa, Charlie and Delta picked the first fight and spot the bodies at the end, then they run past the alley strewn with broken bodies as the grenades and explosions and gunshots and screams sound out nearby.

'YOU!' A German medic runs at them, his grey uniform and his hands covered in blood from tending to the injuries of his comrades. 'Give me that stretcher now . . .'

'My mother,' Emily shouts back. 'She's been shot . . . We need to . . .'

'My soldiers take priority,' the officer barks.

'No!' Emily cries out. 'Please, sir . . . we have to get her through.'

'I will tell you once more before I . . .' He doesn't finish the threat from the shot going through his head as Emily draws and fires, then pivots to fire into the other two medics tending the injured, killing both.

'Go,' she urges. 'GO!'

They set off running again, running as fast as they can while Konrad's shoulders and arms start to burn. He gasps for air, his face flushing a deep red. 'Ben . . . I can't . . . I . . . gotta . . .'

'Keep going.' Emily gets to his side, reaching a hand out to give some lift to the stretcher, not much, but anything helps.

What a thing to do. What a plan to come up with, and right now Ben curses himself for even suggesting a thing of such monumental stupidity. He's risking everyone for one member of the team. Would Miri do that? Yes. Without doubt she would. She might snarl and snap and yell and patronise everyone around her, but she would kill the world for one of her own, and right now Ben might be doing just that.

They cross the end of a street, all three of them turning their heads to the far end and the sight of a heavy truck slamming over onto its side amidst a cacophony of gunfire and explosions. More shouts from somewhere else. Noise everywhere and units of soldiers pouring from the streets, heading towards those noises.

'How much further?' Emily asks.

'Two streets,' Ben shouts over his shoulder as Konrad whimpers, knowing he can't keep going for that long.

A huge bang sounds out and the truck on its side explodes, shooting back across the road as they run into the next junction as the air-raid sirens come to life and the sky above them fills with bombers roaring overhead.

◆ ◆ ◆

Alpha peers over the wall, unaware that Harry, Safa, Charlie and Delta ran past a few seconds ago. He has to go. He has to go right now. Four explosions sound from the street he ran from followed by sustained gunfire, and he vaults the wall and turns the collar up on his stolen tunic and forces himself to walk with the assured arrogance of a German soldier as the tank fires the last shell that whips past Harry and through Safa, Charlie and Delta and past Alpha to hit the truck that explodes out and goes screeching backwards as Alpha simply turns his head to watch it happen.

A second later and he starts walking faster, using the distraction to get away.

The air-raid sirens come to life and everyone around him moves from static, slow and exhausted to full out running in terror for the shelters on hearing the sirens and Alpha runs too.

The bombers come into view overhead, bringing horror to the streets as the allies work to bring the Fatherland to its knees. Alpha runs faster now, cursing at the thick crowds of Berliners streaming against him.

A unit of soldiers stand in the street, monitoring the civilians streaming past. One spots a grey tunic going against the flow and points at Alpha, shouting for his officer, who calls out for Alpha to stop, but the man runs harder, slamming through the dense lines of screaming people as the soldiers give chase, firing rounds into the air to make the people duck and move as a huge explosion rocks the ground, sending bricks and flaming wood into the street, killing several soldiers and many civilians. Alpha goes down, hit by something, and through sheer willpower he rises to run on, his face wet with blood, pain everywhere.

People screaming and crying out, holding the dead and injured in their arms. Pain and suffering in every direction.

Alpha starts to slow, the pain getting worse with waves of nausea pulsing through him, but he can make it. He can find Kate. A grey uniform looms in front and he draws his pistol, aims and fires, then carries on without looking back as his run becomes more staggered and lurching, his feet suddenly heavy, his legs simply unwilling to give him the speed he demands.

One street to go. One final street, where the road has thankfully been cleared to allow the ambulances and trucks to ferry the injured to the makeshift hospital.

There it is, at the end of the road, the schoolhouse. A large brick building with huge white sheets tied together across the roof and a crude red cross painted on it, standing in a sea of rubble and demolished buildings like a beacon of hope to the people who work with bleeding hands and numb feet to keep the access routes clear.

Alpha trudges on with the love of a woman giving him the fuel to keep going. He thinks of her laugh, of her eyes, of the feel of her lips when they kiss, the way she holds him and the soft words she gives. Nothing will stop him now. Nothing.

◆ ◆ ◆

The five agents enter the front door to Herr Weber's building as the air-raid sirens come to life and as one they pause and hold still.

'There wasn't an air raid till later,' Bravo says quietly in German.

'Something's changed,' Charlie says.

'Could be us,' Alpha says. 'Our presence here . . . like a small variance or something.'

'Shouldn't we turn back?' Charlie asks.

'Dear boy, we've come this far,' Bravo says. 'I say we get this done and then go back for tea and cake.'

'You two,' Alpha says, looking at Charlie and Delta. 'Hold the street door. Echo, come up and hold outside. Bravo with me again.'

'Roger that,' Bravo drawls, beaming at the others. 'Such fun we are having, eh, chaps.'

Charlie and Delta share a glance, nodding at Alpha as they take sentry either side of the street door, both of them glaring at Bravo's back as the others mount the stairs to go up and out of sight.

'Prick,' Charlie whispers once Alpha, Bravo and Echo are out of sight.

'Complete prick,' Delta whispers. 'Be glad when this is done.'

Movement in the street door between them. A man coming in.

'Closed,' Charlie says in German, stepping out to block his path as the internal door behind Delta opens.

'Sorry, Affas,' the man in the street door says, grinning as he moves with a blur of speed, driving the point of his blade through Charlie's throat while clamping a hand over his mouth. Delta would react, but the huge arms wrapped round his head lifting him off his feet prevent him doing so and all he feels is a dull crack as his neck snaps.

◆ ◆ ◆

'Almost there . . .' Ben calls back, his own shoulders now on fire, his legs feeling heavier with each step.

Konrad weeps from the agony of it. Fighting with everything he has to keep hold of the stretcher as Emily snatches a worried glance at Miri's deathly form.

The last junction nears. The final one that feeds into Bundesstraße 2, then straight down to Arch 451. So close now. The last corner comes into view and they run on, feeling the tremble in the ground underfoot from the bombs hitting nearby. Hearing the explosions and the screams that follow. Seeing the people streaming past as they flee panicked and wild for the shelters.

'Oh no . . . no, no, no,' Ben gasps, reaching the corner to see the units of soldiers holding position at the end of Bundesstraße 2. Too many to get through. Far too many to get through. Dozens of them. 'Oh fuck,' he adds on seeing the tank trundle into view, albeit a battered old-looking thing. Dozens of soldiers and now a tank. The hope vanishes. The energy they had to keep going abates as all three realise the odds against them.

'Can we go round?' Emily asks.

'Not enough time now,' Ben says, thinking fast. The only option left is to wait for the portal to open near the airfield, but Miri will not last that long. She is barely clinging to life now. Ben tries to think of options, wondering if they can go through the ruins to reach Arch 451, but they'd still have to go through those soldiers and he stares hopeless as the tank lurches towards the units, slewing left and right, stopping and starting in a way that makes the soldiers turn to look at it. 'A fucking tank,' Ben mutters. 'I wish we had a fucking tank . . .'

Delta peers through the slit in the front of the tank, his hands grabbing sticks and pushing things while levering other things while his feet push pedals. 'Delta did a tank course,' he grumbles, mimicking Charlie. 'Delta can drive a tank . . . Bloody thing is ancient.' He curses as it swings left, then overcompensates to bring it too far right while seeing all the soldiers on the junction of Bundesstraße 2 turning to look at him. Then the worst thing happens and he stalls it. Staring wide-eyed at the snorting jolly-faced Aryan bastards laughing at him. 'Wankers,' he mutters. 'Oh, you're for it now . . .' He turns it over, spewing black fumes while Harry, Charlie and Safa share looks as they hunker down behind it.

'You said he could drive a tank,' Safa says.

'I said he did a tank course,' Charlie says.

'Ha! Got it,' Delta says as the tank fires back up to a resounding and very sarcastic cheer from the German soldiers.

'What's he doing?' Ben asks as the tank lurches on towards the German soldiers. It looks like it's going faster. Like it's building speed.

'What's he doing?' one of the German soldiers calls out as the laughs and cheers fade away.

'Yeah, not laughing now, are you?' Delta says, pushing more power into the thing. 'COME ON.' He pushes more, driving it forward as fast as it will go.

'Oh shit,' Ben says, watching the tank charge at the German soldiers.

'Oh shit,' the German soldier calls out.

'Oh yes!' Delta shouts. 'HAVE IT!'

'Harry!' Emily exclaims, a grin spreading across her face at the sight of Harry, Safa and Charlie running crouched behind the tank.

'No way,' Ben says, hardly believing it. 'Right . . . you ready, Kon?'

'No, I'm not bloody ready – my hands hurt and . . .'

'Final push . . . GO!' Ben sets off as the tank speeds up, sending the German soldiers scattering, and Emily runs wide as Safa and Charlie burst out to fire sub-machine guns while Harry vaults to the top of the moving tank, a sub-machine gun in each hand that he fires into the screaming men.

Emily fires her pistol, sending single shots into centres of mass to drop men, striding out with her pistol in a double-handed grip. She empties the magazine, but changes it with a blur of speed to resume firing as Ben and Konrad grit their teeth and run through the bedlam with bullets flying everywhere.

Emily changes magazine again, then runs hard into the melee, dropping to slide at the last second to take out the legs of a German soldier, making him fall as she rises to send her last bullet through his head, then ditching her pistol to snatch his sub-machine gun as she rolls and rises, surging to her feet to strafe the grey uniforms near her as the tank turns into Bundesstraße 2. Into the final stretch and the sight of Arch 451 at the very end.

'BEN . . . GET BEHIND . . .' Harry roars from his perch on top of the tank. 'I'M OUT,' he shouts, throwing his empty guns away as two more get flung up by Safa.

'Kon . . . RUN!' Ben goes for it, gritting his teeth to run across the junction and into Bundesstraße 2 to get behind the tank as Charlie, Safa and Emily move out to cover them.

'Let me have her.' Charlie pushes his arms under Miri's form, lifting her from the stretcher to run at the back of the tank. 'HARRY!'

The big man spins and moves fast, dropping to take Miri from Charlie, heaving the unconscious woman up onto the tank. 'GO,' he roars, thumping the hatch.

'I AM BLOODY GOING,' Delta shouts back.

Ben flexes his hands, grimacing at the pain in his fingers and shoulders as Safa thrusts a sub-machine into his hands and turns him round. 'Get shooting . . . ONE STREET TO GO . . . COME ON!'

The German soldiers rally and start running through the ruins on both sides as ahead more German soldiers come into the street, running past Arch 451 to join the fight, and those odds start stacking again, becoming more and more as the tank trundles with that fresh hope now once again starting to fade.

◆ ◆ ◆

Alpha falls through the main door into the hospital. Sprawling out before pushing up to his feet to turn with almost drunken motion, seeing the nurses and doctors giving aid to the injured dumped in the hallway, who lie screaming and bleeding on stretchers. Someone grabs his arm, but he tugs free to half run and half stagger through rooms full of beds, viewing the faces of the women and children that go by in a sea of distress. So many of them. So many people here.

'Stop!' a male voice calls out. An exhausted doctor who bellows at Alpha, 'No soldiers in here . . . You! I SAID YOU!'

Again he starts to run, ignoring the calls as he mounts the stairs to find Kate. He has to find Kate. He will find Kate.

'KATE!' he roars out and staggers onto the landing. 'KATE!'

◆ ◆ ◆

Echo stands guard outside the door to Herr Weber's office listening to the noises outside. Sustained gunfire and explosions that sound like they're coming closer. Something has changed. He grimaces and holds still. They shouldn't be doing this. They shouldn't be getting ready to drop a nuclear bomb. A creak on the stairs snaps his attention over. Another one. The sound of someone coming up, creaking each step as they rise, and he blinks when the person starts coming into view, then keeps coming into view. A man mountain. Seven feet tall and huge with it. A monstrously big human being.

'Closed. Go back down,' Echo says in German, but the man keeps coming. 'I said to go back down,' Echo repeats, pushing his hand round his back ready to draw his pistol. 'Stop now,' he orders and the arm of the man who crept to his side whips out to whisper the blade across his throat while a hand goes over his mouth, pulling him back and down to die quickly and die quietly.

Inside the office of Herr Weber, Alpha shakes the hand of the Nazi scientist. 'Tomorrow then. Have everything ready,' Alpha says.

'Of course, of course,' Herr Weber says. 'We are ready . . .'

'Well done, old chap.' Bravo grins, shaking hands, then steps to the door, gripping the handle. 'And what a jolly day out it will be.' He twists the handle and steps out in front of Alpha, who nods again at Herr Weber and moves across the threshold to feel a blade at his throat and an arm coming round across his forehead.

'Easy now, Affas . . . Not a word, eh?'

'What the . . .' Herr Weber rushes out and stops dead from the blade sticking in his stomach and the cold hard eyes of Ria Cavendish staring through him. She twists the handle left then right and pulls it free to slice across his neck before kicking him away back into his office, then she turns slowly to look first at Bravo held off his feet by Oleg's huge arms wrapped round his head and Alpha gripped by Jerry holding a blade to his throat.

'Jerry and Oleg are special forces,' Ria says, her voice dull and hard. 'Or they were until they got their pensions. Now they own a café in what used to be Lambeth . . .'

'Best fried locusts in London, Affa,' Jerry whispers into Alpha's ear. 'Isn't that right, Oleg?'

Oleg nods with a simple gesture that makes Bravo shake like a doll in his arms as Ria looks down at the German SS dagger she found in the remains of the bunker now dripping blood and steps to drive the blade into Bravo's chest, staring into his eyes that go wide as the blood drains from his face.

'You killed my mother,' she tells him.

He tries shaking his head, but the blade twists and yanks, then drives in again while outside the gunfire grows closer. She pulls the knife out and watches the life drain from his eyes that grow heavier until he hangs limp in Oleg's arms, who simply releases to let him fall dead.

Alpha squirms in Jerry's grip, the hand over his mouth preventing him from calling out. Preventing him from begging or pleading.

'A dinosaur crashed through the roof of the bunker,' Ria tells him, moving closer. 'It turned the portal off and I spent a year being hunted by packs of velociraptors. They're clever too. Really cunning things . . .' She stops to look at him, staring through him as the blade comes up and he squirms hard, desperately trying to call out. 'Then I went after them,' she says simply. 'Now they fear me . . .' Alpha grunts as the blade sinks in. 'I'm not Miri. I will kill all of you if you come after my brother . . .' The knife sinks deeper, pushed hard by a young woman with strength in her arms and shoulders. 'This is for my mother . . .' She twists and pulls the knife free, severing arteries that pump blood out as he slides from Jerry's arms to lie dying on the floor with Ria Cavendish standing over him. 'Guess what . . . this is a memory of you so that means I get to find you and kill you again . . .'

◆ ◆ ◆

So close. They got so close. Ben ditches the empty sub-machine gun and takes the next one thrown at him by Charlie. All of them bleeding, all of them cut from bullets winging past. Safa's face a mask of blood. Harry's still on the tank, his arms bleeding heavily. Charlie's limping from a gunshot winging his thigh, while ahead of them the soldiers run into the street in front of Arch 451, blocking their path while more come in from behind.

So close. Ben fires back down the street, sending them scattering, but the soldiers find cover and keep the return fire going. Emily screams out, caught by a round scything her arm, but she grunts, snarls and keeps going and it's down to this. To the final two hundred metres that they have no hope of getting through.

Then the tank cuts out. The fuel gone. Delta tries turning it over, but it refuses to start. He works the machine guns inside the turret, but they're broken and useless, so with no other choice he pushes the hatch, clambers and drops down at the rear as Harry scoops Miri into his arms.

'No fuel,' Delta tells the others as incoming rounds ping from the tank. They glance back to the soldiers running into the end of Bundesstraße 2 behind them and forward to more coming, running in front of Arch 451.

Trapped. No way out. The last stand is now and with blood up and bullets flying past, Harry grabs Emily, pushing a hand round her waist to pull her in to kiss as the smoke billows and the bombs from aircraft drop to shake the ground. He kisses hard with fire all around them and Safa blinks when Emily's left foot lifts from the ground as the others look on until Harry pulls back.

'Ach, you're a fine woman, Miss Rose.'

'It's Emily,' she whispers, swallowing while looking up into his eyes.

'I so knew they'd get it on,' Ria tells Oleg and Jerry from the first-floor window of building number thirteen. 'Shall we?'

They lift the three missile launchers taken from the armoury in the bunker just before the dinosaur crashed through the roof, and as one they aim and fire with three missiles slamming through the window to scorch bright trails down the street to hit the ground between the soldiers running in.

'Holy fuck!' Ben shouts out as the missiles detonate. Then he spots Ria, Jerry and Oleg ditch the bazookas to heft fifty-calibre Barret rifles and turn to aim down towards Arch 451. A look between them. From Ben to Ria. A smile shared. A nod given.

'GO!' Ben roars, taking Miri from Harry. 'GO, GO, GO . . .'

They run out as the rifles start firing, with those huge booms filling the street. German soldiers fly backwards off their feet and Ben runs hard with Harry, Safa, Emily, Konrad, Harry, Charlie and Delta all around him, Konrad firing a sub-machine gun with a snarl on his lips and fury in his eyes. Not that he hits anything.

'You said they'd come up here,' Jerry shouts over the noise.

'I thought they would,' Ria shouts back, guessing Ben must have a reason for going that way. They keep the fire on, killing German soldiers and sending them flying while Ben leads them across that final two hundred metres with Harry charging ahead to batter the door in to see the green glowing portal.

'Ah,' Ria says, seeing the shimmering light. 'There's one down there.'

'How many bloody time machines have you got, Ria?' Jerry asks.

◆ ◆ ◆

'KATE!'

He will find her. He has a mission. He is Alpha and he will complete his mission. Kate is the mission. She gave him love and hope. She gave him forgiveness for the awful things he has done. She held him in her arms and soothed his head. She whispered sweet words like an angel sent to make his soul repent for the murders and tortures committed in service for the greater good.

Face after face. Bed after bed. Alpha takes another flight of stairs to the top floor and every shred of confusion vanishes the second he sees her through a doorway sitting on the edge of a bed and he grins a sick smile through a bloodstained, sweat-soaked face covered in grime and filth as the world stops spinning and all the pain vanishes. She is here. She's alive.

'Kate,' he croaks.

She turns to look at him and he takes in the bandage round her skull and the bruises on her cheeks and arms, but she's alive. She's here and alive. He walks towards her, swaying and heaving for air. 'Gotta go,' he says, clearing his throat to speak clearly. 'We've got to go . . .'

'GET OUT,' a doctor yells behind him. 'No men and no more soldiers . . . GET OUT NOW!'

'My wife,' Alpha snarls in German, turning in the doorway to aim his pistol at the doctor, who wilts back in sudden fear. 'SHE IS MY WIFE,' he adds in a bellow to the nurses and orderlies gathering behind the doctor. 'And she is coming with me . . .'

He is Alpha. He will keep her safe. He turns to Kate and moves into the room towards the woman he swore to protect only to see the look of confusion and fear etched on her face and her eyes darting to the side.

'I'm sorry . . . I don't know this man . . .' she says in a timid pained voice in a pure Berlin accent of fluent German.

A click of a hammer being pulled back and the pressure of a gun pushed into the back of his head and in the reflection from the taped glass in the window he sees the black-uniformed officers waiting behind the door aiming Lugers at his back.

Thirty-Seven

The Complex

'We shouldn't be doing it,' Roger whispers urgently.

'Roger,' Gunjeep whispers, his voice edged with warning. 'I do not want a bullet through my head, so I will tell you again to shut up!'

'It's a nuclear bomb, Gunjeep,' Roger hisses, tutting foully as Gunjeep simply walks off.

The chief technician stops at the operating control panel, reading the date and location. 6 FEBRUARY 1945. ARCH 451. BUNDESSTRASSE 2. BERLIN. The agents are on their last visit to Herr Weber now. After this they drop the bomb on London and it's like they're all careering towards a thing that cannot now be stopped. Mother is too scary. The agents are too powerful, so everyone just keeps going, not knowing what else they can do.

Up the corridor in Mother's office, Kate stands in front of her desk, tutting and shaking her head. 'You really do look awful, Mother,' she says. 'Are you even washing? It smells ripe in here . . .'

'People need to think I am losing my mind,' Mother snaps.

'Objective achieved then, I'd say,' Kate replies. 'Right, I'd better go and get ready for my handsome lover's safe return from Berlin . . .

What's that look for?' she asks on seeing Mother's head snap to the monitors showing the live camera feed.

Gunjeep sighs in the portal room. Wishing he'd never taken this on. Wishing he'd never signed up for it. All of this to catch and kill a bunch of people everyone knows are heroes. Harry Madden for god's sake. Harry Madden isn't a terrorist.

'GET DOWN NOW,' Harry Madden roars, striding into the portal room. 'DOWN, DOWN, DOWN . . .'

'GET DOWN.' Safa Patel behind him. Emily Rose, then Ben Ryder carrying Maggie Sanderson.

'Everyone stay calm,' Charlie calls out, limping through the portal followed by Delta.

Mother swipes at the monitor in her office, flicking through the live camera feeds while her heart jack-hammers in her chest. 'It's them,' she whispers. 'They're here . . .'

'Konrad,' Ben says in the portal room while the others gain control, herding everyone together with Charlie and Delta telling them to stay calm. 'We need that portal reset to the island . . . Get the doc in here . . .'

'Gunjeep,' Charlie orders. 'Do as they say . . . Tell him the coordinates,' he tells Konrad.

'We need to get Miri to the medical section,' Ben says.

'Mother needs sorting first,' Charlie says.

'Room clearance as we move then,' Safa says. 'Ready?'

'You said they wouldn't do this,' Kate says in Mother's office. 'You said they wouldn't attack now . . . What are you doing?' she asks, seeing her mother grab a pistol from a drawer. 'Don't be so bloody stupid . . .'

'This is a memory,' Mother mutters, yanking the slide back on the gun. 'A memory . . . Don't attack a memory . . . THIS IS A MEMORY . . .'

Kate thinks fast, watching her mother's increasingly frantic state as she bubbles up into seething incandescent rage. Whatever the reasons are, this is happening, and Kate rushes round to open more drawers, knowing her mother always keeps two guns. She finds one in the bottom drawer, pulling it out to check and make ready. 'We'll take them . . . We can do it.' She looks at her mother. 'We'll take them . . . me and you . . . we can do it . . .'

Mother nods, frantic and shallow. Her eyes bulging. Her skin grey and waxen, the lines so deep. She looks haggard and coming apart at the seams.

'They can't win,' Kate whispers, her voice low and urging, her tone pushing the buttons with an insidious delve into her mother's psyche. 'They can't win again . . . We won't let them . . .'

Mother stares into the eyes of her daughter, seeing the girl she raised and trained to be embedded into covert ops and hidden from the world. Her daughter and the one person in here she can trust implicitly.

'We'll do it, you and me,' Kate implores. 'We're the good guys . . . we are . . . They're terrorists.'

'Terrorists,' Mother mutters.

'They won't be expecting a frontal attack. We hit from the front . . . We take them down . . .'

'From the front,' Mother parrots. This is a memory. It serves no purpose to attack now. It shouldn't happen. It can't happen. It is happening. 'From the front . . .'

Charlie and Delta lead the way down the corridor, pistols up and aimed, with Emily and Safa behind while Ben brings up the rear having left Harry with Konrad.

'Double doors on the right,' Emily says, aiming at the point of danger.

'That's the canteen,' Charlie says.

'You've got a canteen?' Safa mutters. 'We don't have a bloody canteen . . . We had a table in a grotty old bunker.'

Mother and daughter stride down the corridor side by side. Faces blazing with righteous fury and pistols held in double-handed grips.

An energy between them, an understanding that can only come from a connection born of blood. This is Mother's complex. This is her ground and they'll defend it and win. They'll kill the bad guys.

The two sides draw ever closer together. Charlie and Delta going forward at the head of their group while Mother and Kate march towards them.

A bend in the corridor ahead. Charlie and Delta turn to glance back at Ben carrying Miri as Mother lifts her pistol and sweeps round to lock her aim on Safa Patel.

'GUN!' Emily shouts the warning and a single shot rings out that sends a bullet spinning across the short distance into the centre of mass.

Screams fill the corridor. Ears ringing from the firefight in Berlin, then from the gunshots within this contained corridor. Everyone stunned and holding still as Mother staggers back into the wall, sliding along leaving a smeared wake of blood as she drops. She felt the bullet hit, watches as her daughter lowers her gun with a look of absolute coldness on her face that holds for several long seconds before she morphs back into the historian, bursting into tears and wailing. 'Oh my god, oh my god . . .'

'Someone else there,' Emily calls out. 'SHOW YOURSELF . . .'

'Kate?' Charlie shouts.

'I killed her . . . I killed her . . .' Kate stays out of view, her eyes fixed on her mother, who blinks slowly at her daughter.

'SHOW YOURSELF NOW,' Safa roars.

'It's Kate . . .' Charlie says.

'The historian,' Delta adds. 'She's safe . . .'

'Please . . . I think I . . . Oh my god, I shot her . . . She was going to kill you . . .' Kate wails, crying hard with tears running down her cheeks, moving slowly into view holding a gun upside down by the trigger guard.

'GUN DOWN NOW . . . PUT IT DOWN . . .' Safa orders.

'I'm so sorry,' Kate whimpers, lowering on shaky legs to place the gun on the floor. 'She said she was going to kill you . . . I think I shot her . . .'

'Get everyone in the canteen,' Safa orders Charlie and Delta. 'Ben, hold here for a minute.'

'We don't have a minute,' Ben snaps. 'I don't think she's breathing.'

'It's fine now,' Charlie says urgently.

'Negative,' Safa says. 'We hold here. Emily, go with them. I want everyone in the canteen . . . NOW!'

'Ben?' A voice behind. Ben spins to see Doctor Watson rushing towards him with Harry, Konrad and Malcolm. 'My god . . . What's happened? Is that Miri?'

'Shot in the stomach,' Ben says.

'Put her down, gently now . . . Easy . . .' The doctor drops with Miri, lowering to press his fingertips into her neck, checking for signs. 'She's stopped breathing . . .'

'They've got an infirmary,' Ben says as the corridor fills with pan-icked scientists running into the canteen while Safa keeps her aim on Mother still blinking with life as she sits bleeding against the wall.

'MOVE!' Charlie's voice coming closer, leading a woman in blue surgical scrubs who falters on seeing Mother then looks over to see Ben Ryder tending to Maggie Sanderson with an older man and not a second thought is given as Doctor Holmes rushes past Mother to give aid to Maggie Sanderson.

'She's stopped breathing,' Doctor Watson says.

'Into the infirmary now,' Doctor Holmes orders.

'Let me.' Harry bends between them, hefting Miri with ease into his arms. 'Lead the way.'

They set off, rushing up the corridor as Ben pauses to drop at Mother's side while the others go on and the last few scientists run past into the canteen. Then it falls strangely quiet and Ben stares down into the cold grey eyes of Mother as she coughs to bring blood from her mouth that dribbles down her chin.

'How far did we get?' Mother asks, closing her eyes from the pain searing through her body.

'No idea,' Ben says. 'You dropped the bomb, but the world seemed fine and if it's not then we'll fix it.'

She looks at him, seeing the cuts and marks all over his face. He's more handsome in real life. Rugged and pensive. 'This is a memory,' she whispers.

'It is,' Ben says quietly, unaware of the canteen doors behind him standing wide open with everyone in there listening intently. 'We needed your infirmary,' he adds simply. 'But guess what? Changes to a timeline don't affect you when you're not in it, *or* if you leave your time-line and go back to it and I'm guessing you've been in here since this began, right? This is *your* timeline . . . We're in *your* past and I'm betting you're in this place right now feeling like you've won . . . So when we kill you now, you will cease to exist because we are in your direct past . . .'

Mother closes her eyes at the stunningly simple logic and grunts from a fresh wave of pain and when she opens her eyes to look up Ben is gone.

'Hi,' Emily says, holding her pistol with one hand while slowly giving her middle finger with the other. 'Remember me, bitch?'

A single gunshot echoes through the complex making the workers in the canteen flinch and clamp their eyes closed at the brutal execution.

All apart from Kate, who watches her mother slump dead as Emily Rose stands back to holster her weapon and share a look with Safa Patel.

'Round two to us,' Emily says.

'Looks that way,' Safa replies.

Thirty-Eight

The Complex

She looks at the screens in the dark office, flicking through the live feeds to stare with cold grey eyes, then picks up a tablet, activating the public address system.

'All personnel will report for briefing immediately.'

She switches it off and watches the workers scurry from offices and rooms to fill the corridors of the complex as they rush for the briefing room to fill the tiered seats with hushed and excited conversations sounding out, and only when the corridors fall empty does she decide to leave the office because it serves her purpose to walk alone through the complex and enter the room last.

The power to control others is often a fragile, intangible thing and mostly born from perception. A man with a gun can gain power, but he will do so only through fear, and to have control given willingly requires an altogether different set of skills.

At times, she has been hostile, angry, withering in contempt and harsh in voice, but now she is simply restrained as she enters the briefing room that falls instantly silent, and her footsteps echo as she walks to the small raised stage and looks out with cold grey eyes, and the way she waits only serves to heighten the perception of her power.

She looks out across the briefing room, taking in every face staring at her. She knows their names. She knows everything about them from their records. She lifts her chin to speak as a blue shining doorway comes to life, snapping every head over to look at Ben Ryder coming through.

'Are we late?' Ben asks, moving away as the rest disgorge into the briefing room. 'Emily's fault – she was chasing Harry with a pair of scissors.'

'His beard needs cutting,' Emily says.

'Here,' Kate whisper-shouts from the front row, patting the empty chairs at her side while waving. 'Saved you some seats.'

Chatter and noise fill the room as Miri tuts and rolls her eyes from the small stage.

'It's so hot on the island today,' Emily tells Kate, wafting her own face with a hand.

'Can't wait to see it,' Kate says. 'Could so do with some sunshine right now.'

'Hi, Delta!' Hanna calls out, seeing the handsome agent come through the portal with Charlie.

'Oh hey,' he says, offering a weak smile before rushing for his seat. 'She's going to cut my dick off,' he whispers to Charlie.

'Stop having sex with everyone then,' Charlie whispers back.

'Ah, Doctor Holmes, all well?'

'Fine, thank you, Doctor Watson.'

Miri listens and watches, taking it all in, seeing all, reading body language. Her cold grey eyes now a shade more blue. The medications are working slowly. She still feels weak, but she's alive.

She draws breath, clears her throat and coughs quietly with an action that brings a hush to the room, and Maggie Sanderson lifts her chin to address them all.

'I've been called many things. Maureen. Monica. Maggie. Monique. M. Ma'am. Boss. SB, which stands for Stubborn Bitch. MB, which stands for Mad Bitch, and TB, which stands for That Bitch . . .' She pauses to hold the audience in the palm of her hand from a lifetime of experience, with skills used to have control given willingly. 'Now I am Miri,' she adds simply. 'I am OIC and we have work to do . . . We do not know what changes have been wrought as a result of Mr Ryder's actions . . .' She stops to look at him, arching an eyebrow in show of her displeasure. She's already *discussed* it with him and voiced her thoughts on his plan to use the portal in the arch. He just smiled then and he smiles now.

'You're welcome,' he says from the front row.

'As I was saying . . .'

'For saving your life.' He coughs into his hands, making her pause and glare as nearly the entire front row snort chuckles and laugh quietly.

'We have work to do,' Miri says again. 'We have a *lot* of work to do . . . And we will start with going back to the future . . .'

Author's Note

'Which one am I?' my grandfather asked.

We were in my grandparent's kitchen in Birmingham, England. I can remember it so vividly. We had spent the morning playing in the garden, then later my grandfather and I sat in the kitchen and he told me his war stories.

He'd lied about his age and joined the Royal Navy at the outbreak of war in 1939 and trained as a signalman and said that one day he was transferred by winch from one ship to another and as his new vessel sailed off so the old one was hit by a torpedo fired from a German U-boat, killing many.

He told me about the time they were escorting supply ships through the Bay of Biscay and U-boats surfaced between the lines of vessels and how the allied ships couldn't fire back for fear of hitting their own.

He showed me pictures of German sailors in the sea waiting to be rescued after their vessel had been sunk, and he told me, quietly, how the captain had taken a rifle and started shooting at them because his own brother had been killed by the Germans in the last week.

Then my grandfather told me the story of the *Bismarck*, the mighty German battleship, and how he had signalled it to surrender. Years later

I would come to realise how momentous a moment that was and that my grandfather was there, he saw it.

I heard many stories from him, all of them incredible, but more than anything, I remember the dignity of the man and how he didn't tell me the Germans were evil or bad, but that it was war and bad things happened. He'd lost mates, but then everyone had and as the light faded and we drank tea, he brought out a black-and-white picture of a group of men and women in service uniform gathered at a wartime dance and laid it down on the small wooden table between us.

'Which one am I?' he asked.

I looked from him to the picture and studied every single man. I pointed to a few but he chuckled that rich, deep laugh and finally laid a finger on a man with a big dark bushy beard.

'That was me.'

For Ivan Henry Haywood

About the Author

RR Haywood is a long-standing and highly successful Amazon author. He is the creator of the bestselling series The Undead, a self-published British zombie horror series that has become a cult hit with a readership that defies generations and gender.

Living in an underground cave, away from the spy satellites and invisible drones sent to watch over us by the BBC, he works a full-time job, has four dogs and lots of tattoos. He is also a certified, badged and registered hypochondriac, for which he blames the invisible BBC drones.

Should you not have a drone to hand, you can find him at www.rrhaywood.com.